THE

MYSTERIOUS

ALEX BEECROFT
JOSH LANYON
LAURA BAUMBACH

mlrpress

www.mlrpress.com

MLR Press Authors

Featuring a roll call of some of the best writers of gay erotica and mysteries today!

M. Jules Aedin	David Juhren
Maura Anderson	Samantha Kane
Victor J. Banis	Kiernan Kelly
Jeanne Barrack	J.L. Langley
Laura Baumbach	Josh Lanyon
Alex Beecroft	Clare London
Sarah Black	William Maltese
Ally Blue	Gary Martine
J.P. Bowie	Z.A. Maxfield
Michael Breyette	Patric Michael
P..A. Brown	AKM Miles
Brenda Bryce	Jet Mykles
Jade Buchanan	William Neale
James Buchanan	Willa Okati
Charlie Cochrane	L. Picaro
Kirby Crow	Neil S. Plakcy
Dick D.	Jordan Castillo Price
Ethan Day	Luisa Prieto
Jason Edding	Rick R. Reed
Angela Fiddler	A.M. Riley
Dakota Flint	George Seaton
S.J. Frost	Jardonn Smith
Kimberly Gardner	Caro Soles
Roland Graeme	JoAnne Soper-Cook
Storm Grant	Richard Stevenson
Amber Green	Clare Thompson
LB Gregg	Lex Valentine
Drewey Wayne Gunn	Stevie Woods

Check out titles, both available and forthcoming, at
www.mlrpress.com

THE

MYSTERIOUS

ALEX BEECROFT
JOSH LANYON
LAURA BAUMBACH

mlrpress
www.mlrpress.com

Published by
MLR Press, LLC
3052 Gaines Waterport Rd.
Albion, NY 14411

Visit ManLoveRomance Press, LLC on the Internet:
www.mlrpress.com

Cover Art by Alex Beecroft
Editing by Kris Jacen
Printed in the United States of America.

ISBN# 978-1-60820-098-6

2010 Edition

THE WAGES OF SIN

OF SIN

ALEX BEECROFT

Moonlight sucked the colour from damp grass and silvered rising wisps of dew. The deer-park lay dim and still to Charles' left, receding to a black horizon. To his right, the Latham family chapel loomed dark against the lead-colored sky.

Sultan's hooves whispered across the verge as Charles rode past the private graveyard's wrought iron gate and averted his eyes from the white glimmer of Sir Henry's mausoleum. It was one thing to laugh together over newspaper reports of vampires in Prussia while reclining in the comfortable lewdness of an actor's garret—lamps blazing, the magic revealed as greasepaint, squalor and hard work—quite another to think of it here, beneath a slice of pewter moon, in a silence so huge it annihilated him.

A fox cried. Sultan snorted, ears flicking. His own heart racing, Charles gentled the horse over the gravel drive that swept up to the white Grecian pillars of the mansion. They turned towards the stable-yard—coach houses, stalls and groom's quarters arranged about an enclosed square, entered by a short cobbled tunnel beneath the stable-master's rooms. Both of them balked at the darkness beneath the arch, Sultan sidestepping as Charles dismounted. He wrenched his wrist, landed with a slap and slither loud enough to conceal the footsteps of a thousand walking corpses and stood propped against the horse's strong shoulder, gathering himself. Sultan's warm, straw-scented breath spiralled up comfortingly into the pre-dawn sky.

"Easy there, Sultan. Nothing to worry about."

Thanking God that no one was watching his folly, Charles slung an arm about Sultan's neck, took the hilt of his sword in the other hand. Emboldened by the feel of it, he urged Sultan forwards, towards his own stall and rest.

In the pitch black under the gatehouse the several pints of inferior porter he had drunk at the theatre made their presence known again. The night swayed about him and the world receded, until all his reality was the horse hair and leather beneath his hands. *Falling asleep on my feet. Just the state of weakness most likely to attract the devil, or his minions... Or my father.*

There was a more rational threat. As he took off Sultan's tack, fumbled around in the dark making sure the weary animal was supplied with hay and water, the thought of Ambrose Latham drove away all other terrors. *"You wastrel,"* his father would bellow, loud enough to echo in the kitchens and make all the servants sit up in glee. *"You mother's milk-sop boy with your clever friends and your expensive women. Do you think I built up this family's fortune only to have it squandered by you, sirrah? Do you?"*

Having drunk, Sultan nudged his shoulder, leaving a smudge of dirty water and horse-snot on the jonquil silk of his jacket, pulling him up again from his reverie. He still had to get inside without being seen, and it was now less late at night than very early in the morning. If his luck was bad, those very servants might have already begun to wake. They could be standing, watching him as he rolled through the front door with his wig in his pocket and his blond hair singed and sooty from sitting too close to Theo Tidy's spike of tallow candles.

What did you expect, sir, when you sent me to University? That I would slake my appetite for learning in a mere three years, and be content to rusticate thereafter, among a company whose highest pinnacle of wit is to describe their new carriage for four hours together? I honour you for opening my mind to a wider world, but I cannot now go back to the provincial concerns from which you raised me.

A small pain, dull and heavy as a shotgun pellet, caught him just below the breastbone at the thought. Truth was he didn't *want* to be a disappointment to Ambrose Latham, Fourth Earl of Clitheroe. He didn't want to be a drain on his family's resources or a blot on their reputation. But, forbidden as he was to join army or church, in case George should crack his head hunting and a spare heir be required, what else was there? If he could find some subject on which to become an authority, perhaps? If he could get himself invited by the Royal Society to give talks, his erudition the toast of newspapers and coffee-houses all over

London? But what subject interested both the learned gentlemen and himself? They had no taste for plays.

Annoyed by his own hopeless thoughts, Charles nudged Sultan's nose towards the basket of hay, reeled out of the door. By God, did he only have a choice of pathos or fear? Was he to be a coward as well as an embarrassment?

Four steps out of the stables, away from the horses' drowsy whickering, and the answer seemed to be "yes." Silence arched over the world like a collector's dome pressed over a doomed insect. The shift of pebbles beneath his feet sounded obscenely loud. Something snapped a twig as it walked beneath the distant oaks, and it might have been a pistol shot. He tried to think of Theo—actor manager, wit, raconteur. If he could only have some of Theo's relentless cheer to armour him now. It was foolish, childish, to find himself with clammy hands, muffling his breath in case it made him miss the faint noise of the creature shambling behind him… Oh damn!

He stopped, rejected the thought of returning to the stables to sleep. He was *not* a coward! Summoning up Theo's filthiest anecdote, the one he didn't fully understand, he put his head down and walked—*walked* mind you—out to the drive.

As he turned towards the house, Theo failed him. Charles' imagination populated the lane behind him with horrors. What if they *did* exist? In this silence, anything that fed on blood should sense his heart speeding in his chest. Would they make a noise as they prowled? Would he hear anything before the creature's hand came out of the darkness, dragged him to its insatiable mouth?

No, it was nonsense. Absolute tosh. No rational man could possibly believe… And yet, would the Prussians really send officials to dig up graves, make observations and write reports if there wasn't something in it?

He swallowed, panting, and thought about what his father would have to say about this. But even that threat failed. Truth was he'd be glad if Clitheroe slammed open the door, lantern in hand, and gave him a piece of his mind. *Please do, father. A nice long peroration to follow me up to bed and banish my own thoughts. Come down and shout at me. Please.*

But the façade of the house remained shut. Did the marble portico and the sweep of stairs up to the entrance look gloomier than they had? Well, what of it? The moon must simply be going down.

Stopping again, he bit his lip until the blood flowed. Then turned. He clutched at his sword hilt, and slowly, shakily let it go. Yes, the moon had gone behind cloud. The trees of the park sighed in the wind, and that man-like pale shimmer beneath them... was only the statue of General Percival Latham attired in the robes of a Roman senator.

Leaning over to prop his hands on his knees in the weakness of relief, Charles gave a small spasm of laughter. As he did so the wind strengthened, the trees roared, and terror rose out of the ground around him like a fog. His breath hung white in the black air. Cold bit through alcoholic haze, jacket and flesh, piercing him to the bone. The skin across his shoulders and down his arms rippled as the hair stood up, and the little voice of reason within him blew out like a candle flame.

Chest heaving, his shallow breath scorching his throat, he turned again. There *was* something wrong with the house; darkness oozed over it like a coating of oil. A shadow sucked away from the stone and came flooding out towards him in a whispering tide. His legs locked. His bowels froze. He lifted an arm to push the black tide away, and so it touched his hand first. Burning cold. Faintly gritty. Sticky as cobwebs. It slid up his fingers, around his palm, burrowed beneath his cuff. Clammy strands touched the inside of his elbow, the pit of his arm, and then it flowed over his face.

No! Oh God! He pinched his eyes and mouth shut. Strands of it, like the tendrils of long filthy hair, brushed across his lips. Then something groaned by his ear. He heard the wet noise of an opened mouth. Shuddering, he let out a little *'nnn!'* of terror, groping for his sword, his hand pushing through the cloud as if through sand. The thing by his face giggled, and dust pattered on his eyelids. He bit down hard on the mounting desire to scream.

God forbid he should breathe it in!

Dimly, beyond the voice whispering with gleeful hatred in his ear, came a sound like racing hooves. Was it the wind or his own blood stoppered in his breathless body thundering in his ears? Dizziness swept through him and his locked knees gave way. He staggered forward, his lungs screaming for air, agony shooting along his ribs, and thought again of Theo; that half-joking, half-challenging offer of a kiss. Maybe he should have taken the man up on it after all. Sin aside, it seemed a shame to die, never having been kissed.

His fingertips grazed his sword hilt. A final push and he could close clumsy fingers around the hilt. He drew the blade, and as he did so something hit him in the back so hard it lifted him off his feet. For a moment he thought he would crack between the two forces like a louse between fingernails. Then the night air was clean again, and with a confused rush, a red pain in his cheek and shoulder, he was suddenly lying on the drive with a face full of gravel and two men pulling at his coat.

"What? What? Did you see it?" He batted their hands away, scrambled up and made a frantic circle, searching for the *thing*. Was it gone? Let it be gone!

Doctor Floyd's landau stood with lanterns swinging and open doors, all glorious green leather and brass, just in front of him. Beside him, Dr. Floyd—almost a perfect sphere in his greatcoat—reached out a glacially cautious hand as if to restrain him. Charles turned, grabbed the man by his black velvet collar and shouted again, "Did you see it!"

A colourless, fat man, whose professional life seemed to have prematurely embalmed him, Floyd leaned away. He blinked, slowly as a torpid lizard, while propriety and self preservation warred behind his eyes.

"We almost run you over, Mr. Charles." Floyd's groom spoke with the reassuring tone he used to his horses. Protectively, he interposed his beaming red face between Charles and his master, put a gnarled but gentle hand on Charles' wrist. "What you doing out here in the road in the dark anyway? Come to get us, was you? You'd've done better wait in the hall."

Charles shook his head, tried to speak and could not force words past the chattering of his teeth. His grip on the Doctor's coat gave way, and he would have fallen if the two men had not moved in and caught him in their practiced grip.

"The blanket, Sam, and less of your chatter. Here, Mr. Charles, take a drink of this."

A heavy blanket around his shoulders and a long drink of brandy later, Charles let Sam tuck him into the corner of the carriage, concentrated on trying to stop trembling. As he did so, Floyd clambered in beside him.

"I'm most terribly sorry, Mr. Charles. Your brother's message was so urgent. We weren't expecting… And I must say I was looking towards the house. I saw nothing in the road until Jewel clipped you as she passed."

Charles wrapped his arms around himself and chafed his biceps to get some warmth into them. Cold radiated out from the marrow of his bones. But the old felted blanket around him glowed in the lantern light with blue, yellow and red stripes, speckled with dog hair. He basked in wet dog smell, brass polish, leather wax, and Floyd's orange-flower-water cologne. These things and the terror that had passed could not exist in the same world, surely?

"A cloud," he said, in a reedy, shocked voice. "There was a cloud. A black cloud. It… rushed at me, and…"

"Most probably the dust cloud from the landau, sir." Sam spoke over his shoulder as he flicked the whip encouragingly above Jewel's ears.

"No it…"

"Yes, that would account for it. Undoubtedly why we neither of us saw the other coming." Floyd nodded, fished out a handkerchief and wiped his cheeks and forehead with fingers only a little less unsteady than Charles'. "You, um. You fell upon your head, sir. And, mm, if my nose doesn't guide me wrongly, have already imbibed a fair amount of… mm, conviviality. No doubt you are also distressed about your father. I think we need look no further for the cause of a temporary, understandable, overturning of the wits."

"That's not how it…" Charles clutched the blanket more closely, trapped a pawprint between his knee and the seat. The dried mud flaked off and scattered to the floor, and a convulsive choke of disgust forced its way out of him at the patter of falling soil. He smeared it underfoot, looked down blankly for a moment before the words finally penetrated his understanding.

The landau swept through the great curve before the marble steps of the portico. Lights now glimmered in the hall, and as they drew up George flung open the door. His candle showed a white, sickened face, its distinguished lines set in strain.

"My father?" Charles rose to his feet, holding tight to the calash of the landau as it sprayed gravel with the speed of its stop. A fist of dread tightened beneath his breastbone and the waves of shivering returned full force. "What's wrong with…?"

George ran down the stairs. The light shone on his open shirt and bare feet as his scarlet silk banyan trailed behind him. His uncovered hair shone silver-gilt. It was the first time in years Charles had seen his brother so careless of his appearance, and his wild unconscious beauty added a new terror to the night.

Flinging down his candle, George caught Dr. Floyd as he bent to retrieve his bag and hauled him bodily out onto the grass. Floyd raised an eyebrow at the treatment, while George in turn gaped at the sight of Charles leaping down beside him.

"Oh I do have a brother then? No, say nothing, this isn't the time. You'd best come too."

Charles followed his brother's impatient strides past the stone pineapples on the sweep of white stairs. Their footsteps echoed and re-echoed like a volley of rifle-fire against the chequered black and white marble of the entrance hall. A candelabrum set on a table within lit Doric pillars and the portraits of his ancestors with a bubble of amber light. The door up from the kitchen stood partially open. Blurs of white faces, above white shifts, showed ghostlike in the crack.

On the landing, George's valet Sykes stood waiting with a candlestick in his hand, his cravat lopsided and his chin shadowed by an aggressive growth of black stubble. Another twist in the garrotte of fear about Charles' throat. They were normally both of them so impeccable. "George! What's…?"

"Just," George flung up a hand, "be quiet." He took the candle and whispered to Sykes. "Stand outside the door. Mrs. Latham's rest is not to be disturbed under any circumstances. Should Mrs. Sheldrake awaken, you may inform her, but you will not permit her to come in."

"I understand."

They hurried down the passage, their feet silent now on the runner of blue and white carpet. Outside the windows at either end of the corridor, the night pressed inwards. As they stopped outside his father's room, George dropped a hand to the doorknob and bent that exposed, vulnerable head. "I feel I ought to warn you. It isn't… Ah. Well. See for yourself."

Candlelight caught the cream and gold plastered walls, glittered like the ends of pins in the tassels of the bed-curtains and the gold embroidered comforter that lay in a kicked off crumple against the claw-footed legs of the bed. The fire had been made and burned clear yellow in the grate.

Soberly, imagination finally at bay, Charles did what his soldier ancestors would have expected of him. He walked forward into the line of fire, looked down.

Ambrose Latham, Earl of Clitheroe, lay on his back in his nightgown, his limbs fettered by the sheets, his swollen face purple. His open mouth brimmed with vomit. Across his nose, lips and chin the mark of a woman's hand stood out in livid white. His nostrils were stopped with earth.

"What is *he* doing here?" The clock on the mantle struck quarter past six as Elizabeth gestured with her loaded fork. No doubt, Charles thought, his head throbbing, and the side of his face stinging in counterpoint, her advanced state of pregnancy excused the fact that she was still capable of eating. He wished she would do it somewhere else.

Dragging his eyes from the drop of brown grease that trembled on the end of the bacon, he looked where she pointed. The vague sense he had had all night that there were too many presences in the house—a pair of shoes outside a normally unoccupied door, an unexpected number of plates on the sideboard for this impromptu family breakfast, coalesced into a stranger at their table.

He wore the bob wig of a clergyman and a clergyman's black woollen coat. The jet buttons of his cuff glittered, and beneath the stark white powder of his wig, his wing-like brows were just as black. The fan of black eyelashes hiding downcast eyes, and the diffident bend of his neck, could not disguise an angular, almost Spanish beauty; bold high cheekbones and a sullen, dangerous mouth.

"He's here as my guest." George was once more the picture of manly perfection in a suit of emerald silk, but the stick pin in his cravat clashed with his waistcoat, and the lines of strain in his face scored deeper by the hour. Charles swallowed, looked away, conscious that for the first time, George had begun to resemble their father.

"He's father's enemy. Always has been." Elizabeth's white makeup showed cracks and streaks in a dozen places, her handsome face puffy from weeping and her eyes bloodshot. Close to her confinement and with her husband absent at the head of his regiment in Scotland, she had returned home to be coddled with all the attentiveness an expectant grandfather could bestow. And she had always been Clitheroe's favourite.

Charles honoured her for her grief. Despised himself for being unable to echo it.

Outside the tall windows, dawn had barely begun to break. Autumnal rain lashed the panes, rolled in silver beads down each black lozenge. Within the house a melancholy procession of servants passed the door of the morning room: Geoffreys, his father's valet, with an arm full of neatly folded sheets; Cook with jug, basin and towel; and her two daughters following, a can of hot water carried between them. He took another cup of coffee, for the hangover, and looked back.

The stranger's head still bent over the table. He dipped his spoon, ate a mouthful of porridge and the gesture brought his face even further into shadow.

"Melodramatic nonsense!" George speared a devilled kidney and thrust it onto his plate. "Father doesn't have any enemies."

Elizabeth gave a harsh laugh, honey-blond ringlets bobbing with incongruous cheer beside her jaw. "In case you haven't noticed, brother, our father is *lying dead upstairs*. He must have had one enemy, don't you think? And now we're eating breakfast with the prime candidate? That's taking politeness a little too far."

The scrape of a chair. The stranger made to rise and George caught him by the wrist, pressed his arm to the table, restraining him.

At the sight of the stranger's hand, lying as if cut off by the black cuff, the picture of his father's dead face flashed before Charles' inner eye. He too recoiled, struggling to his feet, running to the window, trying to escape it.

"This is not the time for unfounded, hysterical accusations. Really, Elizabeth if your condition did not excuse you I should have to accuse you of running mad. Now *please* keep your voice down. This is the last thing Emma needs!"

By some dint of magic, the stranger had continued his retreat, withdrawing his presence, leaving his body like an old table that sits unnoticed in the corner of a room. But Charles was tired of trying to see his face, being thwarted. "Won't someone introduce us?"

George laughed with surprise. "Don't be a goose! You remember Jasper. Admiral Vane's ward. We grew up together."

Since it was impossible to say "no," Charles leaned back against the window and let the chill of the rain seep across his shoulders. "By reputation only," he said, and watched as Jasper's stubborn chin raised half an inch and his mouth curved in a little bitter smile. "You forget, George, my earliest memory is of waving goodbye as you left for Cambridge. I'm afraid I have no recollection of you at all, Mr Marin. Except, as I say, by anecdote."

At last, with slow grace like the turn of a minuet, Jasper looked up. His eyes, in the broadening light, were sherry coloured—a light, clear brown almost with a tint of red. Had there been room, Charles might have stepped backwards. A jolt of something very like fear went through him. How could he have mistaken the man's invisibility for meekness? It had been all along the quiet of a tiger lying in wait in the long grass. Elizabeth's accusation no longer seemed so laughable.

"Then I wish we could have met again in happier circumstances."

Two heartbeats. Charles had time to wonder if this was some new manner of the paralysis that had come on him last night; time's normal flow suspended. Then the morning room door swung open and Dr. Floyd came in. The scene moved and flowed once more as George rose to pull out a seat for him, and Elizabeth called for fresh coffee.

Floyd sighed, hitched further back to accommodate his belly—which rivalled Elizabeth's in its swell—and reached for the bottle of claret. "I suspect I don't need to tell you that there really wasn't anything that I could have done?"

"I suppose I…" George cut open the kidney and pushed it to the top rim of his plate, grimacing. "I may have been a little overcome myself. I knew—seeing him, I knew—but..." He bowed his forehead into his right hand and rubbed at the frown as though he could erase it. "You understand?"

"Of course. I do. To do nothing is impossible. To wait 'til morning, would be so rational as to be almost heartless in the circumstances." Floyd looked with yearning at the salver of bacon and eggs, and sighed with such feeling that Charles passed over his own empty plate.

Snagging a slice of bread, Charles retreated to the fireplace to make toast. Floyd heaped meat onto his plate. "Your father took laudanum, I understand? A dose in the evening to help him sleep?"

"He had terrible gout," Elizabeth stiffened as though in pain herself, pressed a hand to her flank, looking down as though she could peer through her own flesh at the child growing restless within. Her eyes filled again, gleaming softly, and she brought up her handkerchief to soak the tears away before they fell. "It tormented him nightly. But he was so looking forward to meeting his grandchild..." She hauled herself to her feet and stood with her wadded white hanky pressed to her nose.

"Forgive me. Please go on."

At this rate the conversation would still be winding on by suppertime, and no one would dare ask. "We are all wondering if it was murder," Charles interrupted, too bleary to be anything other than brutal. "My father is known to have enemies."

"Charles!" George half rose, and his look of fragile grief hardened instantly to a compound of fear and outrage. "This is not one of your melodramas! Don't talk nonsense!"

The fog of alcohol and tiredness, the grey slump of absence where desolation should be, lifted from Charles' heart, revealing something bright—a kind of fury. "The mark of a hand on his face, and he lay as though he had been pinned down. How can I *not* suspect murder?"

Elizabeth gasped, retreated towards the door, but Jasper looked up again and fixed Charles with a look of keen interest that made him stumble over his words. "Now…" he looked away from the hunter's gaze. "Now I would be as glad as you to know that was not the case, but I want to know."

"Hm, um." Floyd chewed vigorously at his mouthful of breakfast, but could not swallow it in time to give an immediate answer.

George rose and took hold of Charles firmly by the arm. These days they were of a height, but the extra years had leant George bulk. Charles still felt willowy, ungainly in comparison.

He bent like a reed under the blast of George's force. Bent away a little, literally, as George leaned down to hiss in an undertone in his ear. "Is that what you want? To have the taint of murder thrown on this house? The neighbours gossip and horror? The Admiral telling all and sundry that you murdered Father, or that I did?"

That strange brightness spoke again—the certainty Charles had only ever felt before in philosophical dispute, or pronouncing on the meaning of certain lines in Shakespeare. "I want to know. He is owed justice." Some things were right. They had to be done; not because they were prudent but because they were *right*. "I thought we believed in honesty in this family?"

George's green-grey eyes crinkled at the edges, and the cupid bow of his mouth pursed up as if to shoot a dart. He straightened and knocked Charles on the shoulder with an elder brother's dismissive kindness, catapulting the toast into the fire. "Dear Lord, you are a child still, aren't you?"

"It is not murder." Jasper's voice curled into the room like the smoke from the burning bread, soft, impossible to ignore. "Or if it is, the culprit is long beyond the reach of any mortal justice." The strengthening light gave him a marble look, like a priest of Apollo, a Delphic statue with living eyes, and Charles wondered in a flash of inconsequence what he would look like without that wig.

"Oh please," George sank down with a sigh into their father's chair, at the head of the table. "Jasper, not that. Not now."

"Let me put your minds at ease," said the doctor, draining his glass of claret. "In cases of sudden death I assure you it is common to become prone to fancies, but there is nothing sinister here. A clear case of food poisoning made tragic by the effects of laudanum. Your father ate separately, I understand?"

"He was always rather irritable by dinner time." Elizabeth joined Charles by the mantel, covering her distress by taking down one of the shepherdesses and rubbing at an entirely imaginary spot of dirt. "The pain, you see? He would have his dinner on a tray in his room, take his dose, and then fall asleep if he could."

"Just so." Floyd smoothed a lock of gray hair back beneath his wig and looked imploringly between Elizabeth and George as if to say *is this a subject for the ladies?* Elizabeth brought her fan from her pocket, snapped it open. George pushed aimlessly at the cruet, and in the absence of further guidance Floyd carried on, reluctantly. "Well. Evidently what happened is that your father fell into a drugged, insensible sleep. Some time during the night the food poisoning caused him to vomit, and he, mm well, choked to death without ever waking."

Elizabeth's fan halted, then picked up its pace; she turned her back on the doctor, bowed over the fire. George studied the salt. And Charles said "But what about the hand-print?"

"My dear boy," the doctor loosened a button in the centre of his waistcoat and tucked his hand inside. "The mark was too definite to have been left by an assailant. Pressure of that kind would have left your father's face bruised. Um... scraped. This was nothing of the sort, only a cold white mark. No doubt caused by the blood sinking towards the, mm, nether extremities."

The fan snapped shut. Elizabeth pressed the tip to her mouth as if to keep in a cry, then said, "I'm going to take some breakfast up to Emma."

"Don't..."

"She deserves to know."

George's lips went white with strain. "Even if it kills her?"

"Your wife is not some nervous child, George. Nor does

consumption destroy all the powers of the mind. She frets up there, all alone. I daresay she is more likely to expire from loneliness and ennui than from shock. She deserves to be told."

Grimacing, George gave a deep, weary sigh. He dropped his head into his hand again, waved the other vaguely towards the door. "Do as you will. You always do."

Charles opened his mouth to say *and did food poisoning fill father's nostrils with dust?* and Jasper caught his gaze. There *was* a red note to the color of his eyes, like a thread of blood mixed in with brandy. It made Charles think again of vampires; wonder what it would be like to have the wide, sullen mouth fasten on his throat and suck. But Jasper did nothing of the sort. He just smiled a little and almost imperceptibly shook his head.

As Charles busied himself getting more bread, turning to the fire to disguise the flush, George's longsuffering sigh came again from the end of the table. "Although I never had any doubt it was an accident, I must say it comes as a relief to hear you confirm it, Dr. Floyd. I would hate to have inappropriate remarks made, and I know father would hate it too." He scraped his chair back. "And now I suppose I should begin making arrangements. Thank you for coming so speedily, Doctor. You have set our minds at ease."

∫ ∫ ∫ ∫

Charles shut the breakfast room's door behind him and leaned against it. The rain had drawn off, and sunlight shone from a pale, washed sky, into the eggshell-like dome of the hall. On the ceiling far above, the pink drapery and golden hair of Persephone curled about the pomegranate that Hades held out to her. The Lord of the underworld had long, white limbs scarcely veiled by his indigo cloak. His face, concealed from those below by the flying silk of his jet black hair, turned to her and she smiled.

"Come with me."

Charles started so severely that his feet almost left the ground. He thought for a moment that Death had stepped from the painting and stood before him, but it was only Jasper, materializing out of the shadow of the stairs as if he had stood there, waiting for the chance, since the doctor left.

"You startled me!" Caught between surprise and that odd flutter of not-unpleasant fear, Charles laughed. But he looked down nevertheless. Leather soled shoes. Jasper's steps should echo through this vault as his own did—heavier than his own, in fact, for Jasper was bigger.

"I want to show you something."

"What?"

Jasper bent his head and swallowed a smile, though part of it escaped, lifting the very ends of his lips. His eyes thinned and wrinkled at the edges. The effect was oddly sweet. "I don't think you would come if I explained."

Father's enemy Elizabeth said. And Charles' father—it didn't seem possible. He would sleep soon and, waking, discover it had all been a strangely theatrical dream. But Charles' father was dead. Jasper's shoulders were broad and his step silent. He had the power to hold an old man down while he drowned in his own vomit, and the stealth not to be caught at it.

"I take it you don't believe this was an accident?" Jasper asked.

"No."

"Then come with me."

Curiosity got the better of him. How dangerous could a clergyman be, after all, against an opponent not already stupefied with drugs? Charles nodded, and followed Jasper up the staircase. From the marble-topped dresser on the landing, the statue of a little black boy in a turban watched them both pass out of blank eyes outlined in gold.

Jasper opened the door to one of the guest bedrooms, stepped aside to let Charles in. Regretting the lack of his sword—still hanging in his own room—Charles brushed past. His shoulder touched Jasper's chest, and he stopped, long enough to feel the man's sharply indrawn breath through his own body.

"Your room?"

The green silk wallpaper had faded in the light from the windows, and the hangings of the bed showed an early lacework of moths. The washbasin had not yet been emptied of its grey, soapy water, and on the dresser a *nécessaire* stood open, displaying a shaving kit, an unstopped perfume flask, and a sphere of wig powder tied up in a stocking.

"For a few days." Jasper shut the door and stood in front of it. The quiet click of the latch felt ominous. The room filled with the kind of prickle that presages a storm, and sunlight pressed on the back of Charles' head as he retreated towards the window. From the open bottle on the dresser came the animal, sensual smell of ambergris, like a fox in rut.

Charles took out his handkerchief and wiped suddenly sweaty hands. He had begun to breathe hard again, half frightened, half enthralled. "You wanted to show me something?"

Jasper's tongue swept out to moisten his lower lip. He gave a little twitch as though interrupted mid thought. His voice, when he spoke, was husky as the scent. "I did." He moved to the wall by the fireplace, and when Charles joined him there stood quiet for a long moment. "Do you hear that?"

They might have been in Church; Charles too felt he had to whisper. "Hear what?"

"Closer." Jasper took him by the shoulders, positioned him with an impersonal, authoritative touch. By the time it occurred to him to resent being handled like a puppet, he found himself standing flat against the wall. Its rougher texture proclaimed that they had reached the old house; the Tudor core around which his grandfather had constructed the modern wings.

The wall at his back, and all down his front pressed the living presence of Jasper Marin—the man radiated sensuality like a candle flame's light. Heat kindled in the pit of Charles' belly, and flooded his body. His yard stiffened, and that only redoubled the burn of awareness, and delight. "I don't..." he tried wriggling away, ashamed.

This time Jasper's smile was almost fond. He lowered his head so that his mouth almost touched Charles' ear, and said in that same drifting, intimate voice, "You're nothing at all like your brother, are you?" Lifting a hand, he covered the side of Charles' face, turning him gently to press his ear to the wall.

At first he was conscious of nothing but that hand curved around his cheek, the finger with its jet signet ring resting in the hollow above his lip. The little hairs there stood on end at the touch, and all over his body the rest of his skin tingled in sympathy.

Then a small part of his brain registered that this was a huge hand, much bigger than the print on his father's face. At that sobering thought he felt the cool of the plaster against his other cheek, and the smell of lime and dust made his racing heart shudder to a halt. Through one ear he could hear Jasper's breathing, the long, barely audible tide of it. Through the other came the muffled sounds of the house. Doors closing, feet in the passages. Somewhere beyond it... no, not further, but fainter, *closer* to him, as if echoing through the wood and brick of the house itself, in the hollows of the chimneys and the dust of the hearths, wailed the eerie mewling cry of a newborn child.

CHAPTER THREE

"It's Elizabeth? She's had her baby?"

Jasper shook his head. "No. It's always been here. It grew louder last night, as though the child had been left alone. I lay awake much of the night, listening to it."

"The wind, then. Some trick of the wind across the chimneys." Charles retreated from the wall, turned and did not stop moving until he was at the door. But when he placed his hand on the latch, the little cry, despairing, unremitting, wailed on within the metal.

"You know that isn't so." Jasper's powdered face was so white that beside it the curls of his wig looked discoloured, a helmet of ivory.

"You should wear more rouge."

It almost startled a laugh out of the man. Charles could see the amusement burst like a wave in the back of those extraordinary eyes.

"I am prepared to try it, if it will make you listen to what I say."

"Why?"

"Because there is a curse on this house, Mr. Latham and, if you do nothing to lift it, I am afraid for you all."

Charles stiffened. Abruptly the room and its occupant disgusted him; the incense-like smell and his own deeply atavistic response. "I am an educated man, Mr. Marin. Whatever is going on in this house, I'm sure it needs no appeal to the forces of childish credulity and Papist superstition. If you'll excuse me."

"And I thought you believed in honesty." Jasper raised a sceptical eyebrow, sat down on the edge of his bed. He was human enough, at least, to sink a little into the mattress, leave creases in the counterpane. "Perhaps you are more like George than I thought; happy for a congenial explanation, even when you know it isn't the truth."

"Do not insult my brother to my face." Charles paused with the door half shut. "He is the only reason you are being tolerated here at all."

Jasper bowed his head in the same meek, enduring curve he had used at breakfast. He turned his face away. "Just as you say."

§ § § §

Drawn to the library, as he was every day, Charles could not settle. The high windows poured light on the crimson leather chairs, and the rows of books glowed like banks of gems, their titles picked out in gold. He touched Lady Ranelagh's Collection of Medical Receipts, and snatched back his hand as if scalded. The cry reverberated even in its binding. Beneath the crackle of the fire, up through the legs of the chairs and the struts of the bookshelves, came the cat-like mew of a newborn child.

Once he had begun to hear it, Charles could not block it out. Stopping his ears only made it vibrate through the floor and up into his bones, where it resonated strangely in the sound-box of his skull.

The voice drove him out of doors, at first to the formal garden. But where the house's shadow lay across the box hedges he fancied even the flowers drooped beneath its oppression. Late lavender stood up in sticks, and the snapdragons had grown leggy; sprawling masses of multicoloured jaws. Autumnal leaves drifted yellow on the shingled paths and, as he walked further, a spattering of heavy droplets shook from the screen of cedars and soaked, darker yet, into the black wool of his mourning coat.

He opened the gate in the far wall, and stepped into the family wilderness. It felt cleaner here, the wind making the long flaxen grasses ripple like a lake of champagne. Fronds brushed his calves as he waded in, plump beads of water flashing as they fell. Cold water spread across his shins and wicked up to the kneebands of his breeches. Behind him, his wake could be traced in a trail paler blond against the honey coloured meadow.

About a mile in, a massive tree had been allowed to fall and rot. He clambered up onto the trunk and sat, gazing at the house, waiting for his unquiet thoughts to smooth.

Jasper had no right to call him dishonest. Was it dishonest to refuse to seize the first explanation that came to hand and bend all to fit it? Oh he wouldn't deny that the thing last night had struck him at the time as being uncanny, even evil. But didn't Dr. Floyd's explanation cover all the facts without having to postulate some other world of malicious spirits? His memory might indeed tell him he was attacked first, knocked down after, but surely a blow on the head *could* disarrange the mind, mix fancy with fact? He might be remembering it wrong.

And the baby's cry? That he hadn't heard before Jasper pointed it out, and Jasper was his father's enemy. Jasper had every reason to want him jumping at shadows, ignoring what was plainly in the light. The theatre world had taught Charles that much could be done with suggestion, and Jasper seemed a master of it.

The unreliable sun disappeared behind a cloud, and it grew chill. A fine, light drizzle began as Charles squinted hard at the house. It looked the same as always: the two wings white and orderly, a triumph of classical reason, the core of it a more whimsical Tudor red-brick, with lines of ornament in cream and twisted, exuberant chimneys. Grafted in front, a Grecian portico attempted—almost successfully—to marry the two styles.

It's always been here.

Could that infant have been crying, inconsolable, somewhere within the fabric of the house, even as he played in its corridors? Could he have grown up with that sound embedded in the very makeup of his being?

Maybe that explained why he seemed to have no room, within him, to grieve for his father? Maybe it excused the wicked ingratitude of such a hard heart.

Sighing, he leaped down from his perch on the tree, his stockings striped brown from the trunk, and the back of his black breeches striped green. Perhaps George and Floyd were right after all; there was no mystery, only a tragic accident that could be mourned and buried safely. The third Earl Clitheroe would become the fourth, and life would go on in much the same untroubled path it had travelled before.

He thought of years sifting slowly, weightlessly down, like feathers. Years, settling in soundless melancholy, piling up, until death fell like a flit of shadows at the end. Then eternity in the dark streets of Hades, where the spirits were too weary to whisper. His father was dead, and it didn't seem to matter.

He slogged his way back towards the garden gate. Its wrought iron fancywork left an orange stain in his palm as he opened it, and he found himself pausing, looking down, while that one colour remained bright, and all around him the hues drained from the world, until he might have been a ghost himself.

Perhaps some sleep? Even now the thought of his bed—feather mattress, feather quilt, linen smelling of lavender, scorched warm by the coal and hot brass of a bed-warmer—had a delicious quality. He closed his eyes and rested his cheek against his palm, sliding the fingertips up into his hair, covering again the skin that Jasper had touched. Remembered heat replaced the trickle of drizzle as he flushed. Life still pulsed in him somewhere then, at least.

Rubbing his hand clean, he turned right this time, away from the front of the house, and walked through the kitchen gardens. Apples shone yellow on branches trained in rectangles. The whiff of cherries succumbing to mildew mixed with the fat green smell of cabbage. As the drizzle thinned and sun peeked out again, the ash pit shone as if covered with sheet silver. A dazzle of raindrops flickered at the tips of rufous spikes of fur.

The ash pit's sewage stench floated in a miasma amid the damp air, but that glimpse of russet drew Charles despite it. His feet slithered on the boards above the piss coloured liquid that seeped from layer upon layer of ash, night soil, and kitchen scrapings.

A slurry of discarded food covered the top. He recognised the dregs of last night's dinner—bones of chops, lumps of stew washed clean of gravy. That was what had drawn the fox, no doubt. It lay rigid amongst the rubbish, its thin black lips drawn up over needle teeth, its wrinkled muzzle flecked with foam, lolling tongue red amidst a yellow mess of vomit.

Murder then. Charles had time to feel and detest the flare of relief as bright as joy, before his newly purposeful strides brought him to the kitchen door.

Inside, the red tiled floor smoked from a recent scrubbing, and the long, wooden table was cluttered with bowls. Mary Dwyer and her sister Kitty squeaked together as they heard his footfall, and bobbed the best curtseys they could manage; Mary with her jacket off and her bare arms soapy to the elbow from washing plates, and Kitty with a mixing bowl of pastry tucked beneath her elbow and her hands floured to the wrist. The turnspit boy slept by the hearth, and Charles stopped Cook before she could struggle to her feet and kick him awake.

"Please. I don't mean to interrupt."

Cook knocked her pipe out into the fire. It was strange to think that Mary and Kitty—Mary particularly, with her nut-brown hair and eyes like absinthe, freckled face clear and fresh beneath her petals of white cap—would one day grow to be like her mother. Cook's face was red as rare meat, and the upright chair on which she sat entirely disappeared beneath her. Her chin rested on the shelf of her breasts, and her eyes were shrewd.

"We're all right sorry for your loss, Mr. Charles," Mary spoke up unexpectedly. "He were a kind man, the master."

"Mary!" Cook ladled water into the kettle and settled it on the trivet over the fire. "'T'aint your place to make observations to Mr. Charles. You just get on with them dishes."

Mary's jaw hardened. "Reverend Ollerson says we'm all equal in the sight of God, Mam. I can say how sorry I am if I like."

Cook rolled her eyes and brought a slab of chocolate from a drawer beneath the table. "Them Wesleyans with their strange ideas. Little better than popery, that's what I say."

"But still," Charles interrupted the incipient argument with a smile, "thank you, Mary. It is a shock, I admit."

"I tell you what else is wicked," Cook broke off a square of the chocolate and pulverised it with a half dozen practiced whacks in a mortar. She waved the pestle at Charles like an accusing finger. "That Doctor Floyd, saying as how it was *my* food what killed the poor man!"

"I don't think anyone is blaming you, Cook." Charles leaned back against the dresser opposite the fireplace. Blue and white china crowded by his shoulders, and the scent of jugged hare arose from a bowl by his elbow. "The butcher, now, I daresay he passed off some inferior cut or diseased animal…"

"Ooh, Mr. Charles!" Cook added warm water to the ground up chocolate and whisked it with what seemed unnecessary fervour. "As if I couldn'ta told! That stew was as wholesome as lemon barley water, which I'd have given it to my infant did I have one."

"And we ate it too." Kitty looked up from her rolling pin, only to look down again quickly before Charles could meet her eye. The mouse of the family, clearly.

"You did?"

"Yes sir." Mary placed the final plate in the rack and dried her arms on her apron. Round, white arms, she had, a shade lighter than her face. He thought she had thinned somewhat over these past three months, and her features grown sharper. If that was the case, however, it had not yet begun to damage her beauty.

She caught him looking and dipping her head, gave him a coy little smile from the corner of her eye. But her reply was all business. "Four bowls out of that there pot. One onto a tray for the master, and three we ate ourselves. Then the tureen filled for the dining room and the boy and the grooms scraped the bottom when they supped."

"My father's food went into the hall though, didn't it? And waited for his valet to take it upstairs to him." Charles felt sure from their intent faces that they knew very well why he was asking.

Cook nodded carefully as she fetched a cloth and lifted the heavy kettle from the flames. She poured water, whisked again, and handed Charles a blackjack of foaming chocolate. "It did, sir."

"Might it have sat there long enough to grow unhealthful?" A shudder wormed its way past his guard. He wrapped his hands about the mug and sipped to cover it.

"I should hope not! Not without going cold. It does sit on the sideboard in the hall not more'n five minutes. The master... the old master, that is, wouldn't have stood for no cold dishes in the place of hot."

Tainted food, the doctor had said. But if they had all eaten the same thing with no ill effects, it could not have been tainted at the source. Something introduced later, then. Deliberately.

He sipped the chocolate again. Thick, frothy and bitter it cleared his mind a little of the lingering fog. Some human feeling returned in the amorphous press of dread. *Someone murdered my father. But why?*

The kitchen fire hissed gently over its coals. Cook returned to her chair, filled her pipe and lit it with an ember. The ribbon of smoke smelled acrid-sweet, like tweed fresh off the roll.

"Why" led him to places he didn't wish to visit. "Why" led him to George; George with his debts and his horses, his terror of being seen in the same suit twice. George who had just inherited an Earldom and whose credit was now almost infinitely extendible.

But it also led him to Jasper. The Admiral, Jasper's guardian, had been in dispute with Charles' father for years—some long lying aggravated feud over field drainage and pasture land that only the two of them fully understood. Could a neighbourly dispute, carried on more as a hobby than through any real malice, truly have led to murder? Might the ward have taken up arms on behalf of his guardian, struck out like a medieval avenger, defending his family honour? It seemed unlikely, but there was no denying the man was odd. Suppose he had some deformity in his moral makeup, and thought it his duty to exact a revenge entirely disproportionate to the injury?

And then again, George and Jasper were old friends. Suppose they had worked together, Jasper seeding this story of a curse to draw off suspicion of human malice?

"Why" brought no answers, only more questions. He put the blackjack down on the well scrubbed table, nodded thanks and went out. Better to concentrate on how and see if that proved clearer.

A flight of steps and a bare, white panelled corridor led him from the kitchens back to the entrance hall. His ancestors looked down on him from their frames with unanimous disapproval as he came out of the kitchen door. If the pictures were to be believed, the Lathams continually bred true to type—slender, of a middling height, blessed with open, handsome countenances and pale hair. The chapel, indeed, boasted a stained glass window of St. Stephen the martyr, whose frank beauty and powerful innocence was said to have been drawn from Sir Henry Latham—the most notorious rake of his age.

Sir Henry's portrait hung above the black and gold half-table, and disconcerted Charles by being too much like looking into a mirror; seeing himself a hundred years ago, with a pointed beard and a devil-may-care glint in his eye.

This was the table where the tray with his father's food had stood, waiting to be taken upstairs. Now nothing graced its black marble surface but a pair of golden candlesticks, their exuberant curves echoed in the bows and swags beneath it. He picked them up one by one, looked at their bases and their sockets and put them down again, feeling foolish. What on earth did he expect to find there?

A chinoiserie vase, decorated with golden chrysanthemums, stood to one side of the table, and he picked it up, looked inside and found only the cigar butt he had dropped in there himself a fortnight ago.

Flanking the vase on the other side of the table a second

lacquered pot contained a plant of some kind—horticulture was Elizabeth's area of expertise. Still, Charles knew enough to guess that the drooping, flaccid leaves, yellow as jaundice, were not signs of good health. He poked the thing warily and it rocked sideways, the roots showing like shrivelled worms. Surface soil shifted, and beneath it gleamed a snow white heap of powder.

Charles took a pinch between thumb and forefinger, rubbed it. Square crystals ground into dust at the pressure. Prepared to spit, he lifted the finger to his mouth and touched the end with his tongue. Salt!

Salt? Someone had hated this plant enough to salt the soil beneath it? He shook his head with perplexity and went up to see if Emma was awake. She'd had a sharp mind before the onset of her illness, and was lucid enough still, when propped up and not in pain. Perhaps she could help him pick it all apart.

"I suppose it would be difficult to buy poisons?" Charles tried not to bury his nose in his cravat as Emma coughed and hacked, blood spreading over the handkerchief she held to her mouth. She lay back at last against her pillows, and her nurse sponged the streaks of gore away from her face and hands, held a glass of water for her to sip. Her hair seemed the only thing left to her which still had strength; a loose mass of auburn, russet as autumnal leaves. The shape of her skull gleamed through flesh gone colourless as glass.

"Simplest thing in the world," she whispered. "When I ran the estate, I bought arsenic by the sack. There should still be a pile in the barn."

He found himself kneeling by the fire, feeding in lumps of coal and watching the amber light dance fierce between them. It was hard to look at her, almost harder than it had been to look at his father's corpse. Death stood in the room here too, and she had made an intimate of it. "Why on earth?"

"You never did learn the ways of the farm, did you?" Her blue eyes in that whey-blue face looked luminous as the sky, too tired for tact. "We make a... we put it in water. Put the seed-corn for the fields into the liquid before sowing. It keeps off the birds until the corn can sprout. After that... they don't like it."

"I had no idea," he said, frustrated. He had thought he could at least interview the local apothecaries, ask who had bought rat poison, find some answers there. Now it seemed anyone at all could have gone into the barn and come out with their pockets full of the stuff. "Is this something George would have known?"

"Of course," she said, and pinched shut her blue-veined eyelids. Her brows twisted like copper snakes. "George... Why must he stay away? I should have liked to see him one last time. To say goodbye."

Charles forgot the hand he was using to feed the fire. Flames licked his fingers and he drew it back, reddened, stinging, just as a worse pain twisted in his chest. If it felt like this for him, he didn't wish to imagine how much George would suffer, sitting here watching her die. "I imagine that is the very reason he dare not come."

∫ ∫ ∫ ∫

Charles thought he was dreaming at first. Dreaming the splish and splatter of rain on the window and the warm enveloping float of his featherbed, darkness tinted brown by the dying ashes of his fire. Someone stroked his face, two fingertips across his forehead, light as a draft of air, barely stirring the ends of his hair. He tipped his head back, drowsy, just dreaming, and the touch grew firmer. Cool fingers gently brushed across his eyes.

Jasper.

His cheek flamed where it had been touched and, swaddled in its cocoon of feathers, his body blazed into life, sweat prickling behind his knees, beneath his arms, in his lap. His prick stirred and strained against the sheets.

Against his hot face the fingers that slid slowly down towards his lips felt rimed with frost. They traced the contours of his mouth and began to push inside.

His father's dead face. The white handprint. Evil—the certainty of evil—came over him and every particle of his body shocked wide awake with a jerk. He reached up, grabbed, and felt a wrist like two twigs in a dirty blanket. He pulled and pulled with all his strength and the fingers edged on, inexorable, cold and wet into the cavity of his mouth.

No! No! Oh God no! Daytime doubts could not touch his terror. He heaved and arched, threw himself off the bed, and it was gone, sinking back into his pillow like the lady beneath the lake. He crawled to the corner, grabbed his banyan, and fled into the corridor.

A floorboard creaked, and the house settled with a faint groan. Moonlight and rain drew shifting blue patterns on the floor, and as Charles collapsed against the wall he heard again the echo of an infant's voice in the brick. Wrapping his arms around himself he hugged tight, tucked in his head and rode out the wave upon wave of shudders. *A dream. It was only a dream.*

As his panting breath calmed, the floor creaked again beneath him, and the sound of vehement whispers drifted through the boards. A thud, and then a long murmur in a passionate, persuasive tone.

Charles drew his many coloured dragons more firmly around himself and stood. Long experience of sneaking home in the early morning let him find the silent spots in the slowly seasoning planks underfoot. He prowled down the stairs and into the rarely used east wing, following the sound of urgent secrecy.

He pushed open the studded door of the family chapel and went in. On the wall behind the altar a lamp flickered ruby red above the tabernacle where the sacrament was reserved. His bare feet brushed over grave-slabs. His mother's name, deeply incised into black slate, poked into the pad of his heel.

The vestry door stood open. Yellow candlelight spilled out, over the mosaic floor of the chapel, lighting a swathe of St. Werberg's drapery, her solemn Anglo-Saxon face. Charles put a foot in the centre of it and drew closer to the vestry, looking in at wardrobes, a hanging chasuble bright as a slice of enormous emerald.

A shadow moved in the small room, as a body passed before the candle. George's voice, quavering on the edge of a sob, gulped, "Not even you could be that heartless!"

Charles paused, then picked up the brass bound family bible as a weapon and slid closer. He flattened his back against the wall and peeked cautiously around the door jamb.

George had both of Jasper's hands in his, pinning the clenched fists. He leaned in, imploringly, shuffled forwards. Charles had only ever seen that beseeching look turned on Emma before, sea green eyes wide and trusting and the fine mouth half open, trembling with anticipation like a flower beneath dew. But this iteration had an entirely different quality, something not quite sincere about it, coquettish and false as the sob.

George's hands slid from Jasper's fists to his flanks, fastened with firm possession around the man's waist.

Jasper turned his face to the wall, grimacing. "It's so long dead and buried, George, there is no part of it that doesn't stink."

George laughed, a little whispered breath of certainty and amusement. He drew the taller man closer to him, and reaching up, dragged down Jasper's face to his own. The first kiss was not shocking at all, a chaste and beautiful butterfly touch of closed lips. Charles, watching, felt only that he had wandered back into the realm of dreams, the safe place where such imaginings did not touch the outer world, could not be called anything so sordid as sin or crime.

"No?" this time the chuckle was sweet and thick as treacle. George pressed closer, the skirts of his robe sweeping forward to enclose Jasper in crimson silk, and the second kiss began open mouthed, not chaste at all, their lips wet in the candlelight, their cheeks hollowed. Jasper's hand came up to cradle George's cheek as he made a sound of half protest, half bliss. The line of his body, braced against the wall, sagged as he opened his mouth wider to take in more of George's tongue. Tears gleamed gold beneath the tight shut black line of his lashes.

Charles slammed the bible back into its stand. At the ringing boom, they scrambled apart, Jasper drawing cuff, shirt sleeve and the back of his hand furiously across his mouth. "No." He took a step back into dark shadow, a blur of white face and hands for a moment, and then he was gone, as quickly and thoroughly as the ghost. George pulled his robe tight around him and knotted the belt like a noose.

Running back to the door, Charles eased it shut, stood resting his hot hands and sweaty forehead against its floral ironwork as though he had only just entered, swung it closed with a bang.

"God in heaven, do you mean to wake the whole house?"

George was still so very George. Still so elder-brotherly, so stuffy, so pompous. How could that be? He'd meant to pretend he saw nothing, found himself asking instead, "What was that?"

"What was what?"

This narrow eyed look he had not seen before. He felt as he had, years ago, playing with a rapier in the armoury as a child, when it slipped and pierced his thigh in earnest. Why had he thought playing with murder would be any safer?

"I heard voices," he said. "I thought there was an argument; that you might need help."

George flashed a fatuous grin. "Oh," he said. "Well, thank you." Returning to the vestry, he picked up his candlestick, and Charles took the chance to follow; wardrobes standing open, shelves burdened under liturgical silk and linen. The smell of dust and prayerbooks and ambergris like incense. Dust scattered in a fan below the panelling where the secret priest's door had opened and closed "But it's nothing you need trouble yourself about."

"I want to help," absurdly, Charles felt his own eyes fill. "I hadn't a chance to be anything other than a burden when father… and I want. I want to make him proud."

"You have a heart in you after all? Who'd have thought it?" George laughed and shoved Charles companionably in the head. Then he raised his eyes heavenward and said, with complete candour, "It was Jasper. He keeps the monastic hours. I found him saying Nones or Vespers or some such nonsense and represented to him that it was practically blasphemous to parade his papistry at a time like this."

Not a flicker of insincerity. George lied with the fluid ease of a man who has been doing it all his life. "His mother was a Minorcan whore, you know, so it's in the blood."

What is in my *blood?* Charles thought, aghast, just as George gave a careless shrug and asked, "What brings you out into the corridors in the middle of the night anyway?"

Even in the best of circumstances, Charles would not have attempted to converse with his brother on the subject of either nightmares or ghosts. He said, surprising even himself, "I want to look in father's eyes. They say a picture of the murderer is left in the back of the eye. A final impression and accusation."

In the silence that followed, he could hear the hiss of the flame as it ate its way down the wick of George's candle. The pool of red light beneath the nave light pulsed like a heart.

"You little ghoul," said George, almost in a tone of wonder. "And if there is nothing? Will you then give up this mad, unseemly quest of yours and let it lie? No image, no murderer, am I right?"

Charles rubbed a thumb over one of the daisy shaped rivets in the door, burnishing it. Within, relief gave a dull gleam to match. "I just want to look."

"Do we have a bargain? See nothing, and there was no murder. You never knew him the way I did, and I can tell you now, this is not what he would have wanted."

"He wouldn't have wanted justice?"

"Not at the price of our family's good name."

"I don't understand that."

"I know it, goose. I suppose every house must have its idiot." George chuckled again, that rasp of self satisfied humour that made Charles want to punch him. "Go and look, then. I have no doubt at all you are wasting your time."

And that was true, Charles thought, lighting a taper by George's candle, clinging to the thought as to the light. George would not have been smiling with such easy contempt if there had been even the slightest chance his own image lurked beneath the dead lids to confront him.

Charles led the way into the tiny, grilled off room which had once been the Lady Chapel. The Madonna's headless, handless statue still presided in its niche over a stone altar from which every saint had been laboriously chipped. The body that lay on top beneath a fresh lawn sheet looked too small for Ambrose Latham. As he lit the candles at its feet and head, a sense of deep wrongness, like a mortal dread, made his fingers tremble. He approached the corpse as if walking through tar.

The sheet was stained with faint yellow-brown exudations. He put his hands out to turn the material down around the head, and drew them back twice, suddenly very glad for George's mocking presence at his shoulder.

His skin crawled as he finally touched the damp fabric, and his spirit seemed to do the same. He looked down at his father's face, the jaw bound up in more linen, the sunken, sweaty, waxy white of it, and felt only a conviction that whatever this was, it was *not* Ambrose Latham.

The eyelids felt like thinly rolled cold pastry, and the eyes beneath had turned white, mucus-milky as semen. George still watched, so he stifled disgust and leaned forward. The scent of the thing was rotten-sweet.

"Well?"

Not even his own reflection showed in the spheres of cold jelly. He covered the corpse back up again with less reverence. "Nothing."

Blowing out the candles, they left their father's body in the dark. As George closed the chapel door behind them, the cockerel crowed in the kitchen garden.

"Are you satisfied?" George asked, softly.

"Not really. No."

"Then permit me to give you some advice: learn to be. You seem to have forgotten, Charles, that I am the head of the family now. I don't brook disobedience, and I want this dropped. Do you understand me?"

"No. No I don't." He looked at George's thin lips, the crevices of disapproval that newly bracketed his mouth, and added quickly, "But I am trying."

Chapter Five

"Wait!"

The shadows of the yew walk lay inky dark on the neat clipped grass of the path. The morning tasted of autumn, moist and cool. A faint mist veiled all distances, brought the world intimately close. At the back of the house the gardener burned the first crop of fallen leaves and the scent of smoke spoke of winter to come.

Jasper hesitated, walked a pace further, hesitated again, his head down and his back braced, waiting for the inevitable insult. A wide-shouldered, strong back, Charles couldn't help but notice, set off by the flare of coat skirts. His calves beneath them looked almost indecently exposed in their clinging skin of silk.

When he turned it was with the air of a bear who has suffered the taunts of one too many dogs.

Charles stopped in his tracks. His night had been sleepless and sticky with the memory of that kiss. Something he had only dreamed about had been made real before him, fantasy given flesh, and he could not stop reliving it. Over and over, each time with the same shock of disbelief and delight. No wonder the world forbade this as a sin! If not restrained, no one would ever do anything but sit and picture it, and let the world go hang.

Now, though his eyes were scratchy and raw, and his legs weak from fatigue and wet dreams, it swept over him again—ravenous delight. How had he not been aware, before, of the height of this man? Of the way his neck joined his shoulder in that perfect fluid line? Of the way the black waistcoat with its jet buttons clung tight about his powerful chest? Struck by the personality, how had he failed to be aware of the body that contained it, until now?

"Mr. Latham?" The raw, dangerous look faded slightly as Jasper watched Charles stand with his mouth open, looking—he imagined—like a codfish on a slab. "Are you well?"

"I don't…" Charles shook his head. Jasper shouldn't ask complicated questions like that. *Am I well?* "I don't know what I am."

A little resurgence of that inward wave of laughter flickered in Jasper's face for a moment, until Charles said, "I saw you, last night," and it blew out like a candle.

Jasper turned to the hedge, picked up a cobweb, the dew running down his fingers. "Ah."

"With George."

The side of Jasper's mouth twitched; it could have been a grimace, or a very bitter smile. "Of course."

"Is that why you're here? Because George…?"

He wiped the web off, dark glossy leaves snapping and the red berries bounding at the violence of the gesture. The whole hedge trembled, and grey drops of water spattered over Charles' hot face. "Why don't you ask him?"

"Because," Charles thought of his brother's empty smile, the way the good humour peeled back to reveal something unexpectedly hard, "I don't trust him."

Jasper gave a short, harsh bark of laughter. "Half my age and already twice as wise." Fallen dew trembled like gold dust in the mass of white curls that framed his face, and Charles wondered how you did this. He had watched plays enough—whether on the stage or off—to have some idea of what he might say to a woman. None at all for how this worked with a man.

"I wish you wouldn't wear that stupid wig."

This time the laughter was more natural. Afterwards, Jasper heaved a great sigh and let the amusement linger around the edges of his mouth. "Do I gather you will not be reporting me to the magistrate? I have been pilloried once before." He picked one of the yew berries, squeezed it until it gave a little pop and the juice oozed out. "It was enough."

Charles stepped forward and closed his hand around Jasper's wrist. A snap of contact, like the shock of rubbed amber, set him tingling. He could feel, from the size of the bones, the weight of muscle in his hand, that Jasper could pull away any time he pleased. But when he looked up it was to find only a patient, quizzical look aimed at him. Time thickened about him as he drank in the sherry coloured gaze, sweet and warming as liquor. Then the shape of Jasper's eyes changed slightly with understanding.

Pulling out his handkerchief, Charles wiped the cold yew-slime carefully from Jasper's unresisting hand, earning himself another small, bemused smile. "The juice is poisonous."

"I *was* aware of that."

Letting go abruptly, Charles stuffed his hands deep into his pockets and waited, shoulders up to his ears, for the burning of his face to subside. A woman would have spared his feelings, refrained from mentioning her own knowledge, allowed him to be chivalrous and protective. Would it have killed the man to do the same?

But that question led back inexorably to his father's death. Was he not looking for a poisoner? And were not Jasper and George, together or separately, his prime suspects for the task? He should keep his mind there, not on the shape and pent up strength of that palm. "I do intend to go to the magistrate," he said at last, poking out his head from between his shoulders, like a tortoise emerging from its shell. "But not until I have a murderer to hang."

He began to walk down the narrow corridor of dark trees towards the statue at the further end, and Jasper fell into step beside him. "You still believe it's murder then?"

"I have no doubt of it. His dinner had been poisoned. There is a dead fox in the ash pit to prove it."

Stopping still, looking down at him, his gaze emptied of that faint hint of amusement, Jasper said, "No. That can't be."

In deference to the new tone, Charles took his hands out of his pockets and straightened up. "Why not?"

Jasper frowned, began to walk again. They paced together

to the shadowed, temple-like room of yew bows at the end of the path. There a marble urn commemorating one of the many Mary Lathams of the family stood up on its Doric column like a barren tree. "If I try to explain," Jasper said, "do I have your word you will give me a fair hearing? If you are to turn on me as you did last night, let it be at the end, not scarcely a sentence in."

"You have my word."

The archway in the hedge to the left of the column opened on an herb garden, whose spindly overgrown plants ranged in small beds about a pond full of aimless fish. As they sat down on the raised edge of the pool, one of the under-gardeners—who had been cutting down a half-dead stand of wormwood in the corner—packed up his tools, knuckled his forehead and took himself out of the way. He was red-haired, freckled from too much sun, and Charles watched Jasper watch him with a new, imperious jealousy that he almost enjoyed.

"Well then." Jasper dangled his fingers in the water. The carp swum close to lip at them, and he smiled. "I've always been able to see things other people cannot see," he said, stroking the grey fins and silver gilt sides of the fish, making them dart away back into the deep water. "My mother's people say that a boy child born with a caul over his head is destined to become a witch-finder. He has strange powers."

He ducked his head as if to evade a blow. "If a sense one cannot be rid of qualifies as a power, then they may be right. Certainly, when I came here to live with my guardian it was the Latham ghosts I met first. The white lady. The burning boy. The voice in the walls. The charioteer. They are old, most of them. The charioteer, indeed, is pre-Roman, much faded. I don't think he will last much longer—another generation, another hundred years. I don't know. But I do know this, they are newly angry, and a house full of angry ghosts is not a healthy place for the living."

He looked up to gauge Charles' reaction, and seemed not too much dismayed by the numbed, disbelieving stare.

"I have no idea where to start." Charles sat on the edge of the pond and watched the glide of tarnished silver fish beneath water lily pads bearded with algae. "Can any of that be true?"

"I realize as a papist my word may not be worth a great deal."

Facing one another as they sat by the water side, it took only Charles edging forward an inch before their knees touched. At the little press of cuff and stocking Jasper raised his eyebrows. He had, it seemed, an almost inexhaustible fund of small, cynical smiles—this one had a softness to it that undercut its insult. "I'm not sure you know your own mind, Mr. Latham. There's no wonder you can't begin to fathom mine."

"I thought you were a vampire."

Jasper threw back his head and laughed in earnest, all his soft quietness dissolving for a heartbeat into such openhearted hilarity Charles found himself joining in. "And you balk at ghosts?"

"It isn't very logical, is it? My professor would rend his clothes in horror."

"You studied philosophy?"

"And politics. My father…" Still the sense of disbelief, the sideways jerk of his mind like a horse refusing the rein, at the thought that his father was dead. He reached up and combed his fingers through the little tuft of hair that stuck out, brush-like, from the bottom of his queue. The powder came off on his fingers. "My father wanted me to run for Parliament, but on discovering I was a follower of Locke and Swift he changed his mind. Withdrew his support. I have been trying to think of something else to do that might please him…"

Some shadow of wariness was removed by Jasper's laughter. He caught Charles' gaze with sympathetic eyes. "I'm sorry for your loss."

And it seemed natural, inevitable, to tell Jasper what he had not thought to whisper to another living soul. "I don't… I don't seem to care. I try to find grief and all that comes is curiosity." *Do you think there is something vital missing in me? Am I damned?*

Jasper leaned forward, a pressure of warmth on Charles' knee, solidly reassuring. For the first time in their acquaintance Charles found himself thinking the clergyman's suit looked right on the man. It was easy to imagine him in a cassock, with the grill of the confessional slanting light across that high cheekboned, narrow-jawed face. "It's the same for the ghosts," he said gently. "There are things that must be done first before a man can move on to grief—or peace. How can you grieve when you do not know the truth? You know not whether grief is merited, or the degree or quality appropriate. And Justice too must be appeased before you can be free. There you and they are agreed."

"It isn't right though, is it? It isn't natural to stay behind beyond death because your passion for justice is more consuming than the end of life itself? It isn't natural to feel *relieved* when you discover it was murder after all."

"Maybe not," Jasper's smile had become kind, settled there into age-worn creases as if he had slipped on an old, familiar garment. "Perhaps it would be more correct to let go, to leave justice and vengeance to the Lord. But, in my experience, very few of us find it natural to always do what it is correct to do. The perversities of humankind are unbounded."

It was Charles' turn to be startled into amusement. "You say that as though it's a good thing."

"I suppose I am so bad a priest, such a bad man, as to find it reassuring that others have their foibles too."

Charles took in a deep breath of air scented with smoke and musky ambergris. The day had grown colder, light failing rather than broadening. The wind brought fine drizzle and floating yellow leaves.

"Not such a bad priest," he said, comforted. "Though perhaps a little underwhelming as a vampire."

"They cannot hold much of a conversation," Jasper leaned over, squeezed Charles' knee in a friendly sort of way. A rush of pleasure followed the vein up into his crotch, distracting him.

"And those I've seen have been so swollen with blood it leaked out from their eyes. They lay in a pool of it, some of them. Fresh blood, though they had been interred for years."

Charles moved away, suddenly conscious of the cold stone beneath him, the bite in the air. "And then you do this," he said, disappointed.

He stood, his breath smoking away from his mouth. The driving leaves scratched and rustled as they flew, and then with a cold, creeping tingle the hair on his head stood up. Jasper's gaze was fixed on something beyond his right shoulder, tracking it. A pale reflection slithered over the tawny eyes.

"There's something behind me."

"Yes," the priestly voice again, quiet, sympathetic, certain. Then it faltered into normality. "I don't recognise this one. Turn around, Charles."

His back was frozen solid. Dislodging each vertebra took more willpower than he thought he possessed. Darkness lay behind him, as though the garden was but a draftsman's image and some larger hand had rubbed it half away. Light fell into it and was gone. All along the path streamers of soil lifted from the ground, curled into the darkness, and were swallowed.

He wasn't conscious that he'd put out his hand until he felt Jasper's fingers close about his own. "It's not a dream?"

"No."

The smell of lime plaster clogged his nostrils. The thing paused, seemed almost to be watching him, watching them. The marrow of his bones throbbed with cold as time narrowed and narrowed down to some lancet-sharp point of decision.

"Tell me how I can help you," Jasper's whisper could not conceal the shake in his voice. His hand in Charles' slid, cold with sweat. For a heartbeat Charles really thought the thing might answer. He swallowed his own fear like a mouthful of broken glass.

One by one, gently, the pink veined stones of the rockery

floated silently into the air, hung from the sky as if on wires. Then he felt the release, shouted "Look out!" and he and Jasper ran in opposite directions, flinching and ducking as the stones rained into them. They came together again bruised, wiping off soil.

"It *was* real." Charles had never been more grateful for a man who disdained to say "I told you so" as he was now. "It was real after all! Last time, the doctor said…"

"You've seen it before?"

"Yes." Although the influence was gone, taking with it its exquisite terror, this thought had enough horror of its own to make his back prickle anew. "When my father died."

They looked at one another, and then at the path towards the house. Did a darker shadow still linger there, sweeping towards the doors?

"Dear God!" Jasper caught his hand again, dashed away, dragging Charles, stumbling, overbalanced, and furious with fear, in the wake of his swifter, longer legged stride.

♫ ♫ ♫ ♫

The shoved doors bounced against the wall, wood panelling splintering. George stood in the kitchen archway, toying with the ribbons on Mary Dwyer's cap. The girl, leaning away coyly, was still giggling as George's expression went from mischief to thunder. "What the hell do you two…?"

Charles skidded to a halt, sides heaving. Mary dropped her broom with a clatter, picked it up, the smile lingering around her lips, and ducked back into the kitchen corridor. Jasper stood in the centre of the hall, eyes closed, chin up, like a man trying to hear a faint call. "It's upstairs."

The purple of George's indignation made his green eyes stand out like bruises. "None of your nonsense in this house, man. I won't have it." He set himself like a wall in their way, and Jasper balked. But Charles shouldered past his brother, took the steps two at a time and heard the lecture grow fainter behind him as he rose. "And I won't have you roping in that young fool in your schemes. He is fanciful enough alone."

Upstairs, Charles leaned on the landing table, gathering his breath under the eye of the onyx boy. His father's rifle, lying across the polished surface, pointed accusingly towards the corridor, and he wondered if he should seize it. It was kept primed on his father's orders, in case of burglars, but against the thing that had passed him in the garden, what use would it be? What use would any weapon be against the dead?

The doorknob was so cold it burnt his fingers, and for all the mad scurry to reach the room his courage failed him now. It took the sound of footfalls on the stairs behind him—George and Jasper coming to investigate—to force him to turn the handle.

The latch snicked out of its socket. Holding his breath he pushed the door slowly open. "Emma? Emma, can I come in?"

Her curtains had been opened and her maid had helped her into a bed-gown yellow as primroses. She lay propped against a drift of clean pillows, fragile as a bird's wing. The book she had been reading lay smouldering beneath her hand.

Someone must have made and lit her fire earlier in the day, for the room was coated in ash, and spilled embers lay winking on every surface. Threads of smoke spiralled gently into the utter stillness of the air.

One had fallen in Emma's hair, eaten its way through, leaving the auburn curls a mass of stinking frizz. It lay on her shoulder now and flared orange as he leaned forward. She had been almost a skeleton herself, and so it seemed fitting that across her tightened skin lay a white imprint of the spread sticks and knobs of five finger-bones.

The whisper of movement behind him, and then a hand settled on his shoulder, anchoring him. At the warm reassurance of it he could have turned, buried his face in Jasper's shoulder and screamed protest—if he had still been four. Though he didn't move, inwardly the feeling was the same.

"No." George moved as though his every muscle hurt. "Emma?" He brushed the smouldering ember away, placed his burnt fingers reverently on her throat. "No, love."

Collapsing forward, he sank to his knees beside the bed, gathered up her limp hand and pressed it to his mouth. "I'm sorry. I'm sorry. I kept meaning to come but... I just couldn't stand..."

At the sob, Charles looked away, found Jasper watching George's tears with a half-sympathetic, half resentful look. Jasper jumped, startled, when Charles touched his arm.

"Help me put out the sparks."

"What? Oh... yes."

Here was an emotion, boiling up out of him like scalding tar. "If you can possibly tear yourself away."

Jasper's wide, generous lips clamped closer together. He bent his head and turned, in a flurry of black skirts, to face the wall. Charles took a step forward, opened his mouth to address the turned back, and thought better of it. They put out the infant fires one by one, closed the door in silence behind them when it was done, leaving George alone with the corpse of his wife.

CHAPTER SIX

"I want him out of this house."

Returned from a morning in town with a cradle in the back of her carriage and a basket full of new linen for the baby, Elizabeth had spent most of the afternoon patiently, lovingly preparing Emma for burial. Her hands had been steady and tender as she brushed Emma's hair, twisted it up into a style that hid the burned, brittle ends. She had chased George out upwards of a dozen times and washed the body with only the Dwyer girls to help. Dressed it in white and bound its limbs so they would stiffen in dignified repose.

Now though, Emma lay beside Ambrose in the chapel. Elizabeth took her place at the dinner table and picked at the lace around her cuff, her calm unravelling like a thread.

The day's drizzle ended with a bloody sunset, and the dining room was filled from end to end with garnet light. Shepherdesses disported themselves on the dinnerware. Knives and wine glasses glittered. But not even the pink light could give a blush to George's cheek. Shadows ate out the hollows of his face. He still moved like a puppet pulled by someone else's strings.

Elizabeth lowered her swollen eyes to her belly and stroked the lump that visibly moved there. In the gap between the lacings of her corset a little fist or foot beneath the skin bulged out the black silk of her gown. Uncanny to watch, it must have been uncomfortable to suffer, for her constant look of endurance deepened and she pushed the lump down. "Did you hear me, George? I want that man gone. Send him home to his father."

Opening her fan with a punctuating snap, she gave a mock gasp of contrition. "Oh, forgive me, I mean his *guardian*. I never understood why we allowed his sort in the house in the first place, but now, look, God is punishing us for it."

Jasper spooned pork chops and spinach onto his plate, pretending to be somewhere else, but George's stunned look flickered, disclosing an instant of fear. "His *sort?*"

"Take your pick. Born a bastard, raised a Catholic. He spends all his time impressing the credulous with wicked, arrant nonsense. I wouldn't put it past him to have frightened Emma to death. She was so…" She choked on a sob, covered her face with both hands. "So frail. Maybe… maybe I shouldn't have told her about father. Maybe it is I who am to blame. I can't bear the thought of her lying up there, the thought of it preying on her mind until…" She covered her face with her apron, tears turning the material translucent beneath her fingertips.

Jasper grasped the edge of the table and stood. He stepped away, tucked his chair neatly back under the cloth and rested his hand on its back. "She's right. I'm intruding on a time of grief. I don't belong here. I should go."

"No!" Charles' silent denial was echoed from the head of the table by George. "You can't. I need… we need you."

The aura of George's authority had popped like a soap bubble. Charles almost felt it indecent to be in the same room as him; to see how little was left of him when the airy conceit and self-love had been exploded. "I won't say I've believed you in the past. Hell, I didn't believe you this morning, but if there's half a chance there's something in your babble… If there is some malignant spirit killing us one by one, then we need you to exorcise it. You're a priest, aren't you? Do something. Cleanse the house. Help us."

Jasper gave a shout of laughter, and then another, harsh as the rattle of a mill. "You need me? It's a little unfortunate then that you come so late. You need a priest? I am afraid I cannot help you."

"Jasper…"

Jasper eased forward, all but vibrating with intensity, until his mouth was inches away from George's ear. "In case you have forgotten, I cannot help you because *I am not a priest any more.* You know why not."

Straightening, he brushed the dust from his arms, avoided

Charles' eye, and sketched a slight, impeccable bow. "I wish you all good day."

ʃ ʃ ʃ ʃ

That great stride of his ate up the distance. Even running it took Charles until the stables to catch up with him. Jasper flinched from the hand on his arm, tearing it away, turning aside to brace himself on the wall beneath the archway. "What do you want, Mr. Latham?"

Sunset stained the cobbles red. The head groom and his apprentices passed, leading out the horses for their final exercise of the evening. Sultan whickered in greeting and Charles reached out automatically to pat the arched neck. But all those other curious glances raked over his soul like steel spikes. Jasper too, hand over his eyes, withdrew into himself as he had earlier done at the table. The buttons of his cuff trembled with the shaking of his hand.

When Sultan's trailing tail swished out of sight and the hoof-beats trailed into the distance, Charles seized Jasper's wrist, drew him into the shelter of the empty stalls. "She had no right to speak to you like that."

Jasper's chin twitched, his smile a gesture of defiance. "It is only what I've become accustomed to from your family." He covered his eyes again, rubbing at his temples, then laughed. "No, that's unfair of me."

To the right of the door, wooden steps led up to a hayloft; a glimpse of barrels and old, stiff tack hanging from pegs. Jasper perched on the lower steps, drawing up one long leg, wrapping his hands around the knee. "She's lost a father and a sister in the same week. She's husbandless and alone in a state of helplessness, confined to a house full of death. I would be less than gracious myself in such circumstances."

He reached up and grasped the rough rope of the stair rail, rested his face in the crook of his arm. "In truth I *have* been less than gracious myself. I do not make allowances enough for grief."

Faced with this forgiveness, Charles remembered his own conduct with shame; the misjudgement and accusation, which Jasper had born with this same patient, gentle resignation. "We have all made a scapegoat of you."

It startled a fleeting smile out of the man. "Well, that is an honourable task for a man of my profession."

Outside the door, the level rays of the sun had turned deep topaz. They gilded the downcast face, picked out the foreign, exotic cast to its beauty. Jasper's eyes were almond shaped, slightly slanted in bones that looked archaic as the pyramids. Cast in gold by the sunset, his might have been the face of a pharaoh. A god-king, not a priest.

"Your profession?" The thought pushed the pendulum of Charles' sympathy back towards suspicion. He reached down and rubbed the material of Jasper's cuff between thumb and forefinger. "Yes, tell me about that. You dress as a clergyman. You told me…"

"I know," Jasper twitched off the accusing fingers, hauled himself to his feet.

"So you're a liar. And what else? A charlatan?" He shoved Jasper hard in the chest, but the man barely swayed. He moved his foot back half an inch and then stood, immovable. It made Charles furious. "I will admit you have a charming, plausible way with you, but you are a liar." He pushed again, and again it was like jarring his palm against a wall. "Have you been gulling my family, and me? Worming your way into our sympathies. Taking advantage of our loss to… what? Get back at George?"

Jasper shook his head. His mouth twitched, and then he broke out again into that open-hearted laugh of his, though it had a faint high note of strain in the peals. When Charles hit him a third time, he caught Charles by the biceps, pulled him forwards. Caught off balance physically and emotionally, Charles stumbled. His fists tangled in dark wool and he felt the chest beneath it, firm and warm, lift in a gasp. That fear was back in him—the fear that felt like yearning. He struggled to find a firm foothold, somewhere to push away from, but Jasper lifted him bodily off the ground and slammed him into the supporting pillar of the stairs.

The jolt of impact felt as though it had winded him, or perhaps it was the look on Jasper's face that made his chest feel hollow, his lungs forget how to take in air. His heels knocked against the wood as he thought again of vampires. He wanted... didn't want... It didn't matter what he wanted, for though he set his fists in Jasper's hair and pulled with all his might, Jasper's head bent down to his. The wig fell, a white blur, to the ground. Charles' panting breath burned in his throat and dizziness washed over him. He could feel Jasper's breath against his lips, and instinctively he tilted back his head, offering himself.

The first touch of skin to skin, delicate as a falling petal, and his whole body jerked involuntarily as if struck by lightning; sweet, liquid, erotic lightning. The hands that had been forcing Jasper away pulled him closer, and an itch of pleasure stuttered down his arms at the feel of the man's thick hair tangled about his fingers.

Pinned still against the pillar, he arched up, feasting on the hot mouth on his. He licked and it opened. Jasper pushed harder against him, his tongue slipping into Charles' mouth, and Charles' whole body shuddered with the second shock, the invasion so personal, so unthinkable, so *oh God*, so fantastic. He made a little whining gasp he scarcely recognised as his own, and picked both feet up, winding his legs around Jasper's hips.

That was... oh dear God, that was... so much *more*. The silk of his breeches scratched across the sensitive skin of his inner thigh, even his calves tingled, pressed into Jasper's buttocks, and his prick raged and rejoiced, tight against Jasper's belly. He shifted and felt it rub almost painfully over the hard mound of Jasper's prick. Through four layers of linen, silk and wool, the sweet intense heat made his stomach clench. A black taste of iron in the back of his mouth, and mindless, rutting need seized on him made him do it again. The second time was better.

Jasper's fingers trembled, clamped bruisingly tight around his biceps and the little shudder of them felt stupidly tender. Their kiss broke apart, Jasper mouthing over his jaw, biting his chin. He offered his throat, tightened his legs, pulling Jasper closer in, thought of taking off clothes, and then of nothing but the build of blood, the clench of his balls, the hot dry rub of his prick against Jasper's prick. Sweat soaked out from his groin, made the fabric of his shirt tucked tight between his legs cling, damp as a tongue.

Jasper's mouth closed on his throat. A little biting pain, tongue lapping wet at the mark. The suck went straight to his bollocks. As he squirmed, his wet shirt pulled out slightly, stroking arsehole and the tender flesh between his legs. Pleasure teetered on the edge of pain, rolled over him. He shut his eyes and held on tight while the world ended in fire.

And then it started up again and he found himself soaked in sweat and come, smelling of sex and horses, with Jasper's arms around him and the wide forehead resting damp against his own. There was a blessed moment of warmth—gentling breath against his face and a sense of safety—and then Jasper gave a soft laugh and said "You see why I'm no longer a priest. I'm sorry."

It was dark in the stables now. They both trembled. "Put me down, please."

"Yes, of course."

The strength had left Charles' legs. He clung on to Jasper's solid form for a moment longer, just to catch his breath, then leaned down and picked up the fallen wig. "I wanted to see you without this. Now it's too dark."

The voice over his head was warm and soft as his featherbed. "There will be other chances."

"Do you think so?" Lord, how was he to explain this to George? To Elizabeth? Walking back in to dinner with a bruise the size of two sovereigns on his neck and a wet patch all the way to his knee. Was he insane?

"Loathe though I am to agree with George, he's right on this. You must bring in an exorcist. It doesn't need to be me."

The shirt that had been so delightful earlier now chilled

against his skin. So, this had resolved nothing, changed nothing. "But you won't be going far?"

He guessed the smile from the tone of voice. The world had become a place of scent and touch, the big hand around his cheek seemed a spot of light only because it was so warm. "Just to my own house."

"Good."

"Charles, are you well?"

He reached up, pulled the hand away. Held it a moment in the darkness and then let go. "I'm splendid. Good night to you."

"Goodnight then." The whisper, with its faint tone of regret, followed him out into the colder dark of the drive. He stood for a moment fighting the urge to go back, to argue more, or go somewhere they could make love properly. Then he sighed and headed to the kitchen gardens, where if luck was with him, he could climb from the apple tree into his chamber, unobserved.

§ § § §

The morning brought rain. Heavy, persistent rain that fell like silver rulers on the grey gardens and gurgled through the downspouts, pouring from the mouths of the gargoyles at the eaves of the roof. When he could skulk no longer in his own room, Charles wound an overlong cravat about his neck to hide the bruise, tucked the breeches guiltily between the mattress and the base of his bed and rang for his valet.

The man went through their morning ritual—coffee, shave, newspaper, stockings and breeches, more coffee, the appraisal and dismissal of a half dozen waistcoats—with no apparent consciousness that he was breathing the same air as a sod. Some of Charles' jitters eased. Perhaps it wasn't something, then, that displayed on the skin like a rash. Perhaps he could do this, get away with it, after all.

Dressed, he avoided the breakfast room, opened a door into the library. But there sat George and Elizabeth, on either side of the fire, pretending to read while staring into the flames. So he shut the door again silently, and made his way down the corridor to his father's study.

Far more of a sense of trespass on holy ground here than there had been in the chapel. He had been permitted in this room only twice in his life before; once when he left for university, once to be told the pocket borough he had been promised would be going elsewhere. He edged the door open warily, as though a terrible authority inhered in the very carpet.

A scuffed, rather worn carpet of blue and pink flowers, with a geometric peacock in its centre. The large bay window had been left curtained, and as he opened the heavy blue velvet, a scent of cigarillos and pomade engulfed him. His shoulders ached, and he turned, expecting to find his father in the chair, watching him with white ringed blue eyes from the centre of his own cloud of smog.

But only the chair was there, its red leather seat stretched and sagging. He drew up the sash an inch to let the smell out, then ventured over to touch the tapestried coat of arms on the back of the chair as if it was a holy relic.

He was going to do blasphemy. But he had broken so many rules this past night, why not add one more? So he drew out the chair and with a little frisson of guilty pleasure, he sat down at his father's desk.

Guilty pleasure, that was the phrase indeed. What had he been thinking? It was one thing to indulge oneself in fantasies at night, quite another to act on them. He'd never really thought of himself as the kind of pervert who ended up on the gallows. Yet no jury in the land would hesitate to put him firmly in the same category.

What had he been thinking? Yet how just was it to bitterly punish something so sweet? This sin so heartily abhorred by all—why? What harm did it do to any?

He reached down and traced the brass lockplate of the topmost, left hand drawer. Inlaid ivory and walnut glimmered in cream and gold spirals about it, and the delicate brass handle made a satisfying click as he flicked it up and down again. He drew the drawer out gently and lifted the pile of papers within onto the scene of nymphs and satyrs who cavorted across the desktop.

Spreading out the dog-eared bundle of old bills and letters, he found his gaze wandering again; the picture of the monarch stag that hung beside its preserved head, Ambrose's smoking jacket hanging from an antler. A family portrait; himself like a little girl with his golden ringlets and white dress, the sash around it cornflower blue as his eyes, sitting primly upright on the lap of a mother he could not now remember. George, a rapscallion boy with a fishing rod; Elizabeth very demure, with a pet linnet.

Jasper could not have been more right; he neither knew his own mind, nor could predict what it would fasten on next. And perhaps this thing between them, this mad oscillation of desire and rejection, suspicion and trust was responsible for that. It was a sin because it drove men mad? But wasn't love also a divine madness?

Love! He tapped the papers back together, raised them like a shield against the thought. Whatever lay between them, it was at present the least of his problems. He read through a tailor's bill, the date a month ago, and by the time he reached its obsequious signature his flutter of spirits had calmed a little.

Here were letters from the doctor, some still with the stain and sharp tincture of opium smell folded into them. A ledger from the drawer above his knees confirmed the letters; entries for the purchase of laudanum stretched back, page after page, twice a month for the past five years.

Only the initials changed by each entry; DF must surely be Doctor Floyd. DS puzzled him for a moment until he reckoned in the other items—fishing licence, a new rifle, an ostler's bill for feeding and stabling the coach horses. Doctor Samuels then, from the estate in the Cotswolds, where Ambrose took his regular holidays.

A cluster of entries for Samuels caught Charles' eye. *Night visit, two pounds, 4 shillings and sixpence. DS in attendance all day; 5 guineas. Four guineas to DS for services rendered.* And the curious *To Mrs. M, four pounds, the bedclothes and a quart of spirits.*

A day later and a DC paid back some of this bounty; *received of DC two shillings and a hunter watch,* but this name eluded Charles entirely. He knew of no family doctor with a name beginning with C.

Three months ago. Yes, he did recall that his father had returned from that trip looking wan and nervous. Some shooting accident, perhaps? Or a duel, hushed up for the sake of his reputation? Charles made a pencilled note on the edge of the ledger to remind himself to find out. His father's valet would never betray a confidence, but Ambrose had, as always, taken half of the household servants with him. One of them might be persuaded by coin or loyalty to disclose what they knew. He could even journey to the Cotswold house himself, make enquiries on the spot…

Rain still tapped on the windows, and it was cold and damp in here, with the wind blowing in and no fire. Charles went over to close the window, and as he did, a faint shadow of grief came over him; such a lived-in room, now as empty as the body it had housed.

Sighing, he returned to the desk, opened another drawer and pulled out more paper. The chill made him wish at first for a fire, and then for Jasper—for that moment of more than physical warmth as they clung to one another. More than that, he wished for the man's voice, his company, his half-mocking, half-comforting presence, and his thoughts.

As he rubbed his weary eyes, the wind skirled down the chimney. With it sharp and close came the crying of that bodiless child, melancholy, unending, hard to deny. He snapped the ledger closed, turned to the next pile.

Here on top was an inventory of his mother's clothes, with a tick placed against certain items; a cap, a light sprigged shift with lavender ribbons, a fichu "of silver-blue moiré silk," a sack dress "of mulberry brocade, the hem much torn." Beneath that, a stack of letters from creditors, demanding money.

Slithering out from between a wine merchant's begging missive and the slightly more frosty tones of the bank of England, a folded letter fell to the desk top. It had been torn in two pieces, and shook out from the bundle like waste paper.

Charles gathered the halves, his heart speeding and a little wash of excitement going over him at discovering from the address it was from Admiral Vane. He smiled at the bold handwriting for a moment, before recollecting himself. Dear God, such sentimentality, he would be keeping a lock of Jasper's hair in his pocket next, tied up with ribbon.

You infamous rascal!

The first words shoved his undecided heart, sent it swinging once more over to the other side of its oscillation. Straight from tenderness back to accusation.

Receiving your communication of the thirteenth, I have treated it as it deserved and wiped my arse with it. I send it back to you now that it has served its office, that you may treasure it as you treasure all your dung.

How dare you think to rebuke me with my birth? Your place in society you hold on the merits of your ancestors, such as they were. Mine I have earned by my own virtues.

Chief amongst those virtues is the inability to endure any stain upon my honour. You, sir, have done me calumny, and since you are so cowardly as to refuse me satisfaction, like a man, I must treat you like the rat you are.

You will regret making an enemy of

Admiral Sir Harold Cheveley Vane.

What did it mean? Charles rested his forearms on the desk, and looked at the ripped paper in his hands, while wind blew the rain against the panes and the sobbing in the walls rose in pitch, frustrated and angry.

"Be still," he told it, bowing his head, touching the paper to his lips, remembering Jasper's touch there; the warmth and softness, the bold, plundering authority of his touch. The voice cried on. A loose hair, missed when his wig was dressed, fell over his face like a cobweb. He blew it away, raised his head. "Did you hear me? Be quiet!" And the hair settled gently over his eye, catching in his lashes, tickling his nose.

He plucked it out, felt the others shift in their ribbon, ready to unravel themselves. The child cried on. Charles put down the two pieces of death threat and pushed them together with stiff, unwilling fingers. So Elizabeth had been right. She must have known of this, perhaps even been watching Jasper in dread of what he would do. *The Admiral makes a threat, he sends his ward, and soon after his enemy dies, like a rat, of poison.*

The door sucked closed, rattling against its frame. His heart plummeted into cold, fear making his hands prickle as he looked up. But it was only the wind. *Jasper* he thought. Somehow the man had convinced them all there was a ghost at work. Like the wicked family who had faked the Cock Lane ghost in order to get their tenant hanged, Jasper must have faked the apparitions for his own purposes—to make himself indispensible, to cover his more mundane mission.

Charles pressed two fingertips to the mark on his throat. The deep throb of the bruise hit his lungs like a perfume, arrowed on to his groin. In the walls the little cat-like roar of an angry baby scaled again to a pitch that should have brought all the servants running. He plugged his ears and it travelled along the bones of his fingers. His pulse raced, panicky, in his temples.

"Shut up!" Leaping to his feet he bared his teeth and bellowed it at the whole house. "Shut up! In God's name, shut up!"

And a woman's scream answered him, pealing down the stairs, shrieking in the great echo chamber of the hall. He had swung back the door, was racing down the corridor, his heart racing with a kind of exaltation, his body light, swift, buoyed up by battle ardour, before it came again; a tearing, gibbering wail.

Elizabeth! He reached the stairs, ran up them, three at a time, almost colliding with George as he pelted from the library, his banyan like red wings. But it couldn't be Elizabeth. Elizabeth was tough as ivy, sharp as rose stems, braver than her whole male clan. Nothing, nothing on earth could bring Elizabeth to make a sound so inhumanly afraid.

Her door was jammed shut. He tried to lift the latch but it would not shift. "Let me!" George struggled with the handle, light catching the new grey hairs of his brows, the cruel slashed lines on either side of his mouth. "So help me, if you do not let me in, whatever you are, I will have every stone of this house blessed against you. I will have you cast out and cursed to a hell fifteen levels below the one you currently occupy."

To Charles' astonishment, this threat appeared to work. The handle turned in George's hand. He threw the door wide and Charles' shoe scraped his heel as they scrambled through.

His first thought was "thank God!" Elizabeth huddled in the far corner of the room, with one of the curtains of her bed in a great swathe of gold cloth clutched around her. Her eyes and nose streamed and she was crying with hysterical sobs, the high pitched bubbling wail wet with tears and snot. But she was alive. As he ran to her side something gritty on the floorboards ground with a squeaking sound beneath his shoe.

George had reached her already, his arms around her shoulders. She turned and clutched convulsively at him, burying her sodden face in his pearl-embroidered shoulder. "It was…" Her grasping fingers dug in with such force they ripped the centre seam of his coat. "It was…" He stroked her braided hair, the tears rolling down his own face as they rocked in place.

Charles looked away, embarrassed for them both. He moved his foot, and beneath it there lay a little fragment of white plaster, now ground to dust. More dust scattered over the floor, white and soft, slippery underfoot. Here to the side of the fireplace lay another, larger fleck, white on the outside, tan within. Three ragged hairs the colour of chestnut emerged from it and trembled as his footfall approached.

Above the dust, the wall had bulged out oddly. Trickles of grit and soil wept through the cracks in the wallpaper.

"I..." Elizabeth raised her head, took off her nightcap and mopped her face with palsied hands. "I was tired. I'm always tired these days. I came back to bed and the..."

She sniffed. Without her white makeup she was a pitiful spectacle, her face blotchy and red, her eyes and nose swollen. Charles offered a handkerchief and received a determined smile in return.

"I thought I was dreaming at first. I... It seemed to come out of the wall. Over there."

"Maybe the plaster gave way, and the sound of it suggested a particular nightmare?" Charles rubbed his thumb over the hairs, then dropped the crumb of plaster and wiped his hand on his sleeve until it was sore.

"Don't be an arse, Charles." George rested his cheek against Elizabeth's hair, all gentleness for her, his ire reserved for Charles. "No nightmare killed Emma. I have no notion how you dare suggest it."

"Something," Elizabeth pinched her trembling lips together, swallowed, "whispered by my ear. I felt something... wet. Ah. Like a..." Her chin crumpled again, and she pulled the fallen curtain more tightly around her. "Like a hand. A dead hand. It..." Fresh tears coursed down chapped cheeks. The breath stopped in Charles' body as he remembered what that had felt like himself.

"It touched my belly, where the baby is." She covered her face with her hands and shook with gentler, more desolate sobs.

"I knew it could pass through the... It started to push through my skin. I think it touched the baby. Oh God, I think it killed the baby!"

"You two men go along now." Cook's voice from the doorway startled them all from the daze of horror. She bustled in with an armful of linen and a steaming jug of water, Mary following her with a tot of brandy in a glass.

"Cook?" George dashed the tears from his face, stood up, "what?"

"Ain't it the baby coming then?" The big woman looked crestfallen. "With all that screeching I said to the girls for sure it was Mrs. Sheldrake's time. Kitty's done run for the doctor."

"Ere, drink this, miss." Mary knelt at Elizabeth's side and wrapped her shaking hands around the brandy glass, watching with an almost maternal look as she sipped. "This house ain't a happy one, and that's for certain, but I'm sure, whatever it is, it ain't got nothing against you."

The spirits eased some of Elizabeth's trembling, loosened her grip on the curtain. She took George's lowered hand and with his help rose to her feet. "I want to go home, George."

"You can't travel in your state. Cook's right," George smiled at the servants, his eyes lingering a little on Mary. She looked very fine indeed today, particularly when compared with Elizabeth's swollen, dishevelled bulk. The silver-blue silk of her fichu brought out the vivid shade of her clear, peridot eyes. "You must be very close to term now."

"I'd rather give birth by the side of the road than in this house."

"Yes, well, I would rather you didn't."

Charles watched the two of them glaring at each other with a strange feeling of melancholy. He was a late child, a surprise child after a long barren gap, and he had never quite managed to catch up to the fondness of the rest of the family for each other. "Perhaps I can ask the Admiral if you could stay there instead?" he said, "Just until you are delivered of the child."

He had no idea where the thought had come from; fully expected Elizabeth to remind him that Vane had killed their father. Perhaps that was what he was asking for, the voice of reason telling him not to run straight back to Jasper.

But Elizabeth finished the brandy, took her bedgown from Mary's hand and pinned it closed. "Yes," she said, in the kind of voice her soldier husband might have used for agreeing to a death or glory charge. "If you would, please, Charles. I'd be grateful."

"Mr. Charles Latham." Admiral Vane's butler exuded a salty air. It was probably the wooden leg, and the appalling mess of the right hand side of his face. He bowed Charles into the orangery as if welcoming a captain on board his skiff, and was not above accepting a small token of esteem before he left.

The orangery too bore a faint nautical flavour; the stones whitewashed, the lime trees trimmed into severe regularity, the slate of the floor roughened and dulled by incessant holystoning.

The Admiral sat at a small table, surrounded by dark green foliage, amber moons of oranges and the scent of citrus. He wore a great wig, more suited to the past century, its cascading curls the glossy blond-brown of new cut oak. A plump man. When he smiled, as he did now, his shrewd brown eyes all but disappeared into the round cheeks. His bull neck was swathed from collarbone to ear in a cravat that looked soft as gauze and lay in a limp bow over his uniform waistcoat. "I won't rise, Mr. Latham," he said. "Waiting for death, hey?"

"I beg your pardon?"

With a rustle and flap the man at the Admiral's side put down his newspaper, emerging from the white screen like a butterfly out of its chrysalis. Jasper. He had left off his clergyman's garb, dressed now in a suit of garnet silk that clung about his arms and shoulders, shadows suggesting the curves of muscle. He had swapped that awful wig, too, and the plain, clubbed style of its replacement emphasised the hawk-like Spanish lines of his face.

Charles took a step backwards, cursing the fiery rush of blood he could feel thundering to his face. *A murderer, remember?* But his body listened to his reason not at all, prick stirring and straining uncomfortably against the pinch of his tucked shirt. The blush made his lips tingle and he swore he could still taste the kiss there. A wash of panic went over him. The Admiral would notice! Surely he was bruised all over, visibly, like his throat? Impossible for anyone to miss it!

"Mean that literally, young man." Vane laboriously pushed a spare chair with his foot, moving it an inch. As it scraped on the floor, Jasper leapt to his feet and pulled it further.

"You must not strain yourself, sir."

He gave Charles a little smile, sneaking it sideways beneath his long black lashes. Such a smile! Sweet and uncertain and wicked all at once. Charles' lips twitched in answer, his back straightened and chest puffed out with joy before he caught himself doing it and scowled.

"I will not be treated as an invalid, Jasper. The thing swells by the day, caution will buy me little more than minutes."

"Forgive me…" Charles took the chair from Jasper's hand, watching the welcoming smile fade. "I'm not following."

"This thing." Admiral Vane cautiously unwound his extravagant cravat, revealing a bulge of pulsing flesh about the size of a fist emerging from the side of his throat. His expression, as he watched the change in Charles' face from shock to curiosity, reminded Charles suddenly of Jasper's trademark cynical amusement. "Could pop any time, I'm told. Blood all over the shop. Dead in under a minute. Not a bad way to go."

"I," Charles leaned forward, watched the fragile balloon surge with each heartbeat, the skin pulled tight and red over it, thin as paper. "I had no idea."

"Indeed. But if my son had been doing the job I asked him to do…"

Jasper ducked his head, reached for the teapot, and made a performance of pouring straw-coloured green tea into blue and white porcelain bowls. "Circumstances rendered it impossible, Father. Forgive me?"

"Always. Always, lad. Just wish you'd gone to sea. Could have done more for you. A word in a few ears, could have got you a good ship, made you Post. Captain Marin, hey?"

Charles sipped the tea, its watery, tannin taste and fragrant smell bracing. If not for his own problems, and the grotesque growth that the Admiral was now gently swaddling in gauze, he might have found the exchange amusing. Were all fathers alike? This blend of pride and disapproval? Did they all nag in place of praise?

He put his hand in his pocket and touched the torn edge of the paper. The letter's blood and thunder vengeance roared on in ink there, but he felt now a little foolish to have been so convinced of its absolute truth. He brought the two pieces out, handed them to Vane, who juggled them between his teacup and a little kickshaw of puff pastry in his other hand, from which warm gooseberry sauce bubbled. It was not the dramatic reveal it would have been on stage, with the lights flaring up and the villain caught in the act.

"Ah yes," Vane lowered the pastry to his plate and attempted to scrape syrup and icing sugar from the declaration of war. "It all seemed so important a half year ago. I had a fish pond dug, you know," he gestured gingerly to the East. "Over there. Wanted it deep enough for porpoises—miss them. Miss the sea when I'm ashore. O'course, your father claims it's drained his best acreage of wheat, halved his yield. What am I to do about that? Tell him to plant somewhere else then."

Charles laughed, remembering his father pacing from end to end of the hall, declaiming this perfidy to the whole house, while servants and children hung over the banisters and grinned. "Yes, sir. I heard of that from the other side."

"So he opens his fences, sends his deer herd into my rose garden, damn the man!" Vane's purpling face fell, and his colour returned to a more neutral brown. He coughed and waved over the servant who stood rigid and blank-faced by the door. "Not spending my last hours drinking this slop! Bring us the Aguardiente."

He fixed Charles' gaze with his clear brown eyes. Jasper must have inherited the startling force of his personality from this parent, for the Admiral's regard, sympathetic though it was, could have stopped a rhinoceros in its charge. "Don't mean that, by the way. About being damned."

"Thank you, sir. But that was when you wrote this?"

"No," Vane laughed, a little wheezing sound, his shoulders hardly moving. "That was when I anchored my fleet at the end of your garden and encouraged my Captains to give all their men shore leave at once." His eyes disappeared altogether into fleshy slits as he whispered a roar of laughter. "Nothing like a couple of thousand sailors on the lawn for a lively time. Riots and mayhem! Took us two weeks to hunt them all down again after. Never did find the last sixteen of 'em."

"'Course, your father was apoplectic! Thought he'd burst his spleen with rage. Limped across three miles of fields to wave his stick in my face." Vane's watering eyes emerged from their folds, suddenly chill. His jowls ceased trembling. "He said some things to me, regarding my birth, Jasper's mother, that I could not tolerate. I challenged him. And he, the fucking coward, told me I wasn't gentleman enough to fight with him. Refused me."

The Admiral's fingers tightened around his teacup until the porcelain gave a faint groaning crackle. Charles shifted forward to perch on the edge of his chair, concerned, and Jasper closed a hand around his father's wrist, "Sir?"

Vane shook his mass of glorious horsehair curls and gave a tight smile. "Hm! Yes. *That's* when I wrote that letter. Don't know what I intended. Break out the long nines and bombard his house, maybe." He raised a hand as if to touch the swelling on his neck, but did not complete the gesture. "Glad, in a way, this stopped me. He was a poor old man, hobbled with gout. Not much honour in defeating such a foe."

The servant returned with a decanter of brandy and a silver bowl filled with marchpane in the shape of strawberries. Vane put down his teacup with excessive gentleness and gulped the brandy. "Besides, he was right. Who am I? Just a boot black's son made good." He moved his hand in Jasper's grip until their fingers interlaced. "Should have married your mother, boy. Thought I was too good for her. Thought I could do better. Never did."

A hardy autumnal wasp whined in irregular loops closer and closer to the sticky green spill of gooseberry syrup on Vane's plate. Jasper swallowed, and in the moment's profound silence bent his head over their linked hands.

A bastard, thought Charles, allowing his gaze to rest on the crown of Jasper's head. So the malicious whispers had been true, and Jasper was not the Admiral's ward but his natural son. Just a bastard trying to pretend to be a gentleman. No wonder he assumed so many respectable guises and rang false in each one.

The admiral tapped his letter on the table with a prickly, high pitched rap. "So, death staring me in the face, suddenly none of it seems so very important. Felt sorry for the old curmudgeon. Called Jasper home from whatever it is he does in St. Giles', sent him over to bury the hatchet. Then Clitheroe goes and dies on me."

"I am sorry."

"No, we tried. Now I'm all ship shape, ready to go. Just a matter of waiting for my tide."

"I thought," a peaty smelling wind with a hint of ice bent the grasses on the side of the river and hissed among the reeds. "When I found that letter I truly thought you'd killed him at your guardian's request."

Jasper walked down to the edge of the private quay, its weathered oak fading in the dim afternoon light into the pale silver of the water. The Admiral's barge rocked against it with a comfortable thud, red sails furled. He skipped a stone that went bounding three, four, five-six-seven times over the surface, leaving a trail of widening rings. "When my mother sent me to him, he could as easily have sent me to a workhouse, sold me to a chimney sweep, as claim me for his own. That deserves as much loyalty as I have to give, but even I draw the line at murder."

He wiped his hands. In the sombre light the deep red of his suit had an ecclesiastic air, a dull, dark richness that Charles associated with Italian basilicas. "You think very little of me," Jasper said, "if you suppose me capable of such an act."

"I want to think well of you," the petulant whine that came into his voice when he said this dismayed Charles. "But the more I learn the less confidence I have."

They had walked down to the riverside in silence, an unspoken understanding between them, knowing that Charles could not leave, not yet. Charles had been certain that all he waited for was an opportunity to speak in private. But now it had arrived and he wasn't sure what to say.

"Don't you find it cold?" Jasper pulled the light silk of his coat around himself just as a line of ragged clouds, sailing like the coal barges down the Thames, passed overhead. Rain drove chill into Charles' face as Jasper strode up the slope from the water's edge and paused by his side. Water soaked through his eyelashes, stinging his eyes, and as he closed them Jasper's hand caught his chin, turned his face. Soft linen, impregnated with the musky, sensual smell of ambergris, brushed across his brow, pressed gently on his closed lids.

More rain hit his back, slid down beneath his collar, carrying a gluey paste of wig powder with it, but on his dried face and all down the front of him the heat of Jasper's tall, sturdy form beat like a minor sun. "Don't," he shut his eyes again to avoid seeing the tender, intent look on the man's face. "Don't. I can't. Not without answers."

"I wasn't going to do anything," Jasper gave another of his fund of small, humourless laughs. "But we had, perhaps, better go inside. Thank you, by the way."

The downpour turned the path into a river of milk, loosened the side curls of Charles' wig. He could feel them sagging with every step. "For what?"

"For not telling my father I had been defrocked."

"I'm not sure I was aware of it myself." Charles kicked at the stones, feeling bruised about the heart. "I find I know nothing reliable of you at all, except that you are the Admiral's natural child—a fact that does not fill me with confidence."

"And one for which I feel I cannot be fairly blamed."

A styal completed the ruination of Charles' powder-blue breeches, leaving smuts of lichen and moss on his knees. He came down with a splash that spattered his ankles, trickled inside his shoes. Lifting his foot, he shook it angrily. "It's all of a parcel with your current behaviour. You lied to me."

Though the rain was easing off as they trudged up the hill, crested the rise and looked down on the crisp golden sandstone of the Admiral's modern residence, the wind had picked up again. Charles' coat clung, sodden at the back, and at the blast of icy air, he shivered, teeth chattering. Jasper struggled out of his own coat, swung it—warmer and bigger than his own—about Charles' shoulders, and at that moment he felt he hated the man so bitterly he could scarcely draw breath. "How hard would it have been to just not make the claim at all, if it was false?"

"Let me," they had reached the bowling lawn that stretched

before an empty dance floor. Walking over the great, rectangular yellowing marks where sails had lain out to dry, Jasper opened the iron and glass door, ushered him in. "Let me tell you everything. From the start. After that, you may decide what to do with me. I will abide it, whatever your decision."

"I suppose."

A few hollered commands brought servants with armfuls of towels and clothes. A footman with a gold hoop earring in his ear and a cutlass scar along his jaw thrust into Charles' hands a quilted robe. "Throw your suit out the door and I'll 'ave it dried in the kitchen in a trice. Oy! Badger, look lively now an' set a fire in Mr. Jasper's study. You won't mind changing in there, will you, sir, on account of it'll just be one fire to lay instead of two."

He took Charles' flabbergasted look as confirmation, and rolled off with an apelike gait. Jasper smiled a smile of deep amusement. "As you see, decorum is left at the door in this house."

Jasper's study seemed to radiate warmth. Charles trailed his fingers along yards of tawny brown leather volumes, their gold stamped titles gleaming against title-plates of crimson. The walls—what could be seen of them beneath the bookshelves— were papered with gold silk. Two chairs by the fire steeped in its leaping lemon light, their plump upholstery a mismatched green and blue.

"Refugees," Jasper smiled, seeing his reaction, "from other rooms. I normally sit at the desk."

It was jammed against the wall beneath the window, cluttered with quills and sand bottles, a sextant and an orrery clock under a glass dome. Sheets of paper rolled into every alcove, and towers of stacked books stood dog-eared with bookmarks. To the right of the desk a crucifix hung on the wall, the crown of thorns gilded and the blood red as poppies. Above the desk the window showed bleak and grey. The rain had returned and drummed down on the path outside with a steady, soothing hiss.

Its sound made Charles shiver once more. He drew closer to

the fireplace, peeling his two layers of sodden coats off to let its warmth reach his skin. At the rattle of the curtains closing, he felt a shift, as though the room had been taken out of the world, made into a refuge, somewhere outside time. He swallowed and fumbled with his waistcoat buttons, the buttons of his breeches.

Behind him came the rustle of Jasper doing the same, and he bit his lip as he fought the urge to turn around and watch. *Answers first.* But his body didn't listen, his prick stirred and his skin awoke in anticipation of being touched. Without turning round to look he could not tell if Jasper was watching him. It made taking his shirt off an act of risky surrender, the drag of its damp warmth over his shoulders once more delightful. Even the air, as he stood momentarily quite naked, brushed over him like feathers. He trembled with the mute, unworthy hope that Jasper would forget his promise, and press his naked chest to Charles' sensitized back. The nape of his neck cried out to be kissed.

But the moment passed. He drew on a dry shirt and a pair of canvas breeches, both much too large for him, and shrugged the quilted banyan over the top, uncertain whether he felt disappointed or relieved.

Jasper gathered up the wet garments and, opening the door, passed them out to one of the servants, receiving in exchange a tray of bread and butter, plates and glasses, claret and porter.

"Not more food?"

Jasper put the tray down before the fire, looked up with a smile Charles hadn't seen before; purely happy, with none of the undertones of cynicism and oppression he was wont to use. "Father believes that toast is medicinal after a chill. I'll just…" he returned to the door and turned the key in the lock. Charles' heart fluttered in his throat at the sound of it.

"It was George," said Jasper, moving through the intimacy of the candlelight with a soft tread. "No that's not… I mean…" He knelt down before the hearth, speared a slice of bread on the toasting fork and held it out. The yellow flames had died down, and their warmth had barely begun to reach the coals, crackling and hissing beneath them. "We grew up together, as he said. He was so beautiful. Indeed, he looked like you, though his eyes were never quite so candid."

Charles perched on the edge of one of the chairs, threw its two velvet cushions onto the floor and looked down at Jasper's bent head. Wigless, his drying hair was springing into tight black spirals touched with a hint of red. Ruby port and dark chocolate. Charles caught himself wondering what it would taste like and said "Go on."

"I thought myself very much in love with him, but he thought of us—and there were many of us, youths and maids—as a sort of convenience. Like a chamber pot into which he could void his bodily waste. I contrived to ignore this. I was very young." Jasper looked up, his gaze the same as it had been at supper when George refused him permission to leave, like a slave bowing beneath his chain.

"But when he went away to Cambridge and I to the seminary in Douai, my heartbreak transmuted very rapidly into a feeling of relief. Freedom."

Drawn by the melancholy of his voice, Charles pushed the chair away, settled himself cross legged on the hearth rug, put out a hand to touch Jasper's bare ankle and drew it back at the last moment. Jasper threw down the fork and caught his hand. "But of course, there was his grand tour. He called upon me expecting to be obliged. I... could not think of an excuse. You must understand; I'm the bastard son of an upstart, and he's the son of an Earl. So I yielded, and we were caught."

"George had it covered up. His allowance was ample and his connections the most exalted. The seminary allowed it to pass this once on the grounds of my youth, and George's high birth, but my superiors were told."

His fingers tightened on Charles', and the little rub of his thumb across the back of Charles' knuckles tightened his belly and balls. Terrible to sit here and watch the bowed, bitter expressions flit like shadows across Jasper's eyes, and still be able to feel desire. Did it make Charles a very evil person to find the bitten down anger handsomer on the man than his smile?

"George returned to England and fell in love with Emma, whom he married. I became a priest and was sent as a minister to the Irish community in St. Giles. All was very well, for a number of years, until Emma fell ill. Then George, feeling that he had a right to comfort, sought me out once more."

Charles covered Jasper's hand with his own. In the fire, the coals settled and a faint warmth drifted over the side of his face. "And it happened again?"

"He's not," Jasper smiled, slid his fingers up beneath the wide cuff of the banyan to stroke the inside of Charles' wrist. Charles closed his eyes against the rush of guilt and need. "He's not very good at secret trysts, your brother. Too certain of his immunity, I suppose, to feel the need for caution. But yes… I told him no, he kissed me, and we were caught."

The caressing thumb stilled. Jasper drew back his hands into his lap, knotted them together, huddling over them as if they hurt. "Because I had said no, George settled for having his own name removed from the affair, left me to be punished. I was tried, convicted, defrocked. I stood in the pillory two days, and the whores threw bricks at me for undercutting their trade."

The frown scored a deep arrowhead of grief between his brows. When Charles touched his shoulder he found it tensed against blows, the memory of pain stored even in the muscles. Charles turned away, blew up the fire until the coals caught and glowed cherry red. "I'm sorry."

This time he could fully appreciate the little chuckle for the gesture of bravery it was. "Not your fault. But my broken bones had scarcely healed when I received my father's letter asking me to come home because he was dying." Returning the bread to its plate, Jasper pushed the tray aside, pulled the cushions from his own chair and hugged the last one to him. "I didn't wish to lie to you, Charles. I forget that my vocation has been cut away from me like a limb. I feel its phantom presence and I cannot believe it's gone."

The picture above the mantel was of St. Sebastian, tied to a pole, pierced all over with arrows. Jasper smiled at it, his eyes mercury with tears. "I grew up with that picture. I thought it so romantic; martyrdom. Jesus Christ, I had no idea!"

Charles tried to shift position, got tangled in the overlarge folds of the banyan and shucked it off. It was warmer now, much warmer. The beeswax candles above the fire gave out a thin, sweet smell of honey.

Jasper soaked the tears into his cuffs, pressed his lips together firmly. "And I have been dressing as I used to, playing the part since I came home, because I didn't want father to know. He has at most a month to live and he's made peace with that. This... no. How could I possibly burden his last days with this?"

"You couldn't." Charles reached out and took the other man's face in his hands, brushing away the faint dampness with careful fingertips. Leaning in, he touched his lips to each eyelid, and then to Jasper's lips; little butterfly touches, barely more than a breath and a brush of warmth against his mouth. "I'm so sorry."

"I don't want you to do this because you're sorry."

The overlarge shirt slipped on Charles' shoulder. He gave a little twitch to encourage it to fall down entirely, pool in worn, soft folds in the bend of his elbow. "No." The breeches had already slipped to his hips, were barely clinging on there. He got to his knees and made a little shuffling step forward that made them slide lower until they outlined the curve of his buttocks through the thin shirt. "I want you to do this out of your own free choice. Please?"

Jasper gave a peal of delighted, astonished laughter. "Oh God, you are nothing like him, are you?"

"Do we have to keep talking about him?"

"About who?" Jasper grinned. He touched his finger to the butter in the butter dish and traced the line of Charles' exposed collarbone with it, making it glisten. As Charles watched curiously, thinking how strange this was, he leaned in at one end of the line and sucked the butter off. Charles yelped with surprise, clutching involuntarily at Jasper's wide, silk clad shoulders, his prick alert and throbbing, as a fever of pleasure burst from the bone. Jasper licked and sucked his way along the line and Charles wriggled beneath him until the breeches were around his knees and he could shift forward and sometimes, just occasionally brush his prick against Jasper's kneeling thigh.

His hands felt their way down the slopes of Jasper's back, his flanks, hot beneath a single layer of linen, fumbled with breeches buttons, just as Jasper leaned away, lips glistening and that big cat smoulder back in his whiskey coloured eyes.

The next line, gleaming gold in candlelight, he drew slowly down from the row of bruises across his chest, pressed two dripping fingers to Charles' nipple, circling it, rubbing the oil in. The burst of pleasure built from fireworks to a constant rushing tingle. Charles leaned back onto the scattered cushions, bringing Jasper down with him. Now he could arch up into the mouth that seemed intent on marking him all over with little bruises. Jasper's hair trailed over his sweating skin, making him shiver with delight, and his nipple drew up tight, peaked with anticipation. When Jasper closed his teeth over it, the tug and nip were molten gold down his spine.

Kicking his loose breeches off, Charles pulled the shirt up, over his head, and lay back down, completely bare, rolling the bigger man back on top of him. Silk and thin linen dragged hot and soft against that abraded nipple. The rougher canvas of half buttoned breeches teased his belly and his engorged cock. And the weight! God! The weight of Jasper drove all the breath out of him, filled him with a black ache of need that he had to have satisfied now or he would die.

He thrust up almost painfully against the rough canvas, but Jasper drew away, gave him that lion-eyed look again and growled "I'm not finished," in a voice that dragged up his cock like a tongue.

Sitting back on his knees, Jasper drew his own shirt over his head, and even in his need-drunk state of abandon Charles breathed in sharp at the sight of him. He felt like Pygmalion; he had fallen in love with a Greek statue of an Olympic wrestler, and here it was, brought to life, pale as porcelain. He lifted his hands to worship the curves of shoulder and bicep, feel the sculpted column of his throat, the strong heartbeat beneath a powerful chest, and the arrow of dark hair that led down beneath the slipping waistband of his breeches.

The hard-scrabble, greedy need abated slightly at the sight. Yes, he wanted... but slowly. After he'd felt every inch of that skin against his, sucked those brown nipples into hard pebbles against his tongue, until he couldn't tell whose sweat drenched him, whose spit filled his mouth. "You... are a paragon," he said.

Jasper laughed and stepped out of his breeches. Heavy hips, ridged with muscle, and a cock sized to match him. Charles' mouth went dry, and prickled. He couldn't tear his gaze away.

Jasper nudged Charles' thighs further apart and knelt down between them. "If you're still using words like that, I'm not doing my job." Though the words were challenging, his hands as stroked them down Charles' sides were gentle, brushing over his hips, ghosting soft fire across the curve of his backside. Reaching for the butter again, he wrote a word on the inside of Charles' thigh, and leaned to kiss it away.

Charles scrabbled to find more cushions, propped himself up so that he could watch the dark head dip between his legs. Jasper's rough hair teased the base of his prick, a thousand little licking sensations a chorus to the slow lap of Jasper's tongue across the hollow of his thigh. The sensations welled up the great vein there, hit him in the small of his back and his belly. His prick hardened and swelled until it was almost painful, the thin skin pulled tight. A drop of pre-come fell into his belly button and a wave of shudders swept over him as if he was cold. He reached down and pulled at Jasper's hair, trying to get him to look up so that he could say "please!"

But Jasper just shifted forward a little and closed that clever mouth around the tip of Charles' cock, licking the slit clean. Charles bent like a bow, arching up, his shoulder blades digging hard into the hearth stone, small pain subsumed in this rush of red, astonished bliss. He gave a strangled cry, half shock, half keen of ecstasy, and it stopped. It stopped!

"Sssh!" said Jasper, straightening from his crouch. His right hand rolled Charles' balls gently, his fingers slipping every so often behind to stroke the flesh there with a deep pressure that aroused even the marrow of his bones.

"I… I don't think… I can't…"

Jasper's swollen lips twisted in a self satisfied smile. He reached out and clamped his left hand about Charles' mouth before bending back to his work.

Charles' whole world narrowed down to the hand on his balls, the hand over his mouth, his own little gagged whimpers making him tremble harder with desire. And his prick, surrounded in wet heat. It was too much, all of a sudden. A black, ravenous need swept over him, he reached down, grasped Jasper's head, held it steady and thrust. Jasper's hands got underneath him, lifting his arse from the floor, and Jasper matched his strokes, pulled him closer. The need in him built like anger, like fury, like—*oh God! He was going to spill into someone else's mouth!*—and then it broke, came pouring out of him in a huge cleansing, purging rush, and joy came after it.

Jasper licked him clean. Pulling up the two robes he covered Charles with them and wriggled beneath. They fitted themselves together; Charles arm beneath Jasper's neck, Jasper's thrown over him, pulling him in tight so that at last he felt the velvet luxury of touching Jasper's skin with his whole body. Some panic, some dogged haunting cloud he had scarcely been aware of had gone out of him with his seed, and he fitted his head beneath Jasper's chin and kissed the hollow of his throat in sodden, golden content.

The fire gave a comforting crackle and settled a little. Jasper's prick, still splendidly erect, burned against the soft, sleeping form of his own. "Forgive me."

"For what?"

Sleep beckoned. "Should not have issued in your mouth. It's…"

Jasper chuckled, the deep reverberations shaking his chest, shaking loose something in Charles too. Jasper's big hand closed about the curve of his arse, stroked it firmly, making the skin there come alive, new tingles of interest stirring in his stomach. At the second stroke, the sensation was stronger. He shifted closer, tightening his grip, so that he could press his trails of throbbing bruises against the damp silk skin of Jasper's chest. Jasper curved his fingers and drew his nails gently down one arse cheek and then the other, and by the next stroke Charles found his hips moving of their own will, pushing back to intensify the caress like a cat arching up beneath the stroking hand.

Leaning up on his elbow, Jasper put his mouth to Charles' ear, the soft movement of lips against the skin making him shiver with delight almost as much as the whispered "I hope to have my revenge."

At the flare of intimidation and lust, his prick twitched, half filled. He put down a hand and closed it about Jasper's cock, feeling the length and weight of it, the heat, the skin satin smooth. The head of it rested in his palm like a heart. "Do your worst," he said, with only a tiny quail of nerves, and Jasper closed his eyes and murmured "mmm."

The butter again. In the fire's amber light the lines of Jasper's muscles gleamed like topaz as he cradled the flashing liquid in his hand. He dripped it, yellow gold, onto the darker fallow curls of Charles' groin. It slid, oily smooth, over his newly hard prick, eased over his bollocks and insinuated itself, trickle by trickle behind them into the crack of his arse, coating all his secret places until they glistened. He felt deliciously wanton, dressed for consumption. When he wriggled, the slide of his arse cheeks together sent a thrill through him that made his face burn.

Then Jasper handed him the bowl. He filled his own hands and worshiped Jasper's cock with them, leaning in to taste the tip, his senses filled with the smell of clean sweat, musk, and the creamy fat smell of the butter. Jasper's breath came ragged and he thrust in the circle of Charles' hand. The slide of heavy shaft, foreskin and hot head through his slippery fingers gave him a little jolt of delighted power.

Determined not to show himself for the virgin he was, he got up on hands and knees and cast a challenging look over his shoulder, but when a big hand closed about his hip, holding him still, and the other stroked down from his tailbone and touched the defenceless pucker of his arsehole he still jerked as if stabbed from the shock.

How could that feel good? And yet it did. It was positively the most intimate thing that had ever been done to him. And the reaction in kind was deeper than he had ever felt. He was tempted to run away, for a moment, to huddle back into the shards of his bodily integrity, not to let a stranger breach his bounds. He found himself breathing hard, his muscles tense all over.

The hand around his hip moved to rest reassuringly on the small of his back. "You haven't done this before, have you?"

"No."

Jasper's little laugh sounded awed. Cool air hit Charles' damp back as Jasper stood up, moving away to the mantelpiece. But before Charles could wonder what this meant Jasper returned, kneeling down once more, his belly and chest curved protectively over Charles' back. He kissed Charles' shoulder. "You could fuck me instead."

"No. No." That gorgeous cock—Charles wanted it in him, wanted to be able to feel it with his whole body. "Please. I want this."

Jasper's voice was smoky dark, soft as steam. "Hush then. Don't be anxious. It's good, I promise you. You'll like it." He stroked Charles' hair and shoulders, easing the tension away. Gentle touches all over his back and chest, and the feel of that big cock shifting with each movement, rubbing against his balls and the cleft of his arse. More butter, and the delirious slide got better. His arms shook and the riot of need made him push back against that hardness, forgetting his fear.

"Yes," Jasper leaned forward, opened his hand and showed Charles the candle he had taken from the mantelpiece, its base smooth and round, its tapered length a little wider than a finger. Charles almost choked on his indrawn breath. His balls tightened and his stomach twisted as a throb of gleeful, horrified, fascinated joy swept through him. Jasper drew the candle down his backbone. He closed his eyes and pressed up against its slide. When it dipped between his legs he had no reluctance left; the cool, hard touch on his hole sent a rush of bone deep pleasure up his spine.

It slid in easily. He felt it push through walls of muscle, emerge, within, into a more welcoming cavity. Every slight movement sent that same deep swirl of dark, sensual bliss through each fibre of his body. The round wax tip swept across something inside him and his mouth opened in silent disbelief at the throb of wondrous need. With a little pleading whine, he pushed back, taking in the candle all the way until he was pressed tight against the knuckle of Jasper's thumb.

"Better," said Jasper, withdrawing the candle with a slow, maddening drag. Charles might have protested at its loss, had his lover not shifted his weight and pressed something better there instead. Something blunt, unyielding, softly sheathed in hot, hot skin and slippery as sin. "You push when you can."

Charles could. Imagining himself as a slave boy in the harem of a Sultan; practiced, eager, long broken in, he spread himself wider. Pushing, writhing, the buttery slide of heat and hardness more than making up for the slight burning graze, he forced himself onto Jasper's cock, until gradually that barrier within him yielded, and the whole long length of it slid inside, heavy and hot.

Prickles of pleasure, little hooks of delight, plucked at him all over. Sweat rolled down his arms, and the love bites stung, and he felt too full to breathe. Even when he did, the shuddering inhale seemed only to make him more aware of the other man inside him. He trembled on the brink of some vast mystery. Then Jasper pulled out slightly, slid back in, and all fine observation went out of the window. He braced himself, pushed back to meet the next thrust, and Jasper's deep, ragged groan made his hanging prick leap. "Oh please," he said, reaching for it. "Please. Harder."

It was over too soon, both of them too keyed up to last. They met the little death together and clung to one another panting and trembling with aftershocks, in a mess of oil and semen and sweat.

Charles' turn to mop up—he used his pocket handkerchief, which he could conveniently lose on the way home—and to draw the impromptu covers over them both. Jasper lay on his back, his mouth lax and his eyes closed. In a fit of sentiment, Charles leaned down and kissed the tip of that bold Spanish nose. Jasper smiled up at him, pulled him down into an affectionate hug. The hollow of his shoulder made a pillow just the right size for Charles' head.

Charles amused himself by tracing each one of Jasper's ribs. His whole body felt creamy with satisfaction. The room floated, an elvish bubble, gold and amber, outside time. Jasper's breathing mixed with the sigh of the fire.

"I am trying to feel guilty," Charles said at last. "But I find I cannot manage it."

"No need."

Rolling to the side brought the picture above the mantel into view once more. St. Sebastian's serene face looked down on him as he supposed it must have done all the while they were coupling like hyenas. "No? That's not what I expect to hear from a priest."

Jasper turned the same guileless, loving smile on the crucifix. It made Charles feel jealous. "He and I have come to an agreement on that point. Not one that's shared by the church, perhaps, but then that's no longer my concern."

Sitting up, he looked ruefully at the empty butter dish, the full plate of bread. "Yet that will raise eyebrows in the kitchens. Here." He passed over a couple of slices on a plate, uncorked the claret and poured two glasses. "We'd better eat some."

As Charles dunked his bread in his wine the symbolism of the gesture struck him. "*Can* the church take away from you what God gave? If he doesn't mind, I mean. If he made you a priest, aren't you a priest whatever they say?"

Jasper's hands clenched. He winced. Charles wondered how many of his fingers had been broken when he stood in the pillory. "I'll… think on that," he said, heavily. Tossing the wine back, he found his shirt and shrugged it on.

Looking round for something less painful to say, Charles remembered, "Oh, I meant to ask whether Elizabeth could stay here. Only until she is delivered of the child. We hoped you had invented the ghost, but if it's real…"

"No, of course she must come to us. I hope in fact you will all come, at least until the malignancy can be removed from the house."

"The Lathams couldn't possibly all flee in terror!" Charles donned his borrowed clothes with reluctance. He could feel the unlocking of the door coming, and all those problems waiting outside it like a swarm of wasps. He thought about the barge that bobbed against the jetty at the bottom of Jasper's garden, and all the experienced mariners in Jasper's household. "But you could do me a different favour if you wished?"

CHAPTER TEN

"I'll keep an eye on the Admiral for you." Charles moved aside as the footman of earlier raced down the slope and out onto the quay, carrying a barrel of beer. He deposited it in the Admiral's barge, looking a hundred times more natural in his slops and headscarf than he had in livery. The scar gave him a rakish, piratey glamour.

Jasper too was dressed for work, in a tarpaulin jacket and slouch hat, from which the rain ran off in cascades. He sheltered a lantern in one hand, and in the other held a leather satchel, where a fine silk suit and expensive wig lay rolled together in the smallest possible space. In the deepening autumn darkness the whole scene had an air of Cornish smuggling village that was only intensified when the four men on board began to hoist the topsail.

"I mean to return as fast as ever I can." Jasper's look down into his face was as golden as the lantern, though he did not venture to say anything more personal. "We have enough men for three watches. We can sail through the night." He looked over his shoulder at the footman who now, relieved of his barrel, stood by one of the ropes, ready to cast off. "How fast would you say, Gibson?"

"In this wind, sir, and wet canvas? She'll do a good twelve knots, maybe thirteen. Should be to Lechlade in less than a day, touch wood." He suited his actions to his words, squatting down and touching the gunwhale of the barge. "So long as we don't waste no time, sir."

"I believe that was a hint." Jasper's little smile was limned by rainwater. Flickering in the light of his lantern, it slid into the corner of his mouth and gilded his lips. Charles tore his gaze away before he yielded to the wish to lick the little droplets dry. Though the wind that filled the sails and creaked in the ropes drove his borrowed greatcoat into his legs and plucked chilly around his ears, he still felt enclosed in the warmth of the study; glowing with it. A mixture of sexual satisfaction and joy must be rolling off him in a buttery wave, surely? It astounded him that no one seemed to notice.

"God willing, he will not pass until I return. And you… Take care, Charles."

There was so much to say, and none of it could be said here. The great red mainsail of the barge sheeted home, the foresail following it, in a straining red triangle at the bows. The wind knocked the leeboard against the jetty, and Gibson cleared his throat meaningfully.

"Good luck."

Scrambling on board, Jasper threw his satchel into the hatchway behind the main mast, picked his way forward to stand at the bows with his lantern. He gave a jaunty wave as Gibson threw both painters on board and leapt after them. They were underway at once, leaping forward like a greyhound from the leash. Gibson replaced the man at the tiller, settled in with the rope of the tiny mizzen sail under his foot, the tiller beneath his elbow, cutting himself a quid of tobacco as he steered.

With a final wave, Jasper crouched down, bringing the lantern low at the bow, looking out for obstructions. The rounded stern of the barge swung towards Charles, gilded with extravagant curlicues and mermaids fit for an admiral, all water-blue in the failing light.

He watched the lantern dwindle to a pinprick, sweep about the bend in the river and wink out. Then he folded his arms across his chest and pressed the heel of his hand to his bruised nipple, feeling suddenly, extraordinarily tired.

It was fully dark before he got home, and in the gusts of wind the little childish wailing voice floated out from the walls to meet him, an oppression he had not noticed until he had once escaped it. The entrance hall was brightly lit as always, but he fancied he *could* feel the malignancy Jasper had spoken of like a grey stain smeared lightly over all.

His footsteps echoed in the great empty place, and he shivered.

But the library was welcoming as always. Collapsing into an armchair by the fire, he moved the embroidered screen so that the heat would hit him in the face and waited for someone to bring him a drink. What an astonishing day! The embers of the fire, vivid, transparent shades of orange and sunny yellow, were a portal through which he could see again the events of the last few hours; the intimacies of the study, and the great, new found land of love, rich and endless as the new world. How good to have an ally. How good to have a friend, who would drop everything and go on a hard journey, on a dark night, merely because he was asked.

The thrash of rain against the curtained windows made him look up and give thanks that there had at least been somewhere on the boat for Jasper to sleep dry. As for himself, he would make no progress on this matter by sitting here in a daze of tender contemplation. Getting up, he combed the section of family history for anything that might mention the ghosts. Where did you look for a white lady? Or how put a name to a voice in the walls?

As chance would have it, it was the charioteer he found first, in a biography of Sir Henry:

Ye gentlemen, being Obliged to give up the Hunt by reason of their great Wounds, whereby not one of them could Sit a Horse, grew restive and declared they would find Sport enough at home. To this End Sir Henry Declared he feared no nightly Apparitions, but would rather put the fear of God into the said Ghosts.

Over the course of his Return to Health, he and his Noble Friends thus stalked ye Phantoms of Latham House inasmuch as the Hunter stalks ye Boar, setting up sundry and various Traps and Devices, viz Bells upon Wires across the passages and Balls of Chalk dust upon the doors, the which would Descend upon the unwary Spirit as it passed and Reveal it to All. By these means they at once espied the Hideous Spectre of a Rude Celt upon his wagon in the Laundry Room.

Sir Henry, with great Fortitude, discharged his Dragon at the Apparition, when it was observed that the pellets passed straight through ye Unfortunate Celt and Buried themselves in the Wall. The Ghost, however, with a look of the most Severe Affront, sank into the floor and has not been Heard of since.

"If in doubt, shoot the bugger," appeared to be Sir Henry's motto on all occasions, Charles thought with increasing distaste as he scanned the later pages for anything else. His mother's pet dog, his father's prize hunter and his own valet had fallen victim to the man's blunderbuss pistol. The valet received a flesh wound, but the brother of one of Henry's paramours had not been so lucky—left crippled for life. And this when he had come to Henry in distress, searching for his vanished sister. The chronicler, since the young man was a Catholic, appeared to think the event an amusing tale of noble high spirits, but Charles found he could no longer agree.

The servants were extraordinarily lax this evening. When the door finally opened, Charles was ready with a quip about having died of thirst, but had to swallow his words when he realized it was only George.

"Oh, you're back," George positioned himself in front of the fire, absorbing all the heat, and measured a line of snuff along the back of his hand. The woody, cinnamon smell was a burst of orange in the white panelled room. "Took your time."

Charles shifted nervously in his chair. Here was the guilt, hanging on the ends of George's greying blond hair, played by his fingertips like a harpsichord. A ball of burning pitch seemed to lodge in the back of Charles' throat at the sight of George's easy nonchalance, the confident way he leaned his elbow on the mantel. "It rained," he said, reluctant to share a moment of Jasper's company, even the memory of it, with his brother. How could George be so shameless as to look Jasper in the face after what he had done, let alone have the nerve to try it again?

"You don't say?"

But he couldn't risk George's suspicions, so he swallowed the lump down, where it lay gently seething with jealousy and resentment in the pit of his stomach, and said, "But they say Elizabeth may stay. We can take her there tomorrow."

George chuckled. "Goose! She's been upstairs these past four hours, in travail. You're a little late."

"Oh." Charles looked down at the portrait of Sir Henry on the fly leaf of the book open in his hand. It had a smile so similar to George's he felt time-sick with it. "If it's any comfort, I'm coming around to your opinion about father's death. With such ghosts in the house, murder on top seems extravagant."

"I thought you'd see it in the end." Having toasted his back, George drew up another chair, settled into it, unlatching the diamond-studded buckles at his knees with a sigh of relief. "What brought about this conversion?"

"I find," Charles pressed a hand to his lips as if it was the feather of a quill pen and he composed his thoughts before putting them down on paper. "I cannot see any reason for any of us to do such a thing. Moreover, you showed no concern when I looked for the killer in father's eyes. Elizabeth loved him, and is genuinely distraught. Jasper had been sent here by the Admiral to forgive the old feud, rather than avenge it. And I was in London at the time, at the theatre. There is no one left to accuse."

But the salt in the plant pot? The fox in the ash pit? He shook his head at his ancestor who grinned back up, unabashed, fox-like himself with his pointed tuft of beard. Neither of those things killed Emma, scared himself and Elizabeth half out of their wits.

"So I'm wondering about the ghosts. Is anything known about them?" He raised the morocco bound volume so that George could see the title. "Sir Henry met one, according to this, but it seemed inoffensive enough."

"Sir Henry is supposed to have *made* one." George opened the door and shouted for brandy and cigars. The house settled a little, creaking, and it was so quiet Charles fancied he could hear the women talking above his head, crooning encouragement over the little gasping grunts of someone determined not to scream. The mystery of it came over him like a wave. No wonder Jasper was religious, when this life touched eternity at so many points, coming from the unknown, and returning there, tarrying here for so short a time.

"How's that?" he said.

George regarded the empty corridor outside with a scowl, returned to throw himself disconsolately back into his chair. "Oh, Sir Henry? He had a mistress, you know. Well…" he laughed, "one of many. But this one gets herself pregnant. Nice Catholic girl—she's afraid Daddy's going to pack her off to the nunnery. So she comes to Sir Henry and says 'you said you would marry me, we'd best do it soon.' 'Course that's out of the question. He can't marry a Catholic. She should have thought about that before she let him under her skirts, stupid trollop."

"At any rate, that's the last anyone sees of her. Her brother comes looking for her and gets an arse full of shot for his trouble. 'Course, the rumour is that Sir H had killed her, buried her under the parterre, but no one dares ask. Three months later, the White Lady's first seen on the stairs, and she's been with us ever since." He laughed, a quiet hiss of breath through the nose. "Quite an heirloom. If it wasn't such a hit and miss affair I'd be tempted to add one to the collection myself. Nothing like it for ensuring your posterity."

"You are a piece of work, George." Giving up on the drink, Charles knelt on the bare boards to make up the fire, feeling his brother's gaze like a weight on the crown of his head.

"The same blood is in you, my lad." George spread his arms wide along the back of his chair, and tipped his head back with a weary sigh. "I do hope she isn't all night about it. I need my sleep."

∫ ∫ ∫ ∫

The morning brought an early fog that eased into one of those autumnal days that felt as though it had been seeped in cider. As Charles burrowed deeper under his coverlet, reliving in slumbering content the press of arms about him, the sweetness of breath on his cheek, his valet cruelly flung open the curtains and allowed chill saffron sunlight and a scent of wild garlic to scour in a tonic blast throughout the room.

The early post brought missives and play-bills, but not the letter he waited for. He knew it could not; not yet. But still it was a disappointment.

News came down from Elizabeth's room that the new baby too was not all that could have been hoped for, being a girl, but that mother and child were both alive, both sleeping, and would not be receiving visitors until the morrow. So Charles selected the most interesting of his plays and went down to London to watch it.

Theo was in the crowd, with some members of his troupe, encouraging the audience to heckle their rivals, and supplying mouldy oranges for throwing. Charles spent all evening avoiding him, and returned with no notion of what he had seen, sober as a judge.

Still no post the day after, but the wind had risen and shifted direction. The chimney pots hummed and dank grey leaves rushed past like the wild hunt, but the house felt homely again; an encircling, protective presence. He noticed, as he went up to Elizabeth's room around noon, that he was no longer obsessively checking the shadows.

He had no desire to be fond of babies, in the general course of things, but when he was allowed to hold his niece, he was charmed despite it. The wriggling creature in white bonnet and long dresses regarded him with a frown, as if trying to puzzle out what he was. She smelled milky-sweet, like a sleeping puppy, and lay trustingly in his arms. She had a thin crop of copper hair, an empurpled look about the face from the exertion of being born, and eyes like Chinese porcelain—blue even about the whites.

"Ugly little thing, isn't she?" he said, pretending not to be affected as the tiny hand reached out and grasped his neckcloth.

"Not worse than you at the same age." Elizabeth's eyes were

bruised with fatigue, but it felt like the first time in months he had seen her smile. "I really thought she was dead; that I was going through all of that to bring forth a stillborn. Knowing she's alive, I'd love her if she had two heads."

He carried her away from the window's light, and perched on the side of the bed with her, so that Elizabeth could run a caressing finger from the curve of snub nose to chin. The child smacked her lips as the fingertip touched her mouth.

"Does she have a name, this niece of mine?"

The door opened to admit Mary Dwyer, and a comfortably round matron in her forties with a child of indeterminate sex toddling behind her.

"Harriet." Elizabeth cast a lazy glance at the women, then stiffened like a pointer dog and whipped back a newly intent look. Her face hardened into war-like lines. "Her name is Harriet. And thank you Mrs. Price, you come in excellent time. She is about to be hungry. Please take her into the nursery and feed her. Mary, would you tell Lord Clitheroe I need to speak to him at once."

The change from pliable new mother to mistress of the house was so extreme it took Charles several breaths to catch up with it. By the time he did, she was in the middle of saying "Charles, you stay. I want you to hear this too."

"What…?"

She waited until the door had closed before answering, tucked her plaited hair up under her cap and motioned for him to pass her bedgown. "Please call for two of the menservants."

"Why…?"

"Just do it, Charles. I have a good reason but I'm tired and have no desire to explain this more than once."

The wind rattled the windows, and as Mary came in on George's arm the leaping candle flames twinkled in the deep purple jewel of her pendant, tied about her neck on a ribbon as green as her eyes. She dropped a little curtsy. "Lord Clitheroe, mum," and, smiling, headed back towards the door.

"No Mary, stay a moment." Drawn and deflated as she looked, there was still the iron of the Latham family will in Elizabeth's quiet command. Mary was arrested between one footfall and the rest. Noticing the footmen who stood like sentinels, one on either side of the door, she turned slowly back, looked from Charles' face to George's, in innocent appeal. "Yes, mum?"

"Where did you get that necklace?"

Mary's eyes flickered as though she had closed an inner eyelid, opened it again, fast as a snake. "It's mine, miss. My young man give it me."

A nicely cut amethyst in the centre of a cluster of tiny seed pearls. The setting looked to be made of gold. Fine for a servant girl, Charles thought, maybe a little too fine, but not something he would have looked at twice. Yet here was Elizabeth vibrating with righteous indignation, and George, having leaned forward to examine it close, gasped, his mouth and eyes drawing thin as wire.

"You are a liar as well as a thief." Elizabeth's firm voice chilled even further. "That is Emma's. It's the drop from one of her earrings. I'd know it anywhere."

"Damn me if it isn't." George picked it up, his knuckles brushing Mary's breasts. "I'd have seen it as part of the pair. I didn't recognise it on the ribbon." He pulled her slightly closer by the neck. "Where did you come by my Emma's jewellery, girl?"

Mary raised her chin, looking splendid and vivid as an orchid and not at all abashed. "She didn't have no use for it any more. And my young man *did* give it me, or leastways, he should have."

"What on earth do you mean?" Elizabeth drew herself up, outrage burning her cheeks. Amongst her satin pillows, surrounded by her silver-bullion laced curtains, she might have been the goddess Hera on her throne, completely certain of her own power and the justice of her cause.

But Mary pried George's hand off her finger by finger and made a little swirling twirl to look at each member of the family in turn, eyes clear as absinthe, and her face bold. Fearsomely brave and quite undeterred. It was the completest thing. "When I'm Lady Clitheroe it'll be mine anyways. So yes, it is mine miss, or it will be soon enough."

"When you're Lady Clitheroe?" Despite her fierce beauty, the thought made Charles laugh.

At his snigger she rounded on him in a fury. "What's so funny? He said he would marry me. Didn't you George? And Mr. Latham is a fine gentleman, so of course I believes him."

Scarcely a week ago, Charles' laugh would have expressed his every thought on the matter. But that had been before Jasper. He was in love with a bastard. A man! A maidservant seemed a step up. "*Do* you mean to marry her, George?"

"Oh, don't be absurd!" George drew himself up to the full extent of his middling height and oozed contempt. "Marry my father's drab? I think not." He caught Mary's chin, his thumb in the centre squeezing until it turned livid white, and sized up her face as though buying a horse. "I could buy a dozen of you at the local tavern."

There was still nothing like fear in her eyes; her back straight, her fists clenched, and her face pure. "Then it's you what's the liar and the thief. Taking what don't belong to you, breaking your word after."

George's face suffused with blood, purple as young Harriet's. He beckoned the footmen over with a savage jerk of the chin. "Take her and lock her in the coal cellar. Then Jones, you run for the magistrate. Insolent slut! I'll see you hanging from the gibbet in the marketplace before the week's out."

The footmen took her by the upper arms. She didn't fight, merely dropped a mocking curtsey and smiled sweet as sugar-plums. "You want to watch your language, sir. You know what the Bible says about the wages of sin."

When she had gone, the silence thickened about them like clotting blood. Then at last Elizabeth sighed. "Poor child. George, really…!"

George rolled his eyes. "Oh don't let her wounded virtue trouble you. I inherited her from father, like the other secret passages. She was well trodden by the time I got her."

Elizabeth bent her head into her hand and rubbed her eyes. "Even so, I wish you would keep your hands off the servants. It makes the management of the household so tricky. Lord knows, if you have her hanged we must expect to have to part with Kitty, and Cook too. And it will be Christmas soon!"

CHAPTER ELEVEN

It began with a creak as the library door swung slowly open, and a wave-front of cold air broke over the back of Charles' seat. The flames of the fire sputtered blue for a moment and then blew out. Ash came up in a plume from it, rolled out, gritty, warm as flesh, about his knees. From the chair opposite, George looked up with a brittle, frightened smile. "Dear Lord!" he whispered. "I hoped it was over!"

Charles forced himself to his feet despite the fear pressing him down. A faint, persistent breeze came in from the hall. The walls wavered as if seen through thick glass and a crawling horror seeped out of them, chilling him.

Silence. And something moving. He felt its approach mutely, as a shepherd might sense an oncoming storm. George moved jerkily towards the door. They looked at one another and from the expression on George's face Charles knew he too was thinking *which one of us does it want?*

Wordless terror floated like ice in George's sea-coloured eyes, then he turned abruptly, strode across the room and threw open the sash. Leaves blew in, and moss, and fog. "It's coming this way. Out the window!"

Mist filled the room, spreading in strange spirals, chill and wet on Charles' face. He took a shaky, wary step towards George and as he set down his heel the whole house shuddered beneath him. Doors burst open. The frame of the window snatched itself from George's grip and slammed itself shut so violently that every pane shattered. George yelped with fury and pain, leapt away. He scrambled to Charles' side, holding his wrist. Blood dripped with a patter like rain from the fingers of both hands, and he looked at it wide eyed. Unbelieving. "This thing means to kill us."

"Yes." Charles didn't say "it means to kill *you*," but an unworthy part of him thought it; thought of running away, leaving George alone to face a fate he well merited. But George was *his* brother, damn his eyes, and he had lost enough already. "Sir Henry drove the charioteer away by…"

He ran to the mantelpiece where his father's least favourite pair of pistols hung crossed over the fire, wrenched them down and tossed one to his brother. George caught it in slippery fingers, some of the roguish sparkle returning to his eye.

"We need…"

"In the desk drawer."

Two little paper cartridges of black powder met his questing fingers as he rummaged about in the odds and ends of the library desk, but no shot. Charles combed the bookshelves, turned back in defeat to discover George ripping the diamond and silver beads from the embroidery of his waistcoat. They poured a fortune down the barrel of their guns, and tamped it down with wads of silk. Then, with a final glance at one another for courage, they ran out of the room, towards the threat.

She stood half way down the grand flight of stairs, a shroud shaped patch of white barely thicker than the fog that continued to pour in through every gaping door and window. At the top of the stairs, behind and above her, Elizabeth crept from her room with a fire-poker held like a sword in her hand, her other hand clamped about her mouth as if to keep in the scream.

The white shape drifted slowly forward, oozed down a step, a suggestion of fluttering at its base. Charles lifted an arm that felt heavy as a continent, levelled his pistol at the place where it should have a face, and with a weightless unhurried drift it turned towards him, looked straight at him.

He pulled the trigger. He thought he did. He meant to. But as in nightmare, the link between body and soul had been severed. Command and rage and weep with frustration as he might, he could not move, his blood congealed, his muscles clamped in death's rigor.

Another step down, and she was clearer now, swathed in a long veil from toe to crown, white as quicklime. Dust pattered on the stairs as she passed.

Opposite the portrait of Sir Henry she stopped. His yellow hair was as ghostly as she in the fog, and his painted dark eyes seemed to glitter. The shrouded shape bulged in the middle, and then finger bones like white spiders crept out from beneath the fabric of the veil.

Terror was delicate as the bones as it skated up Charles' spine. He didn't want to see her face. He didn't want to see! But the shroud lifted, spiralling away into the fog.

Dry white skin, a dead and beautiful mummified thing. Her eyes were closed.

George! Do something!

But George was as trapped as he, pinned like a butterfly to its board.

Outside the main door thunder rolled down the drive like flying hooves. The ghost opened her eyes. Dust packed them, spilled out over her cheeks like tears. Dry plaster and dirt trickled from the corners of her mouth.

Her shoulders lifted as if she tried to breathe in, but he realized with a lurch of sick sympathy that she could not. Every part of her face was stoppered tight. For the last century and a half she must have spent every moment struggling to breathe. Pity added a strange soft colour to the edges of his terror. He felt poised unbearably on a point like the moment before one vomits; the need to do it, and the sickness, and the inability an exquisite, maddening torment. Was that what she felt like? Was that what she had felt for the past hundred years?

He breathed in, conscious of the drag of air down his throat, whooping with relief, just as the bottom of her jaw unhinged. It dropped to her waist, her face stretching like a rubber sheet, dust tumbling out of it. Black clots of debris and a fine flying black cloud of dust and hair spewed out of her lips. It looked almost as though she turned herself inside out, boiling up from the feet, bursting out of that grotesque distended mouth in a thick organic fog that mixed with the mist inside the house and flew straight into George's face.

Released from the spell of terror, Charles dropped his aching arm and spun. He could see nothing of his brother, engulfed by the jagged-edged rubbed out nothingness of the ghost. But he knew what it felt like. This was the thing that had come upon him the night of his father's death. This was the creature that had left its bony handprint on the faces of his family. He dared not shoot for fear of hitting George, but taking a deep breath like a diver he ran hard as he could into the centre of it, shoving with all his might against anything he found there.

His shoulder collided with silk. George reeled out of the edge of the cloud, collapsed onto hands and knees, spitting out plaster, his sides labouring. And then the darkness closed around Charles. Cobwebs, thick and sticky, smeared across his face. Something pried at his closed mouth.

Sudden red, shocking pain slammed into his shoulder. The slice of agony made his hand open. The pistol fell from his grip, skittered across the marble floor and away out of his sight. He gasped with pain, and webs swarmed inside his mouth. His throat began to fill with sand and ash.

The thrown fire poker bounced from his shoulder and clattered away. As he collapsed to his knees, fighting to cough, the cloud thinned enough for him to see Elizabeth above, apologetic and horrified, George curled into a foetus like ball, arms around his head. He coughed, and in the spasm after breathed in more dirt. Dust reached down into his lungs, withering him from the inside. His ribs ached from being forced in and out like a creaky set of bellows. His eyes streamed. The ash turned his tears into acid.

"Exorcizo te, omnis spiritus immunde, in nomine Dei Patris omnipotentis, et in noimine Jesu Christi Filii ejus, Domini et Judicis nostri, et in virtute Spiritus Sancti."

Jasper swept through the open doors like a storm wind, still in his rough travelling clothes, his hair tangled and pointed by the rain. Water streamed from the skirts of his greatcoat, and his hand clenched tight around the crucifix at his throat. His voice, clear and confident, rang with all the authority of a cathedral bell.   *"Ut descedas ab hoc plasmate Dei Caroli, quod Dominus noster ad templum sanctum suum vocare dignatus est, ut fiat templum Dei vivi, et Spiritus Sanctus habitet in eo."*

The fog lifted and drew away from Charles, beaching him, letting him hack up the muck from his throat and spit it out in long filthy strings. Clouds drew together, retreating back to the stairs, and in the centre of it there glimmered again the pale, almost radiant form of what had once been a beautiful woman.

Dizzy as he was with breathlessness, his lungs rubbed raw, Charles forgot everything in a rush of possessive awe. If there had been hints of power before in Jasper's mystery, here was the full glory of it unveiled. He looked like a wild man burst in from the rain, but his eyes, those extraordinary clear russet eyes, shone with certainty; so completely unafraid he seemed scarcely human. Alexander the Great must have looked like this when he conquered the world, if Alexander the Great had been known for his kindness.

"Margaret," Jasper said firmly, "remember yourself. Can't you hear your child crying? I can give you both comfort, let you sleep, if you will have it. No more pain. No more hatred. No more endless dying, choked and suffering for all time. You were more sinned against than sinning. Let it go, Margaret, and be at peace."

The ghost's desiccated skin cracked as she frowned. She leaned forward and peered at Jasper with her blind, crumbling eyes. And as she did so, the glass over Sir Henry's portrait shivered to pieces. She ripped off his painted face strip by strip. The shards drove in a twinkling blast at George, who curled tighter around his pistol, shielding the firing pan and his face with the skirts of his coat.

"I know." Jasper smiled, held out both hands, palm up, as if offering himself to the ghost's examination. "Believe me, I do understand. But is Sir Henry worth tying yourself to this prison for eternity, when you might forget him and move on?" He laughed, and Charles felt a surge of new admiration for anyone who could laugh so naturally—no hint of hysteria—while a murdering, animated corpse hung over his head.

"Going on to happiness despite him may be the worst thing you could do to him. He'd be flattered, I think, that you think him worth hating so much."

The white lady turned away. Her shroud went whispering up two stairs. When she turned back a suggestion of living eyes glimmered in the sockets of her face, grotesque and pitiable, indigo blue. She tried to speak, but only lime plaster, burning dry, spilled out of her lips. Charles watched, afraid to move, to disturb whatever process of decision teetered there between revenge and resignation. But as he stared at the ghost's mummified face, something black, like the shadow of a woman, lurched from the kitchen corridor and scrabbled on the floor.

"Go comfort your baby, Margaret. His father is not his fault. And he's been crying such a long time!"

The ghost thinned on the air. Her face softened a little, the cracks closing as the skin grew supple as flesh. She looked over her shoulder, up towards the nursery, and for a moment she seemed nothing more horrific than a painting of a woman held up to the light. A slight, dark haired lady in a green velvet dress with a wide lace collar.

She looked so sad, so fair, that even George stood up. Elizabeth came out from behind the landing curtains. Jasper smiled and began gently to say the service for the burial of the dead, "I am the resurrection and the life, saith the Lord: he that believeth in me, though he were dead, yet shall he live…"

"No!" A dark figure rose up out of the archway to the kitchen. There was a hiss and deep throated boom, a plume of fire the length of an arm, and Jasper's voice broke off mid sentence with a cry of pain. Mary, black with soot, dropped Charles' discarded pistol, clenched her fists and shouted "You ain't making her go away! She's my friend. She's going to make things right for me."

Charles scrambled to his feet, his legs shaking. He looked between the girl and Jasper and as he did so a little rose of blood opened on Jasper's chest, soaking slowly through his shirt. Then another, and a third.

"That George is going to marry me whether he likes it or not."

"Fucking little bitch!" George raised his pistol, took aim.

Charles ripped off his neckcloth and pressed it to Jasper's wounds. Jasper leaned heavily on his shoulder, head bent, taking deep breaths. As he supported the weight Charles' fear transmuted into eviscerating rage. *Kill her, George! Shoot her down!*

Mary's eyes widened, emeralds tossed in a blanket of dirt, as the flaring mouth of the pistol steadied on her face. The ghost disappeared once more into a swirling gritty murk of cloud. And then there was a click, and a hiss, as the pistol's firing hammer came down and the powder in the pan lit. Cloud coalesced about the barrel, dust pattering into it, forcing its way in, clogging it. George's mouth rounded in surprise. It was possible to see the impulse to let go travelling down his arm. His hand loosened. And the pistol exploded in his grip.

Hot iron thrummed through the air. George screamed as the flesh and bones of his hand splattered after it. The stock of the gun burst into splinters and drove into his face. He crumpled forward, a thick crimson rain falling from the gash beneath his eye, his cheek laid open to the bone and falling forward down over his chin.

Mary broke out into a peal of delighted laughter, interrupted by a deeper *boom*! She jerked sideways as if shoved. Blood pumped from between her ribs, gushed over the hand she pressed to her side. Tripping over her feet, she went sprawling, twitched twice and then lay still. In the sudden silence after, the smell of black powder settled like sulphur over all, and Charles looked up into Elizabeth's blank, shocked face as she set her father's rifle back in its place with the air of one backing away from a dangerous beast.

Jasper's hands tightened about Charles' shoulders, his thumbs moving in a secret caress along the collarbone. With only a slight wince, he straightened up and looked the ghost in the eye. "It is best for people like us not to touch this family. Best for us to walk away, if we can, and be at peace. Will you go? Before your revenge kills any more of your friends, will you go?"

The words struck Charles' raw heart like a betrayal. He shook off the comforting hands and knelt by his brother. Tearing the tail off his shirt he wrapped the mangled hand tight. He lifted the hanging flap of face and pushed it gently back into the gaping hole from which it had been torn. George held it there silently, while threads of blood worked down between his fingers.

"I will go."

She had a voice like an oboe. Hoarse, rough and musical. At the sound of it the mist that filled the house began to pour away, sucking away out of the windows until nothing was left but a faint oval of light floating about five feet above the stairs. Then, with a rushing sensation, even that vanished. The chandeliers swung and tinkled. The pat of blood on stone ticked twice. And a roaring, grumbling thunder came from upstairs. The frame of the house groaned.

Elizabeth's face paled. "Harriet!"

Charles and Jasper looked at one another and as one broke for the stairs. Charles faster, but Jasper's long legs taking him up three at a time, his wide mouth set in pain. They reached the landing just as Elizabeth burst from the nursery. "She's not there! God in heaven it's taken my baby!"

A slice of horror like a scalpel through Charles' viscera. He stumbled, held himself up by the wall. The sound of a baby crying seeped out into his palm. He almost stepped away, swung and punched the house, bursting his knuckles on the cursed plaster, but something... something different stopped him. A note of life, perhaps, the aural resonance of a beating heart. "Do you hear that?"

Elizabeth burned up with energy like lighting. "It's her!" She ran left, stopped and listened, ran back, frustration and terror in the drum-roll of her heels. "I can't tell where it's coming from!"

All the separate strands had begun to connect themselves in Charles' head. He followed the thought like a guide rope. "Your bedroom!"

The ugly pregnant bulge in the wall of Elizabeth's bedroom had grown, bursting out of the restraints of the paper. Great clumps of plaster and half bricks lay tumbled on the floorboards, and through the gap between paper and hole there protruded a tiny bare foot, the embroidered slipper spilled amongst the rubble beneath it.

Elizabeth ripped the paper from side to side in one vicious gesture and Harriet rolled—dirty, grazed and furiously indignant—out of the wall to squall in Elizabeth's fierce grip.

In a long, dry slide after her came lace the colour of dust, handfuls of hair, a skull, and a jaw of fine white teeth. The bones of the child were mere shadows of dark colour stained on the walls.

"I'll…" Elizabeth backed away, Harriet on her shoulder, cheek held tight to her own. "I'll find the doctor. See to George. You…" she waved a hand at the tumble of bones.

"May we borrow your coverlet?"

Elizabeth looked at Jasper as if he had just said "may we convert the seas to beer and get hideously drunk," which sounded to Charles like a fine idea. Eventually she blinked, working it out, "Do. Take anything. I'm burning it all in the morning regardless," and fled.

Charles collapsed onto the bed with a groan. An almost imperceptible tremble travelled up from his fingertips and worked its way through his whole body, leaving his stomach unsettled and his mind grey as spent ash. Jasper flicked out the coverlet on the floor and began to transfer the bones onto it, laying each one carefully in its place, sifting through the rubble for any that were missing. Whatever brightness had been in his face earlier had snuffed out. He looked weary. The spots of blood on his chest had stopped growing, turned brown and stiff.

Outside the window the flittering peep of bats skirled beneath the house-eaves. Inside it was silent. Silent for the first time in two hundred years. Peace filtered in through the cracks.

"Are you…" The bloodstains, flexing with Jasper's movements as he patiently reassembled the skeleton, drew Charles' stinging eyes. "Are you badly injured? She shot you."

"I don't know what she loaded it with," Jasper's sideways smile was tentative but warm. He looked down the front of his shirt. "I seem to be glittering."

"Diamonds."

Jasper put down the final toe bone, turned to begin sifting through the plaster for any patches that bore the imprint of the child. He gave a gruff little laugh. "I have never been so expensively rebuked. But no, there must not have been enough weight behind them. I'm grazed and a little winded, that's all. Not like poor George."

Poor George. Charles bit the inside of his cheek, remembering Jasper putting himself in the place of that evil creature; speaking to her tenderly, one victim to another. *It is best for people like us not to touch this family. Best for us to walk away, if we can, and be at peace.* Charles worried the bitten patch with his teeth. An ache was building at the base of his skull beneath the wig, and another inside his chest, below his breastbone. This was not the time, not the time to be worrying about such things and yet…

"Will you help me get her down to the chapel?" Jasper asked.

"Of course."

And yet what if everything was over now, the good along with the ill?

CHAPTER TWELVE

The two great windows of George's room stood uncurtained. Patches of pearl grey sky showed over the misty greens of the deer park. A few determined leaves clung to the trees, as grey as the branches and the morning.

Within, candlesticks clustered on every surface, and the blue and white panelled walls shone sapphire bright. Set in the indigo canopied, gold encrusted, jewelled splendour of his bed, George sat like a partly-broken egg. His face was swaddled in muslin, and his wrongly proportioned arm—too short—padded and wrapped tight in white linen. His eyes, settled in nests of bruised skin, snapped, impatiently bright. "Do we think this is over?"

Charles propped his hip on the window ledge and listened as Jasper heaved a long breath of release and relief. It took him several heartbeats to realize that no one else in the room had understood the obvious "yes."

"Yes," he said himself. "I think I know what happened and why. If you want, I can lay it out before you now."

His big scene. There should have been a change of costumes, perhaps of backdrop, when he revealed that the mysterious stranger was truly the prince in disguise. There should at least have been a circle of attentive eyes, waiting for enlightenment. Not Jasper's touch on his wrist, and the words "Perhaps you might send for her mother and sister."

George shifted irritably. "Cook? I think not. This is family business."

Jasper raised his head and looked George square in the eye. "She's just lost her daughter. It would be barbaric not to offer her even an explanation. If you want this to stop now then for once in Latham family history you must begin to offer some justice to your victims."

Another dull blow on Charles' heart. He opened the door

and passed the summons on to a waiting servant. Jasper was right, of course, but did he have to rule so clear a line between the Lathams and himself? So clear a line that Charles could have no doubt of being on the wrong side. He'd relived their two encounters often enough to remember now that they'd made no promises. No talk of the future. Perhaps he had assumed a long term interest when there had been only curiosity, or worse. Could Jasper have seduced him out of a desire to prove something to George? To take a small revenge, motivated by the same hurt and anger that had driven the ghost?

He swallowed, forced himself to look at the stump of his brother's arm, clean and inoffensive where it lay outside the bedclothes. If it was so, he had not lost so very much.

Groping his way back to the window ledge, he curled forwards over the unaccountable pain in stomach and chest. The door opened and Cook came in, looking diminished. She dropped a very perfunctory curtsey and collapsed on the seat Jasper offered. He loped over to lean on the wall beside Charles, scruffy as a sailor, surrounded once more by some of that corona of power and peace he had flamed with last night. Afraid of what he might see, Charles did not look up.

George sipped at a glass of laudanum in water. "Get on with it then."

Where to start? There were two separate beginnings and he wasn't sure...

"It begins with Sir Henry," Jasper's diffident voice wound in among the hiss of the many candle flames, taking some of the burden for him. "Who got Lady Margaret Evesham with child and then refused to marry her because she was a Catholic. Instead, when she ran to him for help, he bricked her up alive, their unborn child within her, in the wall of Mrs. Sheldrake's room. There she smothered to death, and in her misery and sense of betrayal she refused to move on. She became the white lady. But other than frightening a few generations of children, she was a largely inoffensive ghost until our second set of circumstances intervened."

When Jasper paused, Charles took up the tale as smoothly as he could, determined to bear his part of this ordeal. "'Circumstances.'" He cleared his throat, conscious of Cook, all that weighty presence of her helpless as a whale on the beach. "Mary... I'm sorry Mrs. Dwyer, but I must say some things about Mary that may be uncomfortable for you to hear."

"I'm listening, Mr. Charles. She were a wild one, I give you that. But I don't suppose she'd be alone in that. And she was so beautiful! So beautiful, my Mary, like a flower..."

"Yes. She was." Charles didn't want this, didn't want to spare pity on the family of a murderess. Above all, he did not want to feel this guilt. "And that was what started the trouble, of course. Mary believed in the doctrine of the equality of all men. She believed in it so strongly that she could not understand that others might not agree."

"I remember us talking about that," Cook sketched the outline of a smile. "In the kitchen, when the old Master died."

As Charles wished in vain for a mug of hot chocolate that he could pass to her, Jasper brought out a flask from his pocket and offered that instead. The scent of strong, raw navy rum joined the lingering odour of bone-saw and blood in the room.

"Father took a fancy to her." It was extraordinarily hard to get this out. He could have done with some of that rum himself. "When he said he would marry her, she believed him. Why not? She was as good as any duchess."

"I knowed she was with him." Cook shrugged, "It ain't like the likes of us have much choice in the matter. She says no, we all get thrown out on our ear."

"I don't think it started with coercion, though. She honestly believed he loved and would marry her. He gave her presents— my mother's things—dresses, trinkets, and she was happy. I don't know what happened to change things."

"But I do." Jasper shifted against the wall. The heel of one shoe and the very extremity of his shoulder brushed lightly against Charles, and a burst of warm reassurance tingled down the marrow of Charles' arm. Deliberate touch or accidental? He couldn't tell.

"Mary fell pregnant." This was Jasper's confessional voice, private, encouraging, unshockable. "She told Lord Clitheroe, expecting to be wed, but instead he removed her to the estate in the Cotswolds. There she gave birth to a child, which he smothered with a pillow. He sold the body to a local anatomist for two shillings and a guinea watch."

"No!" Elizabeth slapped the palm of her hand hard on the bedstead, waking the sleeping babe in her lap. "That's a lie!"

"You're a lying bastard, Jasper Marin." George winced as Elizabeth's blow trembled the bed beneath him. His eyes shone brighter than ever, the patch of throat between bandage and nightgown flushed pink.

"I have statements from the doctor and midwife in attendance that the child was born alive, and a statement from the surgeon who purchased the body that in his opinion the cause of death was smothering."

"They're fucking liars too. You suborned them!"

"Let him alone." Their furious gazes mobbed Charles like crows. He looked away, scratched at a flake of paint on the sash until the flapping died down, trying to dredge up from the well of humanity some drops of horror. He shouldn't feel like this, not satisfied, as if a piece had slid into place. "The payments, in and out, are recorded in father's ledger. I wondered what they meant. I asked Jasper to find out."

"I had thought to send you a letter with the details, but the wind changed in the night and it seemed likely I could arrive back before the express post. So I hurried home."

"I'm very glad you did. You saved my life."

Jasper ducked his head to hide his smile. Charles could practically see the lines being redrawn throughout the room as Elizabeth edged her chair closer to George. He thought perhaps if he could reach up and tip that smile into the light, touch and absorb the warm solidity of Jasper through his fingers, then something frozen in him might break loose. He might feel what he should feel. But he didn't dare to return even the fleeting press of shoulders.

"That explains it," he said.

"Yes. It was as if the white lady's tragedy repeated anew. She saw a chance to end the story differently this time. If Mary could become Lady Clitheroe, in a way her own suffering would have been worthwhile. Justice would finally be done and she could depart."

Outside the window the clouds thinned. Sunlight feathered over Jasper's shoulders, drawing steam from the soaked grey wool of his coat. His little snort of laughter was sympathetic, wry. "Of course, Margaret was quite insane, and I dare say Mary, unhinged as she must be by the death of her child, was not wholly to blame either. At any rate, they agreed between them that Clitheroe was to die for what he had done, and that Mary would marry George."

"Emma!" George sat up abruptly, choked on the bolt of pain and coughed deep hacking coughs that had to be soothed with more laudanum. "That's why it killed Emma? Dear Lord, to get at me?"

"I'm afraid so." Jasper rested a reassuring hand on Cook's trembling shoulder. She gave a great pig-like sniff and a brave smile. "If it helps, I believe that was Margaret's idea. Emma was dying already. I'm sure Mary would have been content to wait. But the white lady was beyond such fine distinctions. Clitheroe's death though, I can't fully explain."

"But I can." Charles felt their gazes like a graze on his cheek, and again he turned away to watch the spirals of steam, the change of colour from dark grey wool to a lighter slate blue, the lift and lower of Jasper's shoulders the heartbeat that let him continue. "I found salt, tipped into the plant pot next to the table where father's meal stood waiting to be taken upstairs. You know what a drift of salt he took with everything. He would pour it on as if he meant to cover everything with a layer an inch thick."

"So," Charles' gaze slipped down from the shoulder to the square, strong hand. His hips tingled with the imprint of those fingertips, bruises not yet faded. He concentrated on their loving little throb, to avoid thinking too hard about anything else. "It was easy enough for Mary to fill a twist of paper with the arsenic we keep in the barn. Only a moment's work to tip the salt out of the salt-cellar, tip in the arsenic, and leave father to scatter the poison on his own food. Father dies, Mary gets to comfort his newly widowed, distraught heir. Nature takes its course, the ghost is placated and can find peace. All is set to right, the curtain falls." Charles smiled, exasperated and affectionate, at George's glower. "Except that you didn't play the part written for you, George. And Mary was too sure of success and caught Elizabeth's watchful eye too soon."

A long silence. The yellow tongues of the candles hissed, and in the grate the fire gave a sigh like the sea, settling. Elizabeth closed her eyes, pressing her cheek against the baby's cheek, the suave, round line of the baby's face looking soft as a boiled pudding. Cook looked at her clenched fists and George at his stump. Jasper moved just enough to slide his hand behind Charles' back and rest a palm soothingly on the bunched muscles about his spine.

"What a god-awful sordid affair," said George at last. "On reflection, I don't put it past the old man to have done exactly as you say. Gentler times than Sir Henry's, but the blood will tell."

"You'll stay with us, Cook?" Elizabeth lowered her imperious voice, and a faint flavour of intimacy among women, secrets and hardships shared, tinted the room, shutting Charles and the other men out.

"I will, mum. But if that Mr. George Latham lays a hand on my Kitty, I promise you, mum, I'll geld him meself, with a kitchen knife."

Elizabeth laughed, startled, and smoothed down her skirts. "Should the occasion arise, you may apply to me for some soldiers of my husband's regiment, to hold him down."

∫ ∫ ∫ ∫

The Thames slid away under afternoon sunshine. Burnt cornfields on either hand sent up a smoke of delicate blue and a scent of caramel. Reeds nodded by the water's side, rustling. Beneath the sun's thin warmth, an edge of winter's ice insinuated itself.

"So there's an end of it," said Charles, squashing the petals of a purple mallow into the mud beneath his shoe.

"Not quite." Jasper stood a little further up the bank, his head and shoulders level with the surrounding land, hand propped on a tree root. The blue organic light softened the angles of his face, idealized him. "There are still the funerals."

"You'll come?"

"To Margaret's, certainly. To the others… if I'm welcome."

Charles wondered if some of the dirt, a clot of the wall he had been forced to breathe in, had lodged within him. He could almost feel it, a solid lump somewhere at the base of his throat, and another in his belly. Swallowing did not dislodge them. "For my part you will always be welcome."

Smoke caught at his eyes, making them sting. He shook his head angrily and felt the tremor of the wet land beneath his feet as Jasper strode down towards him.

"What is it?"

How could he possibly explain? The end had come. Jasper would return to St. Giles, he would return to his life of petty idleness, and all the glory of the world would burn up like the fields. Charred stalks and ashes, barren smoke from this day onward, this burst of death and beauty gone. Gone forever.

"Still nothing," he said, reaching out and lacing his fingers through the other man's. Jasper's face lit with his secret, uncomplicated smile. He pulled himself closer, until they were standing toe to toe.

"I feel nothing," Charles said. "It's over and I should grieve now, for my father, for Emma, and Mary, and Margaret, even for poor George, maimed as he is. Where is my grief? I don't feel anything unless you're here. You unfreeze me. You make me live."

Jasper freed his hands and cupped them around Charles' face. Charles felt the clear gaze fall warm as brandy on his lips, and closed his eyes, opening his mouth, in the hope of drinking it in.

Jasper insinuated his foot between Charles', one hand slid round to the back of Charles' head, cradling it, the other dropped to his waist and hugged tight. The kiss was slow and gentle, savouring his mouth. He slipped his arms inside Jasper's coat and clung to the warm and breathing firmness of his body. Comfort surrounded him, filled his mouth, slicked his damp and swollen lips. It smelled of ambergris and heat, Jasper's sweat, and caramel-scented smoke.

When he broke the kiss it was because he was crying too hard to breathe.

He set his face in the hollow of Jasper's shoulder and wept until the silk waistcoat was quite sodden, and the linen shirt beneath seemed ready to dissolve. He wept until his throbbing eyes rested, wrung out, against a sturdy collarbone, and he felt the pulse of their two hearts rock synchronized through them both. Jasper had drawn his coat close about them. They stood resting together as the light drained, and the waterbirds took off in a flight of whirring wings.

"I've been thinking," said Jasper at last, his voice threading over Charles' head, quiet, unembarrassed, "that we are good at this."

The arms and thick woollen coat about him were secure as a chrysalis. As Charles stepped away from them he felt quite new. "Bawling like infants?"

"Investigating. Hauntings, murders, both together. With my sight and your agile mind we could make a profession of it. Now that I'm no longer a priest, I need some other employment. I think you do too."

Sunset tinted the western sky with shades of amber. A wherry, and then a coal barge, slid into view around the curve of river, tall stained sails reflecting gold from the sun. Charles fought happiness, wishing with every fibre of his being that it would master and overwhelm him. "It would hardly be respectable."

"Perhaps not. But it would provide an excellent explanation for why we were always seen about together." Jasper inclined his head, looked down on Charles from his greater height, with a sweet, shy smile. "And we need that, don't we?"

Charles surrendered, and joy broke over him like a tide. As the ending reshaped itself around him into a beginning, he seized it with both hands, greedily. "Yes. Yes we do." *Together from now on!* "God yes! May the world never run out of ghosts, so long as we can hunt them together. Here's to a long and successful partnership to us both!"

THE DARK
FAREWELL

JOSH LANYON

To my dad -- whose own stories brought history alive for me.

The body of the third girl was found Tuesday morning in the woods a few miles outside Murphysboro. Flynn read about it the following day in the *Herrin News* as the train chugged slowly through the green cornfields and deep woods of Southern Illinois. The dead girl's name was Millie Hesse and like the other two girls she had been asphyxiated and then mutilated. There were other "peculiarities", according to the newspaper, but the office of the Jackson County Sheriff declined to comment further.

The peculiarities would be things about the murder only known to the police and the murderer himself. At least in theory. Flynn had covered a few homicides since his return from France three years earlier, and it wasn't hard to read between the lines. But there were already rumors flying through the wires about a homicidal maniac on the loose in Little Egypt.

Flynn gazed out the window as a giant cement smokestack came into sight. The perpetually smoldering black slag heap, half-buried in the tall weeds, reminded him in some abstruse way of the ravaged French countryside. His lip curled and he stared down again at the newspaper.

He didn't care much for homicide cases; he'd seen enough killing in the war. And reading about poor, harmless, inoffensive Millie Hesse and her gruesome end in the dark silent oaks and elms of these lonely woods dampened his enthusiasm for the story he was there to cover, a follow-up on the Herrin Massacre the previous summer. Not to write about the massacre itself. More than enough had been written about that.

It had been a big year for news, 1922, between the 19th Amendment giving women the right to vote and the discovery of King Tutankhamen's tomb, but you'd be hard-pressed to find anyone in the States who hadn't heard about what had happened in these parts between local miners and the Southern Illinois Coal Company. Flynn wanted to write about Herrin one year later; the aftermath and the repercussions. Plus, it was a good reason to visit Amy Gulling, the widow of his old mentor Gus. Gus had died in the winter, and Flynn hadn't made it down for the funeral. He didn't care much for funerals, either.

The train had been warm, but when Flynn stepped down onto the platform of the old brick station in Herrin, humidity slapped him in the face like a hot towel in a barber shop. It reminded him of summer in the trenches, minus the rats and snipers, of course.

He nodded an absent farewell to his fellow passengers—he couldn't have described them if his life had depended on it—and caught one of the town's only cabs, directing the driver to Amy Gulling's boarding house. Heat shimmered off the brick streets as the cab drove him through the peaceful town past the sheriff's office, closed during the violence of that long June day last year, and the hardware stores where the mob had broken in to steal guns and ammunition which they had then used to murder the mine guards and strikebreakers.

The cab let him out in front of the wooden two-story Civil War style house on the corner. Flynn paid the driver, picked up his luggage and headed up the shady walk. He rang the bell and seconds later Amy herself was pushing open the screen door and welcoming him inside.

"David Flynn! I just lost a bet with myself."

"What bet?" He dropped his bags and hugged her hard.

"I bet you wouldn't come. I bet you'd find another excuse."

Amy was big and comfortable like a plushy chair. She wore a faded but well-starched flowered dress. Though her hair was now a graying flaxen, her blue green eyes were as bright as ever. They studied him with canny affection.

Flynn reddened. "I'm sorry, Amy. Sorry I didn't make it down when Gus…"

She waved that away. "The funeral didn't matter. And you're here now. You must be tuckered out from that train ride."

She led him through to the parlor. A fat woman in a blue dress sat fanning herself in front of the big window, and in another chair a small, slim girl of perhaps twenty was reading a book titled *The Girls' Book of Famous Queens*. She had dark hair and wore spectacles.

"This is Mrs. Hoyt and her daughter Joan. They're regular boarders. They've been with me for two months now, since Mr. Hoyt passed."

"How do," said Mrs. Hoyt. The fine, sharp features of her face were blurred by weight and age. When she'd been young she probably looked like Joan. Her hair was still more dark than silver.

The girl, Joan, gave him a shy smile and a clammy hand.

"David's an old friend of my husband. One of his former journalism students. He's going to be spending the next week or so with us."

"Are you a newspaperman, Mr. Flynn?" asked Mrs. Hoyt.

"I am, but I'm on vacation now." Flynn knew this old beldame's breed. She'd be gossiping with the neighbors—those she considered her social equal—in nothing flat. And he wanted the freedom of anonymity, the ability to talk to these people without them second-guessing and censoring their words.

There was plenty for people to keep their mouths shut about considering Herrin had a national reputation for being the worst of the bad towns in "Bloody Williamson County". The trials of the men who had murdered the Lester Mine Company strikebreakers and guards had ended in unanimous acquittals, shocking the rest of the nation.

"David was in France," Amy said with significance.

"My son was in France, Mr. Flynn. Where did you see action?"

"I went over with Pershing's American Expeditionary Forces, ma'am."

"As a soldier or a journalist?"

"As a soldier." He had been proud of that. Proud to fight and maybe die for his ideals. Now he wondered if he wouldn't have done more good as a reporter.

"My son fell in the Battle of the Argonne."

The girl bowed her head, stared unseeingly at the book on her lap.

Flynn said, "A lot of boys did."

"My son was the recipient of the Medal of Honor."

"I'm afraid I didn't win any medals."

"Well, let's get you situated," Amy said briskly, breaking the sudden melancholy mood that had settled on the sunny parlor. "I've got David in the room over the breezeway."

"That's a mighty pleasant room in the summer," agreed Mrs. Hoyt. The daughter murmured acknowledgement.

Flynn smiled at Amy. "I remember."

He nodded to the ladies and followed Amy. She was saying, "I've turned Gus's study into a library and smoking room for the gentlemen."

Flynn asked unwillingly, "Has it been tough since Gus died?"

"Oh, you know. I manage all right. I keep the boarding house for company as much as anything. I never was happy on my own." Amy paused in the doorway of another room. "Here are our gentlemen. Doctor Pearson, Mr. Flynn is an old family friend. He'll be staying with us for a few days. Mr. Devereux, Mr. Flynn."

The gentlemen appeared to have been interrupted in the midst of writing letters. Doctor Pearson was small and spry with snapping dark eyes and the bushy sideburns and whiskers that were popular before the war. Mr. Devereux was older than the doctor, but he dyed his hair and mustache a persevering jet black. He had the distinctive features—aquiline nose and heavy-lidded eyes—Flynn had grown familiar with in France.

"Pleasure to meet you," Dr. Pearson said, putting aside his pen and paper and offering his hand.

Devereux was equally polite. "A pleasure, sir." He had a hint of an accent, but it was not exactly French. French Canadian perhaps? Or, no, French Creole?

"Mr. Devereux is a regular contributor to a number of Spiritualist periodicals," Amy commented.

Mr. Devereux livened up instantly. "That's correct. I'm penning an article at this moment for *The Messenger* in Boston."

Flynn nodded courteously. Spiritualism? Good God.

Perhaps Amy sensed his weary distaste because she was soon ushering him out of the room and down the hall.

They started toward the long blue-carpeted staircase. A quick, light tread caught Flynn's attention. He glanced up and saw a young man coming down the stairs. He was tall and willowy, his black hair of a bohemian length. His skin was a creamy bisque, his eyes dark and wide. Flynn judged him about nineteen although he wore no tie or jacket. He was dressed in gray flannel trousers and his white shirt was open at the throat, the sleeves rolled to his elbows like a schoolboy.

"This is Mr. Flynn, Julian," Amy said.

Julian raised his delicate eyebrows. "Oh yes?"

"He's an old friend of my husband and me. He's going to be staying with us for a time."

Julian observed Flynn for long alert seconds before he came leisurely down the rest of the staircase. He offered a slender, tanned hand and Flynn grasped it with manly firmness.

"Charmed," Julian murmured. He gently squeezed Flynn's hand back and studied him from beneath lashes as long and silky as a girl's. It was a look both shy and oddly knowing. Flynn recovered his hand as quickly as he could. He nodded curtly.

Julian smiled as though he read Flynn's reluctance and was entertained by it. It was a sly sort of smile and his mouth was soft and pink. A sissy if Flynn had ever seen one.

"Julian is Mr. Devereux's grandson." There was something in Amy's voice Flynn couldn't quite pin down. Either she didn't like the old man or she didn't care for the kid—or maybe both.

Julian said slowly, "You're a…writer, David?"

"How the hell—?" Flynn stopped. Julian was smiling a smug smile.

"I know things."

"That's a dangerous habit."

"The philosophers say that knowledge is power."

"Sometimes. Sometimes it's the fastest way to get punched in the nose."

Both Amy and Julian laughed at that, and Flynn realized that he probably seemed a little hot under the collar.

Julian nodded pleasantly and sauntered away to the smoking room cum library.

"What in the blue blazes was *that*?" Flynn inquired of Amy as she led him up the staircase.

She laughed but it sounded forced. "*That* is The Magnificent Belloc. He's a spirit medium."

"You're joking."

Amy shook her head. "He's giving a show over at the Opera House every night this week except Friday and Sunday. Friday the high school is putting on *A Midsummer Night's Dream*."

"Spiritualism," Flynn said in disgust. He came from a long line of staunch Irish Protestants.

"Oh sure, there are a lot of fakes and phonies around. But the war changed a lot of people's feelings about spiritualism and mediums," Amy said. "When you lose someone dear to you, well, I guess you'd do anything to be able to talk to them one more time."

Flynn glanced at her and then glanced away. "I guess so."

"I don't put stock in spirits and that sort of thing, but from what I hear young Julian has a knack for knowing things."

"I'll bet."

Amy said mildly, "He called it right with you. I didn't tell him your first name was David or that you were a newspaperman."

"No, you didn't. But you did mention it to Mrs. Hoyt and her daughter." Flynn added dryly, "I'm guessing that The Magnificent Belloc's bedroom is the one over the parlor. Is that right?"

Amy looked chagrined. "That's right."

"I thought so. That kid's as phony as a three dollar bill."

"Oh, he's not so bad. A bit of a pansy, I guess. It's the old man I don't like. Whatever that boy is or isn't, it's that old frog's fault."

Flynn didn't argue with her, but he didn't agree either. Devereux younger wasn't anyone's victim. He recognized that jaded look. Whatever the racket was, The Magnificent Belloc was in it up to his shell-like ears.

Amy continued up the narrow staircase to the second level. Flynn's room was in the former servant's quarters on the far side of the house's breezeway. The roofed, open-sided passageway between the house and the garage was on the east side of the corner property, the "cool" side shaded by a big walnut tree, but there was nothing cool about that sunny box of a room that afternoon.

After Amy left, Flynn unpacked and then washed up next door in the closet-sized bathroom that had once served as a storage room.

Back in his room, he changed his shirt and examined himself closely in the square mirror over the highboy. What had that punk seen? Dark, wavy hair, blue eyes, strong chin and straight nose. Regular features. He was a regular guy. He looked all right. He looked like everybody else. Girls liked him fine. That girl, Joan, she didn't see anything wrong with him.

He shook his head impatiently at the troubled-looking Flynn in the mirror.

It didn't matter what that pansy thought or didn't think. Flynn didn't have to have anything to do with him. He was going to get his story and then he'd be heading back to New York City where people had a little discretion, a little subtlety.

He could smell fresh coffee and frying ham, and he followed the aroma downstairs where his fellow boarders were having a big noontime dinner of fried eggs, ham, sausage, and golden brown potatoes. "Luncheon" they called it in New York, although you wouldn't get anything like this for lunch.

Flynn took a seat at the table across from Joan. He noticed—to his relief—that the disturbing Julian was absent. There was a lively discussion going on about the recent murders in the neighboring county.

"Perhaps someone could ask the Comte about them," Joan said, with a self-conscious look in Flynn's direction.

Doctor Pearson snorted. The older Devereux was shaking his head.

"Who's the Comte?" Flynn asked.

"The Comte de Mirabeau. Julian's spirit guide," Joan replied primly. "He was a French statesman, orator and writer. He died during the French Revolution."

"You're not a believer, young man," Devereux said severely, watching Flynn.

"I believe in plenty of things," Flynn said. "What did you have in mind?"

"Julian is a medium," Joan said.

"A medium what?"

Mrs. Hoyt gave a breathy laugh and scooped up a mouthful of eggs.

The conversation briefly languished, and Flynn decided to ask about the trials of the miners accused of murder last year and the winter. That revived the discussion, but mostly what he heard about was how the KKK and the local ministers were trying to persuade the government and the law to do something about the bootleggers and their roadhouses springing up like toadstools. The massacre was old news. It seemed nobody wanted to think about it.

Astonishingly, these civilized, decent folk seemed to think the best bet for the lawlessness plaguing their county was the Ku Klux Klan. Flynn found it hard to credit. He kept his mouth shut for the most part and listened.

"Thank goodness for Prohibition!" exclaimed Mrs. Hoyt, shoveling in fried potatoes.

Dr. Pearson shot back, "The only thing Prohibition helps is the gangsters and the damned Ku Klux Klan."

"It's kept a lot of boys off the liquor," insisted Mrs. Hoyt thickly.

"Ah baloney," growled the old doctor. "More of those kids are trying booze out now than they were before Prohibition. Forbidding it makes drink seem exciting."

"That's because the sheriffs don't enforce the law!"

Amy said to Flynn, "Mrs. Hoyt is right about that. We've got a poor excuse for a sheriff. He's great pals with half the bootleggers in the county."

"I'm surprised that you, a doctor, would take that view," Mrs. Hoyt said to Pearson. She seemed indignant, but Flynn had the idea this was not a new argument in this household.

Pearson was unmoved. "When drink was legal these kids weren't allowed in a saloon, but these damned bootleggers don't care who they sell their hooch to or who they sucker into gambling away their paychecks. Why I was tending a poor kid over in Murphysboro just last week who died of that damned bathtub gin."

Joan's gaze met Flynn's and slid away.

"But that's exactly what the Klan and the ministers are saying," Mrs. Hoyt insisted. "If the law won't clean this mess up, then the people have to."

Devereux chimed in, "People? Which people? A bunch of anti-union kleagles and clowns dressed up in spooky robes doing their mumbo-jumbo and burning crosses out in somebody's pasture."

The old guy sounded pretty heated. Flynn was willing to bet that with their complexion and coloring, he and the kid had been mistaken for Italians or worse on more than one occasion.

"You're a fine one to talk about mumbo-jumbo," Mrs. Hoyt said tartly.

Devereux bridled. "I assure you, Madame, Spiritualism is as valid and respectable a religion as any other. We simply believe that the door between this world and the next is accessible to those who hold the key, and that through the talents of one gifted with the power to communicate with spirits, we may learn and be advised by our loved ones who have gone before us."

"Speaking of those gone before us," Flynn remarked, "I see your grandson isn't at lunch."

"Julian rests in the afternoon," the old man said stiffly. "He is not strong, and his efforts to act as conduit to the other side tax him greatly."

Flynn managed to control his expression. Just.

There was not a lot of chat after that. When the meal was finished, Flynn excused himself and went back to his room. He wanted to start looking around the town as soon as possible.

He found he had a visitor. Julian Devereux was seated on the bed, idly flipping through his copy of *Bertram Cope's Year*. Flynn had left the book in his Gladstone.

He paused in the doorway, the hair on the back of his neck rising on end. "What are you doing in here?" he asked sharply.

Julian jumped—so much for psychic powers—though his smile was confident. He tossed the book on the green and white Irish chain quilt, leaned back on his hands.

"I thought we should get to know each other, David."

Flynn studied Julian's finely chiseled features coldly, taking in the angular, wide mouth and heavy-lidded, half-amused dark eyes.

"Why's that?"

Julian arched one eyebrow. "You know."

"No, I don't. And I'm pretty sure I don't want to."

Julian tilted his head, as though listening to an echo he couldn't quite place. "I didn't figure you for the shy type," he said eventually.

"I'm not. I'm not your type either." Flynn was careful not to look at the book on the bed. "Now if you don't mind—?" He held the door open pointedly.

A look of disbelief crossed Julian's face. He rose from the bed and slowly moved to the door. For an instant he stood before Flynn. He was so slight, so lithesome that Flynn kept picturing him shorter than he was. In fact, he was as tall as Flynn, his doe-like dark eyes gazing directly into the other man's.

"Have it your way," he said.

"I intend to."

"But if you should change your mind—"

Flynn inquired dryly, "Wouldn't The Magnificent Belloc be the first to know?"

"Those scabs and strikebreakers got what they asked for." That was the view of big Tom McCarty.

"Bullets and pick handles?"

Flynn was genuinely curious about that kind of reasoning, and McCarty's weathered face tightened. He was a young mine hoisting engineer with powerful arms and shoulders, a long-time member of the United Mine Workers. He didn't say he had been at Crenshaw Crossing or Harrison Woods. He didn't say he hadn't been. "The miners were striking for safe working conditions and decent wages. They deserve that. Anybody deserves that. But Lester and the other mine owners shipped in them strikebreakers and scabs and gave away the striking miners' jobs. I stand by what I say. They deserve what they got."

There were mutters of agreement from the other men at Skeltcher's Tavern. Except that Skeltcher's wasn't a tavern anymore. Theoretically it was a soft drink parlor. Every town, every wide-spot-in-the-road now had a small, weather-beaten saloon currently known as a soft drink parlor though the clientele hanging around those joints didn't much look like sody pop drinkers to Flynn.

"What about these stories about cutting the throats of the wounded men?"

"Don't believe everything you read in the papers, pal."

"I won't," Flynn said gravely.

An older man with the cough that came from too many years of cigarettes—or coal dust—chimed in, "If rich, blood-sucking mine owners like Lester get away with using thugs and scabs to break a strike down here in a union stronghold, then the UMWA and the other unions are finished in this country."

McCarty agreed. "Those miners were acquitted by a jury—two juries—of their peers. That's justice."

Flynn nodded politely and stood McCarty to another "root beer". Maybe it wasn't justice, but it seemed to be raw democracy in action. Flynn had read the trial reports and one thing was clear—local sympathy had been clearly and unwaveringly with the miners. An initial inquest concluded that all the strikebreakers were killed by unknown individuals, and recommended that Southern Illinois Coal Company and its officers be investigated in order to affix appropriate responsibility on them. Eventually two trials were held, the first on November 7, 1922, the second that very same winter. Only six men had been indicted for the massacre, and both trials ended in acquittals for all the defendants. At that point the prosecution had given it up as a lost cause. The remaining indictments were dismissed. The prosecutor had summed up the defense's case as "These men were justified in what they did; and besides, they didn't do it!"

You could still hear the echo of that sentiment in Skeltcher's soft drink parlor. It was like the entire town of Herrin, maybe Williamson County, were suffering from a kind of hysterical blindness and couldn't see what the rest of the world saw. Old General Black Jack Pershing himself had shown up in Marion and pronounced the massacre as "wholesale murder as yet unpunished."

And that was very much the mind Flynn had been in when he had boarded the train in New York. How could it be anything else? But listening to these men talk he was startled at their certainty, their lack of remorse, their continuing and abiding anger at the rich men who they believed had forced them to take violent action. Little as he liked it, Flynn couldn't help but suspect there was a grain of truth in the miner's comments about whether Lester and the other mine owners would ever be held to account for the unsafe working conditions in their properties or the men killed in the explosions in their mines.

It was still early when Flynn left Skeltcher's. His thoughts were restless, and he wasn't ready to return to the stuffy quiet of the boarding house, wasn't ready to hear more about how the

KKK was going to save western civilization, wasn't ready to talk to Amy about Gus. Instead he walked along the mostly empty streets trying to reorganize his thoughts, trying to quell his own turbulent needs.

It was all the fault of that young fakir, the sham mentalist with the lithe body and ancient eyes. That kind of thing was dangerous even in New York where people were cosmopolitan and sophisticated and where there were clubs where a man could go for drinks and the company of men like himself. In Harlem, Greenwich and Times Square there were restaurants, cafeterias, cafés and speakeasies where the city's intellectuals and artists and bon vivants gathered.

Little Egypt was a cultural wasteland in comparison. And Julian Devereux stood out like a tropical flower.

So Flynn strode along the brick streets, waving the gnats away, watching the fireflies winking on and off. It was still uncomfortably warm, though the yellow stars were high in the pink and violet sky now.

A poster in a shop window caught his eye, and he stopped to examine it. Fancy swirling script announced The Magnificent Belloc's public exhibition on Tuesday, Wednesday, Thursday and Saturday night at the Opera House on West Franklin Street.

Flynn snorted at the flowery sketch of Julian in the garb of an Indian prince. He was surrounded by highly stylized zephyrs—or maybe ordinary working draughts—with faces both mournful and gay. The spirits he communicated with? Yet even in that strange drawing Julian's mysterious dark eyes seemed to gaze out at Flynn, seemed to hypnotize him.

Amused at himself, but curious nonetheless, he caught the little streetcar and made the journey across town to the Opera House. It was a grand-looking building with a wide arch entrance, terra-cotta trim and sour-looking gargoyles.

"You're just in time," the freckle-faced girl in the ticket booth told him. "We got strict orders to lock the door after the show starts."

"Is it much of a crowd?"

To his surprise, the girl said, "Oh, yes. The Magnificent Belloc impressed a lot of folks last night, and they told their friends and families."

Flynn raised skeptical brows, but he went inside the lobby which was startlingly ornate with dark wood and gilt fixtures and red carpets. An usher held the door for him and Flynn slipped inside the darkened theater. The door closed firmly after him.

Through the darkness, he found his way down a row of plush seats, located an empty seat near the back and sat down. It was only then that he actually looked at the stage. There was a small table with a crystal ball in the center. Behind the table, The Magnificent Belloc was sitting in a large gold throne. Presumably it belonged to the Opera House since it was hard to picture gramps and Julian lugging that piece of furniture all over the Midwest. It was a nice prop, though, and it suited the occasion and the man sitting in it.

Julian looked like one of those French aristocrats from the time right before the people got tired of eating cake and started lopping heads. He wore dark blue leggings and a silver and powder blue brocade frock coat over a soft shirt with bunches of lace at the throat and cuffs. He had caved to the fashion of phony mediums and donned a turban, but it was relatively simple, creamy pale silk fastened with a giant sapphire. There were jewels on his slender hands and pinned at the lace at his throat; they flashed in the footlights every time he moved. The crowd seemed spellbound, and Flynn was not surprised. Julian looked beautiful and exotic and mysterious. He looked unearthly.

Flynn had already missed the introductions and preliminaries, whatever they were. Julian's eyes were shut and he was mumbling to himself, but the acoustics of the old building were excellent and Flynn recognized the occasional French word. Not French as he knew it. It was probably supposed to be the French of Paris at the time of the Revolution, but it was more likely French Creole. Then again, French Creole was supposed to be an older variety of French, wasn't it?

Someone shouted out from the crowd, "What about these here murders we're hearing about? What do the spirits say about them?"

The Magnificent Belloc shook his head, gave an impatient flick of his jeweled fingers and kept concentrating.

There were hisses and shushing from the crowd for the man who had interrupted the mystic's train of thought. He subsided, abashed.

Belloc—it was hard to think of him as Julian in this context—sat up straight and opened his eyes. He had a distinctly French inflection as he said, "Her name is Marie. No. *Mary*. A pretty child. *La pauvre petite*. She was very young when she crossed, yes?"

Reaction rippled through the crowd but no one spoke up.

"She was…confused at first," Belloc said gravely. "The young ones often are, but they…what is the word? Habituate the most quickly." He looked out over the sea of faces, although he probably couldn't see anything beyond the front of the stage. "Mary. She is all right now. Everything is all right now. Who is here for Mary?"

There was a smothered sob as though torn unwilling out of some grieving breast, and an elderly woman stood up, handkerchief pressed to her mouth.

"Ah. *Grand-mère*," Belloc said kindly. "Mary wishes to tell you something. She wishes to tell you that she is all right. She is happy. She is playing with the little lambs and baby angels. She is strong and she is well again."

The woman sobbed into her handkerchief.

"*Non, non, Grand-mère*," Belloc said quickly. "Mary wishes you to be happy for her. She has joined us with one purpose tonight and that is to tell you that she thanks you for all your love and your care, and that she is in a better place now, *oui*?"

The woman buried her face in her handkerchief, and sank back into her seat.

Belloc nodded, well-satisfied with his chicanery, and relaxed in his throne. He closed his eyes.

Already the murmurs were running through the crowd impressed with the evening's entertainment so far.

Belloc mumbled some more French words. He dipped his head as though agreeing to something the spirits were saying. Listening a few seconds more, he held up a graceful hand bidding the spirits to shut it for a sec.

"Joe…Joseph…he is very excited to speak tonight. Who is here for Joseph?"

Four different people rose throughout the audience, and a nervous titter went through the crowd.

Belloc laughed too. "*Eh bien*! We must narrow this down." He turned to consult with Joe for another few seconds, but again it appeared Joe was overeager and a little incoherent.

"Joe was a miner? Is that correct?"

All four members of the audience remained stubbornly standing.

Flynn began to enjoy himself.

Belloc returned to listening to Joe. He cast the audience an apologetic look. "It is a little hard to understand. Joe, he is not… was not…much for conversation on this side. Except perhaps when he had a bit of the…how you say…*moonshine*?"

Laughter rippled through the audience and three of the four standing sat down. Pointedly.

Belloc smiled encouragingly at the fourth. "What is your name, Madame?"

"Mable Gabbay. I was Joe's second wife."

"Oh yes?" Belloc hesitated a fraction. "And the first Madame Gabbay, she is…?"

Mable said grimly, "Joe was nine years a widower when I met him."

Belloc turned back to Joe, who appeared to be requesting a quick word. He listened attentively to Joe, then turned back to the widow. He said with charming simplicity, "He misses you, Madame. There is no doubt of this. He misses you greatly."

"What I want to know," Mable said, "is whether *she's* over there with him?"

The audience burst into nervous laughter. Surprisingly, Belloc laughed too, although he quickly sobered.

"Madame Gabbay," he said seriously, "it is most important that you understand that it is different on the other side. Joe has returned to us tonight for two purposes. The first is that he wishes you to understand that on the other side the feelings and thoughts that trouble us on the earthly plane are gone. They are no more."

Mable bridled at this but didn't argue.

"The second purpose for Joe's presence here tonight is that he wishes you to understand that he loves you. He wishes he had told you this more often. But though he did not say the words, he was not a man for words, he felt for you *la passion grande*."

Mable did not seem to have an answer for that. She stared with a sort of hard, anxious longing at the empty space on the stage next to Belloc's throne before taking her seat again.

Flynn felt faintly nauseated. This was nothing more than base manipulation of people's deepest, most cherished feelings. Belloc was skilled enough, though the act was much simpler than others Flynn had seen. No floating lights or musical instruments, no weird noises or showy stagecraft, no assistant moving through the crowd and feeding him code words and signals. Belloc was doing it all through, no doubt, painstaking research of the community: reading the obituaries and social pages of the local paper, checking the local cemetery, exploring the town and picking up useful bits of info—all that plus using what was no doubt a wily intuition. Given how very at ease he was, Flynn guessed he'd been involved in this mystical fraud one way or another since childhood. It was sickening and it was fascinating.

After the success of Joe and Mary, Belloc moved into high gear. He kept the names flying, kept the audience eagerly supplying him with the cues and information he needed.

He kept up his reassuring prattle about the idyllic happiness on the other side and the beauty and joy of being dead. And the suckers ate it up, every word.

Had it been a different time and place, Flynn would have taken time and pleasure in writing a searing expose of His Magnificence. But he didn't have time and this was not a town to be trusted when angered. Flynn didn't need more blood on his hands.

"Henrietta, Orrin says that you must look in the cellar. There is something valuable there. You will know it when you see it. Peter, Dolly says you must remarry. *Vraiment.* You do not honor her memory with loneliness and grief, but with joy and love. Maggie, your brother Glenn sends his greetings and wishes you to know that he is happy and well. David, Gus says you must not waste time on regret. He is happy that you are here. Your presence will make a difference in the days to come."

Flynn caught this last in frozen disbelief. "You phony little sonofabitch," he muttered. His words carried with unexpected clarity in the pause that had followed Belloc's last remark.

People glanced around looking for the heretic, and there were murmurs of displeasure. On stage, Belloc had fallen silent, fist to his forehead, ostensibly concentrating hard.

"Angela," he said slowly, "I have a message from Bill." He raised his head and stared out beyond the glare of the footlights. "Is Angela in the house tonight?"

A tall woman stood midway up the sea of red velvet chairs. "I'm Angela. Bill was my father. William Robert Tucker. He passed nine years ago." She looked around smiling, and others were nodding affirmation.

In that same tired voice, Belloc said, "Angela, Bill says that you must not feel guilty for going out tonight. He was teasing you, that is all."

Angela seemed to recoil. She said falteringly, "What does he mean? What is he saying? Who was teasing me?"

"Bill...was teasing you." The fakir must have been tiring because he wasn't bothering with the accent anymore.

"*Bill?* My husband Bill? Is that what he means? What does he mean? What is he saying?" She looked around as though expecting answers from the audience, but the people around her were deathly still.

"Bill says he loves you...you must not grieve for the...you must not."

"What are you *saying?*"

The voice dragged on. "When you see the music box he made you—"

"My father never did!"

"When you listen to the tune 'By the Light of the Silvery Moon'..."

Angela screamed, her voice ringing shrilly off the rafters and walls. "It's not true. It's not Bill. It's my father. It's *not* Bill!"

There was stricken silence in the auditorium. Flynn could almost pick up the soft, tired breaths of Belloc. The spiritualist was gripping the arms of the throne with white-knuckled hands, his eyes were closed, his face tense and pained. Alarmed whispers rustled through the spectators like a fox running through tall grass. The whispers picked up volume and velocity as they flowed through the aisles.

Angela made her way through the row of seats, still crying and protesting, "You're lying. You're trying to frighten me. It's not true. It's not Bill. It's not true..." She ran up the aisle followed by her companions, and they hurried out through the double doors, leaving them swinging.

In the wake of her panicked flight a hushed alarm hung over the spellbound audience, all gazes fixed on the man in the golden throne.

After very long seconds, Belloc's eyes flew open and he seemed to recover himself. He offered a tired smile.

"You have questions, no? Let us see if the spirits have answers. Arthur, Madeline says that you must take the time to eat a proper supper…"

Relieved laughter from the crowd. Flynn rose and made his way down the narrow row of chairs and out of the Opera House.

A fake and a phony. That summed up The Magnificent Belloc. But a smart one, a shrewd one. The Bill incident had been eerie, no doubt about it. It had spooked Bill's wife. That was probably no accident. Whether the story was true or not, it would set tongues wagging, and tomorrow night more people would show up at the Opera House and pay their hard-earned pennies to hear that charlatan babble his clever concoction of spooky stories and platitudes.

Flynn walked briskly, lost in thought, and eventually he reached the boarding house. He let himself inside the airless house with the key Amy had given him and went quietly upstairs.

It was still uncomfortably warm in the room above the breezeway, a hot, still night. The crickets chirped merrily and in the distance a dog was howling. Flynn undressed and stretched out on the cotton bedcover. He closed his eyes.

He heard the clickity-clack of the train wheels again, miles and miles of it, and soon he drifted into dreamless sleep leaving images behind like smoke from a train: bloodied miners, white-sheeted klansmen, and a slim dark man in the rich costume of a doomed aristocrat.

CHAPTER THREE

Thursday Flynn woke to the sound of voices.

He opened his eyes and blinked at the glare of bright sunlight on wallpaper. It took him a few seconds to place himself, to remember that he was in Herrin, in his old room at Gus and Amy's.

He winced, remembering the things Julian Devereux had said during his show at the Opera House the evening before.

David, Gus says you must not waste time on regret. He is happy that you are here. Your presence will make a difference in the days to come.

Nothing would give him greater pleasure than to punch that wiseacre in his wide, smirking mouth. But he had to give Devereux credit. He was good at reading people, good at ferreting out the truths people tried to hide even from themselves. In that sense he was like a smart investigative reporter, but he used his skill for making fools of others rather than educating them with the truth.

Flynn rose and went to the window, gazing down. He could see the breezeway below and the striped awning of the old swing as it rocked gently. Someone was sitting in the swing: he could see a flannel-clad bent knee and the flash of smooth brown arm as the swing moved in and out of sunlight. A radio played noisily through the kitchen window.

Flynn went next door and had a quick bath using three pots of water, two hot and one cold. The day was already hot and by the time he'd shaved and dressed he was nearly as sweaty as when he began, but he smelled more civilized.

At breakfast it was Flynn, Mrs. Hoyt and Joan.

Joan was talking about the murders in Jackson County, although she broke off when Flynn entered the dining room.

"Publishers make things up to sell more papers, isn't that true, Mr. Flynn?" Mrs. Hoyt inquired.

Flynn shook his napkin out and said, "Respectable publishers don't."

Mrs. Hoyt's expression indicated she believed the respectable publisher to be right up there with the dodo bird.

Joan, keeping her voice down as though afraid of being overheard, said, "The papers say that the bodies of the women were prepared as though for Egyptian burial. Do you suppose that means they were wrapped like mummies?"

According to Flynn's pal in the AP the women had been left naked, their bodies crudely carved up, their internals organs wrapped in linen bandages and left in mason jars like the hearts, lungs and kidneys of ancient pharaohs had been placed in canopic vases for burial. Of course that could be a rumor, and even if it wasn't, Flynn wasn't about to share it with the ladies over breakfast.

Mrs. Hoyt said in shocked tones, "*Joan.*"

Joan turned scarlet and explained, "I enjoy murder mysteries."

Mrs. Hoyt was shaking her head at her unnatural offspring. Flynn smiled at Joan. She blushed more.

"I suppose you've covered a few murder cases in your time, Mr. Flynn?" Mrs. Hoyt inquired.

"A few." To Joan, he said apologetically, "They're mostly sad, sordid affairs. Not like the things you read in books. Most murderers aren't that smart. If they get away with it, it's more luck than anything."

"That's what Julian says."

"Julian?"

"Mr. Devereux. I suggested that perhaps he could use his talents to help the police like they say Mr. Edgar Cayce has done."

"And what did he say?"

"He said that the spirits didn't like to get involved in such sad, sordid affairs. Those were his exact words. That the spirits came to us to teach us about how to live better lives so that we can safely reach the blessed hereafter."

"Did he?" Flynn said dryly.

Amy came out of the kitchen with a great platter of pancakes. She had always been a wonderful cook, although she employed a woman to help her now. It had interested and surprised Flynn, the relationship between Amy and Gus. Gus had been a New York intellectual and radical. Amy was…the salt of the earth. Not the kind of woman anyone would have pegged for Gus. Maybe it was true about opposites attracting. Amy and Gus had seemed as happy as two people could be with each other. Not that Flynn was an expert on such things.

"Did you have a nice time last night?" Amy asked Flynn, forking a stack onto his plate.

Flynn nodded. "It was educational. I caught part of young Julian's show at the Opera House."

"Oh my."

Joan caught her breath and said, "I want to see Julian's show. Mama doesn't approve of spiritualists."

"You're not missing anything." Catching their expressions, Flynn qualified, "I guess I'm not much for spiritualism myself."

Amy said quietly, "There's talk that he foretold the death of a member of the audience."

"No." Reluctantly Flynn added, "It seemed like he might have foretold the death of a woman's husband." He shrugged as the ladies gasped.

"It's the devil's work," Mrs. Hoyt exclaimed.

"But what if it's true?" Joan asked.

"There are things we're not meant to know."

Flynn devoted his attention to his pancakes. He wondered why Joan wasn't married and starting a family of her own. But the war had probably put paid to a lot of women's hopes for that. Over a hundred thousand dead American soldiers meant a hundred thousand less husbands and sweethearts.

"Where *is* The Magnificent Belloc?" he asked abruptly.

"Julian doesn't eat breakfast. He can't the morning after a performance."

Joan seemed to know an awful lot about Julian, given he and gramps couldn't have been staying at the boarding house long. If she was sweet on Julian, that really was a shame.

Flynn raised polite eyebrows, and she continued, "Mr. Devereux rarely rises before noon. And Dr. Pearson is always away by this time of the morning."

"That's because he's the only doctor in this county who knows his business," Mrs. Hoyt said briskly. "I don't hold with those boys fresh out of the university. I don't like a doctor younger than me."

"Now, Mrs. Hoyt," Amy said briskly, "that young Dr. Anson in Carbondale is very pleasant and very knowledgeable."

Mrs. Hoyt was unswayed, and Flynn went back to eating his pancakes and trying not to listen to them. He had a lot planned for the day. He wanted to hurry and finish this story; he could no longer remember why he thought traveling to Illinois was a good idea. Murders and mystics…

When breakfast was over Flynn nodded goodbye to the ladies and walked out to the breezeway to have a smoke.

Most of the houses in town were single story, designed with a front porch where people could sit on their swings in warm weather, fan themselves and say unkind things about their neighbors in relative comfort. The boarding house swing was at the west end of the breezeway making it a shady and fairly pleasant place to sit in the hot afternoon. Cream-pink roses wound up the walls of the arbor.

Julian Devereux sat idle in the swing. He looked up at Flynn's approach and offered that sly smile. "Good morning."

Flynn nodded curtly. He leaned against the wall and lit his cigarette, studying the younger man with a level eye.

"Did you enjoy the show last night?"

"Not particularly."

Julian chuckled. "Why not? I heard I was very good."

Flynn said evenly, "You want to know what I thought? I thought—think—you're a two-bit four-flusher in fancy dress. You winkle out people's deepest, most treasured feelings and you use that knowledge to take advantage of them."

"No, I don't," Julian said calmly. "I give them hope. And reassurance."

"Hope and reassurance? Is that what you were feeding that woman last night when you hinted her husband was dead?"

Julian's smile faded. He stared out at the street where two women were strolling along with shopping bags. "I don't remember that."

"I bet everyone else does."

Julian raised a negligent shoulder. Flynn puffed on his cigarette and eyed the younger man's sharp profile.

"I notice you don't deny it's all a bunch of hocus-pocus."

Julian's dark, wide gaze turned his way again. He said mockingly, "Deny it to a smart big-city reporter like *you*, David?"

"Why did you tell that woman her husband was dead?"

"I told you I don't remember that." He sounded mildly irritated.

"That's convenient. How long have you been in this racket?"

Julian smiled with sudden disarming sweetness. "Oh, I come by my trade honestly. I was, as they say, born in a trunk. The only offspring of Count Amadeus and Zaliki the Seer. In fact..." his voice dropped for apparent dramatic effect, "...my mother foresaw my father's death during her final performance."

Flynn's smile was sardonic. "The Astral Plane by Louisiana way?"

Julian cocked his head inquiringly. "I'd think with the things you must have seen in the war you'd want to believe there was something more, something better waiting for us."

"You don't know anything about it."

Julian continued to stare at him with an intensity that made Flynn uncomfortable.

"What was that book in your luggage?" he asked unexpectedly.

"You saw it," Flynn said shortly.

"I saw you turn white."

"I don't like people going through my things."

"You don't like people." Julian was smiling again. "You'd rather write about them, turn them into characters like in a book, than have to deal with flesh and blood."

Flynn dropped his cigarette on the walkway and ground it with his heel. "You better stick to fortunetelling and leave the psychoanalyzing to the experts."

Julian's laugh was suggestive. "I'll tell *your* fortune if you like, David."

It irked Flynn the way the pansy kept saying his name, *David*, with that certain knowing intimacy. He had no right to take that tone. He didn't let his irritation show as he replied, "I thought spiritualists didn't predict the future."

"I'll make an exception in your case."

"Thanks. I'll work it out for myself."

Julian said quite seriously, "All right. But don't take too long, will you?"

Flynn gave a dismissing laugh and walked away. He was annoyed with himself for going out to the breezeway in the first place. He'd had a pretty good idea Julian was sitting out there, but as much as he disliked the other man, he'd headed straight out there after breakfast. It was peculiar. He understood part of the uneasy draw. He and Julian did have one thing in common, but that only made it worse. Julian was the kind of twilight lover that embarrassed men like Flynn. It was only when he saw sissies and pansies like Julian that he felt ashamed of what he was.

The Hoyt mother and daughter were back in the parlor when Flynn grabbed his coat and hat and left for the soft drink parlor and pool hall. With Amy's permission he borrowed Gus's Model T and drove into the center of town rather than walking in the bright shimmering heat.

Milo's place looked exactly like it was: a rundown old pool hall. Flynn walked down a narrow hallway dividing a small office from a store room. A scrawny, squint-eyed man sat in the office, watching the back entrance. A well-chewed cigar was clamped between his teeth and a double-barreled shotgun lay on the big desk in front of him.

Beyond the office was another room with two card tables and door on each end leading to the front. The right door led to a couple of beat out pool tables set off from the bar by a five-foot curtain divider. Two men lackadaisically knocked colored balls around with pool cues and cursed each other amiably. The left door opened on the front of the soft drink parlor. The tall wooden bar was scuffed and battered but someone had made it their business to keep it and the tall stools before it well-polished and gleaming.

The bartender was a Hungarian named Earl. He asked what soft drink Flynn wanted, and Flynn ordered a Dr. Pepper. The Dr. Pepper turned out to be half a soft drink bottle full of fine Canadian whisky. He drank it and ate salty Georgia peanuts while he talked to the natives. For a bloodthirsty lot they were surprisingly good-natured and frank.

"People around here are sick and tired of Williamson County being called Bloody Williamson," said a man the others referred to as Monty. "We're sick of being called murdering hillbillies by newspapers all over the country."

"Twenty-one men dead, two trials, and not one conviction," Flynn pointed out.

"That should tell you something right there."

It did, but apparently not the same thing it told the gentlemen of Herrin.

"I tell you what I feel bad about," said a man with a long scar down the side of his face. "I feel bad that W.J. Lester didn't get what his boys got."

The other men gave him warning looks, but he ignored them. "Hell, this is the strongest union area in the entire country, but Ole King Coal thinks to hell with that and he brings in a bunch of scabs, mine-guards and hoodlum strikebreakers from Chicago. Pride goeth before a fall. That's what the Good Book says. If anyone should have reaped what he sowed, it was that bastard. But he walked away scot-free like the rich always do."

"The coroner had it right when he said the real criminals were the officials of the Southern Illinois Coal Company."

There was a muttered chorus of agreement.

Monty said, "The miners stood their trial and they were acquitted fair and square, but you'd never know it to hear these bastards talk. Look at that union-hating jackass Harding and his baloney about 'free Americans have the right to work without anyone's leave.' He and the big-shot mine owners figure if they can bust the UAWA in Illinois then they can bust any union in the country. Or that other bastard Pershing and his bullshit about 'inoffensive people having the right to earn a livelihood.' Inoffensive, my ass! It's easy to stand in judgment when you've never been hungry or had to see your kids go hungry."

Flynn was silent. He had a lot of respect for Black Jack Pershing, but he'd covered a mine disaster in his time. And he remembered hearing Gus talk about the mine conditions before the unions: working in water up to your hips, gas-filled rooms, cave-ins, and all that for a buck fifty a day—a buck fifty if you were lucky.

Rough justice. That was the consensus of Milo's pool hall and soft drink parlor and a couple of hours of talk and drink didn't sway them an iota. They were resentful but not remorseful. And there was still a lot of bitterness and hatred boiling not far below the polite surface.

When he figured he'd learned all that there was to learn at Milo's, Flynn got in the Model T and drove out to Moake Crossing, about half a mile from where on June 21st the previous summer, the miners and a mob of about five hundred—and growing—had finally forced W.J. Lester's mine to shut and the workers to surrender.

This was the road the miners had marched their prisoners down after their surrender. This was the place where McDowell, the mine boss, had been taken off the road and shot to death.

It was a harmless-looking place on a sunny July afternoon. Nothing but farm fields and forest. It seemed a long way from town. The sky was cloudless and the air so still you could hear the hum of every insect.

Flynn put the flivver in gear and continued on. He had read the accounts many times. The prisoners were walked along the railroad tracks, their arms in the air until they came to the powerhouse. Then, the story went, the Union President Hugh Willis supposedly drove up and warned the miners not to kill their prisoners on an open road where women and children might see.

Maybe that part of the story was the fantasy Willis and others claimed. Certainly nothing had been proven against Willis. But it was no fantasy that the strikebreakers and guards had been herded north of the powerhouse, across the tracks to a narrow strip of wood and brush. The mob pushed their captives into the trees, and about a hundred yards from the treeline they came to a fence with four strands of barbed wire. A big bearded man in overalls yelled out, "Here's where you scab bastards run the gauntlet. Let's see how fast you gutter-bums can run all the way back to Chicago."

And then the mob had opened fire.

When Flynn came to the spot, he pulled to the side of the road and got out, walking across to the dense woods and green brush. The pound of his shoe soles on the dry ground sounded unnaturally loud in the unfriendly silence. He was not a superstitious man, but the place had a queer, haunted feel. The barbed wire glinted barbarous and cruel in the unforgiving sunlight. It reminded him of other barbed wire and other blood-drenched ground.

The undergrowth crackled, but when he glanced around, nothing was there.

High overhead on a tree branch, a black crow called out in its harsh, raucous voice.

On the way back to the boarding house, Flynn stopped and bought an electric fan at the hardware store. He parked the Model T in the garage and carried the fan inside the house. In the parlor he could hear Mrs. Hoyt complaining; he didn't catch the words, but he knew the tone. Her daughter's voice murmured in acquiescence.

Farther down the hall, in the study where Gus had typed his Pulitzer prize-winning series of articles on the national coal strike in 1919, he could hear Dr. Pearson and Mr. Devereux bickering, but it sounded mostly amiable.

"David," Amy called.

Flynn glanced around. Amy was coming his way, a fair-haired, broad-shouldered man in tow. The man carried a suitcase in each hand. For one shocked instant, Flynn thought the man was Paul. Then reality reasserted itself. Aside from the light hair and the broad shoulders, the man didn't resemble Paul at all.

"David, this is Mr. Lee. He works for the Queen of Egypt Medical Supply Company and stays with us regularly." To Mr. Lee, she said, "Mr. Flynn is an old family friend."

Mr. Lee's tilted green eyes met Flynn's briefly. He looked away then his gaze returned and locked. He shifted his samples bag and offered his hand and a smile. David shifted the fan he was carrying and shook hands. He smiled back. Mr. Lee was blond and boyishly handsome.

"Casey."

"David."

"Well now, I'll leave you two to get acquainted. Mrs. Greer's daughter is ill and she had to leave this morning." Amy was already turning. "I need to get back to the kitchen." She hurried away, and Flynn and Casey Lee were left to climb the stairs to the second level on their own.

"Medical supplies?" Flynn asked. He thought he recognized a fellow veteran. It was the way Casey held himself and the quick, no-nonsense way he'd sized Flynn up. During the war there hadn't been time to waste.

Casey laughed. "Yep. I'm the original snake oil salesman. We sell everything from elixirs to remedies for warts and asthma." He gave Flynn a sideways smile.

"You must travel around quite a bit."

"I'm on the road pretty much all the time these days. I was in Marion yesterday." He grimaced. "Day before that I was in Murphysboro."

"Yes?"

"The whole of Jackson County is talking about those murders. People are pretty worked up."

"I bet."

They reached the second level. Casey said, "Amy lays a mighty fine table. I always eat too much. I was thinking of going out for a walk after supper."

"I have the same problem," Flynn said. "Maybe I'll join you."

Casey smiled. He turned left to go down the hall to his room and Flynn turned right.

He was still smiling as he opened the door to his room. The smile vanished at the sight of Julian Devereux lying on his bed.

Julian wore a sumptuous plum-colored dressing gown. At the squeak of the door hinges, he turned his head and looked up under his lashes, smiling with deliberate seduction. "I knew you were back."

Flynn closed the door and leaned back against it. "What the hell are you doing in here?" he asked, keeping his voice down.

"Waiting for you."

"You're wasting your time."

"It's my time to waste." Julian sat up, the purple robe falling open to reveal a sleek, honey-colored body. "Although I shouldn't want to waste much more of it."

Flynn shook his head in disbelief. "You must be insane." He truly didn't know what to make of this young maniac. He had neither scruples nor morals. Worse, he didn't appear to have any commonsense. He added deliberately, "Or stupid."

As it slowly sunk in on him that Flynn was serious, Julian's smile faded, lost its confident curve. His bold gaze darkened with something like hurt. "Why would you say that? The moment I saw you I saw that you were just like me. That you wanted this too."

"I'm *nothing* like you," Flynn said with quiet intensity. "Now get out of my room."

Julian continued to stare at him with those wide, dark eyes. "I'm not wrong." He spoke with a stubborn sort of dignity. It was almost disarming.

Flynn, however, had no intention of being disarmed. "You damned fool. You're going to get us both arrested. Or killed."

Julian shook his head. "People don't notice unless you bring attention to yourself. They see what they expect to see."

He said it quite seriously, and Flynn had to laugh. "*The Magnificent Belloc?* I hate to break it to you, Devereux, but you have a way of bringing attention to yourself." He tipped his head toward the doorway. "Get the hell out. I won't ask you nicely again."

"Fisticuffs would draw the attention you're trying to avoid," Julian pointed out, but he rose from the bed, straightening his dressing gown without haste. Flynn had to hand it to him; he wore his own skin with a panache most men only managed when fully and expensively clothed.

Flynn stepped away from the door, intending to open it. Instead, he found his arms full of Julian. He pressed his slender, taut body to Flynn's and wound his arms around Flynn's neck. Flynn could feel the other man's sizable erection poking through the silk of his dressing gown, and his own body automatically responded.

That was biology. It was pointless to argue with it. He tried, though, opening his mouth to blast Julian. The sound that escaped him was surprisingly without force, and then Julian's lips, soft and honey-sweet, touched Flynn's. It was a delicate kiss, skilful but subtle. The body in Flynn's arms felt slight and almost feminine, but the aggression, the hunger, was all male.

Flynn's own body tingled with uncomfortable awareness. It was all he could do not to respond to that kiss with a blaze of hunger. Instead, he grabbed Julian's wrists, forced his arms from about his neck, and thrust him away none too gently.

Julian staggered, but caught himself. He glared at Flynn. His chiseled nostrils actually flared.

"I don't understand you, David."

"I'm making it as clear as I can. I'm not interested."

"No one will know—"

"I'm not interested in *you*," Flynn cut in. "I don't even like you."

Julian considered this, blinking, puzzled. Flynn opened the door, glanced down the empty hallway. "The coast is clear. Go."

Face averted, Julian went without another word.

Flynn closed the door. He was tempted to lock it, but that would be ridiculous. He made room for the new fan on the dresser top, plugged it in and waited for the sparks to fly. But the fan came on smooth and quiet, the metal propellers flying fast enough to chop an unwary finger off, and a wonderful breeze washed through the warm room, erasing the faint spicy scent of Julian's cologne.

§ § § §

The entire household gathered for the simple, hearty supper of navy beans cooked with chunks of tender ham. There was fresh corn bread and cold, tangy coleslaw. Plenty of everything. David still vividly remembered the deprivations of the war years and he gave thanks with everyone else at the table. He noticed that even Julian and Mr. Devereux politely murmured along with the mealtime prayer.

As though feeling his gaze, Julian's lashes lifted and he gave Flynn a long, silent look. Flynn looked away.

"Were you in the war, Mr. Lee?" Mrs. Hoyt inquired.

"Yes, ma'am. I was in France with the 5th Marine Regiment."

"Belleau Wood?" Flynn asked.

Casey met his eyes and nodded.

"My son fell at the Battle of the Argonne."

"Sorry to hear it, ma'am."

"My son won the Medal of Honor."

"I'm sure he was a very brave man."

Mr. Devereux cleared his throat noisily. "Even if Julian's health had permitted, we are firm believers in nonviolence."

Casey raised his brows. "Well, Julian's only a kid," he said politely.

Flynn glanced at Julian. He was very quiet, his face expressionless as he replied, "I'm twenty-six."

"That so?" Casey said, showing the surprise Flynn felt. "No offense intended."

Julian did not respond, his attention focused on his plate. Flynn felt an unexpected stab of sympathy for him.

"Lordy, I know what it is to suffer from ill health," Mrs. Hoyt said, and she proceeded to describe in detail her many physical woes.

Joan sank lower in her chair, and Julian had apparently removed himself to the astral plane, but Amy listened politely and made sympathetic comments although she had surely heard all this a hundred times. Dr. Pearson contributed with his own occasional acerbic advice, and Casey cheerfully recommended several Queen of Egypt products with miraculous healing properties.

He was personable and quite a talker; Flynn bet he was a great success in his line of work.

When Mrs. Hoyt had worn out the topic of her own ill health, she asked about the news around the county, and Casey admitted he had been in Murphysboro two days earlier.

"Why that was right around the time of those brutal murders," Mrs. Hoyt exclaimed. Joan brightened and the rest of the table eyed Casey expectantly—except for Julian who continued to stare at his plate as though he could foretell the future in the navy beans.

"Well, I was only there when they found the last girl, Millie Hesse," Casey hastened to say. "Although the whole county's been talking about it ever since the first murder."

"Anna Spiegel," Joan said eagerly. "She was the first. Then Maria Campanella, then Millie Hesse."

"I knew Anna," Casey said. "That is to say, she was a regular customer of mine."

"Was she in ill health?" Mrs. Hoyt asked with interest.

"No. Not that I know of. Anna used our beauty products. Our lip salves and rouge papers and kohl eyeliners. She was a very pretty girl." He smiled at Joan. "We carry the finest all natural and all quality beauty products."

Joan blushed and reached for her coffee.

Casey grinned at Flynn who tried not to grin back. Casey had an irrepressible good humor that was hard not to respond to. Looking away from him, Flynn happened to catch Julian's eye and his smile faded. Gramps might be a pacifist, but the expression in the back of Julian's eyes was definitely violent. He looked from Flynn to Casey and his mouth tightened.

It seemed he wasn't kidding about his instincts.

"Was she a nice girl?" Mr. Devereux asked with what appeared to be unwilling fascination.

"Not if she used cosmetics," Mrs. Hoyt retorted.

Casey objected to this. "Sure, she was a nice girl. At least as far as I could tell. They were all nice girls from what I heard. Not the kind of girls to get themselves into trouble. That's what no one can understand. How this fiend could get close to them. He must be very clever."

"Or very evil," Devereux added.

"Excuse me," Julian said, rising. "I have to prepare for this evening."

"There's peach cobbler for dessert," Amy told him.

He shook his head.

"I'll save you a piece for later," she promised, and he smiled at her. It was a genuine smile, warm and friendly and uncomplicated. It surprised Flynn.

Nearly as much as the realization that he was aware of every move Julian made.

When Julian left the room there was a pause and then Mr. Devereux said, "My grandson is very sensitive to the vibrations of evil."

Dr. Pearson snorted. "What that young man needs is fresh air and sunshine and exercise. A few early nights wouldn't come amiss either."

"He has always been most delicate."

"What's wrong with him?" Casey inquired with interest, no doubt mentally running through the catalog of Queen of Egypt remedies and elixirs.

Mr. Devereux shook his head. Casey said, "Sorry if I offended him. I guess he's got one of those baby faces. Must have been hard on him not being able to serve his country."

Mr. Devereux opened his mouth, seemed to consider the company, and said, "My grandson has been called to a higher purpose."

Mrs. Hoyt sniffed disapprovingly.

After the peach cobbler, Casey mentioned that he was going for a stroll and Flynn said he'd join him.

They grabbed their jackets and hats and stepped out into the warm twilight.

"I know a place we can get a real drink," Casey said, lighting a pipe.

Flynn nodded.

They talked about the war and France. "Do you miss it sometimes?" Casey asked as they watched the street lamps blinking on all down the long silent blocks.

"Miss it? No," Flynn said.

"I do. I never felt as alive as I did in the war." Casey gave him that wide, friendly grin. "I guess that sounds peculiar."

"No, I think I know what you mean." Flynn added, "You never feel as alive as in those first seconds after you just miss getting your head blown off. I just wonder what the hell it was for. I lost a brother, an uncle, and two of my best friends in that war. I miss 'em every day." And Paul. He'd lost Paul too, but he couldn't talk about that. Not to anyone. Rarely did he even let himself remember.

A sniper's bullet on a sunny day. One moment Paul had been warm and alive, the next he was dead. *Dead.* No warning, no reprieve, no deferment. Dead and done.

"Yeah. I know. I lost a lot of pals too. Every one of the guys I joined up with went during that damned war."

"It changes you," Flynn said quietly. "It changed the men here. Were you around last year?"

"You mean the so-called massacre?"

Flynn nodded.

"I saw a damn sight more than I wanted to," Casey said grimly. "But you know, my granddad worked in the mines back before the union. Things were different back then—harder, meaner. My granddad worked for fourteen hours a day in a shaft that was only three feet high, sometimes up to his ankles in water. He spent all day bent over, loading coal onto mule carts. The mules used to go blind from so much time in the dark. Granddad died in the mines from bad air."

"Everyone died back then," Flynn agreed. "From the bad air, or collapses, or shaft fires."

"That's right. The lucky ones who survived the mines ended up dying of black lung. It's not that long ago. People still remember those days."

Flynn thought of the stories he'd heard: a man using his pocketknife to cut the throat of the wounded, a woman holding the hand of her child as she led him to see the dying, a man urinating on the corpses. As bad as anything he'd seen in the war. But then this *had* been war—or at least a battle in an ongoing war.

"You know," Casey said, "a lot of those people on the road and at the cemetery where it all ended, they weren't miners. They weren't even from Herrin. They were the no-account trash that gathers any time there's trouble."

Flynn nodded. It was something to take into account, true enough.

"Why do you care?" Casey asked. "You're not from around here. You're from…where? New York?"

Why *did* he care? Why was it so important to understand what had happened? Understanding it wouldn't change it. Probably wouldn't even prevent it happening again someplace else.

Flynn said, "They took dynamite and blew the draglines and the shovels and bulldozers of the Lester strip mine. They blew that mine apart. It'll never operate again."

"Maybe that's a good thing."

They had reached the Lafayette Hotel. It was one of Herrin's nicest lodgings, designed to recall European splendor before the war. It had done a brisk and lively business before Prohibition, but now, like a lot of businesses, it was struggling to stay afloat. Small iron balconies and window boxes decorated the outside. Inside, the walls were paneled in a red wood, ornate amber chandeliers hung from the ceiling, the carpet was an elegant pattern of fruit baskets and flowers on a field of black.

They went inside and ordered "soft drinks" which they sipped while they continued to talk, although they steered clear of such serious subjects as the war or the massacre. Casey was easy to talk to and Flynn found himself opening up in a way he rarely did anymore. He bought the second round. Their conversation grew less focused.

By the third round, Flynn was impatient for what would surely follow—the reason they had both walked out that evening. He was already trying to calculate the logistics of it. This was not New York where they would find a sympathetic club or speakeasy.

They would need to find a quiet alley or a deserted building or a corner of the park.

It had been awhile since he had to sneak around like that. He lived in a Greenwich Village brownstone, and while he was cautious, he didn't have to exercise the kind of care necessary in a small town like Herrin.

He wondered what it was like for a man like Casey. The war had probably simplified a lot of things for him. No wonder he missed it.

"Another?" Casey asked, half-rising.

Flynn didn't want another drink. He wanted Casey's body which was enough like Paul's body to fill him with a fierce hunger. A hunger that had sparked, oddly enough, when Julian had pressed his slim, hard form to Flynn's.

He hesitated, but Casey was giving him a meaningful look, so Flynn nodded. Maybe Casey had to get drunk to do it. That was sad, but it wasn't uncommon.

They had a fourth round of "soft drinks" and then, finally, Casey said, slurring a bit, "We oughta start back, ya think?"

They rose and went out, down the front steps and started walking back. At first Casey was whistling softly, "Ain't We Got Fun", but then he fell silent, seeming increasingly morose.

Their footsteps echoed loudly down the quiet street. Flynn was all but positive he hadn't misread him, but wondered if Casey had changed his mind.

But as they came to the set of stairs leading to the small corner park, Casey grabbed his arm and they ran up to the iron gate. It wasn't locked and they slipped inside, easing the gate shut behind them. It closed with a ghostly clang.

The park was dark and shadowy. The street lamps didn't reach beyond the tall maple trees lining the spiked fence, and they made their way down the dirt path to the small, open-air gazebo. Flynn started to climb onto the gazebo, but Casey pulled him back.

"No. Not there. Over here." Casey led him behind a great flowering barberry bush and unzipped his trousers, freeing himself. Flynn unfastened his own trousers.

The fact that they'd had a good deal to drink, and that Flynn had been craving this release since…anyway, it made it easier. Made it simple to push aside the faint dismay that their joining was so blunt, so businesslike. What was he looking for? This was not Paul, this was not romance, let alone love. He didn't look for that at home, why should he look for it here?

They stumbled together, and Flynn could feel the heat coming off Casey through his clothing. They were both perspiring with excitement—and humidity. He could feel Casey's heart thumping against his own as though he were scared to death. They clutched each other like drowning men. Casey's hardness jutted against his hip. His hands were going to leave bruises; his mouth was like a cave, dark and empty. It opened to Flynn's and their tongues slid together, wet and hot and slick.

Strangely, in that moment, Flynn remembered that delicate, expert kiss Julian had pressed upon him in his room. He remembered how Julian had felt in his arms: light and ardent as a raw flame.

The impression was gone in the next instant. The tang of Casey's sweat and the sweet scent of his hair oil mingled with the sharp, acidic scent of the barberry bush. Casey's fingers dug into Flynn's buttocks, urging him closer. Flynn pushed against him, rubbed against him, hunting eagerly for the release he knew was coming.

Casey's mouth opened wider, his tongue pushed deeper. Flynn drew back from that fever heat, from the bite of the whisky and the unfamiliar taste. He didn't want kisses, he just wanted the relief. He slicked his palm with spit, reached down, got both their stiff cocks in one hand and began to work them, rubbing them together.

Casey groaned into his mouth and then tore away, tipping his head back and gulping great lungfuls of night as Flynn rolled them forward, shoving them along. They humped and fumbled against each other, nearly overbalancing in their thrusting, grinding, frantic…like two stags rutting.

A roiling blaze of heat soared between them, and Casey made a sound like he was choking to death. Hot wet come spattered between their bodies. Breathing hard, they hung onto each other—mostly to keep from falling over.

Then the hasty, limbs trembling, business of wiping off, doing up the zippers and buttons, moving quickly, putting it behind them.

They looked each other over, not that there was much to see in the uncertain light, and they moved in accord down the dirt path back to the iron gate. They stepped through it, the gate shutting with a faint chime behind them. They walked down the steps to the pavement.

To his horror, Flynn realized there was a man a few feet in front of them. He must have just passed by the park as they were reaching the gate. Flynn felt a sudden, guilty alarm that they would be discovered—what they hell explanation could they give for being in the park at that hour?

Casey must have realized their danger at the same instant. He stopped in his tracks. The man must have sensed their presence, for he glanced over his shoulder and jumped visibly.

"Didn't see you behind me," he said. His hat brim hid his features, but he sounded nervous. "Were you in the theater too?"

Casey appeared struck dumb. Flynn said, "Yes."

"Wasn't that the damnedest thing?"

"I—"

"Not that I believe in that superstitious mumbo-jumbo." The man gave an edgy laugh. "But it was strange, certainly."

"Yes."

They were now all three of them walking in a small herd, Casey bringing up the rear. Moonlight shadowed the beautiful old houses and the churches as they stepped briskly along their way. Warmth still radiated from the bricks of the building and road.

"The rest of it, well, any good huckster could come up with that pabulum. Your Auntie May wants you to wear a scarf in cold weather, your grandpapa still loves you." The man snorted in amused disgust. "But predicting Bill Doyle's death? And that thing about the murders."

Flynn felt a chill slither down his spine. Abruptly he knew that the man had been to the Opera House and that he was talking about Julian.

He said carefully, "But maybe we misunderstood him? Maybe that's not what he was saying at all?"

"What else could he have meant?" the man said. "He said— she said—whoever that was supposed to be said that she was lost on the far side of Crab Orchard Creek. That the other girls were with her. Four girls. And one of them doesn't know she's dead yet."

When Flynn and Casey reached the boarding house they found everyone out on the breezeway drinking lemonade and talking. It was clear that the news of Julian's announcement had already, in the mysterious way of small towns, reached home.

The three ladies sat on the wide swing, their shadowy faces lit by the street lamps a few yards away. Their paper fans fluttered like the wings of dying moths, languidly waving back and forth. Dr. Pearson sat smoking at the edge of the brick walk, the red tip of his cigar glowing in the darkness.

Amy instructed them to bring chairs outside and pour themselves a glass of lemonade. Casey and Flynn obeyed. They sat a few feet away from each other on the breezeway, sipping their cold drinks. Casey sniffed discreetly a couple of times, and Flynn was tempted to elbow him in the ribs.

Mrs. Hoyt made a disapproving noise and said, "I don't need to ask where you gentlemen have been this evening."

For a paralyzed second Flynn thought she meant…but then he realized she was talking about the alcohol they had consumed earlier.

"Are the Devereuxs back yet?" he asked, ignoring her.

"No," Amy replied. "Any minute now, I expect. We heard the show ended early."

"Did it?"

"They're saying it was true about the man whose death he predicted, that his wife came home and found him dead."

Joan's shadow shivered in delighted horror. Mrs. Hoyt exclaimed, "Table tilting and spirit writing. Bell ringing and levitation and invisible hands playing musical instruments. At worst it's blasphemy and at best it's nonsense!"

"It's harmless nonsense, I guess. And it's fun," Casey put in, and Flynn saw the white flash of Joan's grateful smile turned his way.

Mrs. Hoyt said, "From what we've heard from the neighbors, I don't think people found it much fun tonight."

"How can that be Julian's fault?" protested Joan. "Anyway, he doesn't deal in spiritualistic phenomena."

"How would you know, missy?"

"I asked him. He said that's for people in traveling shows and carnivals."

"And what is he? The child of a fortuneteller and a vaudevillian."

"Now, Mrs. Hoyt," Amy remonstrated amiably, "the Devereuxs are my guests. I don't want you speaking ill of them. I don't have any complaints about either of them. Julian's a sweet enough boy."

Casey gave a derisive laugh as he lit his pipe.

Flynn stared at him, at the handsome features looking mask-like and foreign in the brief illumination of the pipe bowl. He asked, "Is it true he prophesied another murder?"

"He didn't prophecy," growled Dr. Pearson from the gloomy corner of the breezeway. "He announced she was dead. According to Mrs. Muenster next door."

"He must have heard it on the radio," Mrs. Hoyt said. "Or he simply made it up to frighten people. To get more people to come to his show."

"The radio wasn't on when he came back," Amy said.

"When he came back from where?" Flynn asked.

"I don't know where. He was gone most of the day. He goes out every day. Of course they only arrived on Monday. He said he went to the dime museum today."

"Where were he and the old man before they came here?"

"Cairo."

Joan said, "Cairo, Illinois that is."

"Where else would it be?" Mrs. Hoyt retorted. "Those two are homegrown hucksters."

Amy said, "According to Mr. Devereux they traveled the Continent before the war."

"There is only one continent worth traveling and that is the United States of America," Mrs. Hoyt pronounced.

Flynn asked, "How long were they in Cairo?"

Mrs. Hoyt laughed jarringly. "It's easy to see you're a reporter, Mr. Flynn. You ask so many questions."

"A reporter," Casey repeated in a funny voice.

"Well, well." Dr. Pearson sounded amused.

David flicked his cigarette butt in the damp grass and slapped at a mosquito. "Reporters take vacations too."

"But you're not on vacation," Dr. Pearson said shrewdly.

"No," Flynn admitted. "I'm writing a story on Herrin one year later."

"Not much of a story there." Pearson didn't sound troubled about it, but then who in this godforsaken town did?

"Most people I've talked to seem to see it your way. The rest of the country still wonders whether what happened here could happen someplace else."

"Of course it could. People forget about Ludlow now because that was before the war mostly. But women and children died in that one. And that time it was the mining companies doing the shooting."

"Gus covered the Ludlow story," Amy said quietly.

"I remember." Flynn looked her way although he couldn't read her face in the dim light. Gus had helped dig out the dead women and children killed in the fire set by the Colorado National Guard.

"These are evil, godless times," Mrs. Hoyt pronounced.

"It's not the gods who've forgotten—" Dr. Pearson broke off at the sound of voices inside the house.

"I don't want to talk about it anymore." Julian's irritated voice carried clearly through the open windows. Through the lace curtains they could see his silhouette and the silhouette of the old man as though they were watching a Punch and Judy show. Devereux senior had a fierce, unforgiving profile. Julian had taken off his turban and his longish hair and ruffled collar gave him the aspect of a prince in a fairytale.

"You're going to ruin us with that kind of prophesying," the old man snapped.

"It wasn't a prophecy."

"Whatever it was, it has to stop. You're frightening people. You're frightening *me*. Prophesying is for...for lowlifes and scallywags."

"It wasn't a prophecy."

"People walked out. People left the theater tonight."

"I know. *I* left the goddamned theater."

"Cursing and blaspheming. What devil possesses you?"

Julian said with sudden anguish, "Leave me alone, can't you?"

Their voices faded as they went up the stairs.

"Well!" Mrs. Hoyt said at last.

"That guy's nuttier than a fruitcake," Casey observed.

"Maybe he's telling the truth," Joan said defiantly. "Did you ever think of that?"

Silence followed her words, so perhaps no one had.

Casey went upstairs when Flynn did.

"You didn't say you were a reporter," he said softly, as they reached the top of the stairs at the second level.

"Does it matter?"

"I guess not." But Casey was giving him a funny look.

"What?"

"I don't know." Casey shrugged his wide shoulders.

Abruptly, Flynn was fed up with Casey, fed up with the evening, fed up with himself for ever traveling to this hick town. "Good night," he said curtly, and went down the hall to his room.

He opened the door, stepped inside, closed the door. It was difficult to see in the silver-edged darkness. Was he alone? He stood still, waiting, but no one spoke. No one moved. He turned on the lamp, and the room was empty, the bed neatly made, the window open to the hot, still night.

He was conscious of disappointment.

What had he expected?

Perhaps it was better not to examine that.

He went next door, splashed his face, brushed his teeth. Casey was waiting in the hall when he stepped out again. Flynn nodded curtly. Casey nodded curtly back.

Flynn went back to his room, turned on the fan, turned out the lamp, lay down on the bed. He stared up at the shadowy recesses of the ceiling.

He remembered Julian's face when he'd told him, "I'm not interested in *you*. I don't even like you."

Flynn closed his eyes. He didn't want to think about that. When had he grown so cruel? After Paul had died, he supposed. But a lot of people had lost someone they loved during the war. *Most* people had lost someone they loved. What gave him the right to…to close off the way he had? Yes, that was the truth of it. After Paul's death he'd turned off something inside himself.

Anyway, what was so different between Julian and him? Or Julian and Casey? Julian might be a nut but he was honest about what he wanted. And, face it, his instincts were pretty sharp.

Flynn listened to the muted voices down below on the breezeway. Mrs. Hoyt had gone up before Casey and him. It wasn't long before the rest of them went inside. He listened to the rattle and gulps of the old plumbing, and then the sounds of the house settling down for the night. The squeak of floorboards, pops and cracks of timber and rafters.

And then a complete silence.

And yet…there was something alert in the silence. He could feel it. Feel an…intelligence awake and listening. Flynn listened too.

He waited.

And waited.

The ripe lemon moon shone brightly through the window, making it difficult to sleep. He sat up, considered pulling down the window shade, but that was liable to cut off what breeze there was. Even with the fan circulating, the room felt stifling.

Flynn swung his legs over the side of the bed. Maybe he should get dressed and go for a walk. Lying here staring at the ceiling was accomplishing nothing.

The door swung open soundlessly, Flynn felt the disturbance in the air. He stared at the doorway and the tall, pale form standing motionless. Flynn straightened. The hair rose on the back of his neck, and for one hazy moment he wondered if he was staring at a ghost.

"David?" The whisper was so soft it could have belonged to anyone, but Flynn knew.

He whispered back, "It's all right. Come in and shut the door."

The white shadow slipped inside the room and closed the door. Julian came over to the bed and sat next to Flynn. The mattress springs squeaked. "I'm sorry," he said breathlessly. "I know what you told me, but I can't be alone tonight. Do you…" He swallowed the rest of his sentence. He sounded unsure, frightened to death, in fact, and Flynn reached to cover his hand. He found it ice cold.

"What's the matter?" Instinctively he took the chill hand—both hands—in his, chafing them.

"I can't." Julian stopped and tried again. "Do you ever—?"

"Sure. Everyone does," Flynn said easily. He had the strangest sense that he understood everything Julian was not saying. Julian's trembling fingers clutched his as though Flynn were leading him back through the Underworld.

"What happened tonight?"

"Did you hear about that?"

Flynn nodded, realized Julian might not be able to see him, and said, "Yes. They're saying you predicted another murder."

"I didn't predict it. She's already…" He stopped and then gulped out, "And then this house tonight."

"What's wrong with the house?"

He saw the glimmering outline of Julian's face turning to him, but he didn't say anything. Flynn's scalp prickled. "What's wrong with the house tonight?"

Julian's whisper was so faint he had to bend closer to make out the words. "Can I stay with you till morning? I won't be a nuisance. I want to sleep here, that's all. I'll sleep in the window seat if you like."

Flynn absorbed this quietly. "Sure," he said. "But the bed's big enough for both of us if you don't kick too much."

There was a pause. "Are you sure?"

"Yeah." Flynn stood. "Go on. Lie down."

Julian slipped out of his dressing gown. It pooled to the floorboards in a silken sigh, and he crawled onto the bed. Back to Flynn, he lay on his side in a neat, self-contained line, illuminated by the moonlight. Flynn stretched out beside him. There was only about a hands-length between them. Julian's scent was light and clean, like summer wind and spiced oranges. Fine tremors ran through his body. Flynn touched his arm.

"How can you be cold on a hot night like this?"

Julian moved his head in denial. "I'm all right."

Flynn reached for him, and Julian turned, biddable as a babe, wrapping his arms tightly around Flynn. Flynn was thinking…but no. Julian was completely unaroused. He was seeking comfort, that was all, and Flynn responded instinctively, wondering at himself. When was the last time he had laid with another man for any purpose but sex?

Paul.

Paul was the last time. Strangely, tonight the thought of Paul brought no pain.

Flynn stroked Julian's back. His skin was smooth and unblemished as a child's. His hair was fine as silk. As he grew warm, his body relaxed, went boneless, and soon he was breathing in the soft, deep pattern of sleep. Flynn's arms grew tired, but he continued to cradle the other man until he too dropped into sleep.

A mouth brushed his own, light as a spring breeze, the kiss working itself into his dreams.

Flynn smiled and woke. The room was growing light. He had the impression that the bedroom door had just closed. He was alone, but the pillow next to his was indented with the shape of a head, the sheets still warm.

Not a dream. At least, not entirely a dream. His lips still tingled with that kiss, real or imagined.

He was surprised at how well he had slept, how relaxed he felt. He rolled onto his side, stretching comfortably, closed his eyes and fell back asleep.

The next time he woke it was to the muffled sounds of disturbance. The sound of crying filtered through the floorboards. Footsteps were moving rapidly up and down the stairs. He could hear voices; muted, but the tone was clear enough: trouble. Serious trouble.

He rolled out of bed and dressed hastily, hurrying downstairs.

Amy met him in the main hall. Her plain face was worried and weary. "I'm sorry. There's no breakfast ready. The house is in a bit of a commotion. Mrs. Hoyt passed during the night."

"She's *dead?*"

Amy nodded.

"How?"

"Doc Pearson says stroke. He thinks it must have happened soon after she left us last evening. Joan's mighty upset."

"I bet."

"Doc Pearson has her sedated, poor kid. Anyway, can you manage for yourself this morning?"

"Of course."

Amy patted his arm and turned away. Flynn said suddenly, "Amy, is there more I can do?"

She looked at him with surprise. "Why, no. Not just now, David. Thank you for asking."

Dr. Pearson poked his head out of one of the rooms down the hall and called to Amy. She excused herself and hurried away.

Flynn went back upstairs and waited for the bathroom to be free. Casey stepped out and Flynn explained to him what had happened.

"Can't say I'm surprised," Casey said. "She was a prime candidate. Had all the symptoms."

Flynn raised his brows. "Are you a doctor?"

"Er, no. But we're taught the basics." Casey gave Flynn a sideways look and asked, "Feel like going to grab some breakfast? I have time before I have to start on my rounds."

"Sure." It was not so much that Flynn wanted to have breakfast with Casey as he wanted out of that house. What he really hoped was to see Julian that morning, but there was no sign of him so far, and he had no idea which of the rooms down the hall belonged to whom. Walking in on *Grand-père* Devereux would not be good. "I'll get my hat."

They walked down to a small diner and ordered eggs, hotcakes, ham, and coffee for thirty-five cents.

They didn't talk much. Flynn was preoccupied with thoughts of Julian and the night before. Had Julian sensed Mrs. Hoyt's death? Flynn didn't, in theory, believe in that kind of thing, although he couldn't deny odd occurrences during the war; men who had sensed that they or other men would die the following day. "The sight" his dear old superstitious Irish granny had called it. Some folks had it; you could only chalk so much up to coincidence.

"How long are you staying at Mrs. Gulling's?" Casey asked. "I'm here for the week."

"I'm staying a few more days."

"Maybe we could get a drink tonight?" Casey's green eyes were bright and alert. His smile was wide and warm.

Flynn smiled back, but he felt disinclined to take him up on his offer. Casey was nothing like Paul after all. He said noncommittally, "We'll have to see how things are at the house this evening."

"Nothing to do with us, is it?"

Us.

No it was nothing to do with them. Since the war Flynn had made a point of not getting involved in things that weren't his business. At least...to avoid personal involvement. He wrote about the injustices he saw, but he didn't take them personally. He didn't look for trouble and he didn't make trouble his own business. As much as he had admired Gus, the way Gus had thrown himself heart and soul into the causes he'd covered in his stories, the war had convinced Flynn that a man, especially a writer, could do more good by keeping a certain distance, a certain detachment. Like a surgeon.

Perhaps that detachment had spilled over into his personal life. But without Paul...

But he didn't want to keep dragging up Paul's memory. It was beginning to feel uncomfortably like he'd been hiding behind Paul's ghost. Using the memory of Paul as an excuse for, well, participating in his own life.

He opened his mouth to say…something, but the waitress came to their table, cheeks flushed, eyes bright. "Did you hear? There's been another murder over Carbondale way. A girl named Theresa Martin. They found her by Crab Orchard Creek and they say it's exactly like the others."

"What's like the others?" Flynn asked.

The waitress lowered her voice to a stage whisper. "What it was he did to her."

She bustled away and Casey reached for his coffee cup, saying grimly, "Damned ghouls."

Flynn was inclined to agree, but maybe it was reassuring that even in a place like this people were still shocked by such violence. Wouldn't it be a bad sign if they took it for granted?

After breakfast he and Casey walked back to the boarding house. A black hearse was pulling away as they arrived. A police car was parked in the front.

"Swell," Casey said. "The cops are going to be crawling all over this place thanks to that escapee from a freak show."

Flynn stared at him, at the unexpected venom in Casey's voice.

A sheriff deputy stood outside the front door, and they had to identify themselves to get inside.

Amy met them in the front hall. "What's going on?" Flynn asked, removing his hat.

"The sheriff is questioning Julian."

"Why?"

But he knew why even before Amy said, "Because of the things he said during his show last night. I think they must believe he knows about the murders."

Flynn could hear the murmur of voices from the front parlor. "I thought they were in Cairo last week. Didn't the old man show them his train tickets?"

"He went down to the train depot this morning and I haven't seen him since," Amy said. "I've had my hands full this morning." She hesitated. "That boy isn't… He's not equipped to… Do you think you could…?"

From the parlor he heard a voice say, "You're some kind of colored, aren't you?" This, followed by Julian's murmured answer.

Flynn nodded grimly to Amy and went into the parlor. There was a deputy standing inside the doorway, but Flynn said, "I'm representing Mr. Devereux."

"Are you a lawyer?"

Julian was seated on the sofa. He had not even had time to shave before being rousted out of bed. His hair was uncombed. He wore gray flannels and a white T-shirt. He looked thoroughly disreputable as he glanced up hopelessly at Flynn's entrance. His somber eyes lightened, but he bit his lip and said nothing.

"Who are you?" the sheriff asked, taking a cigar from his mouth. He was a short man with a big belly, a bushy mustache and mud brown eyes.

"David Flynn. I'm a reporter for *The Atlantic Monthly*."

"A reporter! That's what we don't need around here."

"But that's what you've got," Flynn said. "I'm here to make sure this kid's not being railroaded."

"Railroaded! What the hell do you mean railroaded? We're just asking this young man a few simple questions about how he knows things he's got no business knowing."

Julian leaned forward, elbows on his thighs, head in hands. "I don't know anything," he groaned. "I keep telling you."

"You got up in front of three hundred people and told them where Theresa Martin's body was lying."

Julian shook his head without looking up.

"I take it you're not a believer, Sheriff...? Sorry, I didn't catch your name."

"McFadden. No, I'm not a-a *believer*. I'm a Baptist, for chrissake."

"Is that McFadden with an 'Mc' or 'Mac'? We like to spell names right in *The Atlantic Monthly*."

McFadden's gaze—reminiscent of a bear's small, suspicious eyes—flickered. "I don't see much of a story here, Flynn. We're only asking—"

"Mr. Devereux's cooperation? As Mr. Edgar Cayce has helped the police on occasion with their most difficult cases?"

"He has?" McFadden looked plainly taken aback. "He did?"

Flynn nodded. He had no idea if it was true or not.

Julian raised his head. "You don't understand. I can't...control it. It just happens."

Flynn gave him a warning look and he fell silent, his mouth not steady, eyes sullen.

"Sure, and I can see why you would think that way because it's a great story and it would get you great coverage in the papers. And nothing else makes sense because the Devereuxs were in Cairo when these first murders happened."

"So we've all heard a couple a times, but can he prove that?"

Flynn and McFadden turned to Julian. Julian sounded frightened as he said, "I gave shows Tuesday through Saturday at the Gem Theater on Eighth Street. And there will be the train ticket stubs. *Grand-père* will have those."

"*Grand-père*," the sheriff said disgustedly.

"The Devereuxs are from New Orleans," Flynn said. This area had been settled by French and German and English and Irish settlers, so he wouldn't expect to see the same prejudice that Italians or colored found.

"I know French!" The sheriff had his dander up. "I do find it convenient his grandfather is absent this morning."

"The Devereuxs could hardly be performing in Cairo and committing murder two counties away. Unless you think young Mr. Devereux really is a sorcerer?"

"I don't believe in that hocus-pocus hooey," the sheriff snarled.

"Then there's your answer."

McFadden stared at him. "And you don't believe in that mumbo-jumbo either."

"That's not the point," Flynn said. "The point is, without magical powers, Devereux couldn't be in two places at one time."

The sheriff continued to eye him grimly, only partly convinced.

"Think what a fine story it would make," Flynn suggested. "This young man using his talents to help the police in their investigation. Why, the public loves this kind of thing. It would be nice to appear in a national paper for something other than the massacre, don't you think?"

The sheriff stuck his cigar back in his mouth and chewed on it thoughtfully. "Meybee so," he said reluctantly. "Meybee so."

CHAPTER SIX

"I never know when it's going to happen," Julian said, staring at his hands.

"Speak up," McFadden ordered.

Julian's throat moved and he said more loudly, "Before I turned sixteen, the voices—the spirits—came to me all the time. But then when I turned sixteen, I-I became ill. The spirits only come once in a while now."

"Come every night you've got a show, don't they?" McFadden asked. He added sarcastically, "Or are you charging folks a pretty penny on the outside chance the Count of Monte Crisco is going to show up?"

Monte Crisco. Well, that was appropriate from this pigheaded fool. Flynn was careful not to let what he thought show on his face. He said calmly, "You're doing fine. Just tell the truth."

Julian swallowed hard. He didn't look up. "Last night, during the performance, I heard a woman talking to me. A spirit. At first I was confused. Unsure of why she had come to me. She didn't understand." He looked up, but he was talking to Flynn not McFadden.

"What didn't she understand?" Flynn asked.

Julian closed his eyes. "She didn't understand she was dead."

McFadden turned to Flynn and Flynn shrugged.

"What happened?" McFadden questioned.

Julian drew a deep breath and opened his eyes. "It's difficult when they don't know yet. She didn't come to me willingly. She came because she was lost and heard my voice. She's trapped on this side. They all are."

McFadden asked, "Who?"

"The murdered girls." Julian said carefully, "It happens sometimes with a-a violent death. They don't have time to…to transition. And he's done something to them."

McFadden's voice was dangerous as he demanded, "Who has? What's he done?"

"He…cut them up." Julian put his long, slim hands over his face. His voice was muffled and shaking. "He's cast some spell on them. An ancient spell. They're held here, prisoner—"

"Horseshit!" McFadden jumped up, looking as though he wanted to strike Julian. Flynn rose too, watching him, ready to intervene. Whatever McFadden read on his face stayed his hand, but he said in a trembling, deep voice, "You're a goddamned liar."

Julian lowered his hands. He looked terrified. "I'm not lying. Why would I lie? I don't want it to be true—"

"What's the name of this murderer then? She must know it, this spirit gal. What's the name of the man who killed those girls?"

"I don't know."

"Because you're a liar. A goddamned liar and a-a mountebank."

Flynn cut across the sheriff, his voice calm, although listening to himself he thought he must sound as loony as Julian. "Did you ask Theresa who killed her?"

Julian shook his head, his shoulders hunched defensively. "I had to tell her she had…crossed over. It was a shock to her and she fled. They do sometimes." His wide dark eyes were absolutely sincere as they met Flynn's. He might be a mountebank or he might be mad—or both. He believed what he was saying.

"All right then," Flynn said. "You could summon her and ask, couldn't you? You could hold a…whatchamacallit? A séance."

"You're as crazy as he is," McFadden exclaimed.

At the same time Julian said with great definitiveness, "No."

Flynn ignored McFadden. "Why not?" he asked Julian.

"I told you I can't control it."

It was the first thing he'd said that Flynn suspected was a lie. "You could still try. You said she's trapped on this side. She came to you once. She might come to you again." He heard himself but dismissed the thought of what he must sound like. Maybe it *was* crazy, but it was logical too, wasn't it? "You could summon her and you could ask her about the last thing she remembers."

Julian was shaking his head with that exasperating scared stubbornness.

McFadden looked from Flynn to the younger man and said, "You know what I think? I think it was a lucky guess. I think he knew eventually there was going to be another murder. That's what everyone's been saying. His kind like to shock and frighten folks. He said it to get a bigger audience. It just happened to be true."

"He knew the dead girl's name," Flynn pointed out.

"Who says? Today everyone knows her name, so they're saying he knew it last night. There's no proof that he did."

Flynn opened his mouth to argue the obvious, but McFadden said, "Either he's a fake or he's a killer, but I don't believe in magic and I don't believe in ghosts or spirits talking to the living. You want to turn this huckster into a big story for your newspaper like that sacrilegious conman Edgar Cayce, you go right ahead, but you're not making a laughingstock out of me and my boys."

"What's going on here?" Julian's grandfather stood in the doorway, glowering at them all. "What is this? What has he done now?"

The sheriff turned to him with something like relief. "I understand you have in your possession ticket stubs that will prove you and your grandson were in the town of Cairo last week?"

"Yes?" Mr. Devereux's eyes moved uneasily from Julian to Flynn. "What of it? Why are you interrogating him?"

"I need to see those tickets."

"Very well." Devereux's suspicious gaze rested on Julian's pale face. He turned away reluctantly.

The sheriff followed him. He stopped in the doorway and threw back to Flynn, "If you do learn something in this séance of yours, you let me know."

When their footsteps had died away, Flynn seated himself facing the sofa and Julian. He wanted to sit next to Julian, put his arm around him—Julian looked sorely in need of comfort—but that was, of course, out of the question.

He said, "What happened last night?"

Julian's face worked. "David, I've told you everything."

"What about Mrs. Hoyt?"

Julian's mouth opened. No sound came out.

"You knew she was dead, didn't you?"

He closed his mouth and shuddered. He nodded.

Flynn stared at him for a long time. "So it's true," he said at last. "The dead speak to you."

"Through me. I'm only the messenger." He tried to smile, but it was a sad, unsteady effort. "And not a very good messenger. It's true what I said. When I turned sixteen it stopped. And I was glad. But *Grand-père...*"

"What?"

Julian shook his head.

Flynn said shrewdly, "The show must go on—and you're the meal ticket. This is the family stock and trade." He considered this. "But now the phone line to the spirit world is working again and you're starting to get calls."

Julian said nothing. He looked all at once much older, older than his age. He met Flynn's gaze and said quietly, "Please. I can't bear it from you."

"Can't bear what?"

"Don't…ask."

"What?" But Flynn already knew what he was going to hear. Yet the idea had not occurred to him until the second Julian spoke, so how could Julian—

"You want me to contact Paul for you."

It took him a moment to command his voice. "You could do it?"

"I don't know." He sounded anguished. "Perhaps."

"Well?"

Julian shook his head.

"Why not?" And even Flynn was surprised by the anger in his voice.

Julian studied him and the wounded expression in those doe-like eyes troubled Flynn, disturbed him. "Do you never think of anyone but yourself, David?"

"Me?" Flynn was astonished. "What do you think I came in here for a few minutes ago if it wasn't to help you?"

Julian's eyes glittered with quick, angry tears. "I think you thought it would make a good story to write about a medium working with the police to capture a killer."

"You're wrong."

"I wish that was true." Julian wiped hastily at the tears. His smile was bitter. He rose and left the room before Flynn could decide on an answer.

Listening to the fading footsteps, Flynn realized that Julian *was* wrong—although not entirely.

Amy was in the kitchen when he wandered in a short while later. Water boiled on the stovetop. She was greasing a heavy skillet. Death or disaster, people still had to eat.

"There's cold buttermilk in the icebox," she told Flynn, looking up at his entrance. Her smile was tired.

Flynn got a glass and the bottle of milk out. "How's Joan doing?"

"That little girl is heartbroken."

Flynn couldn't think of anything to say. Mrs. Hoyt had seemed a foolish and tiresome woman who would probably become more so the longer you knew her, but even newspapermen tried not to speak ill of the dead.

"How's the story coming?" Amy asked and he realized he'd barely had a chance to talk to her since he'd arrived. Or had he arranged it that way?

The buttermilk was refreshing. As he drank, he considered her question. She would be viewing this situation from whatever angle Gus would have seen it, and Gus had always been pro-Labor and pro-Union and pro-Miners. But how would a man as conscientious and civilized as Gus have viewed a massacre?

"I don't know," he answered. "For all the complaining folks are doing about lawlessness and godlessness, I can't find anyone who thinks Lester didn't deserve what he got or who wants to see those miners prosecuted."

Amy didn't answer for so long he thought she wasn't going to. "It's a mighty shocking thing. I think most people still…"

She didn't complete the thought. Flynn gave a short laugh. "I guess so."

She looked up then and there was an odd glint in her green-blue eyes. "I'll tell you this, no charge. W.J. Lester was and is a fool. An arrogant, greedy, college-educated fool."

As fond as he was of her, Flynn couldn't let that pass. "Amy, my God. They murdered those men. They tortured them and then they murdered them—after promising them safe passage."

Her face tightened. "I don't have to tell you I don't approve of murder. I know that's what it was. Everyone knows that's what it was, plain and simple. People are angry and ashamed and frightened. Frightened about what they learned was inside them." She folded her lips and stared down at the pan on the stove. After a brief struggle, she said, "But you want to hear the truth? The truth is that bunch of thugs Lester imported from Chicago had already stirred up enough hate to get someone killed before the massacre. They'd been harassing farm people and berry pickers for using roads they'd been using for fifty years. Pushing them around, cursing them, shoving guns in their ribs, even robbing a few of them—and threatening to kill them if they went to the sheriff."

She added shortly, "Not that the sheriff cared to get mixed up in it."

"I've heard a few of them were thugs and gangsters. But that mob killed twenty men that day. And even if every single one of them was--"

"You killed men in the war, didn't you? It was them or you, wasn't it?"

Flynn stared at her. "Is that what Gus thought?"

Her face quivered. She turned back to the stove. "No." He could hear that she was close to tears. It seemed to be his day for making people cry.

"Gus said 'Each man's death diminishes me, for I am involved in mankind. Therefore, send not to know for whom the bell tolls, it tolls for thee.'"

Hearing Amy quote John Donne in that flat, plain, unvarnished way struck Flynn absolutely silent.

Maybe it was as he'd said to Casey Lee the night before. Maybe the war *did* have to do with it. A few of those miners had been in France the same time he had, and had seen and done the things he had. If they were like Flynn, they'd come back changed men. Harder and rougher than when they waved farewell to peacetime.

He'd been so sure of the answers when he had arrived on Wednesday morning. He'd planned to write a simple article about the aftermath of violence. He'd wanted to set it straight in his own mind, see it in black and white, saints and sinners, but the reality was many shades of gray. It wasn't anything that was going to be fixed anytime soon and writing more about it wouldn't change that. Plenty of people were already writing and speech-making about it.

Flynn found himself wanting to do something. Something...

"Where's Julian?" he asked.

"Out. He don't like funerals," Amy said cryptically.

Flynn walked down to the courthouse to poke around, but he'd already lost whatever enthusiasm for the story on the massacre that he had started out with. The truth was, he was looking for Julian. He told himself that he wanted to take another shot at convincing him to try a séance; that this would make a better story than his original idea of writing about the massacre. Instead, he would write about these murders—and Julian.

But if he was honest, he wanted to find Julian.

He wasn't sure how or why his feelings had changed, but he felt a singular mix of pity and fascination for that strange young man. And, well, a certain amount of lust.

So he walked along the streets, nodding politely to folks, lost in his own thoughts.

It was hot, but there were lots of cloth awnings and shady roofs along the storefronts so it wasn't bad that time of day. He passed the corner park where he and Casey had stopped the evening before. It seemed like a lifetime ago.

In front of the courthouse the old timers were enjoying the latest gossip over their cigars and chewing tobacco, probably exactly what they'd been doing since the Civil War.

He paused for a shine at the old shoe-shine stand. The grizzled old colored man made pleasant conversation while he swiftly polished Flynn's shoes till they shone like glass.

He went into Skeltcher's and had a "root beer" and then walked back to the boarding house. He was walking up the sunny street when he spotted Julian coming from the opposite direction. He raised his hand in greeting, and Julian paused at the house walkway, waiting for him.

"What time is your show tonight?" Flynn asked.

"There's no show tonight." Julian looked weary. "And before you ask again, no, I won't hold a séance for the police."

"It's clear you're not a mind reader," Flynn remarked. "I wasn't going to ask you to give a séance. I was thinking you might like to drive out and have supper at a roadhouse this evening."

Julian's astonishment was almost comical. "Why?"

"Wouldn't you like to?"

"Yes."

The naked—though fleeting—vulnerability of the other man's face made Flynn's chest hurt. What the hell was Julian's life like that the idea of dinner with a friendly stranger should mean so much? But then he probably didn't have friends. He had that crazy old coot of a grandfather driving him from town to town like a gypsy with his dancing bear.

"All right then," he said gruffly. "We'll tell them we're going out to the roadhouse dance."

Julian said hesitantly, "There'll be a viewing for Mrs. Hoyt, won't there?"

"You don't want to have anything to do with that, do you?"

He shook his head, but his eyes were unhappy. "It might seem disrespectful, though."

"I didn't realize you were so worried about appearances."

The slender brown column of Julian's throat moved as he swallowed. "My grandfather isn't...very happy with me."

He hadn't sounded particularly concerned about what the old man had thought the night before. Flynn wondered what had changed. "It's moot in any case. The viewing is tomorrow night at the funeral parlor. You'll have a show to perform."

He knew he didn't misread the relief on Julian's face. Yes, getting Julian out of that house tonight was a good idea for everyone. And there was no denying how much Flynn liked the idea.

Much more, as it turned out, than old man Devereux did. He could hear them down the hall when he went to use the washroom after he and Julian went upstairs. He couldn't make out the words—the Devereuxs were used to conducting their quarrels under other people's roofs—but the tone was most definitely unhappy on the part of both parties.

He was heading back to his own bedroom when he heard Julian say clearly, "I'm neither a child nor a half-wit however much you wish it might be true."

The old man's response was muffled, but the tone was venomous, and Flynn felt a stab of alarm for Julian. That was not a tone to use on someone you loved, and he had an idea that Julian had fewer defenses than some.

When they met downstairs twenty minutes later, Julian was neatly, even dapperly dressed, hat, coat and tie all present and correct. His eyes were shining and he was so obviously happy that Flynn couldn't help an inward flinch at the responsibility.

Mr. Devereux was downstairs as well.

"Going to a dance, eh?" he inquired acidly, his midnight eyes raking Flynn up and down. "Planning to meet a couple of gals and Charleston the night away?"

It was instantly clear to Flynn that the old man knew about his grandson's proclivities—which meant he now knew about Flynn. He said evenly, "That's right."

Devereux opened his mouth, but closed it as Amy came into sight.

"Now don't go picking up any flappers," she warned them as she went around picking up stray items in the hall and parlor. She was holding one of Joan's books on Cleopatra and crocheting that had belonged to Mrs. Hoyt.

"You're the only gal for me, Mrs. Gulling," Julian said charmingly, and Amy laughed.

They met Casey on their way out the door, and he looked plainly taken aback to see Flynn and Julian together. The surprise on his face gave way to an unfriendly expression, but Flynn tipped his hat and kept Julian moving with an unobtrusive hand on his back.

The sun was setting as they backed the old Model T out of the garage and were on their way at last. Flynn glanced over at Julian and said, "I don't think Grandpapa likes me."

"No." Julian was smiling a lazy smile, and Flynn wondered if part of his attraction for the other man was tied up in that fact. He was surprised to find he didn't like that idea.

"Where's the rest of your folks?"

"Dead."

"*All* of them?"

"The ones I know about. My father was killed in a train wreck. My mother predicted it."

"So you mentioned once before. Count Amadeus, that would be?"

"Yes. He was a magician." Julian smiled faintly. "My mother was Zaliki the Seer. She was a fortune teller by trade, though she was also clairvoyant."

"Like you?"

"Yes. But she preferred telling fortunes." Julian's smile faded and he stared ahead through the windshield.

Prophesying is for...for lowlifes and scallywags.

"What happened to your mother?"

"She killed herself."

Flynn's hands tightened on the steering wheel. He consciously relaxed them. "Why?"

"She missed my father, I expect. *Grand-père* says she went mad. Perhaps she did." He sounded peculiarly disinterested.

"*Can* you tell the future?"

Julian was studying him again, mouth curved in a sly smile. "Sometimes. Sometimes it's not hard to know what's going to happen."

Flynn's face warmed.

They passed scattered houses, gardens, fields and big green lawns that were actually nicely mown weeds. The woods were deep on the edge of town. They passed through them and then the woods thinned to a couple of miles of cornfields, and Julian leaned forward, pointing and saying eagerly, "There it is."

The Dance and Dine Inn was a big white two-story house set back away from the road, welcoming lights gleaming from every window. There were lots of cars and a couple of buggies in the front yard, and several shining roadsters parked on white gravel in the mown field next door, expensive ones, lined up all in a row and watched over by two tough characters in straw hats sitting in chairs by the gate.

Flynn pulled up not far from the side-door entrance. They got out and walked across more white gravel and up the big wooden steps of the long front porch. A tall, very black Negro in a white mess jacket greeted them with a big smile and a suave, "Welcome to the Dine and Dance Inn, folks."

As they stepped inside, Flynn took note of two large gentlemen sitting watchfully in a small alcove to one side.

A pretty colored girl in a French maid's outfit led them to a table near a window.

The best tables, the tables on the screened-in porch, were already filled, but it was nice in the main dining room too, and they got one of the last tables by the windows on the far side of the room. The walls were papered in flocked dull red. Alphonse Mucha posters of women in nimbuses and flowered headdresses decorated the walls. Ceiling fans turned slowly over head stirring the warm air, and small polished brass lamps shone gaily on every linen-covered table.

Flynn studied the menu. There was no booze listed of course, only "soft drinks", ciders, and a beverage called "Grape Drink Français."

He pointed this out to Julian whose mouth curved in that habitual sarcastic smile. He nodded approval to the grape drink and went back to gazing out the window at the moon-shadowed yard.

"Do you know what you're having?" Flynn inquired. Julian hadn't looked at the menu.

"I'll have what you're having."

"You don't know what I'm having," Flynn pointed out.

"It doesn't matter." At Flynn's expression, Julian made a face and said, "Oh well. Have it your way. I can't read."

"You mean there's something wrong with your eyes?" Was this the mysterious illness both Julian and the old man had referred to?

"No." Julian seemed amused. "I never learned how. My grandfather didn't think it was important. For me."

This offended Flynn on so many levels that he spluttered before he finally got out an outraged, "Didn't think it was important? *He* reads. He writes articles and essays for those damned spiritualist magazines."

"That's true." Julian said it placatingly. "I believe he thought it was for the best. That there would be less chance of people claiming I was a fraud if it could be proved that I couldn't read or write."

"Jesus. You can't read *or* write?"

Julian reddened. "You don't have to shout it to the world."

"Sorry." Flynn was still fuming though. He stared down at the menu. When he had himself under control again, he asked, "What do you like to eat?"

"Ice cream."

"Ice cream?"

"Lots of things," Julian amended in an apparent desire to please.

"I'm going to have T-bone steak."

"All right."

Flynn scanned the menu. "They have breast of chicken a la rose and crown roast of lamb and roast duck."

Julian gave this due consideration. "T-bone steak, I think."

Flynn was still trying to come to terms with the notion that Julian couldn't read. Not that plenty of people couldn't read, but Julian's grandfather was a literate man, so to deliberately leave Julian ignorant and uneducated horrified him. Not that Julian *appeared* ignorant or uneducated, but clearly there were considerable gaps.

Untroubled, the object of all this worry studied the crowded room with the same innocent pleasure of someone watching a play. "There's Sheriff McFadden," he murmured, and Flynn, following his gaze, saw that he was correct. The portly sheriff was dining at the roadhouse with an equally portly woman in a puce-colored silk dress. Julian pointed out two policemen, a judge, and a couple of well-to-do Herrin merchants. He was sharp-eyed as any reporter, but that was a necessity in his line of work.

"The law-and-order crowd," Flynn commented.

Julian said sardonically, "Prohibition means bootleggers are running this place instead of honest businessmen."

Their waiter, younger than Julian, arrived, uncorking the bottle of grape drink as he would have decanted a bottle of wine in the good old days. He poured it into Flynn's glass. Flynn sampled it. It was wine all right. Good wine. It might even have been imported.

Flynn nodded, and the waiter filled Julian's glass and departed.

Julian sipped his wine. Meeting Flynn's gaze, he smiled, seemingly relaxed and happy.

"Your grandfather seems to know…certain things," Flynn said neutrally.

"Well, he could hardly miss them," Julian pointed out.

Flynn was still trying to work through that when Julian added, "Why don't we talk about you for a change? I feel like you're interviewing me for a newspaper article."

"What would you like to know?"

"Everything."

Julian gazed at him with such unabashed and unfeigned interest that Flynn felt himself coloring.

"I guess my life is about as different from yours as it could be."

"Not in all ways," Julian said serenely.

"Oh. No. Not in all ways. I was born in Portland, Maine. I graduated from the Fryeburg Academy like my brothers before me. I went to Brown University—that's where I met Gus, Amy's husband. I got a job at *The Daily News*, but the war was on and I enlisted."

"And that's where you met Paul?"

"That's where I found him again. We'd known each other at Brown." He fell silent, gauging the extent of pain within himself. It was…tolerable, surprisingly so. He said calmly, "After the war I got a job as a contributor to *The Atlantic Monthly*."

"But you live in New York?"

Flynn nodded. New York and his tidy, quiet brownstone seemed a lifetime away.

"What's that like?"

"Very different." Flynn thought for a few moments. "I guess…things were too easy for me growing up. It leaves you unprepared for the bad times that come."

"I don't know. Maybe it gives a kind of foundation. Having an education. Knowing that you're loved." Julian said it simply, seriously, and for some reason Flynn's throat closed tight. Too tight to say a word. What Julian said was true. Those things should have supplied Flynn the bedrock of philosophical and spiritual certainty. Why hadn't they? A lot of people had suffered through the war and the terrible influenza epidemic that followed, and they hadn't closed themselves off from life and love.

Here was Julian who hadn't had half the advantages of Flynn, was about as isolated and lonely a man as Flynn had ever known, and yet he possessed a calm confidence and an almost childish optimism.

"If you could do anything you wanted in the world, what would it be?" he asked Julian.

Julian's eyes widened as though Flynn were really offering this, as though he had the power to give him whatever he would like. "I'd like to own a café."

"A *café*?"

"Like in France before the war."

"Were you in France before the war?"

"A couple of times. When I was a child. I loved it." He smiled, remembering. "They have these little cafés. Bistros, the Russians call them. I'd like to open one. Omelets stuffed with mushrooms and cheese, *coq au vin*, mussels in cream sauce. And I'd like to sing there in the evenings."

"Sing?"

Julian nodded. His eyes were bright and mischievous. "Yes."

"*Can* you sing?"

"Er, a bit." He was still smiling, and studying him, it occurred to Flynn that it wouldn't matter if he could sing or not. People would love him. In Greenwich? They would adore him.

He put that thought away, and said, "Well, why don't you? You can't do this forever, surely?"

"It seems you can." Julian's smile had faded. He sounded bitter.

"You could surely stop if you didn't want to do it any longer? You're free, white and over twenty-one."

"And what would I live on?"

"What happens with all this money you earn?"

"*Grand-père* controls the purse strings." He was staring out the large window again, his profile hard.

"Don't you get a say in how the money you earn is spent?"

A second or two passed and he thought he wouldn't get an answer, but then Julian turned back to him and he was smiling again. "Anyway, it's a nice dream. Did you get to try much French food when you were over there?"

"We were a trifle busy," Flynn pointed out.

"But you went on leave, right? Once in a while?"

Yes, once in a while they'd had leave. And he and Paul had enjoyed themselves very much. It gave happiness a special shine knowing it could end any moment.

Their meals came then, and that line of conversation died a natural death. Along with the T-bone steak were Potatoes a la Hollandaise and Asparagus Tips au Gratin. The kind of food you'd expect to find at the Waldorf Astoria, not in a hick roadhouse in the middle of nowhere.

They ate their food and talked and drank more of the Grape Drink Français. It was far different than the evening he'd spent with Casey. The funny thing was that while Flynn had pegged Casey as more his type, he'd never have considered spending an evening like this with him—well, not after the first couple of drinks at Hotel Lafayette. In fact, he was enjoying himself more than he could remember in years. Julian might be illiterate and more than a bit odd, but he was handsome and witty and very charming when he put his mind to it. Flynn found himself laughing at Julian's sly observations and comments more than he had laughed in a very long time.

"Would you like dessert?" he asked, not wanting the meal to end.

Julian's wide mouth curved. "Yes."

They had a dish of Venetian Ice Cream each.

Finally Flynn paid for the meal and they exited the rear side door, watched over by another dark, smiling gentleman in a white dinner jacket.

In a companionable silence they followed slightly tipsy couples through the warm moonlit night and down a hedge-bordered walkway to the big barn where buttery light streamed into the summer evening, and a jazz band could be heard tentatively warming up.

A couple of St. Louis-style bruisers sized them up inside the entrance, looking them over for flasks or pistol bulges.

Inside the barn, the floor had been polished like black glass. The walls were dark paneled and the lights mellow. A few ceiling fans moved the air languidly overhead.

They got a table away from the dance floor but with a good view of the band. A big-bosomed hostess left them a small paper list of soft drinks.

Flynn studied the list. "What do you want?"

"I prefer gin. Did you ever have a New Orleans Fizz?"

Flynn shook his head. "I don't think they have anything like that here."

"No. Prohibition's spoiled everything."

When the waitress came back, Flynn ordered two Juniper Jennies, which were gin and tonics by any other name.

Flynn watched the small back door of the bar and noticed a tall, short-skirted lady open a door in the partitioned area and smile over her shoulder at the young man who followed her in and closed the door behind. He didn't doubt stairs in there led up to the former hayloft. They were making hay all right, though it was doubtful any bales remained.

The thought of sex with Julian caused heat to pool in his belly, made his groin ache.

He looked across the table and Julian was watching him steadily with those dark and knowing eyes.

Julian smiled and turned his gaze back to the dance band.

Their drinks arrived and they sipped them, Flynn with sudden and uncharacteristic self-consciousness.

It was increasingly warm inside the barn as people got up to dance. Half the men were in their shirtsleeves by now, and Flynn loosened his tie and slipped out of his jacket, hanging it on the back of his chair.

Julian raised eyebrows at this lack of decorum.

"Half the fellas in this place have their jackets off," Flynn observed.

The people around them seemed like a cross-section— although there were no old people—an even mix of middle-aged couples and bright-eyed kids. Some of them, especially the girls, looked way too young to have been served hooch in a saloon, but nobody was asking questions at the Dine and Dance Inn.

Scattered here and there were a few single guys hoping to meet the girl of their dreams or getting up the nerve to shell out cash to the ladies of the evening casually strolling about or demurely seated by twos and threes near the edge of the room.

Flynn could easily pass for such young men. Julian…Flynn glanced across the table. Julian was staring alertly at the crowded dance floor as though these were the fascinating customs of South Sea Islanders.

Flynn felt an odd surge of emotion. Amusement? Affection? He wasn't sure.

A muted cornet sang out over the chattering crowd, and a good imitation of Paul Whiteman's version of "If I Could Be With You" rang off the rafters of the old barn.

The drinks were strong and the music was good but suddenly Flynn was wondering what the hell they were doing there.

Julian sipped his drink. His lashes lifted and he gave Flynn such a direct, naked look that Flynn's heart seemed to leap and then seize.

A scream—more of a squeal—broke the spell. Flynn spotted two young men at the edge of the dance floor flailing away at each other. Close by was a would-be vamp in a red dress wringing her hands and yelling at them.

Before the knights errant could do much damage, two rough-looking country boys in their first ties and jackets came sailing across the empty dance floor and yanked the combatants apart.

One of the portly Saint Louis-type gangsters, cigar clamped tightly between his teeth, joined them, and it was clear even from across the tables what was happening.

Flynn opened his mouth and Julian said, "Yes. Let's go."

Flynn shrugged back into his jacket, and they made their way through the crowded tables.

The tenor on the bandstand started a song made familiar to Flynn from the war. A few of the boys at the tables began to sing. That impromptu male chorus sent a funny chill down his spine as he and Julian strolled out through the wide doorway into the warm moonlight. The voices faded behind them.

There's a long, long trail a-winding

Into the land of my dreams,

Where the nightingale is singing

And the pale moon beams.

There's a long, long night of waiting

Until my dreams all come true,

Till the day when I'll be going down

That long, long trail with you.

The Model T jogged and bounced across the mowed field, past the hoods in the straw hats, down the gravel drive, and then they were on the main highway headed back for Herrin. Julian scooted over in the seat next to Flynn. The wind whipped his hair back from his forehead. He was smiling that private smile.

Despite the ripe golden moon hanging low in the sky, it was dark and the road was mostly deserted. Flynn took a chance, pulled Julian closer and put his arm around him. Julian snuggled nearer, the heat of his body warming Flynn all down one side of his body.

"I like this." Julian's warm breath against his ear sent shivers across Flynn's scalp. "I like flying through the darkness like an arrow in the night."

"Do you know how to drive?"

Julian shook his head.

"I'll teach you," Flynn said recklessly. "It's not hard."

There was a funny pause and Julian faced forward in his seat again. After a moment, he said, "I don't expect we'll be here long enough for that."

It caught Flynn off guard. He should have expected it; of course The Magnificent Belloc would not be staying long in any one place. That wouldn't be lucrative. Or wise. He was only here for a short while himself.

"When are you leaving?"

"Monday morning."

Flynn nodded. He didn't know what to say.

The bobbing headlights stabbed into the pitch-black night, and the breeze felt good against his face as they sped along. The wall of woods flashed by, tree trunks white in the headlights.

By the time they crossed the bridge over Crab Orchard Creek, Julian was back to business, his nimble fingers caressing Flynn's crotch, making it difficult to keep an eye out for deer or other wildlife.

He risked a glance at Julian's bent profile. Even in that poor light he could see Julian was smiling.

Julian's lashes lifted. He murmured, "Flynn, stop the car."

As though he'd been waiting for that signal, Flynn yanked the wheel and the Model T bounded to a rough idling halt on the dirt turn-off. He turned off the engine, the lights winking out. It was only the two of them sitting in the dark, listening to the breeze whispering in the leaves of the wall of trees a yard or so away. In the distance a fox was barking.

"Come on." Julian vaulted out of the automobile, waiting till Flynn followed. Frogs croaked accompaniment to the crunch of their footsteps as they crossed the clearing to the shelter of the trees.

Flynn glanced uneasily over his shoulder at the car sitting in the moonlight. The road was dark and empty both ways for as far as he could see. He ducked under the low branches.

Julian had found a soft place beneath the trees and ferns. They undressed and lay down in the cool grass and wild mint. The pleasure of coming together, naked and unfettered, was almost unbearably sweet. They held each close and kissed without haste or fear.

"Let's try it this way," Julian said abruptly, sitting up.

"What?" But Flynn followed Julian's silent command. They stretched out alongside each other, cock to mouth, mouth to cock. It was far too dark to see anything beyond the pale outline of the other, so they were reduced to a kind of night writing, a sensual brailing as they touched and tasted, fingertips tracing, lips exploring the textures of silky hair and smooth skin, of bones and muscles, teeth and fingernails, nipples, eyelashes, balls... everything seemed fantastic and unknown in the Delphian shadows scented of sex and damp earth and decaying leaves.

At last they settled down to it, hot, wet mouths closing over each other's rigid hardness. It was unreasonably difficult to concentrate on anything but the intense pleasure building in his groin and swelling cock, but Flynn tried. He tried to give as good as he was getting—what he was getting was very good indeed. Julian used everything from his warm breath to the slick tip of his tongue. He sucked hard and fiercely and then so soft and sweetly…

It was torture and delight to have this done to him at the same time he was trying to return the favor, growing hot inside and out, skin glazing with honey dew. Flynn buried his face in Julian's crotch and breathed in the damp, musky male scent. He traced his tongue around Julian's balls, and they were tender as sweetmeats, sweet as cherry cordials, those sweet intoxicating sacs…

Julian made a strangled sound but kept pulling and sucking like a trooper, and the great, rolling wave far out in the distance, built speed, growing in height, a wall of pleasured release sweeping inland, knocking down all restraint, all thought, all considerations. That tidal wave of wild delight crashed into Flynn, washed him along in its powerful current. There was nothing like it, flooding him from the ends of his hair to the soles of his feet.

And at the same time he became aware that he had burst the cherry, a wet, salty-sweet rush filled his mouth, like tears of laughter or life-bringing primordial tide. He sucked and gasped for breath and sucked some more.

Later they lay entwined, hearts calming, breath evening, and watched the fireflies flickering overhead and heat lightning flashing along the distant ivory clouds to the south. The only sounds were the crickets and the katydids and the faint splash of the river far behind the trees.

The river's keening song reminded Flynn that a madman was prowling only a few miles away, and that it might not be wise to linger. He kissed Julian's warm, salty mouth. "We ought to think about getting along home."

"I wish we could stay here all night," Julian murmured.

"Be more comfortable in my bedroom."

Julian shook his head. "Not tonight. *Grand-père* will be watching."

"How can you live like that?"

Julian said calmly, "People live however they must."

"Why don't you tell him you don't want to perform anymore? Take your money and go open your café."

He was shaking his head.

"Why not?"

"It's not that simple."

"Why shouldn't it be?"

Julian said irritably, "In case you haven't noticed, I don't actually *know* how to run a café. I can't read or write or cook. I know how to do one thing."

"Con people?" Flynn hadn't meant to say that, it slipped out.

Julian pulled out of his arms and sat up. He said in a silky tone that raised the hair on the back of Flynn's neck, "Oh, it's not all a con. I could tell you things if I wanted to."

"What things?" Flynn was sitting too, reaching automatically for his trousers.

Julian didn't answer, and he repeated harshly, "What things?"

Julian was on his feet now, dressing quickly, ignoring Flynn. He said finally, "I know you don't think so, but it helps people to say farewell to their loved ones."

"But they're not saying farewell to their loved ones. You're making it all up. You're pretending you're hearing voices."

"Sometimes I am hearing the voices."

"But most of the time you're not, you admitted it today to the sheriff. Most of the time you're lying to them."

Julian made a small sound of contempt. "Oh, you're so smart Mr. Big City Newspaper Man, and yet you don't understand the simplest thing. Didn't you ever notice funerals aren't for the dead? They're for the *living*."

He slipped his shoes on and started back for the flivver.

Flynn caught him up in a few steps, fingers sinking into Julian's arm. "What do you mean, you could tell me things if you wanted to?"

Julian stared at him. In the weird moonlight his eyes looked like the black holes in a skull. Flynn dropped his arm.

Julian said in a low, spiteful tone, "Do you really want me to contact Paul for you? Are you *sure* you want to know what he would say?"

"You *sonofabitch*." Flynn leaped forward, fist raised, and Julian stepped warily back. Flynn grabbed him by his shirt collar, but at the last minute he shoved him down rather than punching him in the face.

Julian sprawled on the ground. Half propped on an elbow, he stared up at Flynn. He said mockingly, "That's what I thought."

"I should let you walk back to town." Flynn turned away. He crossed the clearing in long, angry strides to where the Model T sat outlined in silver moonlight. Behind the trees the night sky flashed with lightning, like an electrical short behind a purple black curtain.

Climbing inside, he slammed the door and waited. Julian joined him a few moments later, brushing his clothes down.

Flynn cupped the crank handle, started the engine. Neither spoke on the rest of the drive back to Herrin.

$$\int \int \int \int$$

It was late when Flynn woke on Saturday morning. He had a bad headache and his body ached as though he'd been rolling around on pebbles all night. For a time he lay there wincing as he thought over the events at the shank of the evening.

The fan on the dresser was still droning. A light rain had left the morning cool and fresh. His anger seemed a distant, vague thing now. He was ashamed of having shoved Julian.

He washed his hands and face and followed the smell of coffee down the hallway to the kitchen where Amy was sitting on her own. She looked up and smiled at him.

"How about some flapjacks? I still have batter left."

"Sounds good." Flynn dropped down at the big maple table, avoiding looking directly at the bright sunlight flooding through the open window How could birds be *so* loud?

"You all didn't drop in on one of those illegal roadhouses last night, by any chance?" Amy inquired, readying the heavy iron skillet.

"Perish the thought."

Amy chuckled sentimentally. "Now if Mrs. Hoyt were still with us, she'd be dishing up the Demon Rum sermon right about now."

"It was more like Demon Gin." Flynn asked belatedly, "How's Joan today?"

"Poor kid." Amy flicked water on the skillet and the beads sizzled. She poured the batter into the pan. "She's taking it hard. She hasn't got anyone here. There's an aunt in Missouri. She'll be coming out for the funeral I guess. She could stay on at the house, of course. Joan, I mean."

Amy went on chattering about Joan and Joan's future. Flynn listened with half an ear. What he really wanted—and dreaded—was to ask about Julian. The words wouldn't come.

He realized that Amy had fallen silent. Her back was to him as she flipped the flapjacks in the hot skillet with brisk efficiency.

Flynn stared at the wide, comfortable outline of her. He said, surprising himself, "I'm sorry I didn't come down after Gus died. I should have been here. To pay my respects."

Amy turned. It was almost as though she had been waiting for this. "That didn't matter. After Gus was gone, it didn't matter. He knew you respected him. He'd have liked to see you, though. I wish you'd come then: when he was still well—after you got out of the army. He used to talk about you a lot." She said it without reproach. She was being honest, and Flynn heard her out without defensiveness.

"I should have. I meant to. I kept thinking there was time for all that. You'd think the war would have taught me that lesson." He'd wasted a lot of time grieving. Not only grieving though, because that was maybe forgivable. He'd also wasted time feeling angry and sorry for himself. He'd hurt other people and it couldn't all be repaired. He could tell Amy that he regretted his action—or lack of action—but it didn't change anything. And he couldn't tell Gus...

Perhaps he understood why Julian thought he was helping people when he let them take those dark farewells of their loved ones.

Amy sighed and said, "I guess it's a lesson we all need to learn a few times before it sticks."

He understood why Gus had loved her despite their many and obvious differences.

Despite the turbulence of his emotions—and his hangover— Flynn's appetite was not affected much, and he kept eating pancakes as fast as Amy kept them coming, buttering them and spilling syrup on their pale faces reminding him of that big golden moon over the trees the night before.

The screen door behind him creaked. He turned, uncomfortably aware that he hoped the newcomer was Julian.

It wasn't. It was Casey.

"Well, you're home early," Amy greeted him.

He nodded and set his sample case on the table, pulling out the chair and sitting down heavily. "I thought maybe I'd take Joan out for a drive today. Get her out of the house."

He met Flynn's surprised gaze pointblank.

"Well, that's a very nice thought," Amy said. "She's down at the funeral parlor right now, but she ought to be back anytime soon."

Casey smiled rather unpleasantly. "The old frog was stocking up on remedies for the kid last night," he informed Flynn.

"What remedies?"

"Bromide salts mostly." He was enjoying himself, clearly. "Tincture of belladonna. He's a very sick boy, your pal."

"What the hell is supposed to be the matter with him?"

"Can't you guess?"

"No." Flynn added shortly, "Should you be discussing this with all of us?"

"Now that you mention it, I guess not." Casey smiled again. Funny how Flynn had first found Casey attractive and his grin engaging. He thought now that though he was handsome enough, his smile had a hint of cruelty.

Casey pushed the chair back, picked up his sample case and left the room.

"Where is Julian?" Flynn asked Amy.

"He went out this morning early."

Gathering information for the evening's show, no doubt.

She said uneasily, "What do you suppose he meant about the boy?"

"I don't know. He seems okay to me." All things being relative.

She had a look on her face as though she were remembering something.

"What?" Flynn questioned.

"Oh, I don't know." She seemed flustered to be caught gossiping. "But the old man was closeted with Dr. Pearson for a time yesterday. I did wonder..."

Flynn wondered too, but he realized he had already said too much about it.

Finishing his breakfast, he asked Amy if he could make a long distance phone call. She assured him anything in the house was his to use. He waited until the coast was clear, then went into the hall and called his editor, Ellery Sedgwick, at *The Atlantic Monthly*. He told Sedgwick the massacre story seemed to be hitting a dead end, but he had a new angle on spiritualism and sleuthing.

"I thought you couldn't wait to get back to New York?"

"I can't. But since I'm here I need to make the trip worth my while. I simply don't think there's much story in the massacre. Nothing that hasn't been covered."

"I tried to tell you that."

"You were right. But this spiritualism angle, well that's new." He told Sedgwick about the murders and Sedgwick heard him out in thoughtful silence.

"Well, one thing's for sure, you haven't been this excited about a story for a long time. I'll be looking forward to seeing what you come up with. The spiritualism racket is still news."

Flynn was thoughtful when he rang off.

The house was empty and hushed with a funereal silence when Flynn left for the Opera House that evening. The Devereuxs had departed for the theater earlier to prepare for their final performance while the rest of the household was at the funeral parlor viewing for Mrs. Hoyt.

Flynn took the street trolley and arrived at the Opera House in plenty of time—which turned out to have been a wise decision. It was a full house, every one of the nearly five hundred seats filled. News of The Magnificent Belloc's conversation with the latest victim of the "Little Egypt Slayer", as the local papers were now terming the maniac, had spread far and wide.

Flynn listened absently to the discussion floating around him.

The stage had not been broken down from the high school theatrics on Friday evening, and before the stage crew drew the long red curtains the whispering audience was treated to an inside peek at *A Midsummer Night's Dream* forest fairy kingdom. A golden lantern moon hung in the fanciful swirls and star-swept blue black night. Shy woodland creatures peeked out behind painted trees and rocks. Glowing fireflies and fairies were strategically placed about the *mise en scène*. Flynn was reminded of the evening before. There had been a kind of magic in that woodland bedchamber.

Eventually the houselights dimmed. From behind the curtains a Victrola offered a scratchy rendition of "Angel Friends". The audience sang along.

> *Floating on the breath of evening, breathing in the morning prayer,*
> *Hear I oft the tender voices that once made my world so fair.*
> *I forget while listening to them, all the sorrows I have known,*
> *And upon the troubles present, faith's pure shining light is thrown…*

The spotlights went on, the curtains slid slowly open on the fairy kingdom, far more realistic and beautiful now that the main houselights were dimmed. Julian—The Magnificent Belloc—dressed once more in the finery of a doomed aristocrat, sat in the golden throne. He was smiling remotely as the audience finished.

> *Bless you Angel friends, oh never leave me lonely on the way,*
> *For your gentle teachings ever meekly may I watch and pray,*
> *For your gentle teachings ever meekly may I watch and pray.*

Pretty ghastly stuff in Flynn's opinion. The audience trailed off, and someone killed the magnified rolling gallop of the Victrola.

Belloc rose and strolled to the edge of the stage.

"Good evening."

"Good evening," the crowd rolled back like thunder.

Julian smiled one of those practiced, charming smiles. "You will not be surprised to learn a great number of people are still under the impression that clairvoyance is a mysterious art, practiced by peculiar individuals who seem to be invested with singular—even sinister—powers, which they exercise within the confines of a dark and mysterious room. The séance room."

The audience tittered at his friendly mockery.

"These ignorant ones are unaware that many persons of considerable and various abilities have had psychical experiences of a veridical nature, and are familiar with the power of seeing either past or future, or both, as well as events that are happening at a distance."

He strolled casually to the other side of the stage. "Seeing the past and becoming aware of the possibility of witnessing people or happenings at a distance that cannot be perceived by the physical sight alone should bring us nearer to a comforting realization of the unity of all life and the existence of other spheres, of hitherto unexplored conditions in which dwell those whom we have known and loved in their earth lives, and later have mourned, because the physical process called death has removed them from the limitations of our physical sight and hearing."

The hall was silent, only the occasional cough or throat clearing interrupting the solemn hush.

"This is reassuring, is it not?"

"Yes," thundered back the audience.

"You have all heard of the well authenticated and numerous cases which have been recorded. It becomes evident that this faculty of clairvoyance is a natural one, and can be used under natural conditions by perfectly natural people. The séance room is merely a laboratory, a quiet place where suitable and harmonious conditions can be assured, unhampered by the noise and distractions of the outer world."

He paused as though giving the opportunity to object. A pin would have sounded like an anvil hitting the floor in that silence.

"Tonight, this hall will serve as our séance room as we attempt to contact those who have gone before us."

Belloc returned to the golden throne and threw himself into it with careless grace.

"We will now summon my guide in the spiritual realm, le Comte de Mirabeau. He is your true host this evening."

Closing his eyes, Belloc bent his head, fist against his lips as though he were deep in thought. For a long time no one spoke, no one said anything. Then he lifted his head and murmured in French. There were rustles and whispers in the theater. Flynn smiled cynically, and yet he couldn't deny that he was engrossed along with the rest of the audience.

Belloc's eyelids fluttered, he straightened and opened his eyes. He had a distinctly French inflection as he said, "This one has been waiting, hanging back. He does not wish to grieve you, *monsieur*, but you must relinquish hope." His bright gaze stared past the footlights. "He was a soldier. His name was Christopher, *oui*? Lt. Christopher Thompson. Reported missing in battle." Julian shook his head regretfully, and a collective sigh seemed to escape the audience. "Who is here for Christopher?"

An elderly gentleman rose and stood erect as possible as he gripped his cane.

"He died bravely, monsieur. He wishes you to know that. And he wishes you to know that he is…how you say? Adjusting well to the…er…rules. In fact, he says there are far fewer rules on the other side. Love abounds. Heaven is and will be perfect love and harmony."

The elderly man nodded curtly. He seemed to struggle to speak, but in the end he lowered himself slowly and painfully once more. Belloc withdrew and closed his eyes again. More mumbling in French.

"*Ah, grandmere. Helen. Qui est ici pour Helen?*"

Sighs and rustlings.

"She died during the beginning of the influenza epidemic."

More whisperings.

No one laid claim to Helen, and Belloc shrugged and went on. "She wishes you all to know that the dead do not sleep. They are alive, as you are alive. Do not forget. Do not forget them for one moment."

Belloc subsided once more. On this evening the spirits seemed to be mostly those of soldiers and people who died in the Spanish Flu epidemic. Belloc was sincere and fluent, but something seemed off to Flynn. Slowly it dawned on him that whatever Belloc's attitude, Julian was nervous.

He wasn't sure how he knew, but he knew it.

"Maggie, Cyrus says that you must take the old tonic. The pink-colored one you were accustomed to take. It is better for you. Thomas, your dog is at Harrison Farm. Patrick says that he is happy and well again and free from pain. Martin is watching over you and the children, Louise."

Julian caught his breath. He clutched the arms of the throne and his knuckles turned white. "David, Paul says you...Paul says there is nothing to forgive."

Flynn heard this with a shock of disbelief. He sat very still, barely breathing.

Belloc opened his eyes and stared blindly at the wall of audience. "The quarrel meant nothing, would have been forgotten but for a German bullet. You know it is true."

People looked around, but Flynn didn't move, didn't breathe.

Belloc exhaled a long ragged breath and went on, sending messages to the mothers and wives of dead soldiers and sailors. Flynn continued to sit deaf and unseeing. A sob tore out of the woman next to him. A middle-aged man took out a handkerchief and blew his nose.

What was Belloc saying now?

Flynn forced himself to listen again. Shook off his numb preoccupation. But there was nothing to hear or see. Belloc was leaning back in his gold throne, exhausted. His face was white and strained, harsh breaths seemed to reverberate in the elegant Opera House. He rolled his head from side to side as though in a fever.

"No."

He sat up and glared stage left. "*No.*"

Mesmerized, the audience watched as he jumped up, putting the throne between himself and another invisible presence.

"What do you want?" Monsieur le Comte seemed to have departed in a rush, taking Belloc with him. There remained a tense, angry young man speaking to what appeared to be…a ghost.

There was a long silence. People looked at each other, moved restively in their seats.

Julian said, "You must go. I can't do anything more for you."

A nervous ripple of laughter flowed up and down the aisles of the darkened theater. The audience began to whisper and talk amongst themselves. Julian glanced at them, glanced back at whatever was on the stage with him—or whatever he was pretending was on the stage. But, no, Flynn didn't believe that. As difficult, as bizarre as it was to conceive of, there did seem to be some…presence on the stage, hiding in the painted woodland.

Julian made an anguished sound. To the audience, he said, "Theresa is here again tonight. She says she can't rest—none of them can rest—until this murderer, this madman is caught."

He stopped, biting his lip. The words seemed torn from him. "He is among you even now. You must *trust no one.*"

There were gasps and cries of horror and then, terrifyingly, every light in the theater went out.

An absolute pitch black descended on the Opera Hall.

There was an instant of frozen horror and then pandemonium. The audience rose in a surge, shoved their way down the rows of seats, crowding into the aisles in panic, pushing their way toward the doors. Voices cried out for calm, for order.

Flynn rose also calling for reason, for quiet. People continued to try and push past to get to the jammed aisles.

The overhead lights went on.

People stopped their hysterical shoving and pushing and looked around, blinking, as though woken from a nightmare. Flynn looked back at the stage. It was empty.

CHAPTER EIGHT

The house was dark when Flynn let himself inside.

He made his way to the front parlor, turned on a lamp and sat down, resting his head in his hands. If what he had witnessed that night at the Opera House was legitimate, it was the most amazing proof of psychic ability or perhaps supernatural power that he had heard of. And if it was faked, both Julian and Old Man Devereux deserved to be locked up and have the key thrown away. People could have died in that theater tonight. If the lights had not come back on when they had, people probably would have. As it was, three ladies had fainted and had to be carried from the theater.

Flynn did not believe in spiritualists or ghosts or any of that mumbo-jumbo, but he couldn't argue that Julian Devereux had seemed on several occasions to tap into the uncanny. It was possible he had guessed from comments Amy had made and his own psychological insights that Flynn had not been back to Herrin to see Gus for years. It was possible he had guessed from Flynn's behavior that Paul and Flynn had argued the night before Paul died.

He was shrewd and he was clever. It was even possible he had heard rumors of a missing girl named Theresa Martin and taken a gamble that she was the murderer's latest victim.

But it was not probable.

Which meant what? That Julian did indeed have contact with the spirit of this murdered girl? That here was an as-yet-unused tool for finding the killer who had so far eluded the sheriffs? What use were either of those things if Julian refused to utilize this mysterious power he possessed?

Flynn scrubbed his face and sat up. He needed to talk to Julian alone, but there was no telling how long it might be before he and the old man showed up. He switched off out the lamp and went upstairs.

In his own room, he turned on the lamp and the fan and sat on the side of the bed to take his shoes off. He noticed that a book lay on the bedside table. *The Encyclopedia Americana.* There was an envelope inserted between the pages as though to mark the reader's place. Curiously, he opened the encyclopedia and began to read.

It has to be born in mind that the disease is a progressive, degenerative malady, and that the object of treatment does not lie only in an attempt to combat convulsions by sedative medicinal remedies, but to prevent by every possible means the tendency to mental deterioration which is so important a clinical feature of the disease as shown in the impairment of intellect and memory, by impulsiveness, mental irritability, loss of moral sense and partial or complete loss of productiveness. Male patients are often given over to perverted sexual behavior, a condition that is probably part of the co-existent mental infirmity. It is also accompanied by periodic disturbances, transitory attacks of anger, dream-states or automatic phenomena.

Flynn's heart pounded very hard with a mix of anger and horror. He wanted to throw the book away, but he couldn't help continuing to read.

Hallucinations are infrequent, illusions are common during an attack or following a grand mal seizure, and delusions are transitory, being found usually only in the dream-states. Morbid and sudden impulses are quite frequent, sometimes approaching distinct nerve-storms, during which suicidal and homicidal attacks may occur. Not infrequently the afflicted may set fire to their beds or furniture, commit theft, assaults, homicides, expose their persons and otherwise conduct themselves in an irrelevant and insane manner. Treatment should be commenced at the earliest possible time, after the onset of convulsive seizures, and should be continued for long periods, extending for at least two years even in the most satisfactory cases. For this reason treatment is best conducted in institutions, asylums or under skilled supervision, by which means the mental and bodily functions can be regulated and submitted to suitable forms of work, exercise and dietary restriction.

He slapped the book shut, then opened it and read the bookplate on the inside cover: *Casey Lee.*

At first he was too angry, too appalled, to think clearly. The message here was stark in its ugliness as a famine victim, and the target only too vulnerable. A wave of grief for Julian overtook him.

The grief was followed by another wave of angry outrage. The book had been left here in warning, and he did not believe it was kindly meant. Flynn didn't know much about medicine or this particular illness, but he knew none of this described Julian.

It could not be true.

But he remembered Casey saying the old man had bought bromides and belladonna. He remembered Amy saying the doctor had been closeted with the elder Devereux. He remembered Julian's veiled references to his "illness".

Was the book meant to frighten him off?

He considered it objectively. It was possible that Casey's ego had been pricked by the realization that Flynn had chosen Julian's company over his own the night before. But what if it was more sinister? This passage was meant to discredit Julian, even perhaps throw suspicion on him.

Why?

Was Julian somehow a threat to Casey? Why should he be?

Flynn did not yet dare to truly consider the personal implications of what he'd read. The main thing that Casey would know about Julian was that Julian had supposedly made contact with the spirit of one of the girls murdered in Jackson County; the neighboring county where Casey had been selling his wares during the period of the murders.

A light seemed to go on inside Flynn's mind. Casey was a traveling salesman. He moved all around the countryside, all around the state, and the nature of his business—cosmetics and medical supplies—made women his first and best customers. That sample case of his was as good as a pass key to most of the homes he visited. And that sample case itself was a clue. *Queen of Egypt Medical Supply Company.* Hadn't the women been mutilated in a grisly imitation of Egyptian burial practices? That was certainly the rumor. And Casey said he'd received medical training, which probably meant he knew enough rudimentary biology to carve the organs out of his victims.

Yes, it all made terrible sense.

Casey had sat out on the breezeway and listened to the others talk about Julian's performance and the contact with the spirit of Theresa Martin. If he was guilty, wouldn't he hear that news with alarm? Wouldn't he wonder whether it was true? What if the spirit of the dead girl *could* tell The Magnificent Belloc who her killer was? Didn't it give Casey the strongest incentive to discredit Julian as quickly and thoroughly as possible?

Of course it did.

And if it was true about Julian's illness? Flynn swallowed hard. There was no pretending that he wasn't stricken at this news. "The Falling Sickness" the ancients had called it. Flynn had witnessed a couple of convulsions. Not a pretty sight. Not something he wanted to think of afflicting someone he…cared about.

And if it was true, if Julian had the disease, was his supposed clairvoyance simply a manifestation of his illness? He opened the book and read again. *Hallucinations are infrequent, illusions are common during an attack or following a grand mal seizure, and delusions are transitory, being found usually only in the dream-states.*

He forced himself to consider the statement objectively.

Could Julian's psychic abilities be the sad proof of his deteriorating mental condition?

But he had been right about Gus, Paul and Theresa. If he was simply mad—granted there was always the possibility that he was mad *and* clairvoyant.

Flynn raised his head as he heard footsteps down the hallway. Muffled voices. Doors opening and closing. The Devereuxs had returned to the boarding house, and judging by the brevity of the muted exchange, not in great sympathy with each other.

He listened to the washroom plumbing rattle into life. He looked down again at the book he held. Whether Julian was ill or not, it didn't change the fact that Casey had deliberately sought to discredit him, and there had to be a purpose behind that. In Flynn's opinion it gave credence to Julian's clairvoyant declarations if only because Casey was so determined that they not be taken seriously.

And that, in Flynn's opinion, was because there was a very good chance that Casey himself was the murderer.

But how to prove it?

He was now determined to prove it. He couldn't help Julian, but he could pay Casey back for this, for trying to discredit the younger man, for destroying the delicate connection blossoming between them. He forgot completely his own earlier anger with Julian—he had mostly been over it by the morning, if he was honest. Now Casey had effectively wrenched that tentative emotion out by the roots.

Flynn looked down at the tiny print on the page and his anger rose again. *Male patients are often given over to perverted sexual behavior, a condition that is probably part of the co-existent mental infirmity.*

No question what that referred to, and Flynn didn't happen to believe it was true. Didn't believe the love of man for man was perverted or mental infirmity. Society and doctors were wrong about a lot of things. Why not this?

The washroom door opened, closed, opened again, and the erratic plumbing rumbled into action.

After a suitable interval, the washroom door opened and closed once more. The house fell at long last into silence.

Flynn closed the book, set it aside and turned out the lamp. He undressed in the darkness and lay down on the bed. The curtains gusted in and out and there was a not-too-distant grumble of thunder.

He rose, went to the window, lowering it halfway. He turned off the fan.

The bedroom door opened a silent foot, and Julian's tall, pale form slipped inside the room. A flash of lightning illuminated him briefly, highlighting his wide eyes, the elegant, exotic planes of his face, his mouth which whispered, "I'm sorry. I had to see you."

"It's all right," David said automatically.

Without turning, Julian locked the door. Flynn met him in two steps, pulled him into his arms, his lips finding that sweet, eager mouth in a long, hungry kiss.

Julian clung to him and whispered, "I missed you so."

I missed you too.

Flynn didn't say it, but it was true. Already, in these few days—four days—Julian had become important to him. More important now that he knew that anything between them, any real relationship, was impossible.

Because it was, wasn't it? If it was true that Julian had that dreadful malady?

Flynn buried his face in the silk of Julian's hair and skin. His own heart was pounding as hard as Julian's.

"I'm sorry for what I said last night," Julian breathed. "I regretted it all day, but—"

"It's all right."

"And then tonight at the Opera House. The message from Paul. It should have been in private. I swear I didn't know it was going to happen." Julian's arms tightened around Flynn's neck, he leaned his head back and gazed searchingly at Flynn's face. Flynn kissed his yielding mouth softly.

"I believe you."

"I wouldn't hurt you for the world, David." He seemed almost desperate that Flynn should believe him.

Flynn nodded. "I know. I feel the same. I tried to find you today to tell you."

Something about Julian made it easy to let go of his anger, to say he was sorry. Paul had been too much like himself, apologies difficult for both of them. Julian…there was a gentleness there, the kind of sweetness that was unique to the genuinely strong.

Flynn guided them both to the bed. They lay down, freezing at the ping and squeak of old springs and bedframe. Flynn said, "We've got to be careful. The washroom is between my room and your grandfather's, but even so."

Julian nodded.

They fell asleep to the music of thunderclaps shaking the old house to its foundations and the lightning flashes turning the room electric white.

"David."

He could hear the sound of dripping. Flynn opened his eyes. It was daylight; a silvery, cool daylight. Glistening rain was still falling from the eaves. He turned his head. Julian was lying next to him, his gaze fastened on Flynn's.

Flynn blinked a couple of times, cleared his throat. "Hm?"

Julian's mouth covered his. When he broke the kiss, he whispered, "I've got to go."

"Go where?"

"I don't want to be in this house today. After the funeral they'll come back here and it'll be better if I'm not here. Better for me. Better for them."

He was probably right about that, but Flynn didn't want him to slip away. Their remaining time was brief as it was. "Where will you go?"

"I'll find a place to spend the afternoon. I'll be back this evening." He added regretfully, "I'll have to come back."

"I'll go with you," Flynn said on impulse.

Julian shook his head. "It'll cause comment. Better to avoid that now."

"I'll go with you," Flynn repeated. All at once it was very clear in his mind all the disastrous misadventures that might befall someone with Julian's affliction. But even more strongly it came to him that he wanted to spend this final day with Julian.

Tomorrow the Devereuxs would be off to Murphysboro and the Liberty Theater. And after that? Another stop in an endless string of Midwestern towns. It was more than likely Flynn would never see Julian again after tonight.

He said stubbornly, "I want to spend today with you."

Julian's winged brows arched.

"I do," Flynn reiterated, and realized how much he meant it. Wanted it. Needed it. He covered Julian's mouth in warm insistence, and he felt the other's man's opposition fade.

At last they broke the kiss. Julian sat up, raking his hair out of his eyes. "If you're coming, hurry up then."

He scooped his dressing gown off the floor, pried open the door and peered into the hallway. He was gone a second later, closing the door soundlessly behind him.

Flynn rolled out of bed and headed for the washroom where he washed hastily and shaved. He dressed and was downstairs waiting when Julian arrived a few seconds later.

Julian was smiling and that smile seemed to strike Flynn right in the solar plexus. How the hell was he going to let Julian go?

They let themselves out of the house and walked down to the diner where Flynn had breakfasted with Casey a day earlier. He'd forgotten that nothing would be open on a Sunday morning, and they were greeted by a large unfriendly CLOSED sign in the window. Instead they caught the streetcar and traveled out to Ozark's Park. They managed to get cinnamon walnut rolls and hot coffee from a street stand, and they ate contentedly on a bench in the deserted six acres of well-tended lawns and flowerbeds surrounding a luxury hotel and dance pavilion.

Though they talked, it was about nothing in particular. Just easy and comfortable conversation, and they smiled often at each other.

The storm had left the morning damp and muggy as it warmed up. There was an electrical hum in the air, and Flynn could feel an echo of that buzz every time Julian's gaze lingered on his.

When they grew bored with sitting, they walked down to the lake and skipped stones across the blue surface. Julian turned out to be unexpectedly adept at this crucial skill, and they made a friendly wager as to who would buy lunch. Flynn won by a skip, eleven to ten.

At lunchtime they bought a big striped watermelon and split it in half, sitting in the deep, cool shade. Flynn found himself struggling to stop staring at Julian as he ate the ripe, red melon, wiping occasionally at the juice running down his chin, spitting the seeds into the grass with the insouciance of a Huck Finn.

"These murders…" Flynn said tentatively.

Julian sighed and spit a couple of seeds at a rose, knocking the petals from its yellow head.

"I'm not asking you to check with your contacts in the spirit world," Flynn said. "But…what do you think? As a…a citizen?"

Julian lowered his lashes, considering. He lifted a dismissing shoulder. "It could be someone like you."

"*Me?*"

He grinned at Flynn's consternation. "Someone these women wish to talk to, despite the fact that he's a stranger to them. People talk to reporters. They like to see their name in print."

"What if he's not a stranger to the victims?"

"You mean the slayer could be known to the women?"

Flynn nodded. "Someone they've known for years maybe. Someone they trust *because* they've known him for years. Someone who's been a regular part of the community."

"Like a sheriff or a priest."

"Er…yes. Or a peddler or a trader."

Julian gazed at him with sudden alertness. "Like a traveling salesman?"

"Yeah."

He considered it with evident surprise. "You think Casey Lee is a murderer?"

"Do you?"

"Do *I*?" Julian's eyes widened. "What does it have to do with me?"

"I don't know. I thought perhaps your ability might give you insight into people. A feel for them?" He felt silly even saying it, but there was no denying Julian had a preternatural talent for knowing things no one could reasonably know.

Julian shook his head. "I don't think so," he said with shattering honesty. "I'm no good judging him. I'm jealous because you like him so much."

Into that naked revelation, Flynn said awkwardly, "I don't like him so much."

"You did." Julian grimaced. "Much more than you liked me. You wanted me, but you didn't like me." His smile was self-mocking. "I make you nervous."

Flynn said quietly, "You don't make me nervous any more except, I guess, in a good way." He smiled at Julian's uncertainty. "And I do like you. I wouldn't be here with you now, ants crawling in my pants, if I didn't."

Julian's laugh was lazy. "I guess that's true. And I did try to keep you from coming with me. Do you think Casey Lee is the Little Egypt Slayer?"

It felt so strange to discuss it calmly in broad daylight. Flynn said, "Well, there's a lot of circumstantial evidence. He was in Murphysboro or at least nearby in Jackson County at the time of at least some of the murders. And he's a person the women might let into their homes without question. He sells medical supplies."

Julian seemed very involved in finding the right blade of glass to make a whistle. "Queen of Egypt Medical Company, yes."

"And he's got medical training. Those women were pretty cut up from what I read."

"He cast a spell on them, I believe. I couldn't quite understand what I was hearing during the performance last night. I don't think the women knew who killed them. He must have drugged them first." Julian added, still not looking at Flynn, "I don't think it was cruelty, you know. I think the man who killed those women is mad. Mad as a hatter. Lee has a cruel streak, but I don't think he's mad."

"Has he done something cruel to you?" Flynn asked, and he was startled at how instantly angry he was at the notion.

Julian looked startled too. "No. I can see the way he looks at Joan, though, the way he talks to her. He's going to marry her if he can. It's not right."

Flynn stared. Was that true? He thought of the small attentions Casey offered Joan. And he thought of Joan's eagerness, her obvious loneliness. Yes, he could see all that now that Julian pointed it out.

Julian said slowly, thoughtfully, "Maybe you're right at that. Maybe the slayer is someone the women have known for years and trusted. They can't see that he's going slowly insane—and neither can he." He swallowed. "Madness can creep up on you."

Flynn thought of the book that had been left in his room. There had been several pages about the likelihood of patients afflicted with that particular disease going mad. Not everyone, true, but the author had been far more interested in discussing the gruesome probabilities.

He opened his mouth to tell Julian about the book, to ask him about this mysterious illness, but Julian jumped up and said, "I need to stretch my legs. Let's walk back down to the lake."

As he spent the day with Julian talking and walking, Flynn felt more and more convinced that Casey Lee was simply trying to discredit the younger man. There was nothing wrong with Julian. He was smart and funny and jolly company as he described the astonishing and silly things that had happened during performances through the years. He laughed at his own mistakes with the same good humor that he laughed at the follies of his fellow performers.

Flynn stared at Julian stretched comfortably on the green velvet lawn. He was smiling faintly, face tilted to the sky, and Flynn's throat tightened painfully. If only this day would never end. He wanted to lean over and kiss Julian's beautiful, mocking mouth. Impossible of course. Even to take his hand and hold it was forbidden for two men. They had been born several centuries too late.

The day flew and soon it was evening and the acetylene gas lamps were coming on all around them, families and couples leaving the park. Flynn and Julian rose and followed them out through the gates.

They caught the streetcar back to the Gulling Boarding House, reaching the house to find it unexpectedly quiet.

They exchanged puzzled glances. But when they looked in the front parlor they found nearly the entire household there, speaking quietly. Not surprisingly, the mood was subdued after the day's funeral.

"There's plenty of food in the kitchen," Amy told them by way of greeting. There was a curious expression in her eyes.

In fact, the entire household seemed to watch them very carefully. *Grand-père* had been glowering from the moment they appeared together in the doorway. Casey Lee sat in a chair near the cold fireplace. A strange middle-aged lady sat on the sofa next to Joan who was dressed in sobering black. The middle-aged lady, also dressed in black, bore a remarkable resemblance to Mrs. Hoyt minus a few years and pounds.

Joan introduced her aunt Mrs. Packard, and Flynn nodded a polite hello. Julian stumbled through an awkward apology for missing Mrs. Hoyt's funeral. Joan was quick to make his excuses for him on the grounds of his extreme sensitivity to spirits. This brought a politely skeptical nod from Mrs. Packard and a faint, derisive smile from Casey Lee as he met Flynn's gaze.

Flynn, remembering again the book that had been left in his room, met that green gaze with his own stony one and saw Casey's eyes narrow.

Joan, finished describing the hymns and flowers of Mrs. Hoyt's ever-so-lovely funeral, was saying in her pleasant way, "Julian, I know it's a terrible imposition, but it would mean so much if you would only consider…"

"Consider?" Julian asked warily.

"Holding a séance so that I might talk to mama."

Julian's recoil was unmistakable. "I'm… I don't think…"

Tears filled Joan's eyes, she clasped her hands together as though in prayer—much to the obvious discomfort of her aunt and Casey—and pleaded, "You're not giving a performance tonight. You could do it right here in the house. I've already spoken to Mrs. Gulling and she's given permission if you would agree."

Flynn glanced around but Amy had slipped out of the room. Not that he blamed her.

"It would just be us." Joan looked around the room with a supplicant's gaze. "Our family here. You do it for strangers. It's not fair that you won't do it for people you know."

"Assuming you do it for real," Casey drawled.

Julian threw him a look of dislike. He stared at Joan. "It's not…that simple."

He looked to his grandfather, who said tersely, "Julian must have time to rally his energies. He's given four performances this week. The toll on his psychic stamina is considerable. He must have time to rest and recover."

"Plus he wouldn't be paid for this," Casey said.

Julian's mouth opened, but he swallowed his angry words as Joan said, "Please, Julian." Tears spilled from her eyes. "I never got the chance to tell Mama goodbye."

There was a strange silence. Flynn became aware of a sense of foreboding. *Refuse,* he thought. *Tell them no.*

Julian sighed. "All right."

Hearing this, Flynn felt oddly weary, almost let down. Yet the day before hadn't he been hoping for this very thing? He himself had suggested a séance to the police. Now he wondered what he'd been thinking.

Joan was still thanking Julian as Flynn turned and went down the hall toward the stairs. Passing the study, he saw Dr. Pearson reading at the long table. He was so engrossed in his book that he was unaware when Flynn stepped inside the room.

"Dr. Pearson?"

Dr. Pearson looked up and stared at him with an unfocused look. He looked like a man who had received unexpected bad news.

"May I talk to you?"

Pearson seemed to shake off his preoccupation. He closed the book and folded his hands on its blue and gold cover.

"Sorry, young man. I was miles away. You wished to speak to me?"

"Professionally. Consult you, I suppose I mean."

The doctor's silver brows rose. "I see."

"Yes. Except it's not for myself. I wanted to ask you about…a friend."

"Ah." Clearly Dr. Pearson had heard that one many a time. His expression became one of resigned patience.

Flynn came the rest of the way into the room and sat down at the polished table. He lowered his voice as he said, "This friend is subject to convulsions. Seizures. He's—" Flynn took a deep breath. "I believe he's an epileptic."

"*Ah.*" The doctor's tone was quite different. Could a greater tragedy befall anyone? Beside the grim physical and mental prognosis, there was the social stigma. No wonder the idea of marriage for epileptics was so frowned on; the notion of delivering children to a similar catastrophic fate would make any sane person quail.

When Flynn didn't continue, the doctor said with brisk kindness, "Poor fellow. I'm sorry to hear that. What is it you think I can do for you —er, your friend?"

Flynn said carefully, "My question is…does the disease always follow the same course? What I mean is, is there any chance of… of recovery?"

Flynn was so sure of the answer he was taken aback when the old man said calmly, "Occasionally. It depends on a variety of factors. Some patients do achieve remission even after many years of seizures. Occasionally the illness can be controlled through treatment. When did your friend first begin to exhibit signs of the malady?"

"I believe he was sixteen."

"That is more favorable than someone who develops the illness earlier in life."

"Is he likely to die from the seizures?"

"Probably not from the seizures themselves. Are the convulsions frequent?"

"I-I'm not sure. I don't believe so. I don't really know."

Pearson considered this, and then light seemed to dawn. He eyed Flynn with mounting hostility. "Does the patient or the patient's guardian know that you're asking for this medical advice?"

Flynn felt his face heat. "No."

"I see."

Flynn gathered his courage. "It's not what you think, sir. I'm asking out of friendship only."

Dr. Pearson continued to inspect him dubiously.

"May I ask you one more thing? Must the illness always end in…mental deterioration and madness?"

"Of course not." Testily, Dr. Pearson rose from the table and went to the tall bookshelves lining the far end of the room. He put away the book he had been reading, scanned the shelf and pulled another. He flipped through it, muttered to himself, and then silently read for a few seconds. His mouth tightened. He replaced the book on the shelf.

"On second thought, never mind. There is a modern tendency to believe the best course of treatment is to lock these unfortunates away as soon as possible in one of the asylums popping up all across the country such as the Craig Colony in Sonyea, New York."

"I've heard of it."

"I'm sure you have." Pearson came back to the table. "If you want the opinion of an old horse doctor, those well-meaning monsters are responsible for the destruction of far more lives than the wretched disease itself. In fifty years of medical practice it has been my observation that what the epileptic patient most requires is a reasonable routine of rest and activity, interesting occupation for their minds, affection of friends and family, and a diet rich in protein and low in carbohydrate. Mild bromide is useful if the attacks are frequent and severe."

"Is that true?"

"I've no reason to lie to you, young man," Pearson said irascibly.

Flynn thanked him and went upstairs.

Supper was deep-fried catfish, tangy coleslaw, chilled beets, fresh, crusty Italian bread with plenty of butter. Good simple food, and all of it, with the exception of the catfish, left over from the funeral reception.

There was no sign of Julian at the evening meal. The other guests were subdued although Casey Lee did his best to cheer Joan up.

Joan's aunt, Mrs. Packard, eyed Casey tolerantly and asked what she clearly imagined to be shrewd questions about his marital status and income.

After the meal, the household, with the exception of Dr. Pearson who said he didn't hold with such out and out superstitious nonsense, retired to the formal dining room. The large, polished oval table sat with a brass candelabra burning brightly in its center. Julian stood behind the chair at the head of the table. He was dressed in ordinary trousers and a white shirt rather than the rich costume he wore for his stage performances.

His gaze met Flynn's. There seemed to be a message in his eyes, but Flynn was uncertain of the meaning. He moved to take the seat Julian's left.

"I was expecting something quite different," Mrs. Packard announced, settling her self on a spindly chair which creaked ominously beneath her weight. Whether she was pleased or disappointed was unclear.

"Isn't the Comte de Mirabeau going to join us?" Joan asked uncertainly.

Julian gave her an odd look. "No. Not tonight."

The Comte's night off apparently.

"I still don't feel this is a wise idea," the elder Devereux complained, taking the chair at the end of the table. "Julian is not strong."

"Or perhaps you don't feel he should be doing this for free?" Casey Lee said, making sure he was seated next to Joan who was on the right side of Julian.

The old man said querulously, "I didn't say that."

Julian glanced at Flynn, who offered him what he hoped was a reassuring smile. Julian's smile flickered in return.

Flynn pulled his chair out and sat down with the others. They quickly settled, obeying Julian's instructions to rest their fingertips lightly on the glassy surface. Julian looked grimly around the assembly and requested Joan to say *The Lord's Prayer*, which she did in her soft, grave voice.

Casey Lee squeezed her hand reassuringly, and she gave him a shy smile.

Julian eyed them unsmilingly before offering up a brief petition that the spiritual assembly might enable those humble seekers gathered to receive a fuller measure of celestial knowledge to ease their grieving hearts and seeking minds.

There was silence. The candle flame on the tabletop seemed to brighten.

Julian said abruptly, "Make your presence known."

Silence.

Joan gasped, looking around. Flynn heard it too. They all heard it: a sound like the rustling of large wings. Not the flapping of flight, but a gentle quivering, a trembling beat.

"It's a trick," Casey Lee said shortly, and he reached across the table. Joan murmured protest at the same time Flynn's hand shot out to intercept him. The two men locked gazes. Flynn dug his fingers in hard, and Casey Lee opened his mouth in protest.

Julian said in a flat, cold voice. "You must neither speak nor touch me."

Flynn released Casey and the other man sat back in his seat, rubbing his wrist.

They rested their fingertips on the table edge once more.

All was still.

The table suddenly rocked beneath their hands. The shadow of candle flame danced crazily against the wall as the candelabra slid forward a few inches. The elder Devereux snatched it up and placed it safely on the sideboard.

There were gasps and murmurs. Julian said, "Please join your hands together so that all may know that no one is moving the table."

They clasped hands hastily. Flynn's hand closed warmly about Julian's long, cold fingers. He tightened his hold reassuringly and Julian squeezed back.

Amy was seated on Flynn's other side. Her work-roughened hand was comfortingly vigorous. Her profile looked stern.

The table continued to rock and then it slowed and stopped.

Julian asked in a low, almost sleepy voice, "Who are you?"

Silence.

"What was your name on the mortal plane?"

Silence.

"Did you go by the name of Alicia Hoyt?"

Silence.

"Is the woman known as Alicia Hoyt among you?"

Silence.

Mrs. Hoyt's sister sighed restively. Mr. Devereux threw her a warning look.

Joan cried out, "Mama!" She was looking past Julian's shoulder.

Flynn glanced over his shoulder as the others looked up. There did seem to be a pale, glimmering outline of a form, but it did not look precisely human, let alone female. Everyone stared, spellbound.

"Are you Alicia Hoyt?" Julian persisted. He did not look behind. His eyes were closed, his lashes black crescents on his cheeks.

Silence.

"Do you have a message for your daughter, Joan?"

There was a gasp from around the table. A single word appeared in letters of light on the wall behind Julian.

"What does it say?" Joan asked, looking from one to the other of them.

Flynn had to narrow his eyes to make out the small word. "Beware," he read slowly.

There were several intakes of breath. Amy's hand clenched his tightly. Julian's remained cool and lax in Flynn's grasp.

A sound like the rustlings of tree branches—very distinct from the earlier fluttering of bird wings—filled the room, followed by the sensation of wet leaves or wet…something falling upon their hair and skin. Beads of water seemed to rain from the ceiling and splash on the table. They glittered in the candlelight like raindrops or drops of blood.

There was a distinct sound of someone inhaling and then a fiercely exhaled breath. The candles on the sideboard went dark.

"Death shall shine in your starless night." The voice came from Julian but it was several octaves higher than his normal tone and it had an eerie, dreamy quality.

"Who said that?" Mrs. Packard's voice sounded frightened. "What does that mean?"

"Julian?" Flynn asked quietly.

"Don't wake him," Mr. Devereux whispered urgently from down the table. "He's entered into a trance state. It's most dangerous to wake a medium."

"What do we do?" Amy asked. She sounded calm but ready for action.

Mr. Devereux hissed, "We mustn't break the circle of our hands or do anything to shatter the trance."

"But what's the point of it?" Casey asked impatiently.

"Can't you all stop talking?" Joan cried.

A sharp surprised silence followed her words.

"Julian," she said softly through the pitch darkness that blanketed the room.

"There is no Julian," the queer flat voice coming from Julian said. "There is only Millicent."

"*W-who?*" Joan quavered.

"Millie Hesse?" Flynn cut across quickly, softly.

"Millie Hesse," agreed the voice.

"Who's Millie Hesse?" Mrs. Packard demanded. "Where's Alicia?"

"Millie Hesse was the first," Casey said in a thick voice.

"No," Amy said. "The third."

The voice that came from Julian said dreamily, "Millie Hesse is the last. The others have gone now, crossed the great river."

"What river?"

"The Mississippi?"

"What the hell is he talking about?"

"*Iteru*," Julian said in that same vague voice. "First Theresa went, then Anna, then Maria. There's only me now…"

Flynn ignored the nervous babble of voices. He stroked Julian's icy knuckles with his thumb. "What do you want, Millie?"

"Justice for the dead."

"When did you die?"

"The nineteenth of July, 1923. It was a hot, sunny morning when he came to the house."

"Who came to the house?"

Silence.

"Who came to the house?" Flynn repeated.

The voice said serenely, "The sun was shining on the water like silver dust and the leaves in the trees whispered like a hundred tongues. I can't say his name."

"Why can't you say his name?"

"He cut our tongues out in the way of the ancient sorcerers so we couldn't speak his name. I can't go forward. I can't go back. The others have gone. Only I remain. Only I wait for justice."

"This is lunacy," Casey cried. "Ancient *sorcerers*? Devereux is insane. He's a charlatan--or he's insane."

"Shut up," Flynn told him fiercely. "Shut up or I'll shut you up."

"Try it!"

"Don't break the circle," Mr. Devereux entreated from the far end of the table.

Flynn felt the tension go through the circle as though someone had tried to pull free but the others held fast. He urged,

"Millie, can you write the word on the wall like you...like Julian did before?"

Silence.

"Millie, someone—you or another spirit—wrote a word with letters of light on the wall. Can you do that? Can you write the name of your murderer—?"

"You're *crazy*!" Casey roared. "You're a goddamned bunch of lunatics!"

A flash of light was followed by great upheaval in the darkness.

"Casey!" Joan cried out in distress.

Mr. Devereux exclaimed, "He's broken the chain of hands."

Amy let go of Flynn's hand. On the other side of Flynn, Julian's hand tightened on his own with near crushing force. A strange drumming sound from beneath the table and the chair at the head crashed over, Julian nearly pulling Flynn and his chair over too.

"Turn the lights on!" Flynn yelled.

"What has happened to Julian?" shouted Mr. Devereux.

Pandemonium reigned. The floor was vibrating beneath that queer rapid pounding sound. What was it? Flynn felt his way in the dark and found the rigid mound of Julian's tumbled form. He could hear an alarming choked whistling as though air were being pressed from a bellows, feel the severe muscle contractions of the body convulsing beneath his hands. A flailing arm grazed his jaw.

It was all the worse for being in the dark.

"Get Dr. Pearson," Flynn ordered. He reached out, trying to protect Julian's thrashing head from the forest of table and chair legs.

On the other side of the table Joan was screaming over and over in a complete hysterical fit. There was much stumbling around and cursing in the dark.

"What in tarnation is going on in here?" Dr. Pearson's voice demanded above the mayhem.

Julian's fit seemed to be lessening as the lamp at the sideboard against the wall was lit at last.

Mrs. Packard made her way to Joan and slapped her. Joan collapsed in Casey Lee's arms, sobbing. The others stood bewilderedly gazing down at Flynn and Julian.

Julian lay trembling and pale in the aftermath of his convulsion. His dazed eyes moved unseeing from Flynn's face to the ceiling to the table.

Mrs. Packard and Amy attempted to soothe Joan who continued to weep on Casey's shoulder. He swept her up in his arms and bore her from the room, the worried women on his heels.

"Well, well. What have we here?" Dr. Pearson lowered himself painfully on one knee and examined Julian curiously but not unkindly. He took his pulse, checked his pupils. "You're all right now, aren't you?"

Julian didn't answer. Did not seem aware of his surroundings yet. He kept licking his lips and blinking.

"Let's get him to bed. The worst of the attack is over. He'll sleep now."

"He should have been dosed properly. You shouldn't have discouraged me," Devereux said to the doctor. He stroked his grandson's damp hair with a shaking hand and whispered in French.

"If he's having these fits more frequently, then yes, we'll have to dose him with the bromides. You said the fits were rare."

"This is your fault!" Mr. Devereux charged, and Flynn gazed up at him stupidly.

"How is it my fault?"

"You know what you've done. Overexciting him, overtaxing his strength, encouraging him to-to unspeakable—"

Flynn waited in horror for the old man to say it. Rescue came from an unexpected source.

"Gentlemen, gentlemen," Dr. Pearson broke in impatiently. "This isn't doing the young man any good. What he needs now is absolute rest and quiet. Save your dispute for later and help me. Between the three of us we should be able to get him upstairs to his room."

"I'll take him," Flynn said roughly. He bent, gathering Julian carefully in his arms. In fact, Julian, for all his willowy height, was no featherweight, and Flynn did require the assistance of the older men to gain his feet.

He needed their help up the staircase as well, but at last they got the sufferer to his own room, undressed and tucked comfortably inside his bed. By then Julian seemed to be coming back to himself. He clutched Flynn's hand.

"David…"

"Shhh."

Devereux senior moved between them, breaking Julian's hold, and there was nothing Flynn could do or say to stop it. He had no rights here despite the way Julian's tired, dazed eyes sought him out.

He turned around as Amy appeared at the bedroom door. "Dr. Pearson, you've got another patient downstairs. Joan took a fit right after the séance."

Dr. Pearson, taking Julian's pulse once more, looked confounded. "Very well." To Flynn he said, "He's all right now. I expect he'll sleep all night and most of tomorrow. Someone should sit with him, though."

"I'll sit with him," Mr. Devereux said with a fierce look at Flynn.

"David," Julian murmured.

"What are you thinking? Mr. Flynn can't stay," Devereux said sternly. The ready tears of the invalid filled Julian's eyes.

Flynn opened his mouth in protest, but what could he say?

He threw one final look at Julian who was wiping shakily at his tears.

Dr. Pearson had already followed Amy out of the room and down the hallway. Their footsteps rapidly disappeared as the elder Devereux said grimly, "A word, Mr. Flynn."

Flynn nodded reluctantly and Devereux followed him over to his own room.

"If you come near my grandson again, I'll go to the sheriff. Julian is not responsible for the things he does. He's ill. You see that. And you know only a man as ill as Julian would let you do those foul, perverse things to him."

"Julian might be epileptic, but he's not a child and he's not insane."

"That's where you're wrong," Devereux said with bitter triumph. "This filthy disease has eaten away his mind and his will. He's like a child, and for your information, the law recognizes that fact and has placed him in my guardianship."

"He's twenty-six years old."

"He is epileptic. Already he shows the signs of moral insanity." He glared at Flynn. "I've told him and now I'll tell you, if he doesn't obey me in every respect, I'll have him committed for his own damned good."

"You won't have him committed," Flynn said quietly. "That would be the end of the golden goose."

Devereux said equally low-voiced, "But if the golden goose is going to run away with you, Mr. Flynn, then I will have no choice but to have him committed in the hopes the doctors can help him. Or at least keep him from harming himself."

"*Run away with me?*" Flynn repeated, stunned.

The old man stared at him suspiciously, then said slowly, "You don't know? You didn't offer to take him away…?" He laughed an acrid laugh. "There. You see now? You see what that poor sick, young madman made of your using him? You should be ashamed, sir. And if you approach my grandson again, I'll see that you're shamed before all the decent world."

He left Flynn's room, closing the door silently behind him.

For a long time Flynn stood motionless, unable to think past Devereux's words. Distantly he could hear the house still in commotion. He thought that across the hall Julian was crying. His heart squeezed, but he continued to think hard.

There was no way away around it, was there?

He couldn't risk exposure. New York might be more sophisticated in its tastes than Herrin, but it wasn't *that* sophisticated. Nowhere on the planet was *that* sophisticated. Oh, they could easily manage it if *Grand-père* wasn't bound and determined to keep his meal ticket. Julian would be safe enough in Greenwich. Flynn could say that he was his distant cousin or some such thing. He would be safe and he would thrive there, and Flynn could make sure he got the care and attention Dr. Pearson had spoken of, particularly the affection and love.

But not if M. Devereux was going to come after them.

He needed to put the thought out of his mind and go to sleep. But sleep wouldn't come—even after the house settled into a heavy, portentous silence. Flynn lay fully dressed, hands behind his head on his bed, staring out the window at the old, tarnished moon.

It wasn't possible, was it?

The old man had already had Julian placed in his wardship. He was two steps ahead of them all the way. They couldn't run away like children or hobos. Start a new life without money or friends?

Perhaps he was the insane one to lie here contemplating such a thing.

And yet…and yet Julian had told the old man they were going away together. Julian *wanted* to go with him.

Sleep was impossible. He felt uneasy, restless. He needed to speak to Julian.

After a time he rose and went down the hall to Julian's room. He eased open the door. The lamp on the dresser was down low. An ominous-looking bottle and a glass with a spoon in it stood next to the bed. Mr. Devereux sat in a chair near the window, dozing. Julian was lying in bed gazing up at the ceiling.

As the door swung open, he stared at it, stared at Flynn without expression. Flynn came to stand at the end of the bed. "Hello."

Julian nodded politely.

"How do you feel?"

He curled his lip contemptuously, but said nothing. Flynn shot a quick glance at the old man, gently snoring, and came to sit on the edge of the bed. He took Julian's hand. Julian did not resist, but he didn't respond either. Not even when Flynn leaned forward and kissed him.

His lips were feverish and dry and there was the taste of bitter— medicine or bromide, no doubt—on them.

When Flynn withdrew, Julian gave a long, weary sigh. "Now you know."

"I already knew. I knew the day before yesterday."

Julian's brows drew together. "You did? How?"

"It doesn't matter how." Flynn said, "You could have told me. It doesn't make a difference." And he realized as he said it that it didn't. As frightening as the convulsions were, the fear that the disease might—probably would—grow worse, something about Julian made him feel alive and happy in a way he hadn't in too many years. And if the war had taught him one thing it was that happiness was fleeting and fragile. You had to grab on to it and hold tight for as long as it lasted.

"Oh, it matters," Julian said bitterly. He glanced at the old man in the chair. "You asked about why I can't take the money I earn and go do as I like? Because he's my legal guardian. And if I don't do exactly as he likes, he can have me shut up in an insane asylum or an epileptic colony like the one in New York."

"He can't do it simply on his say so."

"Oh, David." Julian sounded both miserable and impatient. "You still don't understand. This affliction is…it's a curse. And people blame you as though you had control of it. There are plenty of folks who think I'm crazy for seeing spirits. Let alone if they saw me having fits. Any doctor would have me committed if he told them even half of it and let them examine me. Let alone if they knew…" He gave Flynn a despairing look.

"There's a way around it."

Julian's eyes widened. "What are you saying?"

Flynn threw a quick look at the sleeping man. "Did you tell him you would go away with me if I asked you?"

Julian's mouth trembled. "I shouldn't have, I know it. I know you didn't ask, didn't plan on asking. But I-I wanted it to be true."

"And if it was true?"

Julian swallowed hard. "You know the answer. You know how I felt from the first minute I saw you. But it's no use."

"How brave are you?"

"I don't know." Julian's eyes were puzzled.

"I've got friends and I've got family and they're a hell of a lot more powerful than anybody on the side of your loony *grand-père*. But it would be a fight and it wouldn't be a pretty one. Do you have the nerve for it?"

Julian's riveted gaze held his, so Flynn saw each emotion flash past: joy, doubt, fear, stubbornness, despair. "For myself, yes," he whispered. "But I couldn't do that to you. You'd be ruined. You don't know what it would be like."

"Neither do you."

"It would be bad."

"Yes. Probably. He's a stubborn old coot. But then it would be good. That's what I believe."

"I…wish I could believe too…" Julian closed his eyes. Wet glittered beneath his lashes. "Sorry, David. I…can't talk anymore. I want to sleep now."

"All right." David squeezed his hand and rose. "I'll come and see you in the morning."

Tears trickled down Julian's cheeks. He ignored them stoically and said, his voice nearly steady, "We're leaving on the morning train."

"Not now, surely? Not while you're ill?"

"Oh yes. I'll be well enough tomorrow. He'll want me away from here—and you—as soon as possible."

Flynn stared down at his lover—yes, he acknowledged, his lover—and squatted down beside the bed so that his face was level with Julian's.

"Julian?"

Julian's eyes opened, red-rimmed and over-bright.

"We'll see it through together, I promise you. I won't abandon you. I have resources and contacts your grandfather doesn't. Maybe he can paint you—and me—in an unflattering light, but when I'm done I'll have him tarred and feathered and run out of town."

"Don't, David." Julian reached out a quick hand. "He's not evil. He thinks he's protecting me."

"Maybe. But he's using you too." Flynn covered his hand, brought it to his mouth and kissed it. "Rest. I promise it'll be okay."

Julian's eyelids were already fluttering shut.

Flynn watched him and in a few seconds he could see that Julian was sleeping again. He looked with far less affection at the old man, starting to snort as he woke himself with his snoring.

Flynn hesitated. He was ready to do battle now, but clearly Julian was not. It would have to wait, but in one thing he was determined. Julian was not going to be dragged off to another performance in Murphysboro tomorrow morning.

He left the sickroom and stood undecided in the hall.

If he was going to do battle, it would be wise to be as well-prepared as possible. He thought of the medical book that Dr. Pearson had started to hand him and then thought better of. He might as well know now what he was committing to, but either way he was committed. Hope for the best and prepare for the worst, that would be his motto from now on.

Flynn went downstairs. The house was in darkness. The silence seemed complete and absolute. There was a single band of light down the hallway beneath a door. Joan's room he guessed. The other sickroom.

He went into the study and turned on the light. Going to the tall bookshelf, he scanned the green, red, blue bindings for the medical book Dr. Pearson had pulled from the shelf. A gold embossed title caught his eye. *The Burial Customs of Ancient Egypt as Illustrated by the Tombs of the Middle Kingdom.*

For an instant Flynn could not seem to process the information. He recalled his conversation with Julian about the Little Egypt Slayer. That the slayer would be someone his victims knew and trusted, someone with medical knowledge and tools, someone who frequently traveled the countryside, someone so well-known and liked that his eccentricities might be taken for granted.

He took the book down from the shelf and it fell open with the loose-leafed familiarity of an oft-read section.

A priest then cut an opening in the abdominal cavity. The internal organs were removed in ritual fashion leaving only the heart. The ancient sons of the Nile believed that the heart contained the individual's essence and was the centre of intelligence...

Flynn closed the book and shoved it back on the shelf, his mind racing to the events of the séance. To those final moments after Julian had seemed to make contact with Millie Hesse and Flynn had asked the spirit whether she could write the name of her killer on the wall in the letters of light.

He left the study and strode down the silent hall to the dining room. He found the lamp on the sideboard and turned it on. The chairs still lay fallen on the floor, the table had moved two feet to the left. The candelabrum was on the floor. Flynn stared at the wall behind where Julian had sat.

It was simply a blank white wall with two prints of optimistically European landscape. No place on Earth that Flynn recognized. He walked up to the wall and peered closely. There was a small black smudge in the center. He remembered leaning out of his chair to see, but the letters were so small he was unsure how he could have made them out. He bent close and saw the letters, perfectly formed, as though branded in the plaster: *Beware.*

That was the word offered at the first part of the séance. Had Millie Hesse left a second part of the message? Flynn examined the wall with meticulous care. He found another smudge half hidden beneath the bottom frame of the unrecognizable European castle.

He squinted, leaned in closer still. He could barely make out the small scripted letters burnt into the plaster: *Pearson.*

From beyond the grave: *Beware Pearson.*

Flynn turned and ran down the hall to Joan's room. He was distantly aware that Mr. Devereux was coming down the stairs. The old man hissed, "I told you what would happen if you came near my grandson again, Flynn!"

Flynn ignored him. He ran to Joan's door and yanked it open.

The gentle lamplight revealed Joan, naked and still on the sheets. On every flat table and dresser surface of the room stood mason jars of various sizes glinting in the glow of the lamps. An array of surgeon's instruments were arranged on a white towel at the foot of the mattress. Dr. Pearson stood beside the bed calmly, placidly unrolling bandages. Behind him, the full moon seemed to loom outside the window like a great golden eye staring into the room.

As the door swung open, however, Pearson's head jerked up and he gazed in instant affront at Flynn. Though it was the same man who Flynn had spoken to a few hours earlier, it was the face of a stranger. He rattled out a string of nonsensical syllables—was it supposed to be Egyptian? Perhaps it really was.

"Stop," Flynn ordered.

The maniacal stranger who wore Pearson's body snatched up a scalpel and flew across the room at Flynn.

Flynn caught the doctor by his wrists, and as fragile as they felt, the man had an unexpected and terrifying strength. *The strength of a madman*, Flynn thought dimly, wrestling for possession of the scalpel.

He pulled the scalpel away and hurled it outside the room.

"What the devil do you think you're doing?" Mr. Devereux cried, reaching the doorway.

Flynn threw Dr. Pearson back. He bounced off the bed and fell to his knees, suddenly an old man again, broken and bowed. Flynn went to Joan, turning her face to see if she was breathing. To his relief he could see the faint rise and fall of her bony chest, feel her exhalations against his hand.

"Go get Amy and Casey Lee," he told Mr. Devereux, throwing the quilt on the chest at the foot of the bed over Joan. "At least, try to wake them. I'm guessing they're all drugged."

"Drugged?"

"He wouldn't want them interrupting."

Devereux stared at him as though it were Flynn speaking in Egyptian. His mouth moved as he stared back at Joan, at the monstrous array of shining jars and gleaming tools in shocked disbelief.

"Interrupting?" he parroted.

"What do you think he's doing in here? Surgery?" Flynn snapped. "This is the Little Egypt Slayer."

"Y-you're mad."

"No, *he's* mad. Stark, staring mad. It was right there in front of us all the time. Who has a better excuse for traveling the countryside with bloody clothes and bloody instruments? Look, we can talk it out later. Go get Amy or Casey Lee. Or phone the damned sheriff." Flynn lightly slapped Joan's face, calling her name.

Still looking dazed, moving like a sleepwalker, Devereux turned to leave the room.

Dr. Pearson uttered a blood-curdling shriek, launched himself from the floor and grasped another of his razor-sharp instruments from the white cloth on the foot of the bed. He darted across the room, plunging it into the throat of the horror-stricken Mr. Devereux.

Mr. Devereux began to make ghastly choking noises, clawing feebly at the silver blade wedged in his gullet. He slumped to his knees as Flynn grabbed Dr. Pearson and slammed him against the wall. Hard. Pearson's head hit the wall with a crack. He went limp and collapsed on the floor.

Flynn dropped down on his knees beside Mr. Devereux. Already the old man's eyes were glazing as he struggled for his final wet gasps. Seeing Flynn, a spark of alertness came into his face. His bloody lips moved, he tried to raise his hand.

Flynn took his hand. "Can you hear me? I promise you I'll take care of him. I love him."

He couldn't tell if the old man heard him or not. Perhaps it was the last thing he wanted to hear. It was certainly the last thing he heard.

For a few stunned seconds Flynn knelt, his mind reeling. Behind him he could hear Dr. Pearson's stentorian breaths. He turned and was struck motionless by the unearthly aspect of the moon, so beautiful, so ancient, so indifferent to all that happened beneath her golden eye.

Unbidden the words of a poem he'd learned back in his school days returned to haunt him.

Ere for eternity thy wings were spread
Alone I listen'd to thy dark farewell.

In two steps he was back at Dr. Pearson's side. He slammed his head into the wooden floor once more for good measure, and ran shouting to wake the household.

Shadows
in Time

Laura Baumbach

"Yesterday upon the stair, I saw a man who wasn't there.

He wasn't there again today. I wish that he would go away."

Nursery Rhyme

Boston

1760

"Shall I take you on the floor tonight? Like a stable mare? What do you say, my boy? Nothing?"

Williams chuckled softly, the harsh sound swallowed up by the thick velvet curtains and heavy bed chamber furniture. He wait a few seconds for his lover's reply then roughly gripped the much younger man's chin, forcing the smooth, angelic face upward. Even so, Neal refused to raise his gaze. Judge Williams pushed Neal's face away with a sharp slap.

"It's just was well. It is not like your preference is of any concern to me."

Contempt always brought such a delicious flush to the boy's fine-boned cheeks. This time was not any different. Williams savored the sweetness of success while he watched Neal try not to squirm. Williams took advantage of the moment to run his hands over Neal's upper arms and shoulders, admiring the trim, firm muscles, the hallmark of a silversmith. They were even more attractive when spread wide and lashed to the foot board of Williams' bed as they were now. Neal's slender body naked and on display for his pleasure as Williams sat on a plush stool in front of the young man, admiring and playing. The long hours Neal spent working metal into delicate wares for his father's silver shop showed. Williams appreciated every curve under the pale skin.

He especially admired the slight curve of hard flesh jutting up from between Neal's thighs. The color was a tantalizing shade of rose, the length just right to fit in the grasp of his hand, the width slim like the body that claimed it as its own. Though it looked thicker now than normal, the tight bands of the hair tie Williams had torn from Neal's dark wavy locks wrapped securely along its length, ensuring the lad stayed hard and wanting until Williams had what he wanted. Maybe even longer.

Grabbing Neal by the hips, Williams pulled him closer, unbalancing him slightly, forcing Neal's arms back as his wrists remained tied to the foot board. His young lover said nothing until Williams slowly lapped at the swollen crown of Neal's cock, his fingers digging into the lean flesh of Neal's buttocks, his stare fixed on Neal's averted gaze. Even then, a gasp was his only reward. It was infuriating that the boy continued to fight him after all these months. He knew what was required of him and yet he fought, embarrassment and shame ruling over reason and prudent decisions.

"Let me hear you say it, boy." He let his fingernails dig a little deeper, not enough to draw blood but enough to leave a reminder of what disobedience could bring.

"*Look* at me and say it."

He watched the convulsive bob in Neal's throat as he swallowed down the words, marveling at the graceful lines of muscle and flesh that led to the square, beautiful, clenched jaw. He rubbed his own stubbled chin over the bound, glistening cock pointed at his face, delighting in the startled jerk of Neal's hips that unintentionally forced it harder against his prickly cheek.

Ah, the eager slide of hot, weeping flesh against his own. He never tired of it even after four decades of life. He could barely wait to possess this passionate young buck, possess him completely, permanently. Neal's future would be *his* future. Whether the boy wanted it or not.

Williams edged forward on the stool, forcing his knees between Neal's spread thighs. He released his hold on the firm buttocks, bringing both his hands to caress and fondle Neal's groin, cupping his sac then teasing the crease behind it. His fingers were dry but that didn't stop him from exploring and breaching the tight opening to Neal's body with one finger. Neal squirmed and shifted at the sudden penetration. Williams used the movement to go deeper. When he could curl his finger forward and touch a hard bead of flesh he stopped and worried the knot.

Neal curled his toes into the thick weave, visibly tensing his body. Williams knew he was steeling himself against the next touch from his "lover's" groping hand. Yet even as the young man burned with embarrassment and revulsion, his cock betrayed him, hard and weeping, yearning for attention. This was everything Williams loved about seducing naïve young lovers, so beautiful and eager.

Soft gasps and shallow pants filled the silence but Neal still wouldn't speak. Williams bent forward so his lips touched the bobbing cock. He exhaled, letting hot moist air mingle with the drops of cream pooling in the folds of the lengthened foreskin, the tiny slit on the smooth globe under it peeking out.

"What do you think my servants will say come morn when they find you here naked and tied to the bed, cock bound and weeping, as you are now? They know better than to blaspheme my reputation or they will find their worthless hides locked away in chains in prison."

Williams reached up with his free hand, twisting Neal's chin until their gazes finally met. Once gained, he held Neal's gaze with the force of his own harsh stare. Without breaking the line of sight he pulled Neal's cock so he could push down the foreskin and suck softly as the newly exposed head.

Neal grunted, a choked sob swallowed down before it fully escaped.

Williams smiled. "But I dare say, you will not be so lucky, young sir." His smile faded and his eyes narrowed. "Say it." Without waiting for Neal to respond, Williams stilled his finger still deep inside Neal's ass as he licked at a few of strips of cock flesh bulging out between the crisscrossed ribbon. The heat and taste almost made him close his eyes in delight.

Neal's face was the color of pale tea roses, a sheen of sweat giving his skin an unearthly glow, like a distraught angel. His china blue eyes were half-lidded with lust, his mouth parted, dry lips revived every few seconds with an anxious touch from his tongue. Arms restrained to each side and back, his hips pushed forward, a jutting, uncoordinated rhythm, a primal rutting looking for release. His forehead was furrowed, a few lines marring his smooth complexion, this and his silence the only indications he was struggling against Williams' demands.

Williams sucked the cock to the back of his throat, sliding a second finger into Neal to massage the hidden pleasure spot inside. Neal trembled, droplets of sweat running down his taunt abdomen to disappear in the dark spare nest of hair under Williams' grasping hand.

"I...c-crave the pleasure of you... inside me." Neal had to force himself to speak clearly or risk having to repeat himself. Williams sucked harder and Neal shuddered adding. "I want you to...possess me."

"And?" *It was marvelous how one's body could betray one's inhibitions and social taboos. Manipulations were so much more enjoyable this way, if no less humiliating.*

"We—we were meant...to be together." Neal could barely spit the words out.

"That wasn't so hard, now was it?" Williams moved his fingers in short hard jabs, delving deeper, nudging the small stone of heat in Neal's channel while sucking hard on the head of the swollen cock. It leaked and jumped in his mouth, scraping against teeth and tongue. The sound of Neal's strangled cries were music in his ears.

$\int \int \int \int$

Neal's gaze fastened on the faint ink that stained the pale fingertips from too many years of handling legal documents. They always left Neal feeling dirty no matter how clean the hands really were, each long, bony caress like a quill to parchment, writing unpleasant truth on his weak and wanton flesh.

Why had God made him like this? Weak to the pleasures of the flesh and easy prey for the more cunning lover. But with the shame came unspeakable pleasure –when his lover decided to grant him it. Neal was less concerned over his lover being a man than he was over the kind of man he had fallen for. Better to face eternal damnation over fornication with a good, loving man than the cruel one that had ensnared him.

"Perchance, tonight I won't take you at all. Just leave you and your pride to wither away from lack of attention."

Williams palmed Neal's cock, the coarse ribbons wrapped tightly around the straining flesh rubbing against the sensitive shaft, forcing the trapped blood to pound in the bulging veins entwined up to the leaking tip. Neal couldn't resist thrusting into the grip again and again, his body crying out for release from the torturous wait.

Each touch brought the stink of unpleasant spices, the ground herbs added to an exotic oil his more experienced partner had specially shipped in from the Caribbean. The smell irritated Neal's nostrils and burned his eyes.

The thick, red oil Williams slathered around Neal's mouth was colder than the room, not even warming to his body temperature. Williams' long-fingered hand slithered down Neal's back to paint his naked ass, sliding between the globes of his backside, leisurely seeking entrance to Neal's taut body a second time. The questing digit found the tight bud and wormed into it, the sudden scrape of fingernail soothed by the glide of slick oil, a relief to the used lining.

Neal grunted at the sudden intrusion, a spark of pleasure stroked by the wiggling, prodding rod igniting the fire in the pit of his bowels. His cock hardened, curving away from his naked body, presenting its modest, hooded length to the spice-tainted air. He shuffle his feet awkwardly further apart so he could remain standing the way Williams insisted he did, feet planted on the center of the weird symbol in the middle of the bedroom rug. It was the same symbol the other man wore around his neck, the pattern burned into the fabric pouch that hung from a sturdy ribbon. The game had been going on for months. Neal knew what was expected of him. So much so that it was ritual by now. And he knew the consequences if he didn't play his part.

He stared down at the foreign mark, trying hard not to imagine a stiff manhood or a licking tongue in the curved strokes. Williams had no intention of giving him any sexual release soon, and wild imaginings only made the wait more agonizing.

Shame burned his face, heating radiating from his cheeks hard enough to make his eyes water. He let the rising buzz of humiliation in his ears drown out his partner's nasal words, the eerie, sing-song chant hanging in the air unanswered.

Neal knew his silence didn't matter to Judge Williams, the pompous Boston barrister actually thought it was his due; that all should bow down and be respectful in his presence. Neal had quickly learned the best way to play to the man's weaknesses in ego and physical desires. It had taken time but Neal finally saw the older man for who and what he truly was.

There *had* to be a way out. No matter what it took.

∫ ∫ ∫ ∫

"Move swiftly, child. That worm of a man is (dialect) gone to a meeting at the tavern, but I never know when he'll see fit to return. If he catches you here now, he'll burn us both. Hurry, child!"

The sound of passing horse's hooves clatter on the cobblestones echoed faintly down the narrow alley he used to reach the back door. The falling snow muffled his much lighter steps, the stench from the emptied chamber pots thrown out in the street stronger here, lessening the amount of foot traffic and prying eyes.

Ayana's hushed words ran together, heavy and exotic, her Jamaican accent painting blue oceans, warm breezes and lazy sun-drenched days for Neal Clifton like they always had despite the woman's current tense insistence. Neal winced when the housekeeper's hard, bony grip squeezed his arm as she pulled him out of the lightly falling snow and into the warmth of the Judge's small kitchen.

"I know, Ayana." Neal clasped his own chilled hand over hers, returning the comforting touch. She was small in stature, her skin smooth and clear like a petite bronzed sculptures in his father's study. She was a beautiful woman, large dark eyes, coal black hair, and a full-lipped, expressive mouth under high, sharp cheekbones off set by her worn but clean white neckerchief. It framed her neck and face beautifully. Neal could see why she had been considered a royal captive, why Williams had needed to possess her whatever the cost—to her or to her people.

"I'm not sure but I think someone saw me. From the Abbot house next door. Coming around to the alley." He resisted the urge to flee before it was too late.

"Then you must hurry." The warmth of the room pushed the chill away from his back as she urged the door closed. The clink of the door blocked out the outside world of prying eyes and accusing fingers. In the sudden silent of the small, comfortable room his nerves calmed and his courage returned.

"I wasn't to leave town for three more days."

"The time is right now, child. The spirits do not lie."

"Then I'll leave tonight. I'll send a message to father to follow as originally planned so he'll be less inclined to suspect a problem. The transfer of the business back to Philadelphia is almost completed." He had lived his whole life in Boston but a change was needed if his was to have a decent life. He glanced anxiously toward the upstairs chambers. "I have to say, with the latest turn of events, I'm no longer reluctant to go."

Philadelphia was his father's place of birth, but Neal had spent little time there. When his father told Neal he had begun arrangements to return to the Pennsylvanian town five years after his mother's death, it seemed natural. But Neal has been surprised by the plan to merge businesses with a fellow silversmith of equal reputation. Surprised but too distracted by his own troubles to pay much regard to most of what his father told him about the new business plan and their new partner.

After years of working as his father's apprentice, Neal was an excellent silversmith but his real talent lay in the business aspects. He had a head for figures and a natural charm and wit when dealing with people, both customers and business associates. It now offered him a legitimate opportunity to leave Boston. Impulsive as always, Neal leaped at the chance to escape his present situation without further thought.

"I know it was unspeakable of me to ask you to do this but I couldn't think of any other way." Betrayed by his lover, the fine upstanding Judge Martin Williams, Neal's friendship with Ayana, Williams' indentured servant, remained intact, the two of them bound together against one evil.

"I know, child. I know. You must not let him keep *anything* that ties you to him." Her dark eyes were like a fierce storm at night, full of power and anger. "If I could get back what he took from me all those years ago I would send his black spirit to the other side of the darkness and never let his filthy soul find peace!"

If anyone understood what a cruel and abusive man the Judge really was beneath his public mask of respectability and moral righteousness it was this proud and defiant woman, forced into service for over a decade, treated no better than the lowliest slave.

Neal knew Williams had some mysterious, unspoken power over Ayana. Whenever Neal had shown too much curiosity about the subject Williams would only give a randy smirk. Neal was certain she had suffered in the Judge's bedchamber, as well as in his household service, at one time.

And Neal knew all about the Judge's bed these last few months. At first they had been deliriously wonderful times, but Williams' true character soon emerged, and Neal realized what a precarious position he had put himself and his family in. He'd been a fool. Now he was here to correct the grave error his naïve heart had made.

"I only wish you could, Ayana. Unmerciful as it is, I *do* wish it after what he's done! I should have listened to you from the beginning. I was blinded by what I thought was love."

"That man knows nothing of love!" Ayana spat on the floor mumbling a few words Neal didn't understand but recognized as her native tongue. It sounded dark and ominous, curses being brought up from hell. "He is the devil's servant. With *no* heart. The only soul he owns belongs to another! Evil! Evil lives in this house, child, evil and darkness!"

The intensity of venom in Ayana's usually gentle, exotic, sing-song voice startled him. It spurred his desire to do what needed to be done and be gone from this house once and for all. Neal gently disengaged her grasp to stride through the kitchen and into the hallway. He was suddenly anxious to be gone from this place once and for all.

His gaze lingering on the small animal bones scattered on the floor by the hearth. Strangely, Williams had encouraged Ayana to keep her heathen cultural beliefs alive, reveling in the exotic, mystical rituals. She clung to them in a fanatical manner Neal wasn't quite comfortable with. She had refused to let Neal into the house until the spirits and mystic signs had told her the time was right. Apparently, the bones favored him this evening.

The bones appeared to vibrate as he walked by them sending a chill through his chest, spurring him to walk faster. He took the staircase two treads at a time, the hallway to Williams' chambers at a trot. Ayana followed, her pace slower but just as anxious, lit candle in hand.

Neal threw open the door and moved into the familiar room with the ease that spoke of many hours spent in the plush surroundings. Too many hours that created too many detailed memories. Memories that echoed off the cold walls to hammer accusingly at Neal. Gone was the pleasure he had first discovered here. Passion and adoration had turned to bitter guilt and shame.

"He keeps his personal papers this drawer." Neal moved to the ornate desk in the corner of the room and lit a another candle off Ayana's flame. Light splashed across the cluttered surface and shadows danced on the walls like demons guarding the gates of hell. The room was chilled, smelling of burnt ash and spices. Neal yanked on the upper drawer of the desk, frustrated but not surprised when it didn't budge.

"The key would be best, but he never takes it off. Even when he's…" Neal paused, embarrassed though he knew Ayana was aware of the things that happened in this room between Williams and himself, "…unclothed." He was surprised by how much disgust there was in his voice. Disgust for the Judge's offensive behaviors but mostly for his own foolhardy actions. He was responsible for the trouble he found himself in.

Ayana touched his arm, her voice low and soft. "You are young, Neal. You think with a young man's heart. A heart that looks at life with passion and love. Do not let this deceiver change your heart. I know of his charms and sly ways." She tapped Neal's chest, a soothing, maternal pat of acceptance. "Yours is a good heart, child. There will be others to share it with, even if your lovers are not ordinary choices."

She nodded a small knowing smile on her full, brown lips. She traced the curve of his cheek and jaw with a tenderness that brought tears to his eyes. If she had been allowed the life she had been meant to have, Ayana would have been a wonderful mother in Neal's estimation. "Love is love and it is meant to be shared. You will find another who deserves your heart. A better man than Judge Martin Williams!"

"That shouldn't be too hard considering the Judge's character, but I doubt it, Ayana. After this, my 'choices' must remain secret, buried where no one can use them against me again. I can never trust another not to betray me. Never. There is too much to lose. My father would never recover from the shock. He is all the family I have left to me. I can't let Williams take that away from me as well."

A letter opener lay to one side on the desktop, its gleaming metal bright and inviting in the glow of the candle light. Neal jabbed it into the lock space and forced the metal to give under the full weight of his slight frame. The drawer cracked and splintered under the pressure. Neal yanked it open. Ayana touched his arm but said nothing. Neal paused, concern for her twisting his inside into knots. She would be here to bear the Judge's wrath at the drawer's destruction, not he.

Ayana shook her head. "Broken lock or not, once he discovers them missing he'll know who took them. Do not fear for my safety, child. I will survive as I have done all these years."

"I'm sorry, Ayana. The last thing I want is for him to hurt you because of me."

"Hush and hurry before he returns and we both feel his displeasure."

Neal stared into her fathomless black eyes and wondered for the hundredth time how this woman had remained so goodhearted while withstanding the isolation and humiliation Williams forced on her. He knew he could not have tolerated it. A few short weeks on the Judge's leash and he was willing to do anything to escape. Including thievery.

Pushing a few loose parchments aside, Neal retrieved a slim bundle of letters out of the back of the drawer. They were wrapped in dark red ribbon, the one Neal had used to tie back his wavy brown hair the last night Williams had seduced him.

Williams had used it to bind his hands over his head the second night they spent together. More recently it had been tied around his shaft while Williams teased and tortured him until he begged for release. Dark stains marred the ribbon, mute testament to his eventual relief. He could feel the burn of shame on his fair skin and the buzz of humiliation in his ears forcing him to turn his back until he could regain control. He had even cut his hair shorter after his last night so as to no longer need to wear a hair tie.

Before he regained his composure, the air in the room shifted and a deep, mocking voice chilled his flesh and froze his heart.

"Stealing your love letters, as passionate and revealing as they are, will hardly be worth the thievery charge, if I still have your thoughtful and rather damning gift, don't you think, Neal, my dear boy?" That nasal, condescending tone rippled over Neal like tainted honey, thick, sweet -- suffocating. Words stuck in his throat like flies.

"Mercy!" Ayana surprised gasp made Neal spin around to face his tormentor head on, sliding the bundle under his waistcoat before he turned.

Williams had the advantage of several inches of height over Neal, his wide shoulders shrugged in an insolent pose of privilege and vague distaste. The sharp angles of his ruddy face appeared more pronounced in the ineffectual candlelight. A sheen of sweat glistened on his forehead, his skin color paler than usual. Neal hoped it was because the Judge had been caught off guard but he knew that outwitting the sly, older man wasn't even a possibility.

Williams' dabbed at his lips with a folded pocket handkerchief, keeping it in his hand to pat deliberately at his face again before speaking, his words slightly hesitant and stilted. "I greatly doubt your father's reputation will hold up under the scandal."

"You won't show them to anyone." Neal's chest tightened. He knew Williams was politically connected enough to escape prosecution but it was all he had. "You'd ruin yourself as well!"

Williams abruptly stepped closer. Ayana held her ground nearby, but Neal jerked back, then stumbled, brought up short by the desk. His resolve to follow through on this mission was still strong, but he was fearful of the power and rage the other man wielded. He'd felt the weight of that rage too often these last few weeks.

The desk candle shuddered sending the shadows into a frenzied riot before it stilled. Their dark grasping fingers retreated but not before Neal felt their empty chill tug at his flesh.

Face uncharacteristically gray like the muted edges of the gloomy room, Williams ran his palm down Neal's face, a tender touch that turned to a grip of iron on his jaw when he tried to flinch away. "You are so young, sweet Neal, all innocent wonder in those wide blue eyes." Williams gave a leering sneer, his heavy lidded eyes tight with scorn. "Even now that you are not so innocent anymore."

Neal's jaw ached with the force of the hold but he refused to look away. A long finger slid back and forth over his closed lips as if Williams was wagging an accusing finger at a naughty child. Williams' hand tightened painfully on Neal's chin then disappeared to return a second later as a vicious backhand slap. The force would have sent him reeling if he hadn't been trapped between the desk and Williams' larger frame.

From the corner of his momentarily blurred vision he saw

Ayana step forward as if to intercede.

William ground out a low, menacing command without turning her way. "Stay yourself, woman. Come near me and you will lose something even more precious than what the boy will."

Ayana spit at Williams' feet, her dark eyes searching his face, a small smile forming slowly on her lips. "I hope the evil you bartered with so many years ago is eating away your black, merciless soul. I can smell it oozing out of your skin. I pray it has a full meal!" She mumbled a few words in her native tongue, rattling the strings of beads and bones she wore around her neck.

One hand nursing his stinging face, Neal brought his other arm up to stop her, but she was already backing away to the edge of the room. He knew he would bear bruises from this confrontation, but he wouldn't be responsible for her sharing the abuse because she wanted to protect him.

"Ever the *chivalrous* gentleman." The scorn was palpable. Williams grabbed Neal by the hair then thrust him away, his fingers suddenly gripping the front of his own chest as he stepped back, pain etched on his face. Ayana and Neal made small, startled noises, both unused to seeing the powerful man hesitate for any reason. Williams let out a hollow chuckle.

"Merely indigestion. Don't squeal with triumph yet, Ayana. No doubt spoiled meat in the pies at the tavern." With an obvious effort to compose himself, Williams patted his cloth to his neck and took a deep breath through clenched teeth. It gave his voice a raw, gritty quality that was chilling. "But I doubt public opinion will be swayed by good manners and a sweet face. In fact, it will probably be your undoing. An angelic face used to try to seduce an older man against his wishes in to the devil's clutches. Unsuccessfully, of course, but others will see how I could be tempted by such a beautiful but immoral, libidinous young man."

The sneer of contempt made Neal nauseous. "My father is... aware of my...unconventional desire in bed partners."

"Yes, no doubt, considering his own randy youth. But does he want the world to know of it as well?"

How could he have ever seen this man as anything else than a monster? "Please, Martin, don't do this!"

"Your actions today leave me no recourse, my boy. Conspiracy with my maid. Thievery." Williams stopped to struggle for a breath. "Your father, the most respected silversmith in Boston, will know his only son –and heir to his sizable fortune-- to be guilty of trying to seduce a respected member of the legal system to engage in a disreputable behavior." Williams' eyes squinted as if he were in pain, his complexion more ashen that before. "What do you think that will do to his current plans to combine his business with that of Wade House? More importantly, what will Wade House think of it?" He paused, letting all the complications sink into Neal's brain. "Unless…"

"Unless what?" If there was a solution to this, a way out without more shame and ruin, Neal needed to hear it.

"Unless you agree to everything and anything I demand. Whenever I demand it of you, inside this bedroom and out of it." Williams leaned against the high, carved footboard in a confident pose but looked suspiciously as if the man needed the support to stand upright.

"Do not listen, Neal." Ayana trembled, her fingers reaching out to Neal as if to snatch him away from Williams' influence. "He weaves more lies with each word from his forked tongue! He will make you his slave as he did me. Take your very soul. You do not want this." Her nails dug into the palms of her hands so hard Neal could see the creases left behind when she unclenched them again. "Trust me, child. Ruin is better than this living hell."

Neal stared at Williams, taking in the satisfied smirk and the expectant tilt of head as he waited for Neal to break under the magnitude of trouble the judge could create for him. Something inside of Neal unfurled and rose up in his chest. He had to work to push the words past the emptiness it left in its place. He could not disgrace his family name. He'd beg if he had to.

"You've taken so much from me already, Martin – all joy in life, my pride, and my self-respect." It was a losing battle to keep the moisture from blurring his vision but he consoled himself that no tear was actually shed before this devil.

"That is the cost of my silence and protection. Take it or not. The choice is yours." He dragged a smug glance up Neal's slender body. "After all, I'm not asking for anything more than you have already given me."

"You mean *taken*. You used me! Used my own untried wants and desires to blind me to your true nature. I was naïve and inexperienced, eager to accommodate a worldly man of professed good standing to introduce me to the ways of knowing another man. Something I had craved but didn't know how to express." He clenched a fist and pounded the desktop. "I had no idea how ruthless and cruel a man you were until now."

Suddenly it all seemed nightmarish and grotesque. Gone was any sense of joy he had experienced the first few times Williams had pleasured him. The weight of the letters tucked into his waistcoat felt like the chains lashed to a drowning man. This needed to end.

Neal straightened and backed a few steps toward the doorway and Ayana. "I have the letters back. You can't prove anything."

"Ah, yes, but you are forgetting something. I still have the most damning piece of evidence of your attempts to persuade me into sin." Williams pulled a gold watch from his waistcoat pocket and tossed it playfully in the air before opening it. He squinted at the inside lid, reading aloud in a dramatically infatuated stage whisper. "*M.W. Let others not Judge our love, Neal.*"

He waved it slowly through the air as if showing the world the traitorous words of love Neal has foolishly engraved on the watch himself. "I especially like the way you capitalized 'Judge'. Such an affecting turn of phrase, don't you think? So cleverly fraught with double meanings. I'm sure the court will be properly impressed by your implicit declaration of love." Williams' smile was strained and thin lipped. Neal wasn't sure if it was irony or pain that gave it a twisted, pinched effect. "Love for a *man*. How impulsive of you, my sweet, pathetic…" His eyes had a faintly wild look in them but he gave Neal another dismissive sneer, clutched the open watch roughly to his chest and slowly let the word drip off his now gray lips. "...*catamite*. Or now that I'm paying for your place in my bed, I wonder, does that make you a prostitute instead?"

"Damn you, you bastard!" Neal lunged for the watch but Williams effectively removed it from his reach, toppling over to the floor. The Judge landed face down, both arms and the watch pinned under him.

Neal stood frozen in place not knowing whether to run while Williams no longer blocked his exit or try to wrestle the watch from the man.

Williams moaned and rolled over to his back. His hands scrabbled at his neck, tearing away his stock and under it, the button to his shirt's neck slit. His eyes were wide open, clear and focused on Neal's face. Pain twisted at his thin lips, a rasping breath rattled in his throat so low and feral Neal couldn't believe it came from a man.

Torn between fleeing and giving aid, Neal's sense of right and wrong pushed him to drop to his knees beside Williams. His gaze darted between the judge's ashen face to carpet, searching for the damning pocket watch.

"I can't understand what he is saying." Neal leaned closer. Under the side of Williams' body lay his watch, the hinge slightly twisted, the face open, the hands ticking away the second of Neal's life. "Maybe he is trying to ask for forgiveness."

"Do not touch him! He is trying to call the dark ones. Trying to summon the power of life after death. He needs a vessel to house his rotten soul in so it isn't taken to the afterlife. Stay back!" Ayana approached Williams' side but stopped short of touching him, instead choosing to kneel several feet away on the thick carpet. On hands and knees, she stared at Williams, watching his hands work a thin ribbon that was around his neck out from under shirt with clumsy fingers, nail beds tinged with blue. Her face lost the rich shade of bronze Neal has always thought of as being more beautiful than the richest brown velvet, her expression one of horror. "Stop him!"

"What?" As much as he wanted the watch, he couldn't bring himself to lean over Williams and grab it. Not while the man's hands still clawed at his own throat, snarling his fingers in the tangle of ribbons and strings that decorated his neck. A black pouch, the desk key and gold ring hung from separate strands. Neal saw them every time he had been bedded by the man. But the judge had never revealed their contents or purpose no matter how many times Neal had asked. Nor did he ever take them off.

"Stop his hands." Ayana grabbed at the air in a frustrated parody of Williams' gestures, every fiber of her being showing a need to dig her nails into the man's flesh. "I cannot touch him while it remains in his possession!"

"What? While what remains?"

"My amulet!" If it was possible to screech in a whisper, Ayana succeeded at it. "The pouch! Take it from him. He must not have its power at his command! If he opens the gates to the darkness we will never be rid of his black soul."

None of this made sense to Neal, he didn't even believe it, but his next protest died unspoken as Williams suddenly stopped all movement. His hands rested on his still chest, the black pouch clenched in his left palm, and his face slack, eyes mercifully closed. The rattle from his lungs died away with a sudden puff of breath that already smelled of death.

Neal traded a horrified, shamefully relieved glance with Ayana then choked on his next breath as a bold knock on the front door echoed up the staircase. Ayana jumped to her feet, eyes lit with a dark, almost insane fear. Neal started to rise but she stayed him with a curt command.

"Stay! Take what you came for quickly! I have much to tell you. My pouch must stay in your possession. Give it only to me!" Her steps quick and silent, she ran to the doorway. "I will send the caller away and return. Make no sound!" With that she was gone.

Neal heard the front door open and the muffled sound of insistent voices, one Ayana's and two males. He couldn't afford to waste time. The Judge's associates treated Ayana as if she barely existed. He knew she would be unable to detain them long if they were insistent on coming in to wait.

Time was ticking away.

The watch lay tucked slightly under the man's flaccid body. Neal stared at the ashen face, seeing none of the wit and charm he had been attracted to, none of the generosity or kindness Williams had pretended to possess in the beginning of their relationship. Nothing of the man he had thought he loved. It had all been a cruel lie, a deception for control and personal gain. Williams had made a mockery of Neal's emotions.

The voices below became clearer, the callers unwilling to be turned away. Unable to tear his gaze away from Williams' lifeless face, Neal leaned over the body to pluck the watch off the ground. The twisted lid clicked closed in his hand. The usual crisp ring of metal to metal was missing, the bent edge leaving a gap in the outer seam. His fingers wrapped around the closed shell, but as he pulled back, cold, strong hands sunk into his shirt and held him in place. Williams' eyes sprung open, the pupils dilated so wide Neal felt like he was staring into an abyss.

"Lord have mercy!" Neal's whispered oath thundered in his ears. Absolute terror gripped his throat. The watch fell from his nerveless hand to land on Williams' chest just above his heart, gleaming gold against too pale flesh.

Neal grasped Williams' clawing fingers, trying to force them open. Williams' strength bested Neal on an ordinary day but now the judge seemed to have the power of three men. He yanked Neal closer, drawing Neal to his face.

Williams' mouth contorted, his cold lips brushing Neal's, his whispered words foreign and curt. There was a rhythm to them that repeated again and again, a chant spoken in a raw broken voice Neal didn't recognize as belonging to Williams, despite witnessing it.

The room grew colder and the shadows seemed to move on their own, creeping closer, long gray talons reaching out from the darkness to push the light from the room. They had a life of their own. Neal felt as if they were reaching for him. A white mist flowed from the judge's mumbling lips, pouring around his mouth to cover his cheeks and eyes, a mask of swirling vapor that hid Williams' human features turning them into a caricature of death. The mass moved as if blown by an unseen wind, forming tentacles that clawed at Neal's lips seeking entry to his body. Its touch brought sharp stinging pain as if he was being stung by insects.

Panic seized Neal unlike any he had even experience. He tore at the frozen fingers holding him down, his frantic efforts finally managing to rip his shirt free. His hands came away with the small black pouch that had been in Williams' hand as well, the thin, worn ribbon breaking under the strain. Neal fell back, hitting his head on the leg of the desk when he landed.

Suddenly the judge went rigid, his eyes blank, dark voids. The mist rose in the air, spinning like a directionless top, uncertain where to find refuge.

It was terrifying but at least the rising chant had stopped. More terrifying were the voices from below. They were growing closer, Ayana's insistent tones respectfully but unsuccessfully trying to divert the callers.

His vision blurred for a moment, the blow on the desk leg harsh to his unprotected temple. In the haze that clouded his eyesight, the room swirled with a white mist. It flew at him. He instinctively raised his hand to his mouth to prevent it from clawing at his face again. The black pouch in his palm brushed his lips, the fabric soft and warm. It made him think of one of Ayana's comforting touches after a cruel night spent with the judge.

The vapor whirled and backed away from Neal to return to Williams' body. It lingered by his gaping, lifeless mouth, then reared up to the height of a man, its ghostly veil transformed into a hideous gray face of rotten flesh and exposed bone. As unnatural as it was, Neal could still see Williams' resemblance in the ghastly form. Its false mouth gaped open wide, tattered lips twisted in what Neal imagined to be a soundless scream. Then the visage sunk down low over the judge's body to disappear under the man's open shirt.

Neal stared at the dead man, disbelieving what his senses told him. This couldn't be real. Ayana believed in such things but God-fearing, civilized men did not. It was shock at the judge's death, terror over being exposed, and the blow to his head that brought these nightmarish visions before him. By the time Neal was back on his feet the room was occupied by nothing but shimmering shadows and flickering candlelight. Reality was back in place. Only the hammering of his heartbeat at his wounded temple and the stinging of his lips told him otherwise.

The fear of discovery was more overwhelming than any fear he retained of the dead man. He plunged his hand under Williams' open neck slit. The watch was hard and real under his touch. He snatched it away and jumped back from the body. Shoving both it and the pouch into his jacket pocket, Neal raced to the bed chamber door and quickly but silently strode to the servants staircase at the end of the hall. Once he made it safely to the kitchen he listened in the hallway, hidden by the shadows.

"He said not to disturb him. He was not feeling well, sir."

The voice of Jonathan Webster carried loud and clear, overriding Ayana's objections. "We understand that, woman. We were with him at the tavern when he took ill."

The more placating tone of George Crisp, a barrister like Webster, smoothed over Webster's more condescending approach. "Mr. Webster and I are here to inquire about his current health. Martin was so unsteady when we parted he couldn't even get his watch into his pocket properly. Your neighbor says he thought a friend of the judge's came by as well. If he's up for young Mr. Clifton's company he won't mind seeing us."

"I sent Mr. Clifton away. The judge wished to be left alone."

"I see. You do look out for the Judge but," He was more polite but also firmer, "we insist."

There was silence then Ayana's strained voice carried more

clearly to Neal's hiding space as he watched her turn toward the back hall where lead to the kitchen. "As you wish, sirs. He retired to his chambers when he arrived home. It's at the top of the stairs." Ayana glanced to the darkened hallway and at Neal as if she could see him standing in the shadows. "I was making him tea. I should go finish."

"Nonsense, woman." Webster herded her up the stairs in front of them. "Announce us! My God, after ten years one would think a servant, even one from a heathen country, could learn proper manners!"

Neal stepped back into dim of the kitchen. This would be his only chance to escape unseen. He would send word to Ayana, keep her trinket safe with him until he could come back to give it to her. It was a pouch of herbs and bones as far as he could tell. If she had survived Williams having it for so long, what harm could a few more weeks do? She would understand. If he were caught here, they would know she had lied to them.

At the back door, he edged it open as quietly as possible, pleased to see the evening light had extinguished. The courtyard was wrapped in a shroud of darkness that would cover his movements from prying eyes. Footprints in the snow would support Ayana's claim he had been there and gone, the still falling snow making it impossible to tell when they had been made if they didn't discover them soon. With luck, no one would be aware of the truth.

It took him extra time to maneuver through the side streets to the place where he'd left his horse. It was wiser to wait until morning to travel but Neal needed to put distance between himself and this place. Needed time to think things through. He'd made a mess of things. Allowed lust and desire to put him in a dangerous position with a man who cared only about using him as Williams used everyone.

He was worried about leaving Ayana there alone to handle things. If Williams' death wasn't accepted for the natural demise it truly was she would be a suspect. He was keenly aware she was a strong, clever woman. A woman more concerned that

Neal remove her trinket from Williams' possession than his unexpected death. Which was ridiculous. With Williams dead, she *was* a free woman, the pouch had nothing to do with it.

Still…

He slipped his hand into his pocket and fingered the crude bag before taking it out. On impulse, he tied a knot in the broken ribbon and slipped it over his head and under his own shirt. When it touched his skin he felt oddly comforted by it. Ayana's gentle, exotic voice whispered in his head "be strong, child, be strong", a phrase she had spoken many times to him in the last few humiliating weeks. She had endured ten years with that monster while Neal had been willing to be branded a thief after only a few weeks under the man's cruel power. Ayana was stronger than any man Neal knew, including Williams.

He slowly retrieved the damning watch from his pocket. The metal was cold and hard against his palm, the uneven edge of the bent cover sharp against his skin. He was a fool to have engraved it. A fool to have given it to Williams. It felt different in his palm — heavier, colder. Touching it now gave him a gathering sense of dread.

Dropping it back in his pocket, Neal decided it was the added guilt and shame it symbolized, the embodiment of a disastrous attempt to find and explore his own identity and needs. He was convinced it was the wrong man not the wrong need that was his error. His parents had taught him that love, a precious and rare thing, couldn't be a sin. No matter what others believed.

He would keep the accursed watch, a reminder of the damage an unwise choice could bring to an unsuspecting heart. Maybe it would keep him from making the same mistake again. He hated to think love was fleeting and there was no such thing as the 'right man', not for *another* man. He wanted to find the right man. But how would he know when he saw him?

An ache pressed up under his breastbone so intense it made Neal swallow hard to try and dislodge it. Unsurprisingly, it didn't work. If anyone would ask, he'd blame the moisture on his face on the melting snowflakes.

ſ ſ ſ ſ

Philadelphia

"Room's at the top of stairs, last one on the left, Master Clifton, the one your father always uses." Amos Ross poured a pint and handed it off to a waiting customer. He rounded the bar top to shake hands, a sincere grin of welcome on his ruddy face.

Ross was robust and hearty. Not a large man but fit for a man of his apparent age. He had an honest face and a clear eye for a man who serviced ale all day. His grip was firm. The friendly pat on the back Neal's balance slightly off and a stinging hand print behind.

"You've only got half your father's bulk, son. Sorry, boy, I'll have to remember not to rough you like I do him." Ross laughed and lightly rubbed where he'd patted Neal's back. The man's good mood was infectious and Neal had to return the teasing, good-natured grin. He could see why his father had been a lifelong friend.

The Ram's Head Inn was as inviting as the redheaded man's rough, warm handshake. The cozy dining room was filled with animated customers and the pleasant aroma of baked bread filled the air. "Will you be wanting a bit of a supper? I could have the cook save a bowl of her dish."

"No, thank you, Mr. Ross. It's been a long, cold journey. As much as I am enticed by the offer, my father having spoken highly of your cook's skills, I believe I'll just retire for the night. It was…difficult to rest on the road."

Neal's fitful attempts at sleep had been filled with disturbing dreams and night terrors. He'd been jarred awake more than once by a stinging at his lips, the touch of cold fingers on his face, the windblown snow swirling gray to white in a menacing dance before him. He hoped once he arrived at a secure, populated inn, the unnatural terrors would fade.

"Call me Amos, lad. Your father and I have been too close for too long for less."

"Amos it is then, sir."

"Good. The fire's being tended to in your room. It'll take the chill right off your bones, yes it will." Amos relieved Neal of his travel bag and walked to the stairs. They trudged up the narrow staircase, Amos in the lead.

"I would like to wash up before I turn in. Rid myself of a few layers of road dust." Neal ran hand over the light stubble on his face. Memories were making him feel dirtier than any grime from the trip, but freshening up might make it easier to face another night.

"There's a pitcher of hot water in your room." Amos reached the last door at the end of the long hallway. The door was open revealing a large bedchamber, almost as welcoming as Neal's own room back home. Amos nodded at a large white pitcher on a dresser and waved a lad of about six years of age out of the room. "Had the boy take it up when I sent him off to tend the fire. Thought you might like that. Your father always does. "

The walls had been papered in a subtle pattern, cheerful but masculine. A door on the far wall had a barrel lock in place. Neal assumed it was a connecting room. Possibly where his father would stay when he arrived. The tapestry curtains were heavy enough to block out the strongest morning light and the inevitable draft that seeped around the windows of even the finest home. A fire crackled in the grate, small flames in the tinder already lapping at the split logs and coal.

Neal moved to the hearth and let the warmth soak into his legs and hands. "Now I know firsthand why my father always choose your company, Amos. This is like being home. Thank you."

"Jonathon will always have a place in my home. Time and circumstances have never changed that between us."

"I know he values your friendship as well, Amos. The bond between you has been unbreakable despite distance and marriage. And now that mother is gone, I'm pleased he will have your friendship to rely on. His health is not its best. I'm confident your nearness will give him comfort."

Amos set Neal's bag on wooden chair in the corner. He nodded at Neal, accepting the compliment with grace and a pleased grin. "Thank you, lad. We're fortunate to get a second chance to make some more memories. It's an honor to have you here, as well. Though I'm a bit surprised to see you here alone."

The man's humble appreciation of his father made Neal's chest ache. He had never experienced a friendship as dear as these two held. Neal had always preferred the companionship of older men and none of them had time or patience for him. Until Williams.

How could he ever have survived the humiliation and shame in his father's eyes if Williams had succeeded in his plan? His heartbeat faster the mere thought of the judge. Dead or not, the man still terrified Neal.

"He'll follow in a few days. I had completed some personal business earlier than I expected and decided to arrive early. I sent a message to inform him I would meet him here. I'm sure he won't mind."

"Did you have any last minute chats with him?"

"No," Neal fought to keep his voice from trembling with the memories. "I'm afraid my leaving was a bit of a whim. Impatient I suppose."

"Jonathan always said you were an impulsive lad."

Neal was too shaken to do anything other than let the comment go. "Since I will be working closely with Wade House's proprietor, I thought it might be a good idea to meet with our new business associate on my own. I'm to take a more active part in the day to day running of things."

Amos nodded sagely, a look on his ruggedly pleasant face that told Neal he knew more about the elder Clifton's personal and business plans than Neal might. "Peter Wade is a good man. As fine a silversmith as there ever was. Almost as fine as your father. Bit of a loner, that one. Single man and all." Amos' jaw cocked to one side in an indulgent smile. He winked at Neal. "But I'm betting a handsome, fine young man like yourself will be just the thing for him. He suits you. Your father has high hopes you'll agree."

"My father?" The conversation has taken a confusing turn.

"He thinks highly of the man. As do I, lad. We've both known Peter since he was a boy. But you'll see for yourself." He winked again, as if sharing a guarded confidence. It was all wasted on Neal. He had no idea what the man was trying to tell him. "If you'll be wanting a nightcap later, you know where to find me, lad." With a nod and another face-splitting grin, Amos was gone and the door closed.

The room was comfortably furnished with a plush bed, a dresser, and a ornate clothes cupboard. His bag sat on a straight backed wooden chair and by the fireplace were two upholstered sitting chairs done in a dark fabric. It was clean, cozy and warming up nicely. Even apart from his friendship with Amos, Neal could understand why his father's practical side chose this place over the more luxurious accommodations he could easily afford. The elder Clifton never forgot his humble beginnings.

The faint scent of lye mingled with the smell of fresh bread and strong ale that drifted up from the lower level. Neal's stomach rumbled in response to the foods but the bed, with its fresh sheets and thick comforter, spoke louder. He made short work of washing, including shaving the light stubble from his face. He might have waited until the morn but bathing made him feel as if had removed a part of the troubles he carried with him from Boston. He wished the frightening vision in his dreams would wipe away as easily.

Embers burned low in the hearth. Neal banked the fire for the night. He sank down on the bed in his shirttails with only the glow of dying coals for illumination. The pocket watch lay on the small stand by the bed where he had placed it when he undressed.

He automatically reached for it to check the time, but hesitated as he had learned to do these last few days.

What was once meant to be symbol of his heart was now a looming, weighty reminder of how empty his life was — empty and destined to stay that way. He'd been foolish to think a man could love another man and find happiness in it. Any burden or pain the watch now caused him was just, a lesson to be remembered.

And it did cause him considerable unease. Touching it made his hands shake. The flesh that made contact with its cold, hard surface seemed to burn as if he had handled a glowing ember, despite there being no evidence of any wound. Each time he had an illogical need to inspect it, sincerely expecting to find it waterlogged with ice or snow to explain the new heaviness to the metal.

And still it kept perfect time. The graceful, slender hands ticking away in their unhurried rhythm, the face maybe a shade darker as if a shadow lay under the glass. At least he assumed the watch still keep good time. He hadn't been able to force himself to pry open the bent lid and look since retrieving it from Williams' body. But he could hear the steady *tick*, even and strong like a heartbeat encased in gold.

Crawling under the comforter, Neal pulled it high, snuggling down. His hands fell to rest over his heart, the steady thrumming reassuring. His gaze darting right and left, staring into the deepening gloom.

The room grew darker as the embers waned and the once small shadows arched high, rearing up, frightened horses in the moonlight. Blood pounded at his temples, his heartbeat thundering in time to the ticking of the watch beside his head. He strained his hearing, listening for some sound of the people below. But the room was well-placed and no sounds reached him except for the faint rattle of the windowpanes against the gusting winds.

Neal shut his eyes, trying to relax, ignoring the unease that crept across his skin. He shivered, part natural chill, part trepidation. Nights had not gone well since Williams' death.

Turning on his side, he drew his lower legs closer to his body and slipped his fingers under the collar of his shirt for warmth. The thin ribbon of Ayana's amulet tickled his palm flooding his mind with thoughts of the woman, his unlikely friend and confidant.

It plagued him that he had left her alone to sort out the circumstances of the judge's death. Both he and Ayana were blameless, but that didn't mean others would see it that way. By all rights it had been a death by natural causes, no matter how unnatural the events afterward had appeared to be.

A slight wailing sound whispered near Neal's head. He buried his face deeper into the pillow and kept his eyes tightly shut. He had heard it every night since leaving Boston. The wind at the windows. It *had* to be the wind.

The wail rose and fell, never louder than a breathy sigh but with a menacing hiss to it that made Neal's stomach churn. His grip tightened on the ribbon in his hand, fingernails raking his chest. Each time this had happened on the trip, he had forced himself to abandon rest and push on, the gray mist seemingly unable to torture him unless sleep was approaching.

Breath, cold and foul smelling, brushed his cheek, the hand of death caressing his face. The sound tormented him, its singsong rhythm so close to the last words Williams had spoken he was sure it was his mind playing guilty tricks.

Neal was determined not to give into an apparition of his own making this time. But when the fiery stings gnawed at his face trying to pry his lips apart, he couldn't stand the terror a moment longer.

Each night the vision had a more recognizable form. Not human but no longer a shapeless cloud, either. The face was better defined tonight, sharp angles and shallow curves around a slash that could be a mouth. The eyes were empty sockets, dark holes with no spark of life or kindness in them. Jagged claws formed from twisted strands of smoke-like gray pierced his mouth, pulling at his jaw, stabbing his flesh until the pain rivaled a horde of wasps. His heart pounded in his chest, his throat so tight he could barely breathe.

Instinctively his hands flew up, ineffectively fighting off the wisps of smoky talons. His fingers tangled in Ayana's ribbon, the sudden movement pulling the amulet from under his shirt. The small pouch popped into the air then fell back when it reached the end of the ribbon's length around his neck. It landed on Neal's lips with a light slap, the faint scent and taste of exotic spice and rich dirt released from it by the impact.

Neal reached to wipe the fine dust away. He froze, his hand on his mouth, the pouch and its dust the only thing there. The mist had reared up, giving a whispered sound that was closer to a screech than the usual chants.

It swirled around the room again and again, building up speed and power then rushed headlong at Neal.

Neal sealed his hands over his mouth, pouch and dust in his palms and braced himself. At the last minute, he rolled out of the way, landing on the floor on the far side of the bed. Tangled in linen and shirttails, he lay there listening and waiting. When nothing happened except his teeth chattering from the cold, he slowly regained his feet. The room was empty, undisturbed except for the watch. It lay on the bed as if it had been knocked from the stand. Neal quickly grabbed it and closed it in the table's drawer.

He was sure he would get no sleep again this night. It took several attempts for him to settle back in bed, but the release of tension and a nearly sleepless week of travel took its toll. The taste of spice on his lips and tongue were oddly comforting, like his mother's pudding when she was alive. Reassuring.

His last thoughts were of Ayana, her precious amulet and his failing mental state. If this was all just his becoming unbalanced with guilt, it was going to be a rapid decline. He wouldn't have to worry about finding happiness.

∫ ∫ ∫ ∫

The city bustled with energy undaunted by the second snowfall in as many days. The streets were frozen, cobblestones slick with snow and ice packed solid by carriage wheels and hooves. The thick, large flakes gave the busy street sounds a muffled grace.

Glancing expectantly up the lane, Peter Wade swept the snow from the stoop of his storefront. As much as he respected, admired and even liked John Clifton, he was nervous. This arrangement was far from ordinary.

"I imagined Neal Clifton to be made from the same cloth as his father, Amos? Thick limbed and heavyset?"

Amos Ross chuckled and shook his head. "I don't want to spoil the surprise." They entered the shop.

Peter poked a bit, wanting more to go on from this wild plan. "Jonathon is easy company for a gentleman of such distinguished reputation and wealth. We have agreeable viewpoints, but his son is said to have a keen head for figures. I'm not sure a squinty-eyed clerk is best suited to my temperament."

"You're an impatient for a man ending his third decade, Peter Wade. And one who can't afford to be passing up an opportunity of this kind. Your financial future in business will be set as well as an end to the lonely days and nights I know you're enduring. So buck up, man. I've never know you to walk away from a challenge. Don't make this one your first."

"My skill with the metal is on equal standing with the fine Clifton Silver's goods." Picking up the piece he had finished last evening, he examined the joining to see if it would benefit from another polishing. "But you know I lack an interest in the more practical end of business."

"Which is way this is a reasonable end to it."

"I feel like the nervous groom in an arranged marriage."

"That's because you are, man! Trust me. Jonathon knows what he's doing. He knows his son and he knows you. Better than your own mother did." Amos gave Peter the look that said it all. "The three of us know the reason you're still a bachelor. Same reason I am. If Jonathon hadn't been a loyal son and given his family what they demanded— a respectable marriage with a heir— he'd have stayed a bachelor as well. And stayed here."

"You're a loyal friend, Amos." Peter was almost envious of the older man. "Twenty some years is a long time to keep a candle in the window."

"Not when the one you're waiting for is the only one you want." It was said with depth of feeling; Peter believed every word of it. To find love, even a love that couldn't be spoken about, was possible. He had to believe that. "You'll learn that. If you're lucky. Neal is perfectly suited to you. He'll see that right off. Jonathon was to have discussed it all with the lad."

Peter gave a frustrated grunt. While it was not uncommon for two bachelors or widowers who worked together to share living space, and develop a longstanding companionship, no matter which side of the trough they drank from, Peter's quiet life had been in upheaval ever since these two older matchmakers had decided he was the answer to bringing respectable stability and happiness to Neal Clifton's young life, while adding companionship to his own lonely existence. It was frustrating.

And so very appealing.

He hoped Clifton was a tolerable sort, and a little more pleasant to look upon than the balding, barrel-chested senior Clifton was.

Not that he himself was a frail man. Being a silversmith needed more than an artist's eye for fine detail and patience. It required a surprising level of body strength, power and endurance. The average household coffee pot took over two hundred hours of firing, shaping, acid baths and hammering, most of it achieved with the delicate application of sheer brute strength.

At the unusually tall height of six foot one, Peter's sturdy frame was solid muscle, most of it in his thick shoulders and arms set on a sturdy pair of long, strong legs all clothed under shirttails, plain brown waistcoat, leather breeches and thick stockings. His hair was not overly long as was the current gentleman's fashion, but he still preferred it tied back with a strip of brown leather that nearly disappeared against the color of his hair.

The hour chimed on the ornate fireplace clock, a keepsake from his late father, a lethargic winding down of time, a reminder of domestic chores still undone for the day. He sighed and put his latest commissioned piece down on the tall table that served as his client display area.

"Put on your best courting manner, Peter. He'll be here soon. Take it from a man who knows, don't let this chance slip away, my boy." Amos patted him on the back and walked toward the front shop, whistling a tune Peter recognized as something the vicar's wife sometimes sang at church gatherings. Usually weddings.

"Amusing, Amos. Very amusing." Amos merely winked at him and continued without losing a note.

The tune was whipped away on the blustery wind as the door was suddenly thrust open. A lean, hurried form swept into the room along with the chill blast of air.

Peter started forward as the new arrival shrugged off hat and scarf and turned to face Amos. The sight froze Peter to the spot, feet suddenly stuck to the flooring as if he had gone completely lame. His stomach clenched, his expression instantly melting into a startled look of delight before he could temper it.

The slight, pale skinned man before him was beautiful. A slender, dark-haired angel with watery, startlingly blue eyes, a delicate straight nose bracketed by high cheekbones, and framed by waves of chestnut brown. Of average height, he stood many inches shorter than Peter. Drenched, he couldn't weigh much more than half of Peter's sizable weight.

Peter could see the elder Clifton in the dazzling smile that instantly animated the slender pink lips. There was no doubt in his mind who this young man belonged to, but Neal Clifton obviously had inherited his mother's attributes—slim, delicate featured, almost petite, but undoubtedly male. The late Mrs. Clifton must have been a truly awe-inspiring, magnificent woman to have given birth to such a man considering her husband's plain, rugged looks.

A small ache of desire hit his gut. This beautiful man would never want him. Peter had to work hard to push the burst of longing back into the furthest corner in his heart where he kept such unacceptable thoughts and feelings.

"Good day, Mr. Ro—Amos." The young man smiled shyly and nodded to the older man. The upturned corners of the wind-reddened lips coupled with the honest pleasure at seeing Amos endeared him to Peter immediately. The young man apparently respected and honored his father's friends. "It's unexpected to see you away from your place of business on such a busy day."

Neal's voice was like buttery soft leather, a little breathless from the cold, but medium-pitched, well-mannered, slightly-hesitant, and self-effacing. A touch of humor to it. There was no trace of snobbery or entitlement, as Peter feared the young son of a wealthy man might have.

He was mesmerized by the small Adam's apple just above the notch of Neal's collar. It bobbed up and down as the young man swallowed nervously, blue eyes darting to skate a quick glance across Peter's face again and again as he smiled at Amos. It pleased Peter more than it really should that he made Neal anxious and unsure. A man that looked like Neal Clifton need never be unsure of his welcome in any company.

Amos chuckled, patting Neal's arm, urging him further inside the shop, herding him toward Peter. "Performing a merciful act, son. Delivered a bit of supper for the two of you so you aren't subjected to this man's cooking come evening."

Peter shot Amos a dark look which the man heartily ignored.

"You'll be wanting to spend the entire afternoon and evening together discussing business and whatnot. Make use of Peter's guest chamber for the night if need be." It was more of a command than a suggestion, one that left both Neal and Peter staring wordless at the other. Neal was the first to recover.

"That's very...kind of you, Amos. But I have yet to even make Mr. Wade's acquaintance let alone impose on his hospitality." Neal acknowledged Peter with an embarrassed glance and tentative smile. "Would you do me the honor of a proper introduction, sir?"

"My pleasure, lad. Couldn't think of anything I'd like to do more." Amos grinned that wide smile that seemed to swallow his face and motioned Peter forward. This time Peter found his feet actually responded to his silent command to move. "Mr. Peter Wade, may I introduce to you your new business partner, Master Neal Clifton."

"I believe you are expecting me, sir." Neal hesitated, hand extended.

"A pleasure. And I do mean that. Your father praised your business sense and talent but failed to mention you were a man of handsome stock."

He casually wiped his hands against his breeches to remove the sweaty sheen that had suddenly appeared on his palms. Despite his best efforts, he noticed a tremor as he gripped Neal's hand. "At your service, Mr. Clifton."

"You flatter me, sir but if I may be bold, please, call me Neal."

The smaller hand slipped into his, warm, smooth and fine boned. He gripped it firmly to hide his own slight shuddering movement and found strength in the slender fingers as well. Strength, charm *and* beauty?

This was going to be a difficult day.

Desire rippled up Peter's arm. It ran down his spine like hot silver poured into a sand mold, beautiful and dangerous. His cock stirred, filling with each pulsing beat of his wildly pounding heart, trapped and hidden by leather breeches.

"Not 'sir'. Peter." He stared down into wide eyes so gleaming wet they were tiny oceans. "If you'll pardon the intimacy of it."

A *very* difficult day.

"Yes, please. I'd be delighted to become more intim—" Peter found the faint blush that tinged the high cheekbones endearing. And intriguing. "More familiar...I mean, it's only appropriate since I have requested you call me by my Christian name." Neal glanced around the shop at the commissioned wares, flitting gaze pulled back to Peter's face time and again, then moving off.

A flirting gesture? Does he know of his father's more personal plans?

Long dark lashes feathered against smooth, clear skin. A thin slice of tongue, pink and wet, darted out to simply touch an upper lip, seductive in its innocence. Peter sighed soundless.

An *impossible* day.

Unthinking past the thrill of Neal's warm, firm touch, Peter raised his free hand and clasped Neal's wrist, effectively trapping the younger man in his grasp. Time slowed, savoring the moment, then Neal eased away, his radiant smile overshadowed by uncertainty. Peter was sure he'd over step his bounds.

Two minutes in the man's company and Peter felt completely exposed, vulnerable. He was allowing himself to be seduced by physical beauty without knowing the man underneath. Maybe Neal wasn't as attracted to him as Peter was to Neal. His hands, still wanting to hold on to Neal, now found little comfort tightly gripping the front edge of his waistcoat.

"Had a traveler stop by the inn this morn, brought news from Boston." Amos casually slipped into the growing silence in the room. "Seems a judge there was found dead. Judge Martin Williams. You might have heard his name."

"Yes, I knew of the Judge. A prominent man."

"He was known to many, even outside of Boston. And feared by most who knew him well. Had a fondness for heathen cultures and black arts. Even kept a voodoo princess as a servant from one of his trips to the black islands. Can't say I'm surprised he's met with a sudden end to his days."

Neal's stomach dropped to his toes. He tried not to let his expression change but the vision of Williams laying on the floor of his bed chamber, ghastly gray and cold, was too much. He felt the blood drain from his face. He couldn't keep his gaze from darting to the darkened corners of the room to check for any signs of the insidious cloud of swirling gray. Coughing lightly Neal used his handkerchief to cover his trembling lips.

"A natural death, Amos?" Peter moved closer, his towering frame and substantial girth solid and reassuring to Neal. He felt the wash of paralyzing fear fade to a tolerable level, his heart still pounding against his ribs but not painfully so.

"Didn't say." Amos pulled his hat on and buttoned his jacket, preparing to leave. "Found him in his bed chamber. Not a mark on him. Some business about a broken desk drawer and a rumor about a man skulking about but there weren't much but gossip at this point. Your father might bring more reliable news when he arrives."

He grabbed the shop's door handle and paused a grim, thoughtful expression tightening his wide mouth into a pursed scowl. "Not that it matters. Not to speak ill of the dead, but the world's a better place for it if you ask me." Amos yanked open the door and ducked his head into the wind. He was gone with barely a nod in their direction. A plain spoken man of action.

An uncertain silence settled around them in the void Amos' leaving created. Neal brought his gaze back to study Peter, then shifted to the man's empty hands. "For such...sizable hands, your work possesses a distinctive grace and skill. I can see why father chose you." He forced his gaze away from Peter's large, graceful hands—and the things Neal's imagination wanted them to do to him. "To...to join our strengths."

Strong hands, ones that used their strength to create beauty not pain.

He remembered every harsh touch and painful grab Williams had inflicted on him. The weight in his jacket pocket seemed to grow heavier. Neal slipped his hand into his pocket to reassure himself all was normal, but jerked back out almost as quickly as he had inserted it, the metal so cold it felt like fire.

Was it the wind gusting under the threshold or did he actually hear a moan whisper past his cheek? Guilt and shame squeezed his chest but a glance at Peter's solid, reassuring presence melted the spasm as if it was never there. Neal felt his face heat and hoped it wasn't too noticeable, though he didn't know how anything could escape the other man's intense, searching stare.

These large hands were different; he could tell by the way Peter had cradled his, fingers supporting his wrist, warming his winter-chilled skin, a firm handshake, but nothing more. No crushing squeeze to show dominance. Just restrained, careful strength. A flash of desire hit. Was there such a thing as a powerful man who was gentle?

Somewhere from a dark corner in the room Neal imagined he heard a soft moan or whisper. He tried to ignore it, but a flicker of white off to one side send a chill down his spine even when he realized it was a wisp of smoke from the hearth. The fire snapped and he nearly jumped, covering the move with brisk rub of his hands as if they were still cold. Which indeed they were, his whole body was numb with a cold that had little to do with the weather.

"I—" Something very personal flickered in the steady stare. Peter's eyes were dark brown as the graphite and clay crucibles used to melt silver and gold. "Your workmanship. They're…" he couldn't resist the pull of the man's hands, "…impressive." Everything about this man was.

Peter Wade was handsome in a rugged, daring fashion that brought visions of the heroes in the stories his mother told him as a child. A towering man, Peter was broad in shoulders with hearty upper arms that sprouted from a muscular chest undoubtedly honed by many hours swing a malling hammer. This man labored hard at his craft.

"While I have learned my father's trade well and enjoy it, I lack the power and endurance that you and he share by virtue of your stalwart bodies."

Peter's gaze measured Neal from head to toe. A small smile tugged the man's firmly held lips into motion. "I've seen your work as well. And *your* appearance suits *you*, sir. Your work possesses a grace and delicate skill. It is obvious to me now where that comes from."

Peter paused, his focus moving off into the darker corners of the room before looking back at Neal, a new daring light in his eyes as if he had made a decision. His shoulders straightened marginally. It seemed to Neal he took on a more confident, assertive air out of whatever thoughts had struck him.

"The day grows long and I have yet to sit down to a warm meal. It would be a shame to let Amos' generosity got to waste by having it go cold. Would you join me? My living quarters are in the back. We'll sit by the fire and chase off that chill wind that followed you into the shop."

Peter shuttered the shop window and locked the door to show he was closed then moved down the hallway, one large, firm hand guiding Neal with a small push on his lower back. The hand stayed there as they walked, its solid presence calming the rippling terror running down his spine. It felt possessive and intimate and...right.

If only the whispering voice would stop! Even Peter's rich timber of speech couldn't completely block it out.

"One of the schoolmaster's daughters tidies up for me and stocks the cupboard a bit, but not more than bread and cheese. A real meal will be an appreciated change. Amos is a thoughtful friend to share his cook's wares. Come."

Wordlessly, Neal hurried along, hoping to leave the disembodied whispering behind.

Down a narrow hallway they entered the tidy back kitchen, a fire dying low, Amos' supper pot warming near the embers. Off to one side a half open door revealed a bedroom, but Neal could see nothing more than a thick rug and a tall dresser as they passed by.

A shake of the grate, and the addition of coal under Peter's expert hands, and the fire crackled to a comforting blaze. The gusting wind whistled down the chimney blessedly silencing the moan that had followed Neal, caressing his cheek like a feathery touch of icy fingers.

The sudden absence of the chilling sound made Neal weak

in the knees. Loss of sleep and little food these last few days didn't help. He stumbled, bracing for the fall, fervently hoping he could blame his unsteadiness on the dim light and unfamiliar surroundings.

An arm wrapped around his waist like an iron band to hold him upright, his fall transformed into a slight stumble. He looked up and was captured by Peter's steady gaze only inches from his own. The man's eyes were three different colors of brown; all jagged edges packed together, bright and shining clear, like tiny stained glass windows. He smelled of leather and body heat, tinged with a faint musky scent Neal recognized as arousal. He just couldn't be sure if it was Peter's or his own. He was back on his feet with nothing more between them than a breathless look. Peter's arm disappeared, but a hand gripped his shoulder.

"Your father mentioned I was a life-long bachelor?" It wasn't what he expected Peter to say but it broke the awkward moment.

"He did share that he thought your life somewhat lacking in companionship." Neal searched Peter's face for some reaction to his words. "Of...any kind."

"Life has taught me to be a man of few wants or needs. And those that I do have I've learned to keep to myself." A curt, automatic reply that had an undercurrent of emotion Neal could feel all the way to the bright buckles on his shoes.

Pausing briefly in his step, Peter added in a thoughtful, vaguely frustrated tone, "Your introduction to my life looks to change that, I'll wager."

§ § § §

They talked over business and politics, silver molds to favored hammering techniques. Neal asked about the best blacksmith to the most able cobbler in town. The conversation started out stilted but Neal's natural exuberance took hold. He gradually coaxed out more from the other man than Peter's quiet, short comments. They relaxed into the pleasure of the other's company.

Despite their outward differences, they discovered they had many things in common. During a rare silence between them,

Neal caught the other studying him—his movements, his clothing, his face—an intent, openly appraising look about him. Neal felt he saw approval in the measured glance. That thought shot a thrill to his loins.

"I must give your father his due, Neal. He is a shrewd man. In his business sense and his assessment of human nature." It was said slowly as if Peter was talking to himself, remembering little things he once disregarded as unimportant. "He foretold that we would be...companionable."

"That we do seem to be, sir. I am ease with you like I have been with no other so quickly."

"He cautioned me that you would be my balance—'a graceful sweep of charm and whimsy to compliment my...more sturdy design'." His smile widened, showing Neal just how handsome he was.

Neal had to stop himself from leaning toward the man, a twenty-year-old's willpower wavering in his mere days-old resolve to ignore his body's physical desires.

"Was he evaluating our craftsmanship or our character?" Neal needed time to sort out the attraction he was feeling—a mutual attraction he hoped.

He was surprised when Peter purposely leaned in close to him. "I believe he may have been clever enough to be referring to both."

Neal smiled brightly, excited by the man's closeness but afraid of misreading Peter's intent. "My father is an intuitive man, maybe more so than I had suspected."

Peter laughed but didn't pull back. "He was right about you. Your presence inspires me to bring more beauty to my life." There was that appreciative glint again, along with a roguish smile.

"You flatter me, sir." He couldn't help the self-conscious smile. It felt good to be treated with kindness and respect. Neal would have blushed if another man had said that, but Peter appeared at ease with making a brash, flirtatious compliment.

This bold attitude intrigued Neal. And scared him. He knew what it was to be drawn in by a charming, assertive man.

The accursed pocket watch weighed heavily in his waistcoat pocket, cold and stark, reminding him of why this wasn't a wise course of action. Which was the reason he had kept it, wasn't it? His conscience in a twisted gold box. One he would gladly dispense with right now.

And just like that, Williams invaded his thoughts, the ghostly specter of guilt. He shoved the memory away and thought instead of Ayana. He'd heard no word on ruling of the judge's death yet but he feared for the woman. He hoped the letter he had left with the stable boy for his father would provide her aid if it was needed. Ayana had never really seemed to need or want anyone. For any reason.

Unlike the way Neal now wanted the man before him. That undisguised glint in those steady brown eyes was surely desire. Neal had seen it in many a man's eye before but he only had the courage, disastrous as that turned out to be, to return the interest once.

Until now. A shiver teased his spine but he wasn't sure if it was excitement or fear.

Undeniably, caution was needed. He had to be sure. He couldn't afford another mistake of the heart. Why was he cursed with these nagging needs and desires of the flesh? But then Peter appealed to him on more than a physical level. In the short time they had known each other he had found a sense of safe haven no other had given him.

"I have heard great praise for Wade House and its proprietor. High praise." Neal's furtive gaze wandered over Peter's towering frame, lingered on the fit, firm torso and well-defined musculature to end at the man's rugged face. Peter's lips, parted in a soft smile, coupled with the unmistakable heat in his stare, grabbed Neal's gaze and held it tight. Desire hit him hard in the gut forcing out fervent, heated words before he could stop them. "And justly so, sir."

With near-panicked effort, Neal tore his gaze away. He needed time to think and he couldn't keep looking into Peter's bold eyes.

His father had nothing but praise--*continual* praise, now that Neal thought about it, for Peter Wade and Wade House. Hard working, respectable bachelor, successful, devoted to his craft, a stout loner with a fine heart and an artist's soul. Neal could see it all in the man before him. That and more. He could see sensual power and gentle hands, soft gazes and bold confidence. Strength and desire, passion and want.

A coldness burned his thigh, a circular pain the size of a watch. Neal shifted, opening his jacket so the pocket fell away from his body. It did nothing to slow the sudden pounding of his heart, the dryness of want in his mouth.

Williams had been a 'respectable' man, too, though the elder Clifton had been outspoken with his dislike of the judge. Neal should have listened to his father opinion on his choice of... *company*. Maybe, it was time he listened now.

Peter pulled the pot off the fire. He set the supper and two bowls on the small table. Mugs followed with a healthy measure of wine in each. The carved wood of the table was graceful but sturdy, meant for service not looks yet still pleasing to the eye. Just like the shop and the cozy back living space. A lot like Peter.

"We'll share supper then I'll walk you back to your rooms when you take your leave. There are streets you should avoid at night. Come, sit with me, Neal."

Neal nodded and moved to sit with his back to the fire but Peter gestured at the chair beside him. "No, no. Sit here, facing the hearth. I'm enjoying the way the firelight strikes your face."

It was overly bold. Inexcusable. Neal should object at the impudence and liberty Peter took with the flirtatious comment. He should reject the offered seat, leave the shop and find his own way back to the inn. Any man would. Any man not attracted to other men.

Nervous, excited, wary and pleased, Neal moved to round the table and squeeze past Peter toward the other chair. He was suddenly uncertain when Peter didn't do the gentlemanly thing and step back to widen his passage through the small space. If anything, the man leaned in, purposely brushing their bodies, face to face, gazes latched on to each other. Neal knew his own stare was as nervous as Peter's was daring.

Peter's breath, warm and alive, washed over Neal's lips. Neal wanted to devour the heat, taste the mouth so tantalizingly near, feel the strength and passion he was sure lay under Peter's calm exterior. It hurt to have Peter so near, to drink in the confusing, delightful, terrifying emotions this plain-spoken man instilled in him in such a short period of time. Neal flushed with hesitation, wanting but knowing he should resist, he should hide away until this business with Williams was over.

The decision was taken from him when Peter slowly slid a hand into Neal's unbound hair and pulled him in. Angling Neal's face with a gentle tug of hair, Peter drew closer. He stared into Neal's pleading eyes, his gaze searching.

"I...I..." Whatever Neal was going to say died on his lips. The fireplace clock ticked off two loud, seemingly endless seconds while Peter gave Neal a last chance to say more.

Neal couldn't utter another sound, breathless with the desire to know the touch and taste of the man who handled him with such gentle power and respect.

Then, as if Neal was made of the most delicate silver filigree, Peter closed the distance between their parted mouths and kissed him. It started out as a slow caress of lips, an exchange of panted breath, a gentleman's introduction. The moment their lips parted, heat, moisture and undeniable want mingled on their tongues. The kiss turned wanton, teeth clicking, tongues licking.

Neal wanted to be swallowed down whole, consumed, to become a literal part of the other man, to chase away the whispers, the chill in his bones, the fear that lingered in his heart. His fists twisted in Peter's shirt, the fever of the man's body seeping deep into Neal's skin, connecting them as if they had been molten silver fused together.

Neal could feel Peter's hardness against his side, thick and hot, curved to his hip as if it fit like a missing part of his body. He ground into the heaviness, letting his tongue stroke Peter's palette and tongue in the same rhythm. He yearned to untwist his fingers from Peter's shirt and seek out the other man's cock, to slide it, naked over his palm, to rub its length with his eager shaft until they found release. But just as he began to loosen his grip, Peter ended the kiss, peppering Neal's mouth with soft caresses, gently pulling Neal's reluctant lips away.

"Peter." The sigh escaped with the last wet slip of lip over lip. It sounded broken and hopeful even over the buzz of pounding blood in Neal's ears. Peter's hand tightened in his hair before releasing him and pushing Neal to an arm's length away. An immediate chill invaded Neal, gooseflesh raising on his arms and neck. Confusion battled with the desire to regain his grip on Peter and pulled him back for another embrace. Peter's concerned expression stilled his impulsiveness.

Peter's palm touched Neal's cheek as it withdrew. "I'd offer apology for what would seem at any other time a vulgar taking of liberties, sir, but I don't think I have misunderstood your father's suggestive assurances. Or the look in your eyes."

"What do you see, Peter?" His gaze was so passionate Neal felt as if it raked over his skin like the sharp tines of a fork. A fresh shower of gooseflesh paraded down his spine. He could not trust his limbs to function.

"My own hunger looks back at me, good sir. Hunger and a rare, superb, unequaled, manly beauty. Now that I have known you, though the time has been mere hours, I would forsake all I have in life to call you mine." Peter paused, his jaw squared, his shoulders straight, obviously resigned to accept rejection if it came. But his raw, pleading voice betrayed him. "Tell me I have not laid my soul bare to you only to have it thrown in the dust."

Pressing a hand to Peter's chest, Neal waited for the speed of his racing heartbeat to slacken. He needed the roar in his head to fade. Reason returned with the ebb of blood. "Relieve yourself of any fear of vulgarity or imprudence to me or my honor. I take no offense at your actions or intentions, Peter. Even if considered a perversion of nature to our kinsmen, we are of a like mind and like bodily desire."

He fidgeted and stepped back. Distance. Neal needed time. So much was left unfinished in his old life, the life he was literally fleeing from. Death and madness did not mix with affairs of the heart or loins. He had no right to drag Peter into his nightmarish madness. The total silence in room was frightening. Not even the ticking of the clock or the hiss of dying flames broke the sudden stillness. "But I must implore of you. I have traveled much this week and find myself in need of more rest than usual. If you will not take offense at the abruptness, I beg you to let me take my leave. I don't wish to stay too late and find the inn barred for the night."

"Surely, the hour is not that late." Peter glared at the mantle clock. "Hell, it's stopped again. The girl that tends to things for me forgets to do it at least twice a week." He moved to the mantle, opened the clock face and affixed the key, turning the gears several times before gracing Neal with a half-amused glance. "Would you care to guess at the proper time? I've lost track for some reason, sweet lips."

It sounded right coming off Peter's lips, a pet name spoken with a comfortable roughness that sent a chill up Neal's spine. But it was the appreciative, lingering gaze that truly distracted Neal. Before he realized what he was doing he had the pocket watch out and its cover released.

His gaze flashed to the pocket watch face, drawn by a sudden sense of cold terror. The creamy white background was gone, occluded by a smoky vapor so dark not even the crisp black hands could be seen. The case vibrated, the audible *tick-tock* of passing time like a disembodied heartbeat pulsing against his sweating, shaking palm.

This couldn't be happening now! Not here, not in front of anyone, but especially not in front of Peter. So far there had been no witnesses to his bouts of madness. He had prayed it would stay that way until he could reach Ayana to find some answers.

The watch burned his hand.

He couldn't bear the sound of the ticking. It gathered strength with each passing second until it thundered in his head. With a cry of pain, Neal threw up his hands to cover his ears, knowing full well he was the only one who heard its accusing beat, but still needing to find refuge from it.

The watch tumbled from his fingers. Gray-black shadows coiled up from the edges of the bent metal, billowing high, gaining length and breath as it rose before Neal's terror-widened eyes. Then suddenly, another movement by the hearth managed to pull his attention away from the horrible, untimely mental aberration.

Peter, expression alarmed, powerful body poised in a defensive stance against the mad man in his home, was all Neal saw before he blocked everything out with a tight squeeze of his eyelids. He would lose everything now. This madness was his undoing. His future was gone and all possible happiness with it.

Willfully blind, he still saw Peter in the blackness behind his closed lids, shocked, confused and ready to physically defend himself.

And the only other thing in the room with Peter was Neal.

This was not good.

Neal was desperate to make Peter understand, but the words wouldn't come. He opened his eyes and stepped toward Peter but the shadows, now a huge, almost opaque mass, opened a black hole like a mouth and wailed its ghastly sound, swirling menacingly between them.

It lunged at Neal.

He fell to his knees nearly weeping, helpless, his shame and guilt exposed and at the mercy of his own dark secret. These were the fruits of his unnatural desires. Neal wanted to curl up and die.

"Neal!"

Peter's voice was strong, concerned but unruffled considering the scene Neal was creating, cowering on the floor, fighting off some specter only he could see.

"Neal, what's happening? What is it?"

"Do not fear me, Peter! Please!" He cringed and ducked as he imagined the shadow striking out at him. "It is but my guilty conscience haunting me, driving me mad."

"The devil that!" It was bold, harsh, forcefully uttered, but not *at* Neal. Neal raised his head to find Peter looking directly at the black specter hovering over Neal's head. "I'm not blind, man! If this is your madness, it afflicts me as well. I see this unnatural shadow."

The room shuddered, another wail bouncing off the plastered walls and bare wood ceiling. Peter seemed to read Neal as if he had known him all his life and understood him at a mere glance. "Here. With us. In this room, Neal. You are not mad. *I* see it. *I* hear its unearthly tongue."

"I'm not imagining it? Truly?" Neal had convinced himself this was all his mind playing tricks, punishment for his own wickedness. It would take more than a moment to dispel the idea, even with Peter's confident insistence.

The gaping mouth stretched wider, the garbled screech wretchedly gruesome. It swayed above Neal then plunged downward, looking for all the world as if it meant to consume him. Neal fell to the floor, a swiping sound slicing the air above him, solid and real. Very solid and real, very unlike the formless mist. He rolled onto his back searching the room for a weapon to fend off his attacker and found Peter had already raced to his defense.

The slicing cut the air again and again, the fireplace poker whipping through the black misty form, powerful, sweeping blows welded by Peter's straining arm. The mist billowed out in trailing clouds of darkness, each blow followed by a bellowed wail of anger.

But that was all the protective blows managed to produce. The ghost was unstoppable.

It dove past Peter, descending straight down on Neal, pinning him on the floor. Its obvious objective was now apparent to Neal, the need to invade Neal's body at any cost. That had been the goal of every attack so far and this one wasn't any different.

"Neal! Neal, *move!*" The air near Neal's head swirled by, the power of Peter's swings singing through the gray cloud.

Body heat touched his skin, intense beside the chill ribbons of cold that still grabbed at his flesh. Peter pushed Neal closer to the floor, trying to insinuate his body between Neal and his attacker. The force of Peter's protective move jarred the watch from Neal's numb fingers. It landed with a thud, the lid snapping shut with a sound as crisp as brittle bone shattering, the rim of the cover staring back at Neal like an empty eye socket.

Long, gray claws tore at Neal's face, prying at his lips then attempting to slither under his hands as he fought to seal off his mouth and nose. When the need for air became too much, Neal instinctively tore at the collar of his shirt, battling to keep the cold, gritty mist from touching his skin.

Suddenly his grasping fingers rubbed over the thin ribbon of the amulet. Ayana's smooth, dark, knowing face swam before Neal's blurred vision. Inexplicably he knew how to fend off the unnatural creature.

Dragging the amulet out from under his shirt he clamped it to his face, holding it over his mouth. The smell of decaying earth and heavy spices was nauseating but the effect was instantaneous.

The ghost rose in the air. Screeches of anger and frustration rattled the window in its pane sending vibrations of terror deep into Neal's bones. The mist seemed to pale to a murky gray, twisted like a spinning child's toy and flew at Peter.

The room spun, Peter's substantial weight suddenly on him then under him. Breath whooshed from his lungs. He was light-headed with the movement, amulet falling away from his face to hang about his neck, the thick scent of earthy spice clinging to his nostril. Cold needles dug at his back. Holding Neal in a fierce bear hug, Peter rolled under the kitchen table.

Gray mist darted at them from every side until Peter reared up, flipping the table on its side, the top facing out, their backs to a wall.

"Back to hell with you, you evil spirit! Be gone!" On his knees, Peter jabbed at the specter, the heavy fireplace poker still in his hand.

The ghostly apparition turned its gaping mouth and talon-like claws on Peter and fear of losing Peter exploded in Neal's chest. It spurred him into action, an unfamiliar clearness of thought guiding his hand.

"Come here, hold me!" Neal rose to his knees, anxiously grabbing at Peter to drawn him nearer. Peter threw him a look that was part confusion, part elation.

"Now?" Peter made it sound like he would consider it if Neal gave him a good enough reason. That unguarded moment, that one word, sealed their future as far as Neal was concerned. His chest burned and his face flushed and something inside of him smiled. He suddenly knew what love was.

Sparing Peter an affectionate, exasperated growl, Neal pulled Peter to him, repeating the bear hug Peter had used only moments ago. He tugged the ribbon on the amulet up and slipped it over Peter's head, the thin fabric thread binding their necks together, their faces brushing.

"It's the only object that it fears! Trust me, Peter!"

He could feel Peter's heart pounding in his own chest, the heavy thud slower than his own racing beat. The ribbon was tight around two necks instead of one, the least little move pulling them closer. Hot breath flowed across his cheek and down his throat, their chests plastered to each other. A thick thigh wedged between his legs, and Neal could feel the swell of Peter's manhood, rigid and hot, though the layers of their breeches. His own shaft stirred, excited by the nearness of the man.

Risking a hesitant glance into Peter's eyes, Neal's gut clenched and a tingling sensation skittered up his spine. Soft brown eyes gazed down at him, questions in the concerned wrinkles around them, but he could see no harshness in the look.

How could a man go through this and not condemn the one responsible was beyond Neal, but it would have to wait until later to be sorted out.

Neal twisted the thread around so the amulet touched both of their lips, their rapid, warm breath releasing the pungent smell of earth, decay and exotic land into the air around them. Peter baulked slightly at having the tattered bag so near but gave in at one pleading look from Neal.

With a final ghostly wail, the pale graying mist swiped at the air with its viciously hooked tendrils then retreated back to the watch, slipping in under the bent lip of the cover.

Quicker than Neal would have thought possible, Peter yanked the ribbon from their necks and dove at the timepiece. He wrapped the amulet strings around the watch tying the lid tightly shut.

An eerie stillness filled the room broken only by the raspy sound of their labored breathing.

∫ ∫ ∫ ∫

The bound timepiece quivered in the dust on the floorboards, but no ghastly shadows or gaping mouth tormented them. A faint moan bounced off the kitchen walls but Neal wasn't certain it wasn't the wind in the chimney. A rain storm has rolled in, the soft patter of falling droplets like angel's tears on the roof.

"Tell me."

Emotions rolled across Peter's face. Horror, disbelief, panic, anger, maybe even grief, a split second devoted to each then the next outrageous realization seemed to strike.

Neal wasn't sure which of them made Peter abruptly drag him close, upper arms locked in the man's fearsomely strong grip, lips near his but nothing like passion or heat in Peter's steady gaze. His voice was eerily low and calm for a man who had just battled a demon.

Battled and *won*. Defeated the specter, at least temporarily.

Chased it back to its unholy berth in the accursed watch and bound it there. At great possible injury to life and limb. Peter hadn't run, hadn't been rendered helpless or struck dumbfounded by the unnatural events.

He also wasn't speechless.

"Tell me, Neal." Peter punctuated Neal's name with a shake, making him listen. The grip on his arms tightened and then eased slightly. "An ungodly demon seeks to take you from me."

Supportive now instead of restraining, that's how Peter's hold felt. He let the other man take some of his weight, exhaustion, relief, hope, draining away his strength. "You braved a specter of death. Without knowing what creature had come upon us, you fought to protect me. You didn't think me mad!" Neal slumped. Peter lowered him to the floor, back to the wall, then took a place beside him, knees touching, one heavy, comforting hand still grasping Neal's arm.

"I don't think you suffer madness now." He pressed Neal's shoulder back, gently forcing him to raise his bowed head to look Peter in the eye. "Tell me what beast treads along your steps, Neal. For it is my path, at present, as well."

"I have been cursed." Neal choked on the words. Guilt rose up to constrict his throat. He felt lightheaded, nauseous that Peter should hear the facts of his past indiscretions. "Maybe not unjustly, but harshly. Stalked by the evil that sought to possess me when it...he was alive."

"And into death?"

The watch shook, metal and cloth against wooden planks, a rattle like the tiny bird bones Ayana kept in a metal lined box. The wind had turned to a whistle in the chimney, the patter of the rain mimicking distance horses hooves in the dirt. All of the sounds more welcome than the one Neal knew was inside the timepiece.

"Yes. You have the right to the truth after what has just occurred." Neal closed his eyes. There was no other way. Humiliating as it was. "Judge Williams believed in a heathen practice, like an ancient religion of sorts. One he learned during his travels in the Caribbean. It has rituals his servant Ayana still practices. She professes to communicate with the spirits of the dead. He used these same rituals to keep her a prisoner. And now he—his evil spirit—uses it to...*pursue* me."

"Even in death he seeks to possess you?"

"As you have just witnessed. Since...knowing him..." Neal searched Peter's face, hoping not to see disgust or condemnation with his next words, "*knowing* him—" Neal broke off his gaze, then looked back up at Peter, his wide stare pleading. "I would say it was an affair of the heart, but I learned far too late that affection had nothing to do with his desire for me. It was a carnal relationship, nothing more. A perversion such as society sees it."

Peter's hand still lay heavy on Neal's shoulder, steadfast and strong. It gave Neal the courage to reach up and cover the man's fingers with his own. It heartened Neal when Peter didn't object.

"I thought to learn how a man loves another man from a caring soul." Nausea rippled through him again. "I was naïve and foolish. I have no excuse but my inexperience in the ways of the world. Williams desired nothing more than a plaything to manipulate."

Bile burned the back of his throat. He had to swallow several times until he was reassured he wouldn't let humiliation win the moment. "At least, I thought that was all he wanted. Until the night he died."

"You were involved in his death?"

"Only as a witness, I swear! Ayana and I." Neal's gaze darted to the mercifully quiet pocket watch before he gave a jerky nod. "In his bed chamber." He realized what vision his impulsive admission might give Peter. "At least, I think so."

"You don't know?"

"I did nothing! I first went to only retrieve letters!" The fire snapped, the flames occasional small fingers of flickering gold, the room's increasing chill sending shivers up his spine and under his scalp. "Ill-advised letters. Written when the affair was new and wondrous." His chin slumped to his chest, exhaustion leeching his lagging energy away. "He threatened to use them to expose me, to paint me as an unscrupulous seducer of older men, to blight my reputation and humiliate my father. I had to prevent reckless ruin to my family name by my own indiscretions!"

"So you resorted to thievery? Violating a judge's home? You didn't think that reckless?" Peter's dry tone and steely glare made Neal feel hopelessly young and foolish.

"N-not entirely." He grimaced. He took a deep breath trying to steady his voice. "I knew where the letters were kept. Granted, I might have damage the desk drawer opening it, but I didn't violate his home!" It fell weak and quaking into the tense air. "Ayana let me in through the kitchen."

"*Helpful* of your Ayana." The frown pulled Peter's lips into a thin line. The resulting wrinkles around his narrowed eyes spoke of disapproval and disappointment. "To aid and abet in your thievery."

Peter apparently had a generous gift for dry wit. Neal felt physically wounded. His cheeks glowed warm despite his chilled skin.

He wanted to wipe away that harsh expression. "They were my letters. It wasn't really thievery. From my point of view."

"No doubt." The frown eased slightly. "Then what happened?"

"He returned earlier than expected. I do not know why. He was paler than usual but still despicable and cruel. But I cared not for his harsh words and ruinous threats. I had the letters back."

Peter sighed, the first encouraging sign that he was relenting, seeing Neal's unmanageable dilemma. "He let you leave with them without protest?"

"Not...exactly." This was harder than he had hoped it would be. "This would be when he died."

"Tell me."

And with that one strictly spoken command, Neal seemed to completely break. Words poured from him without regard to the madness they revealed, parts rattled off in sputtered half-sentences between distraught gasps. The Judge's collapse, his attempts at the heathen rituals while dying, the horrific appearance of the ghostly demon and its unearthly pursuit of Neal, the damning, and damned, watch Neal didn't dare leave out of his care, and the odd magical protective powers of the servant woman Ayana's worn amulet. It was chaos and lunacy, but Peter had a fairly decent idea of what burdens Neal was carrying.

This young man, this beautiful man, was lean of frame and delicate of feature, but he had backbone and nerve if this demonic spirit had been pursuing him for days. Peter's own heart had yet to calm its heavy beating under his ribs.

That frown was back on his face but Peter fought to keep it in check. It was clear Neal was at the end of his rope. His body trembled with the chill dampness of the rain-soaked air, or the frightful assault they had just endured.

Peter rose, gently prying off Neal's desperate grip when the younger man refused to let him take leave. Avoiding the fallen timepiece, he quickly added more fuel to the fire and returned to sit by Neal. This time shoulder to shoulder, backs to the wall, all eyes turned to study the amulet and its tiny gold prisoner.

"I need to find someone who understands the powers of the amulet. Someone like Ayana. Philadelphia is a large and varied a port as Boston. Surely there are some of Ayana's people here, practitioners of her culture, her spirit ways." Neal's face brightened and he began to rise to his feet. "Sailors would know when human cargo arrived. Servants! Slavers! I could visit the taverns by the docks. I could—"

"Sit!" The stern order stilled Neal's actions but Peter's hand pulled him back to the floor. He added a sharp yank to quelling any thoughts of resistance. "My God, do you ever think before you act?"

The cloud of hurt that fell over those dark blue eyes tempered his anger. Neal had been abused enough by others of late. Peter wanted to be the one who made it better. He had to if he ever hoped of a future with this man. "I see impulsiveness is something we'll have to work on. Together."

"You don't think less of me for Williams? For my desires? My...perversion?"

"How can I condemn a man when the same sin lives within my own heart? I cannot look upon your beauty unhindered by society and law, but I hope to live a secret life of perversion, and happily so. If it is with you."

"You are undaunted by all," Neal gestured weakly at the watch, "this?"

"Sometimes you have to fight for the important things in life." Pulling Neal in close, Peter tucked the dark head under his chin and wrapped his arms around Neal's bowed shoulders, delighting in the way Neal relaxed into the embrace. It took less time than he thought before the regular puffs of warm breath on his skin told him Neal was asleep.

§ § § §

Peter passed the hours alternately staring at the watch and gazing at Neal as the other man slept. Eventually, the rhythm of the rain against the windows lulled him into a light doze. He woke to sharp, insistent knocking from the front of the shop. He wiped at his eyes before darting a glance at the amulet bound watch. A second glance at the nearby window showed a muddy gray blur. Night still claimed much of the sky.

Tensely curious about by a pre-dawn caller, he slowly wrestled Neal off his chest, rolling his shoulders to eased their stiffness. If what Neal had said last night about Williams' sudden death, it was not unreasonable to suspect the law could be in pursuit of the young man.

Neal mumbled something, his heavy-lidded eyes bloodshot, locks of dark wavy hair tousled against one cheek partially obscuring the lines on his face from being pressed into Peter's shirt. The faint shadow of beard accented the fine angle of his jawline and fairness of his complexion.

"Peter?"

Even disheveled and incoherent—possibly because of it—Peter was struck all the more by Neal's refined attributes. Undeniably, the man delighted Peter's appreciation and love of physical beauty. No one, man or woman, could gaze upon young Clifton and not be taken by his good looks. He also knew Neal to be prosperous, a skilled tradesman from a respected family, but now he knew him to be of good heart and true intentions, if foolishly impulsive at times. The man beside him was more frightened youth than evil seducer or murder. Peter felt that despite what was happening with this bewitched specter, these events were happening *to* Neal, not because of him.

"Peter, what is it?" Neal lurched to his feet, unsteady, back to the wall, gaze flickering from Peter to the amulet and watch. "Who would call here at this hour? Have they come for me?"

"It will be alright." The moment he had vanished the ghost, nay, more likely from their first kiss, Peter had fallen into the role of Neal's protector. It seemed natural and right like the comfortable fit of his favorite smithy tools against his hand.

Whomever was trying to bang their knuckles raw on his door would the first in what he suspected would be a long series of challenges if Neal remained in his life. At least he hoped so.

"I shall see to it. Whomever it is." He pressed his lips to Neal's forehead as he pushed him back into the shadows of the room. "Be silent and still." Neal's frightened, wide-eyed stare and trusting nod pulled at his heart.

The wind rattled the shutters, but the rain had abated. Before crossing to the door, Peter coaxed an ember to life, pulling a flame out to light a candle. Rumpled, a strand of his thick brown hair hung loose from the cord at his neck. He made no effort to dispel the idea he had been asleep. And alone. If constables were on the other side of his threshold, he couldn't afford to let them become too curious or intrusive. Neither Neal nor a moaning watch in the middle of his kitchen floor would be easily explained.

Releasing the bolt, he cracked open the door, holding the candle out to illuminate the caller. A dark cloak, mud-stained and worn, was draped tightly around a small figure. Brown hands made of delicate bones and callus skin held the fabric close against the grasping wind.

Relieved this was no constable, Peter open the door wider, but remained wary. This was no hour for casual callers.

"Wade House does not open until morning, madame."

"I have not come to buy pretty things, Master Wade."

"Then why pull me from my bed, mistress? Who be you?"

"A servant, sir. I bring news to Master Clifton from his father." Her voice was soft but firm, rich with exotic tone, words oddly clipped, almost musical. Unfamiliar with the accent, Peter found himself straining to understand her.

"Clifton lodges at the Ram's Head." Wind caught the hem of the cloak's hood and pulled it back. Her caramel skin was smooth over broad cheekbones and an oval face. Cat-shaped, wary eyes as black as ink studied him. He felt their penetrating stare drag over every inch of his skin like ghostly fingertips. He absently shrugged his shoulders to shake off a sudden chill. "Seek him there."

A bold gust of air swiped at the candle. It carried the sharp scent of spice and earth to Peter, triggering a mild feeling of unnamed panic. The flame flickered and almost extinguished. Peter hurriedly drew back to shut the door. Woman or not, she affected him oddly. He couldn't be sure she wasn't some extension of the unnatural forces pursuing Neal.

"Please! I beg of you. For both your sakes. Tell him Ayana has come to help." Her pale brown lips tensed in a pursed line. Her fingers gripped the cloak more tightly.

"Ayana?" Peter's head cocked to one side, recognition instantly hitting him. Suspicion ebbed but he was still wary. According to Neal, this woman was much more than an ordinary servant and had played a key role in Neal's present deadly dilemma. "*Neal's* Ayana?"

"Aye, sir. The foolish child's Ayana." Her small smile was wan but genuine. It brought a light to her dark eyes that softened the foreign, black depths. As difficult as it was to judge her age her tone was very maternal toward Neal. "Truer words than you may think, Peter Wade."

"I don't understand your meaning, Ayana, but then I haven't understood much of the last day." Peter swung the door wider and urged her into the room with an impatient gesture. "Swiftly, please. Neal will be relieved to see you safe." He bolted the door.

Towering over her, one hand on her back, Peter guided her toward the back of the shop. Her plain skirt rustled softly, boots tapping on the floorboards in her haste. Ayana dropped her cloak on a chair as she passed it, attention focused in the direction Peter had pointed. He followed close behind.

"Child? Show Ayana your gentle face, boy. Show me I am not too late." Quick, sure steps crossed the small kitchen, unerringly headed toward the shadowed corner of the room where Neal secreted himself.

A muffled, low shriek rattled near her feet, the bound watch quivering against the wooden floor. She stopped cold, eyes wide in fear at the discovery of the evil trinket so close. The wail died away, but Peter felt the air was suddenly thick, heavy with natural tension.

"Ayana?" Neal hesitantly stepped out of the darkness. "Are you truly here? I've prayed to see you every night since this nightmare began." Groggy, blurry eyed, he hurried to meet her but stumbled.

Peter was at his side, righting him, supporting him until he regained his balance. Neal gave him a grateful smile that Peter returned along with a roughly murmured, "*Our* nightmare. You won't be abandoned to manage this on your own, Neal."

"I have come to help destroy this evil, child." Ayana edged around the watch. Once she was at Neal's side she touched his cheek. "You will need my help to overcome this darkness from the grave."

Peter was struck by the dramatic contrast between her rich brown skin on Neal's pale, fair face. This whole event, weeks of trials and horrifying confrontation had pushed the younger man near his limits.

Only slightly self-conscious, he squeezed Neal's shoulder, pulling him closer to his side. If this woman knew of Neal's real relationship with Williams, she knew his heart. Peter wasn't going to betray Neal by hiding his own feelings around Neal's most trusted confidants. Men cut from the cloth that he and Neal were could not let pride nor fear extinguish true feelings in their hearts.

Pressing her hand to his face with his own shaking finger, Neal let the guilt he had been carrying turn his voice into a raspy, anguished whisper. "I thought you might have been blamed for Williams' death. I should have stayed with you to face them."

"No, you were right to go. I forced you to go. It was much easier to explain events without you being present."

Peter wasn't certain what was happening but he knew he needed to stand back and let Ayana put some of Neal's constant fears to rest. Only she could fill in the blanks of these last few critical days for them both. It was her amulet binding the spirit inside the watch, her rituals that might free them. Peter's and Neal's entire future depended on this woman.

"I'm so sorry I left you there to handle the whole thing. It was cowardly of me." Neal's voice broken slightly, the dim candlelight glimmering wetly in his vibrant eyes.

"Hush, child. You did what was best for both of us. You father received your letter, child. He handled everything. He obtained my legal freedom after the Judge's passing and all accepted the death as weakness of the heart."

"What about the broken drawer?"

"They said it was his own doing looking for the powders his doctor had prescribed for him."

"Doctor?"

"The Judge's frequent 'indigestion'. No one knew but his

doctor." Sheepishly, she gave Neal an affectionate smile. "In the end, the Judge had few friends to question his passing."

"And, sir," she bowed slightly, as much teasing as respectful a gesture. "I serve the Clifton household. Your father has been very generous and kind to me."

"But now," her gaze darted to the bound watch, fearful, dark but determined. Voice low, raw, almost angry, her accent became heavy, difficult for Peter to grasp at times. "I have much to tell you, child. Things you will not understand but must accept."

Peter frowned. "I don't like the sound of this."

Ayana's dire tone and Peter's unhappy reaction unheeded, Neal remained focused on the living villain that had occupied his life for so many months. "The watch. Did anyone note it was missing?"

"No. No one. The men with him that night say the Judge was unsteady, ill, last they saw him. He must have dropped it on the journey home. They think it long gone in the hand of a beggar. No one cared that he passed, Neal. No one."

"I can't believe it." Neal straightened, back still to the wall, but the worry lines that marred his face lessened. "I was so sure constables were at my heels." Neal blew out a long breath then froze. "Williams' neighbor. He saw me that night. Going into the house. Mr. Abbott? He said nothing?"

"Abbott had no affection for the Judge." Ayana's laugh was brittle. "He was appointed to the judge's position with the court. He will keep his own counsel, I think."

"Then it's truly over." He slumped further down the wall, head hanging.

Peter wanted to take him in his arms, bury Neal's worried, pale face on his chest and protective him from the world.

Slowly raising his head, he found Peter's anxious, stern face. "I'm not mad and I'm free, Peter."

The watch shook so hard the rattle echoed off the walls. The wail held a note of rage in it, enough so that Neal jerked upright, one hand grabbing Ayana's offered fingers. The other hand stepped away from it to brace his back on the wall. Peter moved with him, angling his body so he blocked the watch from Neal's line of sight.

"*Almost* free, Neal. Almost. We *will* vanquish this obstacle as well. I swear it. Together."

"We must work quickly. The amulet will only hold the Judge's spirit for so long."

"What does it want?" Peter shook his head. "I know it wants Neal, but what does it want him for?"

"An unimaginable horror. A new body. A new life." She placed her open palm on Neal's chest. It rose and fell, fast and shallow, plain for all to see, measuring every rapid breath Neal took. "He practiced some of the most ancient and dark rituals of my people on you. His dark soul called to it. He was preparing for death. His spirit is eager to possess you, Neal, to have a new home so the Judge can live on. He chose this over the grave that awaits him."

Gloom hung in the air, pushing at the walls of the small kitchen, oppressive as a wool cloak. A chill seeped into his tense muscles, his skin hypersensitive to pressure in the room, his body responding to the anxiety, the instinct to protect mixed with desire. He understood the urge a man would have to make Neal his own. He felt it down to his bones, but unlike Williams, it also touched his heart.

Peter turned away to tend the fire. "I would see him put into that grave before this is done."

"Seducing Neal was all part of his plan. Rituals to baptize him with the signs of the afterlife, mark his young body with his own foul scent so his ghost could find Neal at the right time. He knew he would die soon. The doctor's powders did no good. He cared only for himself. Always for himself."

"I should have seen it. He treated me like an object, like that watch. Useful only when he wanted. A possession." Neal colored faintly, looking more youthful than his twenty-two years. "The knowledge it was not real love came to me too late. I was lost by then, my honor gone, my heart dead."

"He was an evil man." The pain on Neal's face was cutting. Peter wanted to embrace him but settled for offering verbal comfort.

For now.

"You didn't deserve what he did to you, Neal. The betrayal. The abuse. He didn't—couldn't care for you." Voice rough, needy. Even across the room his desire for the other man was obvious. "Your heart is not dead." He paused to summon his courage. He would prefer to bare his soul in private, but their world was off center, trapped in unnatural events. He feared they didn't have the luxury of waiting. If the spirit should escape again, all might be lost. "At least, I pray 'tis not. I would wish that you would share it with me."

"After all this?" Neal's expression lightened. He straightened, gently moving Ayana aside, and approached Peter. Hesitation, surprise, hope written on his face. "You remain interested in our...partnership?"

Peter glanced toward Ayana. She had drifted back slightly to let the shadows dull her presence, inconspicuous as possible without leaving the room. He shrugged his shoulder, an anxious twitch, letting his reservations slip away with the gesture. "If you will consider one as an equal. Made of both desires of the flesh and of the heart."

Neal flushed, a pink splash of fever on too pale cheeks. "Peter!"

It was merely his name but Peter heard everything he needed to know in it—anticipation, fear, want, desire, embarrassment and—acceptance. He pulled Neal to him, excitement coursing through every limb. It was meant to be a gentleman's embrace, a hearty slap on the back, a manly display of pleasure.

The heat of Neal's lips on his own, the wetness of his tongue, the taste of his mouth was unexpected. He was surprised at the bold move until he realized it was *his* hands entwined in Neal's hair holding his head at the proper angle to kiss, *his* arms drawing the slighter man up to meet chest to chest, *his* strength keeping Neal in place until the man reacted with his own grasping, needy embrace. Breathless and weak-kneed, it was long minutes before Peter loosened his grip. A sharp rattle of metal on wood disturbed the joy.

Spices and earth peppered the air. A blanket of gritty mixture settled over the bound timepiece. The death rattle stopped abruptly. "I know the ritual that will banish this spirit to the darkness once its chosen host is cleansed. I have the needed ingredients with me. I can perform the cleansing ritual here. Now. But I will need help." Ayana rubbed her fingers over her palm to get the last of her potion off her skin and on to the ghost's makeshift, metal lair. "It is good you are prepared to share yourselves."

"What?" Neal ran his hands through his hair, smoothing it back into place from Peter's insistent grasp. He turned to face the woman, the fact he had momentarily forgotten she was still in room written in his flustered movements. "Why?"

"Because it is the only way for you to be rid of this abomination. You must be cleansed of his scent. Obliterated. Replaced." She cast a meaningful, lingering gaze over both men, eyebrow arched, a small smile on her full lips. "By the scent of another, a new *paramour.*"

"O-oh."

Undaunted by Neal's embarrassed stutter, Peter stepped up close behind the other man, hand confidently squeezing Neal's shoulder, his voice warm and firm. "I don't foresee that as a problem."

♪ ♪ ♪ ♪

Rhythmic chanting, strong, forceful, carried through the closed bed chamber door. Its exotic song, mesmerizing and mystical, darkened the heavy mood of the house. Oppressive as it was, it couldn't dim Neal's anticipation.

Peter built a hurried fire in the hearth to ward off the

pervasive chill, then lit a single candle on the bedside table. Its glow flickered dimly, painting the bed with long strokes of gold and gray, the illusion of warmth and comfort, a welcome contrast to what was happening in the shop's small kitchen.

Hurriedly stripping to nothing more than his shirttails, Neal hesitated, idly touching items as he walked to the bed. The chamber was simple but comfortably appointed. The sparse furniture handsome, sturdy, large, like Peter. The turned back bed was oversized to accommodate Peter's tall height, the matting good quality, thick and firm. The revealed bedding was clean, not the same quality Neal was used to in his father's home, but still cool and smooth under his fingertips. The coverlet's bound edges were ropes of silk, a dark gray wrapped around a massive square of deep blue linen, a shade surprisingly not unlike the color of Neal's eyes. Touches of the same color were used around the room—drapes, chair—obviously a favorite of Peter's.

Sitting on the edge of the bed, he studied Peter's bare back, shoulders long and corded, muscles rippling with every move as the other man crouched, tending the fire. After only knowing each other for a few hours, Peter had stood fast at Neal's side during the ghost's attack, held to the conviction that Neal was not insane, and remained with him through the night. Remained at his side and held him in his arms while he slept, protecting him throughout the night. Peter Wade was a steadfast man, strong, self-confident and unwavering when faced with overwhelming adversity.

Amos liked Peter. His father liked him. Neal liked him. More than liked him. Affection, desire, want, lust, maybe even the start of something more, made his breathing come in rapid puffs, his face warm and his skin tingle. He tore his shirttails over his head and threw them on the bottom of the bed. The damp cold of the room raised gooseflesh all over his body. Despite the cold, other parts of his body responded to the sight of Peter's half-naked flesh. Sliding between the linens, he drew the cover high for warmth and scooted to the center of the huge bed into a position so he could see Peter. And Peter could see him—waiting. Willing.

Wanting. He let the blankets fall to his lap.

If this had been Williams' chamber he would have had to suffer the Judge's cold, dirty touch and embarrassing insults while the man undressed him. Pain, abuse, shame, remorse would follow rapidly.

None of those things would occur here, except some lingering guilt. He wasn't sure that would ever go away. But he could live with guilt if it meant he could have the possibility of a life and working partnership with this man, secret as the intimacy would have to be all their lives.

Dusting his hands on his breeches, Peter stood from the fire and turned, gaze finding Neal, his expression marked by first surprise and then pleasure. He disrobed as he crossed the few feet to the bed. He was completely naked by the time he reached Neal. It was a bold and confident action. Even married couples rarely completely undressed together, even during intimacy. It unnecessary, shameful, exciting and wanton.

Neal knew what strength it had taken for him to completely undress. He couldn't see any of the hesitancy he had felt in Peter's smooth movements. His smile was just as bold as his actions, his intense, needy gaze devouring Neal's, taking in everything. Neal felt desired, hungered for, as if he was the only thing Peter required to be whole.

Peter climbed onto the bed on all fours, a stalking mountain lion approaching its prey. And just like a frightened deer, Neal froze in place, stare lost in Peter's devouring gaze, waiting for the pounce. Peter wrapped a muscle bound arm around Neal's hips and yanked him closer and down.

He lay flat on his back, arms flung over head in the suddenness and strength of the move. Heat radiated into his side, body heat mingling, warming his chilly skin, a blanket of comforting flesh encasing him on one side. Peter bent over him, looming close, a smile of pleasure on his square, rugged jaw, his lips silent yet parted.

Hard and growing harder, every inch of his body tense,

tingling with anticipation and lust, Neal studied Peter's face as it slowly drew nearer. The man was undeniably handsome, brown eyes like the finest burl woods, multi-shades of brown and gold dotted, surrounded a lake of black. Neal liked the way their gaze darted across his own face, followed by Peter's hand, touching his cheek, his hair, his jaw line, his lips, drinking in every part of him, seeing the cut of him, seeing *him*.

Leaning close, Peter slipped one arm under Neal's head, the other curling around his back to pull Neal closer. Agonizingly slowly, Peter touched his lips to Neal's, a soft greeting, gentle and short lived.

A wailing moan, muffled and distant but louder than Neal expected leeched through the closed bedchamber door. The chanting rose for several seconds them lowered as the moan subsided. Neal sighed when Peter broke the kiss.

"Peter?" Did they get this far only to have the man not want him?

Peter lifted his head, barely separating their mouths. "Are you alright? Do you truly wish this, Neal?"

Words couldn't be found to answer adequately so he didn't try to find them. Wrapping both arms around Peter's neck, he pulled the man down, pressing their bodies together. Hard cock knocked hard cock as their mouths met, teeth clicking, jaws open and devouring. The embrace became heated, insistent, almost frenzied. And it was Neal doing the insisting. Their tongues clashed, Peter's demanding possession of Neal's mouth, giving breath and slick wetness over in exchange for control. His lips tasted faintly of salt, stale from their forced night on the floor but rich, masculine.

Desire pushed aside mundane thoughts, the very core of Neal's being flushed with need and wanton lust. His soul cried out for release from the burden of guilt he had been carrying. The urge for acceptance and rakish carnal pleasure blotting out all else. Even the ghastly events happening outside the bed chamber were as distant as a half forgotten dream.

Groaning as his head was angled back by Peter's large hand, blunt fingernails scratching his scalp as his hair was combed out of his face. Lips peppered slow, soft kisses along his brow and down his cheek, over his jaw line and back up the other side. A thick thigh slid between his legs holding them apart as Peter rocked against Neal's body, stiff cock nudging his sac, teasing his shaft, heat and wetness and silk all at once.

"Lord God!" The sensations were almost too much for Neal to tolerate.

True to his nature, Peter used action instead of words even in this. The kisses never stopped, light touches to Neal's closed eyelids, a breathy, moist trail down one cheek, then finally reclaiming his mouth, invading and conquering him all over again. When Neal began to toss his head wanting more, Peter began working his way down Neal's neck and chest, claiming very inch of flesh as his own.

Moaning, Neal arched his back, thrusting up into Peter's long torso. His nipples were hard and burning, wanton, like begging things. Peter pressed his thumbs, hard, pushing and rubbing, making Neal groan with pleasure. His hips worked against Peter's hard abdomen, pinned between flesh and linen. He tossed his head to one side, baring his neck, silently begging.

He thrust up again, pressing his chest into Peter's hands, his rough thumbs. Nails pinched lightly then harder. Neal shuddered, his nipples like glowing embers, burning hard, eager. Peter licked at them in turn then sucked one into his mouth and teased it between his teeth. The other nipple felt abandoned until a rough thumb and finger plucked it back to fiery life.

Hips bucking, Neal grasped Peter's shoulders with both hands, using him for leverage to gain more friction. Peter rolled slightly, teeth still latched on Neal's taut nub. Neal gasped at the loss of body heat. He choked back a protest as calloused fingers brought both cocks together and began massaging the stiff lengths, pulling back foreskins to rub the exposed heads.

A sharp nip at his aching nipple shot rivers of fire like the rays of a sunburst across his chest. He pushed up into Peter's lips, a grunt escaping as the nub was flicked by a wet tongue, suction pulling the crinkled flesh into the heat of Peter's devouring mouth. The sensation raced past pleasure to pain then deep, muffled groans of need that rumbled against his ribs took the pain to a place he could only describe as ecstasy. Several short, harsh strokes on his shaft, a swirl of callus around the rim of his swollen cock head, and Neal tipped over the edge.

"Mother of God! Peter!"

Body fluid coated Peter's pumping hand, smoothing the strokes as the other man wrung the last of Neal's joy from him. Peter licked the sweat from Neal's chest, moving up to take his panting mouth in a searing kiss. As the orgasm faded, he realized the kiss had gentled.

Peter shifted his weight, resting between Neal's spread thighs. Neal was still panting, trying to refocus his vision in the dim room as Peter slowly breached his opening with a wet, smooth finger, both large, square hands under Neal's ass, long arms finding Neal's opening with ease.

"Are you with me, Neal?" The finger went deeper, finding Neal's sweet spot, sending bellows of heat through his lower gut, loosening his instinctive resistance, sending reason and the power of speech to some locked corner of his fevered brain. He nodded. Peter kissed him again then rolled to one side, weight still heavy on Neal, one hand kneading the curve of his ass. Peter lifted to one knee, pulled Neal into a better position beneath him. His cock replaced his finger and he slowly began working deeper, a smooth rocking motion, back and forth, patiently joining them.

Steeling himself against the surge of pain he had come to expect with this, Neal squeezed his eyes shut, fists twisted in the pillow under his head. It took him some time before he realized Peter has stilled and was talking to him, a low soothing murmur, calm but with an underlying thread of strain.

"Neal? Open your eyes. Look at me. Show me you are here, with me. Not with Ayana. Not remembering someone else. Look at me. This is not to be taken lightly."

Eyes open wide, Neal blinked, more to push away his surprise than to adjust to the darkness of the room. The smell of wood, cotton and Peter filled the air. A faint buzzing dulled his hearing, the sound of his own blood rushing in his veins. His cock ached, embarrassingly soft from the threat of coming discomfort, pleasantly sore from the thoroughness of Peter's earlier attention.

His ass clenched, the stretching burn of penetration constant, fresh and sharp, muscles tense waiting. He'd endured this act before, under the ruthless hand of the Judge. He bit back the memory. He would endure anything if it meant being rid of Williams' ghastly haunting. He hoped Peter would be kind afterward. Know some way to make the taking less gut-wrenching but, he was prepared to settle for it being over quickly.

Peter seemed to have other plans. His thumb gently passed over Neal's lips, rubbing over the wet lower one, an intimate, deeply affectionate gesture.

"You already marked me." He slid his palm down Neal's abdomen, the touch sticky, the scent of his own fluids rising up from Peter's hand. "Now if I'm going to mark you as mine, I want to be the man you see when it happens, in your thoughts and with those beautiful eyes. Just me."

Blinking back a sudden wetness that blurred his vision, Neal nodded. He tried to relax against the bedding, taking deep breathes to ease the tightness in his gut. Peter nodded back, then reached out to force one hand under the folds of bedding, returning with a small silver vial. With an ease that told of regular practice, he deftly pulled the top off and set it spinning off into the shadows, the dull thud of metal to carpet marking its journey.

Uncertain, Neal watched Peter work one handed, a drizzle of oily liquid splashing between their lower bodies, coolness running over their cocks as Peter poured it back and forth. Neal wasn't even aware of where the bottle went after the first slippery stroke of Peter's shaft caressed his passage.

The room faded. Peter's steady stare was all he saw, every nerve in his body feeling as if it were swollen, glutted with lust, brimming with sensation. The pain was carried away on the rush of pleasure, the rub and bump of cock head over the spot inside hitting him like lightning strikes. He arched and rocked, seeking more. Distantly he recognized the gasps and groans as his own over a background of Peter's rhythmic panting grunts.

Heavy hands tugged his hair, wiped the wetness from his cheeks, soothed their drying fluids over his fevered flesh, skin alive and tingling as if dotted by sparks of molten silver from the forge.

His own fingers danced over rippling skin, smoothed the valleys of hard muscle, mapped ribs and spine, freely exploring, taking what was being offered, reveling in having found not only a kindred soul, but a good man as well.

Fingers dug into his hips and pulled him further into Peter's embrace. Urged by guiding hands, Neal draped his calves over Peter's shoulders, his cock stiff and curved to point at his belly. All pain cast off, pleasure devoured him. His ass spread wider, his opening stretched so tightly he could feel the bulging rim of cock as it slid out to its head and burrowed back in again, slick, hot, thick. Testicles smacked against his ass, teasing the spread, delicate skin between his cheeks, regular and hard, spanking him like a searing palm.

His nipples crinkled, swollen, taunt, peaked nubs of flesh full of memory of Peter's mouth against them. The sharp tug of teeth, the bright flare of delicious fire that flowed across his chest, racing straight for his cock. His gut was heavy, oddly full like his swollen cock, the knot of desire building larger, tighter until he was sure he couldn't endure more. Then Peter thrust fast and deep, jerky rough strokes, his hands almost crushing Neal in their grip, his lips demanding, hungry, his taste hot, wet, bathing Neal's mouth with Peter's scent just as his cock was burying his essence in the farthest reaches of Neal's body.

Despite all the care Peter had taken, all he had given Neal this night, release still eluded Neal. It was unbearable. Peter shuddered and heaved above him, hips pumping, firing, filling Neal's channel, a thousand pins of ecstasy torturing his body. He couldn't stop the single sob. It burst out under guise of a groan.

He would never be happy, never free of the Judge's humiliation and abuse.

His cock twitched and bobbed, engorged with an impossible weight, a scorching need that seemed as helplessly restrained and bound as the ghost was in the cursed watch.

Warmth wrapped around his cock, fingers, long and callus, still and strong. Neal's face was turned toward the candle glow and held there. Peter stared down only far enough away that Neal could focus on his face, the sternness in the lines around his eyes, the gentleness of his gaze, understand the firmness of his confident tone when he demanded, "Mine. You. Are. Mine."

Lightning struck the room. Or Neal just imagined it had. His body seemed as if it exploded. His cock jerked, spurts of pearly droplets glistening in the light. As they landed, Peter swiped them into this palm to rub onto his chest, licking his fingers to get every last bit. He leaned in the last few inches and kissed Neal hard, sharing the taste of the younger man's release.

Neal moaned at the intimacy of the action, then pulled away, screaming.

The bedchamber door burst open. Hinges scattered, the dense wooden door flapped, swinging on broken wings. A cold wind whirled into the room, smoky clouds of black and gray, thinner, paler than before. It trembled, screeching in a reedy, frenzied call. It flowed through the room in an instant, long fingers grasping at Neal's still screaming lips, its gaping black hole of a mouth desperately trying to seal them together, to swallow down the anguished sounds.

Neal's skin crawled, a thousand insects scurried under his flesh, as if feeding from a decaying corpse. His chest was raw, flames crisped the hairs across his heart, the air in his lungs searing, filled with suffocating fumes that reeked of sulfur and iron. Daggers lanced through his eyes, his scalp tightened, the screams torn from his throat were filled with pain, agony on his ears. He could see Peter trying to fight off the shadow, rolling Neal away, covering his body with his own, trying fiercely to shield him from the darkness.

But still it clawed at him, Clawed and clawed and clawed. Never gaining entrance but still on this side of the gates of hell. This would be the last thing he felt and heard. Not Peter, not the memory of their joining, not the joy he'd finally found. Agony and terror. Williams had won after all. The room faded. Neal knew he was on the verge of blacking out. He wanted his last sight to be of Peter, but his strength was spent. He closed his eyes, darkness preferable to the devil's tool pinning him down.

The darkness lifted. Neal could breathe again. His eyes fluttered open, lungs raw, the taste of evil still clung to his lips. Peter held on to him tightly, cursed oaths accompanying each swing of his fist at the shadowed form.

Ayana stood at the threshold of the chamber drawing ancient symbols from Williams' rituals in the air, her eerie singsong chant, rapid and strong, loud enough to be heard over the spirit's wailing screeches. She called to the demon, coaxed it to her, her amulet hung around her neck, the pouch strings open, the scent of spice and earth mixing with the smell of men and sex.

The ghost answered her. It reared up from the bed and dove at her, weak, frenzied, almost transparent. As it approached Ayana met it head on, tossing dirt into its open mouth. Flames bellowed out of the fireplace, long talons that slashed the shadow into strips of gray smoke. The flames instantly died away, sucking the ribbons of darkness down with them. Stillness filled the room.

A weight lifted off Neal's chest. His head cleared, his body relaxed, the pain gone. Nothing was left behind but the vague sensation of anticipation.

"Thank you, Ayana. Peter..." Suddenly he realized he was in Peter's arms, naked, both of them, with nothing, not even linen between them and Ayana's gaze. Neal wasn't sure he had the energy to find a cover but Peter rose to the occasion, shielding Neal's lower half with a generous thigh. As grateful as he was, this was awkward.

"Ah, Ayana? Do you think you could give a moment of privacy?" Ayana averted her gaze but not as quickly as Neal would have liked. Instead of leaving the room she moved closer.

"I destroyed the watch." She tossed the mangled timepiece onto the bed. For the first time Neal noticed her dress was torn and hair cap missing. She blotted a trickle of blood from her lip with the edge of her apron. "No more shadows in your lifetime, child. Leave the darkness and secrets to others."

"Unfortunately, I don't think my life will be entirely free from the need for secrets, Ayana." He traced the ridge of Peter's broad cheek with a light touch, one that made the other man shiver and put a smile on his face. "I hope I get better at keeping them though."

"You'll have help. Lucky for you I'm excellent with secrets." Peter's voice was rough again, desire creeping back into his eyes.

"Even now?"

"Especially now. I told you, Neal. You're mine."

"You'll both have help." She turned and walked to the threshold, shoving the door upright. "Mister Clifton has sent you a gift to celebrate your...partnership. A housekeeper who can do the wash, cook and clean *and* keep a secret. I have no quarrel with your way of life, if you have no quarrel with mine."

"Ayana!" Pleased, both men rose part way off the bed but quickly dropped back down to preserve their dignity. Ayana laughed and left, the broken door swaying in her wake.

They shared a dazed look, Neal was amazed at how quickly Peter had adjusted to the events of the last two days, his strength, confidence and sense of right were unshakeable, even in the face of unearthly madness.

Peter twisted around and found the coverlet. He swept it up off the floor, tucking it around both of them. Neal grabbed the watch from the bedding to keep it from being lost. It was hopelessly bent, cold, but only the cold of ordinary metal, lifeless and silent.

"Should I keep it as a reminder?" Neal frowned, his mood darkening. "A cautionary tale of the error of letting desire rule reason?"

Plucking it from Neal's hand, Peter tossed it on the bedside table. "No. We don't need any reminders of this day."

Peter rolled to his back and took Neal with him, laying chest to chest, Peter's stiffening cock between his thighs. The look of need in Peter's eyes sent a thrill of pleasure down Neal's spine.

"Besides, Master Clifton, I intend to have a lifetime of you allowing desire to rule your reason. And mine."

ABOUT THE AUTHORS

ALEX BEECROFT was born in Northern Ireland, raised in Cheshire, ALEX has lived all over the UK but nowhere else. She studied English and Philosophy at Manchester University, then read for an MPhil in The Cult of the Horse in Early Anglo-Saxon England. She worked in the Lord Chancellor's Department in London, moved to Guildford to work in the Crown Court, and has hopefully finally settled near Cambridge with her husband and two children

Alex's first m/m novel, Captain's Surrender is an Age of Sail romance set in the 18th Century British Royal Navy of Hornblower fame. Her second novel, False Colors, on a similar theme, comes out in spring 2009 from New York press Perseus Books. Working with MLR has given her the chance to branch out of 'pure' historical into historical/paranormal with THE WAGES OF SIN.

Visit Alex on the internet at: http://www.alexbeecroft.com

A distinct voice in gay fiction, multi-award-winning author JOSH LANYON has been writing gay mystery, adventure and romance for over a decade. In addition to numerous short stories, novellas, and novels, Josh is the author of the critically acclaimed Adrien English series, including The Hell You Say, winner of the 2006 USABookNews awards for GLBT Fiction. Josh is an Eppie Award winner and a three-time Lambda Literary Award finalist.

Visit Josh on the internet at: http://www.joshlanyon.com

LAURA BAUMBACH is the award-winning author of numerous short stories, novellas, novels and screenplays. Her favorite genre to work in is manlove or m/m erotic romances. Manlove is not traditional gay fiction, but erotic romances written specifically for the romantic-minded reader, male or female.

Married to the same man for almost 30 years, she currently lives with her husband and two sons in the blustery Northeast of the United States but is looking for a warmer location to spend the second half of her professional and family life.

Laura is the owner of ManLoveRomance Press, founded in January of 2007. She is also the owner of the promotional co-op for authors of gay romance and fiction, Manloveromance.com. (http://www.manloveromance.com)

You can find Laura on the internet at: http://www.laurabaumbach.com/

http://groups.yahoo.com/group/laurabaumbachfiction

http://www.mlrpress.com/

http://groups.yahoo.com/group/mlrpress/

THE TREVOR PROJECT

The Trevor Project operates the only nationwide, around-the-clock crisis and suicide prevention helpline for lesbian, gay, bisexual, transgender and questioning youth. Every day, The Trevor Project saves lives though its free and confidential helpline, its website and its educational services. If you or a friend are feeling lost or alone call The Trevor Helpline. If you or a friend are feeling lost, alone, confused or in crisis, please call The Trevor Helpline. You'll be able to speak confidentially with a trained counselor 24/7.

The Trevor Helpline: 866-488-7386

On the Web: http://www.thetrevorproject.org/

THE GAY MEN'S DOMESTIC VIOLENCE PROJECT

Founded in 1994, The Gay Men's Domestic Violence Project is a grassroots, non-profit organization founded by a gay male survivor of domestic violence and developed through the strength, contributions and participation of the community. The Gay Men's Domestic Violence Project supports victims and survivors through education, advocacy and direct services. Understanding that the serious public health issue of domestic violence is not gender specific, we serve men in relationships with men, regardless of how they identify, and stand ready to assist them in navigating through abusive relationships.

GMDVP Helpline: 800.832.1901

On the Web: http://gmdvp.org/

THE GAY & LESBIAN ALLIANCE AGAINST DEFAMATION / GLAAD EN ESPAÑOL

The Gay & Lesbian Alliance Against Defamation (GLAAD) is dedicated to promoting and ensuring fair, accurate and inclusive representation of people and events in the media as a means of eliminating homophobia and discrimination based on gender identity and sexual orientation.

On the Web: http://www.glaad.org/

GLAAD en español:

http://www.glaad.org/espanol/bienvenido.php

SERVICEMEMBERS LEGAL DEFENSE NETWORK

Servicemembers Legal Defense Network is a nonpartisan, nonprofit, legal services, watchdog and policy organization dedicated to ending discrimination against and harassment of military personnel affected by "Don't Ask, Don't Tell" (DADT). The SLDN provides free, confidential legal services to all those impacted by DADT and related discrimination. Since 1993, its inhouse legal team has responded to more than 9,000 requests for assistance. In Congress, it leads the fight to repeal DADT and replace it with a law that ensures equal treatment for every servicemember, regardless of sexual orientation. In the courts, it works to challenge the constitutionality of DADT.

SLDN
PO Box 65301
Washington DC 20035-5301
On the Web: http://sldn.org/

Call: (202) 328-3244
or (202) 328-FAIR
e-mail: sldn@sldn.org

THE GLBT NATIONAL HELP CENTER

The GLBT National Help Center is a nonprofit, tax-exempt organization that is dedicated to meeting the needs of the gay, lesbian, bisexual and transgender community and those questioning their sexual orientation and gender identity. It is an outgrowth of the Gay & Lesbian National Hotline, which began in 1996 and now is a primary program of The GLBT National Help Center. It offers several different programs including two national hotlines that help members of the GLBT community talk about the important issues that they are facing in their lives. It helps end the isolation that many people feel, by providing a safe environment on the phone or via the internet to discuss issues that people can't talk about anywhere else. The GLBT National Help Center also helps other organizations build the infrastructure they need to provide strong support to our community at the local level.

National Hotline: 1-888-THE-GLNH (1-888-843-4564)
National Youth Talkline 1-800-246-PRIDE (1-800-246-7743)
On the Web: http://www.glnh.org/
e-mail: info@glbtnationalhelpcenter.org

If you're a GLBT and questioning student heading off to university, should know that there are resources on campus for you. Here's just a sample:

US Local GLBT college campus organizations
        http://dv-8.com/resources/us/local/campus.html
GLBT Scholarship Resources
        http://tinyurl.com/6fx9v6
Syracuse University
        http://lgbt.syr.edu/
Texas A&M
        http://glbt.tamu.edu/
Tulane University
        http://www.oma.tulane.edu/LGBT/Default.htm
University of Alaska
        http://www.uaf.edu/agla/
University of California, Davis
        http://lgbtrc.ucdavis.edu/
University of California, San Francisco
        http://lgbt.ucsf.edu/
University of Colorado
        http://www.colorado.edu/glbtrc/
University of Florida
        http://www.dso.ufl.edu/multicultural/lgbt/
University of Hawai'i, Mānoa
        http://manoa.hawaii.edu/lgbt/
University of Utah
        http://www.sa.utah.edu/lgbt/
University of Virginia
        http://www.virginia.edu/deanofstudents/lgbt/
Vanderbilt University
        http://www.vanderbilt.edu/lgbtqi/

Stimulate yourself.
READ.
www.manloveromance.com
THE HOTTEST M/M EROTIC AUTHORS & WEBSITES ON THE NET

CPSIA information can be obtained at www.ICGtesting.com
Printed in the USA
LVOW070141130112

263687LV00001B/4/P